D0599794

WHEN OUR WORLDS COLLIDED

PRAISE FOR DANIELLE JAWANDO

'Powerful'
Cosmopolitan

'A searing debut novel'
Evening Standard

'Sensitive, moving and engrossing'
i News

'A gripping, Manchester-set tale of troubled young masculinity'
FT

'Thought-provoking and timely, yet filled with hope'
The Bookseller

'Jawando's writing is incredibly raw and real;
I felt completely immersed'
Alice Oseman, author of the Heartstopper series

'An outstanding and compassionate debut'
Patrice Lawrence, author of *Orangeboy*

'One of the brightest up and coming stars of the YA world'
Alex Wheatle, author of *Crongton Knights*

'A raw, unflinching and powerful story that
will stay with me for a long time'
Manjeet Mann, author of *The Crossing*

'An utter page turner from a storming new talent. Passionate,
committed and shines a ray of light into the darkest places'
Melvin Burgess, author of *Junk*

'A beautiful ode to found family, and a compassionate
look at the power of connection borne from
the ashes of tragedy and apathy'
Christina Hammonds Reed, author of *The Black Kids*

DANIELLE JAWANDO

WHEN OUR WORLDS COLLIDED

SIMON & SCHUSTER

First published in Great Britain in 2022 by Simon & Schuster UK Ltd

Copyright © 2022 Danielle Jawando

This book is copyright under the Berne Convention.
No reproduction without permission.
All rights reserved.

The right of Danielle Jawando to be identified as the author
of this work has been asserted by her in accordance with sections 77
and 78 of the Copyright, Designs and Patent Act, 1988.

1 3 5 7 9 10 8 6 4 2

Simon & Schuster UK Ltd
1st Floor, 222 Gray's Inn Road
London
WC1X 8HB

www.simonandschuster.co.uk
www.simonandschuster.com.au
www.simonandschuster.co.in

Simon & Schuster Australia, Sydney
Simon & Schuster India, New Delhi

A CIP catalogue record for this book is available from the British Library.

PB ISBN 978-1-4711-7879-5
eBook ISBN 978-1-4711-7880-1
eAudio ISBN 978-1-3985-0008-2

This book is a work of fiction.
Names, characters, places and incidents are either
the product of the author's imagination or are used fictitiously. Any resemblance
to actual people living or dead, events or locales is entirely coincidental.

Typeset in the UK by M Rules
Printed and bound by CPI Group (UK) Ltd, Croydon, CR0 4YY

MIX
Paper from
responsible sources
FSC® C171272

For Julie Jawando,
for always being there

1

JACKSON

I lean back against the metal railing and look around the Arndale Centre. It's packed. It always is on a Sunday. I'm on the first floor, near this walkway that runs between Victoria's Secret and the Apple store. I'd been waiting outside Victoria's Secret at first, but I didn't want Aimee to think that I was some sort of perv. Just hanging around watching girls buying underwear. So I decided to move further along. I take a deep breath and pull my phone out my pocket – *15.40*.

She's already ten minutes late.

I try not to overthink it. Maybe her bus got held up coming into town. Or maybe she's just pushing her way through all the crowds outside. Or maybe, when she messaged me to tell me that she was leaving, she hadn't even left the house. I click on WhatsApp, but she hasn't sent me anything since:

> Leaving now. Meet u in the arndale xxx

I think about messaging my mate, Harrison, but I know that he'll only take the piss. Especially if he thinks Aimee's stood me up. I shove my phone back in my pocket and try to look as cool as I can. *Casual.* But my palms are starting to sweat and my heart is going a million times a minute. If I'm honest, I'm bricking it. What if she doesn't show up? What if she's decided that she ain't feeling it after all . . . that she ain't feeling me? Not that I could blame her. I still can't believe that Aimee Portas, the hottest girl in school, who could have her pick of any guy she wants, decided to go on a date with me. I pull at the sleeve of my jacket and I'm hit with this strong smell of aftershave. It almost knocks me out. I mean, maybe I overdid it a bit, but I read somewhere how girls like it when a guy smells nice, so I pretty much emptied the whole bottle over myself. It was probably a stupid thing to do, but I want to impress her. Never in my life did I think that Aimee would say 'yes' to me, so I can't screw this up. There's no way I'm going down in history as *that guy.* That guy who had a chance with Aimee, then blew it.

I look around, to try and calm myself down. I turn and lean forward on the railing. I can see all the people below me. Just going about their normal lives.

There's groups of girls spilling out of River Island, teenagers hanging outside JD Sports. People hunched over small tables in

Starbucks, kids crying, mums shouting at toddlers. I see a few security guards moving on a couple of boys who are standing beside the cash machine, then I feel my phone vibrate in my jeans pocket.

I pull it out quickly, praying it ain't Aimee telling me she can't make it. My heart quickens as I open WhatsApp, and a small part of me doesn't even wanna look. Then I see the words:

Soz, bus was longgggg. In town now, where r u? Xx

I breathe out, and I feel this grin spread across my face. I don't care if I look like some sort of goofy idiot either, because Aimee's coming. She's here, in town, on her way to meet *me*. I type a reply, then shove my phone in my pocket again. The nerves are back. What if I don't know what to say to her? Or it just feels proper weird between us? Then there's the end bit – she might want me to kiss her. Not right away or nothing, but if it goes well … I think about what it would be like to kiss Aimee. How her lips would feel … I've thought about kissing her for time. *For three years.* Ever since she first sat next to me in R.E.

I pat down the sides of my hair, and I'm about to turn back around, so that I'm facing in the direction that she'll probably be walking in, when something catches my eye. At first I think it's just some kids messing about. I hear shouting, and then I hear someone scream. And I don't know why but it goes right through me and I can tell that it's more than people mucking around.

There's a spiral staircase blocking most of my view, but I see this boy in a bright red puffa jacket, running. I can't see his face or nothing, only the top of his head. But I watch as he frantically pushes his way through the crowds, barging people out of the way, and knocking this woman over. He doesn't even seem to notice that people are pissed at him for pushing past them, he just carries on running. Looking behind him, like he's trying to put some distance between him and something else. And then I realize: he's being chased. A group of boys run after him. One of them shouts something, but it's so loud inside the shopping centre that I can't make out what they're saying. The boy in the puffa jacket jumps over this metal partition thing and runs down a ramp that leads to one of the exits. The other boys run after him and disappear down the ramp as well. Then, it's almost like it never happened. Like I'd just imagined it … and everything seems to go back to normal.

I feel two warm hands cover my eyes and I jump. Almost stumbling backwards.

'Guess who?' a voice says.

I try not to smile too widely, as I move her hands away and turn to face her.

'You took your time,' I say, and I can't stop staring at her. I'm proper nervous now. More nervous than I've ever been in my *whole* life. I've only ever seen Aimee around school or when we have classes together, and if I thought she was outta my league then, well, this is a whole other level. This is God-would-have-to-be-on-my-side-for-her-to-even-fancy-me-back type of level. Aimee moves her hair away from her face and I have to look away, because I don't want her to see how much I'm checking her out.

She leans down over the balcony bit, and I think, *Jackson, man. Just tell her how nice she looks. Nah, more than nice, you idiot. Tell her she looks gorgeous, or something ... just open your mouth.*

'You got another girlfriend down there or something?' Aimee asks.

'Nah,' I say quickly, and I feel myself getting warm. 'I ain't got a girlfriend. Why would I have a girlfriend? I mean, I ain't saying that I don't want one or anything like that. 'Course I want a girlfriend ... not that I'm tryna ask you or nothing. I mean, that would be a bit much on a first date ... what I'm saying is—'

Aimee shakes her head and even though she's looking at me like I'm from a completely different planet, she's laughing. *That's gotta be a good sign, right?*

'Jackson,' she says. 'Shut up!' I do as I'm told, because I've already made myself look like a right idiot and I should probably quit while I'm ahead. 'You're pretty weird, you know that?' she continues. 'But in the best way ... it's kinda cute.'

I feel myself go all hot. 'Erm, was that supposed to be a compliment?' I ask. Aimee moves closer and I clear my throat. 'You look ...' I say, and I try to find the right words, but she shakes her head.

'Yeah, I know!' she interrupts. 'Now are we just gonna stand here staring at River Island all day, or are you actually taking me out?'

I laugh. 'I'm taking you out,' I say, and I gesture towards the spiral staircase at the other end of the walkway and I start to relax a bit as we make our way towards it.

'Good,' she says. 'Cos it took you long enough. I was beginning to think I'd have to ask you out myself.'

I pause. 'You mad?' I say. 'Been wanting to ask you out for *ages*, I thought you'd shoot me down ... and y'know I'd never hear the end of it if that happened ...' I smile. 'I don't think my heart could take it either,' I say, moving my hands to my chest.

Aimee shakes her head. 'You're full of shit and you know it,' she says. But as we reach the bottom of the stairs, she glances at me. 'You really don't have a clue, do you?' she says. 'I like you, Jackson. Why else d'you think I'm here?'

I swear, I almost go into cardiac arrest. And for a minute, I wonder if I've heard her right. Did Aimee just say that she liked me? Not only that, but she'd been waiting for *me* to ask *her* out? Harrison, Sam and Elliot are actually gonna lose their shit when they find out. And now I really can't stop smiling. I try to think of something else to say, but my throat feels proper dry. We reach the set of double doors that lead out of the Arndale, the same ones that boy in the red puffa jacket ran through and I pull on the handle, holding the door open for Aimee.

She raises her eyebrows. 'Awww,' she says. 'You don't do this in school – you really trying to impress me, or what?'

I smile as we head outside, but I still can't look at her properly; I can't keep eye contact for too long, because of how much I like her. I shrug and I hope she can't see how awkward I am just being around her.

'Well, I'll make sure I do from now on,' I say.

It's cold outside and a sharp gust of wind hits me in my face. Aimee links her arm through mine and I swear I almost pass out. I must be looking at her funny, because she says: 'You don't mind, do you? It's freezing.'

'*Nah!* No!' I say, a bit too quickly, and she laughs. So much for trying to play it cool. There's some large stone steps that lead away from the Arndale and towards the other side of town, and we head down them. A tram makes its way noisily past us and Aimee turns to face me.

'Where is it we're actually going?' she asks.

Up close, I still can't get over how pretty she is. It's mad. She's got these grey flecks in her eyes that I've never noticed before and I feel myself looking down, towards her mouth. Her lips are sticky and shiny with gloss and I catch myself thinking about kissing her again—

'Jackson?' she says. 'Hello??!'

'Sorry,' I say. 'Printworks. I thought we'd go there – there's like Nando's and the cinema and—'

Aimee smiles again. 'I know what's inside the Printworks, Jackson,' she says.

I clear my throat and I feel myself getting hot, again. 'Oh, right, yeah. Soz,' I say. I suck in a sharp breath and I wish we could rewind and start again. All I've done since Aimee got here is make a complete fool of myself. I can just imagine Harrison and the others pissing themselves when I tell them later. Aimee nods but neither of us moves. I see her glance towards my mouth and wonder if she's thinking about kissing me too. But surely she wouldn't want me to do it in the middle of town? In

7

front of all these people. She lingers for another moment, and if that was my chance to make a move, it's gone, because she tugs at my arm.

'Come on, then,' she says, as we start walking again.

'All right,' I say. 'Keep your hair on.'

'Wow!' Aimee says and she bursts out laughing. 'You actually talk like someone's ninety-year-old grandma sometimes, y'know that.'

I bring my free hand to my chest and I pretend that I've been shot there. I even stagger about a bit. 'Ouch!' I say. 'You ain't playing today, are you? I mean, are you actually on this date cause you like me, or have you just come to take the piss? So far, I'm weird and I talk like someone's granny. Any more insults you wanna throw my way? You might as well get 'em out your system . . .'

Aimee laughs. 'Oh, stop fishing!' she says. 'I already told you I like you, I'm not saying it again.' She moves her hand along my arm, then links her fingers through mine. 'There's still time, though,' she adds, and she gives me that look again. Like she's thinking about kissing me too. I try not to make a big deal outta the fact that Aimee's holding my hand. Or that she's flirting with me. Is she flirting with me? There are a few shops and cafes dotted about outside, opposite a large, concrete square. A Caffè Nero, Foot Asylum, Selfridges. We take a left, beside this massive Next on the corner and I nudge Aimee playfully.

'Can't wait,' I say. 'Y'know there's nothing I want more in life than to be ripped to shreds by you!'

Aimee smiles. 'I knew it!' she says.

We make our way along the pavement, and at first I don't get what's going on. Maybe it's because I'm too distracted by Aimee and the fact she's holding my hand. And I'm concentrating far too much on making sure that I ain't holding it too tight, or that my hand ain't too limp or clammy or anything like that. I see a woman a little bit in front of us, dragging her small kid away from something by the hood of his coat. I hear her say: 'Sweetheart, come over here. Don't look! Come with Mummy . . . don't look!' The kid starts to cry and she picks him up and covers his eyes, walking away from the pavement, in the middle of the road that the tram runs down. There's something about the way she says it, something in her tone . . .

And then it's like everything else shifts into focus. I see all these people moving away from the side of the shop, or walking into the road like that woman did, and it's like I can feel it then. The fear and panic bubbling up all around us. I don't even know how to explain it, but you just know, don't you? You can tell. When something awful's about to happen. People are staring or turning their heads, another kid is crying. I see someone gasp, and a few people with their phones out, taking pictures . . . no, *filming*. But everyone's moving away from something on the floor. A knot tightens in my stomach and I feel Aimee freeze next to me.

'Oh my god,' she says. 'Oh my god, oh my god.' Aimee lets go of my hand and I see how much she's shaking as she moves her fingers to cover her mouth. She makes this weird sound, halfway between a scream and a sob, then she turns to bury her face in my neck. My eyes go to the spot that everyone seems to be walking past. The faded concrete squares to the side of Next. And that's when I see it.

The red puffa jacket, in a heap on the floor.

The same one that was weaving its way through the shopping centre while I'd been waiting for Aimee. I stare at the boy. At his brown skin and fade. At the massive tear down the side of his jacket, and the way his body's sprawled on the pavement. He looks proper young, he can't be more than fourteen. If that. There's a girl kneeling beside him, pressing something onto his stomach. An old cloth or something, like she's trying to stop the bleeding. But there's so much of it. So much blood – *everywhere*. I move my hands to my head and I step away from Aimee and I don't know if I want to cry, or scream, or run, or throw up.

My whole body feels weak, and even though I know that there's people around me, it all seems to wash over me. All I can hear is my quick breath and the loud thumping of my heart in my ears. There's a sharp, twisting pain deep inside my chest. I see Aimee leaning over me and I hear her say: 'Jackson, are you okay? Jackson?' But I can't speak. I can't stop shaking, or feeling like I can't breathe. I don't want Aimee to see me like this. I put my hands to my chest to try and stop the pain and I feel Aimee's hand on my back.

'Hey,' she says, but all I can do is stare at the ground. 'Just breathe,' she says. 'I'll do it with you, come on . . .'

Aimee breathes in and then out slowly, and I copy her, as she nods and keeps her hand on my back. The pain starts to ease and I feel the thumping in my chest slow down. The sound around me goes back to normal and I straighten myself up and suck in another deep breath. I half-expect Aimee to look at me like I'm the most pathetic boy in the whole of Manchester when I straighten myself up, but she doesn't.

'My sister has panic attacks,' she says, and she tugs at my arm. 'Come on,' she continues. 'Let's go the other way around, I'm sure someone's already called an ambulance ...'

I don't move. I can't stop staring at the boy in the red puffa jacket. There's tears and snot running down his face and I can see how frightened he is. Everyone else, apart from this one girl, just walks past him. People are crossing over to avoid that bit of the pavement or staring from a distance, and I'm suddenly angry. Why is no one helping him? Is it because they're scared? Or they don't care? Or do they just see this young Black boy and think the worst? That he somehow brought it on himself?

'Jackson!' Aimee says. 'Come on! It's like awful, it really is ... but we don't know what happened ... it could be gang-related, or anything.'

I look at Aimee, but I can't even deal with what she just said right now. *Gang-related.* If it was a white kid who had been stabbed, would she be saying that it was 'gang-related' then? I shake my head. I can't walk off and leave him. I can't walk off and do nothing like everyone else is doing. I take a deep breath and I feel myself start to tremble again. I've never seen anything like this, just a few fights in school, but I know ... *I know* I can't leave him.

'Nah. I can't ... I can't do nothing,' I say, and I head towards the boy.

11

Aimee doesn't follow me and I don't know if it's because she's too scared to get involved, or if she thinks that it's not her problem. Either way, I push it to the back of my mind. Up close, I can see that there's even more blood than I thought and I'm suddenly worried I'm gonna have another panic attack. The girl's trying to stop the bleeding with a scrunched-up T-shirt, but I can't even tell what colour it used to be. The boy turns his head and he catches my eye. The tears are streaming down his face and into his mouth and I see it then. *The fear*. Just how scared he is. He lets out a whimper and even though it's faint, I can tell how much pain he's in.

The girl glances up at me. She looks scared, but she presses down harder on his wound.

'Thank fuck,' she says and her voice is shaky. 'D'you know how many people have taken one look over here, then pissed off? I don't get what's taking the ambulance so long either . . .'

The boy starts to cry harder. 'It's all right, Shaq,' she says. 'The ambulance'll be here soon, yeah?'

But he's losing so much blood. He's already lost so much blood.

'I don't wanna die,' he says. 'I don't wanna die . . . Please don't leave me . . .'

The girl shakes her head. 'I won't,' she says, and she glances up at me.

I feel my chest tighten and I kneel beside this boy – beside Shaq – because I don't know what else to do. I'm not a paramedic, what *can* I do? Apart from try to make him feel less alone. Less scared.

I move my hand towards his and I'm not even sure if it'll make a difference because all I am is a stranger. But he reaches his hand out and wraps his fingers though mine. Like just holding onto me is enough to help him survive.

2

CHANTELLE

You know how you get those people who believe in fate? Who believe that *everything happens for a reason* and *people come into your life cos of it* and all that rubbish? Well, I am *not* one of those people. You can keep your shit Instagram quotes with sunsets in the background away from me, thank you very much. Here's what I actually think. That some people (and, yeah, I'm talking about myself here), are born into shit situations and others get the good end of the bargain. It's not your fault, it's not the 'universe' trying to prepare you for something. It's just the way it is. And you can either make the most of the situation you're in, or you can sit and wallow and cry, and feel sorry for yourself for eternity. Which let's face it, never solved anything.

For example, my current shit situation means that there's no way in hell I would be able to afford the jacket I saw in Lipsy. But my ability to make the most of the cards I've been dealt means that I'm going to take it anyway. Don't get me wrong, it's not like I steal things on a regular basis, and I don't take things cos I think the world owes me something. It's just sometimes there are things that I *really* want, and I know I wouldn't be able to afford them otherwise. It's sort of easy when you know how to do it too. The Lipsy bit has its own section inside the big Next in the Arndale. The jacket is awful. It's covered in all these diamantes and I, for one, wouldn't be caught dead in it, but I know how happy it'll make Marni when she opens it on her birthday next week, so I don't think twice.

I stuff the jacket underneath this dress, then I take loads of items inside the changing room and pretend I'm trying them on. I wait for a few minutes so that it doesn't look too dodgy, then stuff the jacket inside my bag and hand the rest of the clothes to the bored-looking shop assistant.

The next bit's probably the hardest. The jacket's still got the tag on and there's no point in me even trying to get it off, before I'm at home. Otherwise, it will just leave this massive rip, and it'll be no good. I see the security guard watching me, so I pretend to look through a rail of leggings. If you act guilty, then nine times out of ten, you'll be stopped. That's what my friend Leesha taught me, anyway.

The quickest way out of Next is the exit that leads onto Corporation Street and out of the Arndale. Once I'm out I can make a dash for it, but it's all about the timing, cos I know that as soon as I try to go through the exit, the tag will start beeping like no one's business, and I'll definitely be caught. I look around and I see a woman just in front of me. Her pram is loaded with about fifty million bags. Her kid throws a soft toy out the pram and the woman bends to pick it up. She hands it back to her kid and I yank a pair of leggings off the hanger, then walk past, dropping them into one of her bags without her even noticing. She huffs, then pushes the pram down this escalator. I follow her, so that I'm as close as possible, without looking like a weirdo. We reach the bottom of the escalator and both walk out the exit at exactly the same time.

The beeping goes off loudly and the security guard comes rushing over.

'Excuse me,' he says, and gestures for the woman to stop. Out of the corner of my eye, I see him asking her to open all her bags. I don't stop, I just keep walking until I'm outside and away from the shop. I pull my phone out and I send Marni a message:

Wait til u see wot I got u 4 ur bday!!! xxxx

> Wot is it????? xxx

Not telling u!!! xxx

> Plsssss xxxx

I go to reply, but I suddenly hear all this shouting. There's a group of boys standing a few paces away from the stone steps that lead out of another exit from the Arndale. Five of them have got their faces covered and there's only one who hasn't. He's wearing a bright red puffa jacket, with fur around the hood. I recognize him right away from school. Shaqeel, but everyone calls him Shaq. I don't know him well or anything – he's in the year below me – but everyone knows who he is. Shaq's one of those people who you hear before you see. He's got the loudest laugh and he's always messing about, but everyone likes him, even the teachers. Everyone knows how good at football he is too. He's like the next Marcus Rashford! He plays on the school team and I heard that he'd got scouted for United's under-eighteens as well.

I hear one of the guys say: 'Not such a big man now, are you?'

Then Shaq says: 'Nah, don't, please. Please!'

But I can't really make out what's happening. There's this weird flurry of movement and this scream, then the guys all run off. They leg it in different directions, pushing people out of the way. One of them jumps over a low brick wall then disappears into the crowds of people making their way through the concrete square. Another jumps onto a tram just before it pulls away. At first, I don't even think they've touched Shaq, cos I didn't see anyone throw any punches. It didn't even look like a fight, really. Then I see Shaq walking slowly away from that space near the steps. For a minute I wonder if he's pissing about, cos he's staggering all about the place like he's drunk. Or acting like he's taken something. Then I notice he's clutching his stomach and that's when I see it. The blood.

He tries to steady himself against the outside wall of Next, but he can barely hold himself up. He tries to open his mouth to ask for help, but he's obviously in so much pain and shock that he can't form any words. He just makes this whimpering sound. I'm frightened, but I feel the adrenaline kick in. I don't think, I just rush over to help him. Shaq loses his grip and collapses and it's almost like I've stepped out of my own body. Like I'm watching someone else, some other girl, kneeling beside Shaq. I shout for help, but no one does anything. I don't even realize I've made the call, but the next minute, the words, 'Ambulance! I need an ambulance!' leave my mouth. Shaq scrunches up his face and he glances down towards his stomach. He must suddenly realize how bad it is, cos his breathing quickens, and he cries loudly, moving his face so that it's pressed into the concrete.

I hear the woman on the other end of the line say: 'Chantelle? The main thing is to try and stop the bleeding until we arrive ... can you do that? Is there something you can use ... a cloth, or T-shirt? Try to find something and press down as hard as you can. Keep the pressure on the wound. Okay?'

'Okay,' I say. I feel tears stinging my eyes and I don't want to hang up, I don't want the ambulance woman to go, cos I'm so scared. I'm scared that I don't know what I'm doing, and that Shaq might not make it. Every inch of me is trembling, but I reach over and grab my bag, emptying my shit out onto the floor. I've got an old T-shirt in there, this grey one that I was actually going to put on one of the shop hangers, in place of the Lipsy jacket. I grab the T-shirt, then lean over and unzip Shaq's coat, so I can get to the wound better. My heart almost stops, when I see how bad it *really* is. But I try not to show it, cos I don't want to scare him. I scrunch up the T-shirt as tight as I can, and

18

I press it onto the wound. Shaq winces and he turns his head to look at me. Tears stream down his face, but he manages to say: 'You ... you go my school.'

I nod. I don't know if it helps, him having someone here that he recognizes. Someone familiar, but I swear, I see some of the panic go. I press down on the shirt as everyone else just walks past us, and all I can think is, *I don't want Shaq to die.* I wish the ambulance would hurry the fuck up. It seems to be taking for ever and what am I supposed to do? How am I supposed to save him alone? A boy comes over to help, I don't get much of a look at him, but I mumble something about being glad that someone's stopped. I know that there ain't much he can do either, but I'm glad that someone else at least tried, instead of just walking past, like Shaq doesn't matter. Like he's just a piece of rubbish. Something that can just be stepped over, instead of a kid who's badly hurt.

The boy doesn't say anything at first, maybe because he's so shocked. He glances down at the T-shirt I'm holding and I realize why it isn't working: there's just too much blood. He kneels down beside Shaq and I hear Shaq say: 'I'm gonna die, ain't I?' The words come out faint and his voice cracks, and then he adds. 'Don't leave me ... I don't wanna die. I don't wanna die yet. I'm scared ... *I want my mum ...*'

Shaq cries harder and his words sting. My throat suddenly dries up, 'cos I don't know what to say. Am I supposed to lie and tell him that everything's gonna be all right, even though it might not be? Am I supposed to make out that everything will be fine? Even though I can see how bad it is?

I hear the boy say: 'I'm not going anywhere, all right. The ambulance'll be here soon. I'm right here. I'm here . . .'

Another boy comes running over from the tram stop across the road. There ain't much he can do either, but I hear him on the phone, asking how long the ambulance is gonna be, saying that it needs to hurry. Shaq just keeps crying and I hear the faint sirens in the background grow louder. He catches the eye of the boy holding his hand and he says: 'Will you tell my mum that I love her?'

''I will . . .' the boy says, even though he'll probably never see Shaq's mum.

The second boy is standing just to the side of us, and when I look properly I realize he goes to my school too. The noise of the sirens is almost deafening. Then the next minute, the police and an ambulance are here. The paramedics rush over and move me and this boy out the way, saying long words I don't even understand. But they ask me what Shaq's name is as they strap something around his stomach. They lift him onto one of those beds with wheels, then hoist him into the ambulance. One of the paramedics says something about me being brave and how I did the right thing, to try and stop the bleeding. Then they close the doors and drive off. There's loads of people standing around now, watching. Me and whoever this boy is share a look. A look that says: *I hope we've done enough. I hope to god he'll be all right.* I bend down and start to pick all my shit up off the floor. I'm shaking and I just wanna get out of there. Two policemen come over, and I pray they didn't see me shove the Lipsy jacket that still has a security tag hanging off it back into my bag. But they don't seem to notice. The boy who's standing with me does, though. He gives me this funny look, like he's judging me. Like he thinks I'm trash or something and for a minute, I feel embarrassed that I even stole the jacket in the first place. But then I push all that aside, cos it's got nothing to do with him. And who is he to even stand there and judge me, anyway? I shoot him a filthy look and then one of the officers says: 'Hello, do you mind if we ask you both a couple of questions?'

I shrug and I feel the boy next to me tense, but he says: 'No, 'course not.'

The police officer nods. Out of the corner of my eye, in the distance, I see the other boy who came over to help – the one from my school – rush off and disappear into the crowds.

3

MARC

I push my way through the crowds and I keep moving as quick as I can. As soon as I saw the police arrive, that was it. *I was out.* I don't even bother to look behind me, just in case they notice that I got off. I can hear more sirens screeching as I follow the road that runs down the side of the Arndale and up past Shudehill Bus Station. Every part of me is still shaking. *I saw it all.* The whole stabbing. I'd been waiting at the tram stop for Rhys. The thing is, though, I knew that it was gonna happen even before it did. I know that sounds proper stupid, but as soon as I saw those guys run out the exit after that boy in red, I just felt it. I felt the atmosphere change. I suppose when you grow up in a place where violence and fighting can kick off at any minute, you get used to knowing what the signs are. You get used to being able to sense it, just before it's about to happen . . .

I didn't know what to do at first. I was too frightened to go over straight away, in case the boys who'd stabbed him were gonna come back. So I just stood there, frozen. Then I saw this girl from my school go over. This gobby one who told me to watch where the fuck I was going when I accidentally bumped into her on my first day. This other boy joined her and I knew I had to try and do something. I've spent enough of my life scared and helpless. Not being able to do anything when my dad hit my mum and then me, and I never want to feel like that again.

So I called the ambulance again and tried to get them to hurry up. And even though I wanted to run away and curl into a tiny ball, I went to try and help.

I didn't wanna stick around when the police got there, in case they saw me and thought I was involved. I didn't wanna end up being arrested, or searched, like what normally happens. And if I'd have got picked up by the police, then I'd have been in some serious shit with Dry Eileen.

I've spent most of my life around police officers, foster carers and social workers to know that when it comes to it, none of them ever believe a boy like me.

I've been in care for about five years. Before I moved here, I was living in Bolton. It was shit, but no matter how many times I got moved around, at least I was still at the same school. But then about four months ago, I got sent to live with Dry Eileen all the way on the other side of Manchester and I had to change schools. I've already tried to run away twice. Both times my social worker, Emma, caught me. Don't ask me how, it's like that woman's God or something. She can tell what I'm about to do, right before I do it. The first time, I even got as far as the train station. Then as soon as I reached Piccadilly, she came at me out of nowhere, and started going on about how dangerous running away is, how I hadn't even given Dry Eileen a chance. I wanted to tell her that she should try living with Dry Eileen and see how she likes it. But I just got in the car with her and let her drive me back. It's only a matter of time before Dry Eileen says she doesn't want me, that she 'can't cope', anyway. That's what always happens. One minute, you're with a family who are telling you to treat their house like it's your own, the next you're packing all your shit up in a bag ready to be moved *again*.

I don't want to go back to Dry Eileen's, so I decide to walk around the Northern Quarter for a bit. It's the one place I go when I want to get away. And it doesn't matter where I'm moved to or which new carer I have to go and live with, it's the one place I feel safe. I can't explain it, but I just like getting lost down all the side streets and by the old buildings and stuff that are covered in murals and graffiti. I like trying to figure out what the murals mean, or the words say, or who the people behind them are …

Rhys was supposed to meet me at the tram stop, but I don't even know if they'll let the trams come this way now. Maybe they'll just cordon everything off? I pull my phone out and open WhatsApp, but he still ain't responded. Not since I told him I was here. I kiss my teeth.

Rhys doesn't always message back. Sometimes he ghosts me

for days and then just pops up again with a 'hey'. *Hey!!* After he more or less disappeared off the face of the Earth. But like an eediat, I always respond. I check the time – *16.30*. I've been waiting for almost an hour.

I type out another message:

> Some1's just been stabbed near the Arndale!!
> I saw it all happen!!

> R u comin or wot???

> Or shuld I just go?

I stare at the message and I really want him to come more than anything. Cause after what I've just seen, I don't wanna be on my own. I at least wanna be around someone to take my mind off it. I plug my earphones in. If he's not here by the time I've listened to three songs and gone to my favourite mural in the Northern Quarter, then I'm just gonna go. Deep down, though, I know that if Rhys was gonna come, then he'd be here by now.

4

JACKSON

I can't stop staring at the floor. At the space on the concrete where that boy – Shaq – had been. There's even more police here now, talking loudly and moving people on, and I see some of them making their way up the stone steps to tape the exit to the Arndale off. I feel my whole body tense and I try to remember everything I know I'm supposed to do when the police stop me. Hold eye contact, don't answer back, speak properly ... don't use slang. But, most importantly, *stay calm*. No matter what they do or say. If I show that I'm even a bit pissed, they'll say I'm being 'aggressive' or 'intimidating' or 'violent'. And that's when things can get really bad. At least, that's what my dad's told me, anyway.

I see that girl, whoever she is, shove a jacket into her bag and I notice it's still got this massive security tag on it. She looks up at me and realizes I've clocked it, and for a split-second she looks embarrassed. Then she shoves the bag on her shoulder, straightens herself up and glares at me, as if to say: *mind your own fucking business!* I shake my head and look away. Some boy's just been stabbed and all she's bothered about is the jacket she's stolen. She shoots me a dirty look.

Two police officers come over to us, and one of them says: 'Do you mind if we ask you both a couple of questions? Did you see what happened?'

I look at him, and even though I know I've done nothing wrong, I feel uneasy.

'Sort of,' I reply and my voice shakes. 'Well, I didn't see anything happen, I just . . . came over to help.'

The officer stares at me and then he gives me this weird look, after the word 'help'. Like he doesn't believe me. He gestures for me to follow him and I search for Aimee in the crowd, but I can't find her. We stop a few paces away from where another police officer is putting up that plastic tape. He gestures to the girl.

'Do you know her?' he asks.

'No,' I say. 'I saw her with that boy – Shaq, she said his name is – and I went over to see if there was something I could do.'

'Right,' he says.

I feel people staring as they pass. They're probably wondering what I've done. Why I'm the one who's been stopped. Maybe some of them think it was me . . . that I'm the reason Shaq ended up in the back of an ambulance. The policeman pulls a pen and pad out of one of the pockets of his jacket.

'Was he a mate of yours?' he asks. 'The boy who's been stabbed, did you know him?'

I swallow, hard. 'No,' I say. 'I just ... I saw that he was hurt, and everyone was walking past. Except that girl ...' I point back in the direction of where we've just come. 'She was there with him, on her own. So I went over, to see if he was okay – to try and help.'

The last word comes out small. *Quiet.* I went over to try and help, but all I could do was hold his hand. The policeman stares at me again. There's something about the way he looks at me. It's not just the fact that he clearly doesn't believe a word I'm saying ... it's something else. Something, about the way he takes in my clothes and my trainers, and my Rolex, that makes me feel bare uncomfortable. He probably wouldn't believe me if I told him my dad bought me that watch for my sixteenth birthday just gone.

'Help how?' he asks, and his voice is cold. 'What exactly did you do?'

I feel embarrassed and stupid, because what *did* I do? I didn't phone an ambulance like that girl, or try and see what was taking them so long, like that boy did. And I didn't try and stop the bleeding either. I just knelt there and held his hand. Like a total idiot. Why did I even think that would make any difference?

I stare at the ground and I say, 'I held his hand.'

He scoffs. 'You held his hand?' he repeats and I try to ignore his tone. I feel the anger rising inside me, but I push it deep down to the pit of my stomach, like I know I have to. I just wanna get out of here. I don't wanna be standing here talking to this policeman and being made to feel like I've done something wrong, when all I did was try to help.

'Yeah,' I continue. 'That girl had already phoned an ambulance, and he looked ... *frightened*. So I thought it would make him feel less alone.'

The policeman goes quiet. 'Right,' he says. 'So let me get this straight, you didn't see the incident itself? Who did it? What they looked like? You just came out here ... then tried to help?'

I pause. 'Yeah,' I say, and then I remember. 'But I was in the Arndale, I dunno, like ten minutes before it happened and I saw him – *Shaq* – running through the shopping centre. He was being chased by about five or six guys ...'

'I see,' he says. 'And did you see what they were wearing?'

I shake my head. 'Nah ... I mean, *no!* They were all wearing black and they had their faces covered.'

He glances down at my wrist again, and then he says: 'Pretty expensive watch you've got there, isn't it? That yours?'

I stare at him and I feel that anger inside me, again. Pretty expensive for me, that's what he means. Like the only way I could ever afford a watch like this is if I'd robbed someone, or got it another way. Through selling drugs, probably. I want to ask him: *Who else's could it be?* But I bite my tongue.

'My dad bought it for me,' I reply.

He stares at me and I can tell that he thinks I'm lying. 'And what's your name, son?' He says.

I try not to pull a face when he says *son*. 'Jackson,' I reply.

'Jackson what?'

'Campbell.'

I already know what's coming next. I've been stopped and searched enough times to know what he's doing. He reels off some bullshit script and I have to go through the humiliation of it all. In front of Aimee, in front of all these people standing outside the Arndale, who've just heard that someone's been stabbed and see me, getting searched. I feel angry and numb, but I go through the motions of it all, like I always have to. Holding my arms out so he can pat me down, turning out my pockets . . . of course, he doesn't find anything, but he still isn't satisfied. Maybe he was hoping I'd have a knife on me.

'What's your date of birth?' He asks. 'And your address?'

I tell him and he looks at me funny when I say my postcode. 'Give me a minute,' he says. 'Stay there.'

I don't move and he wanders down the pavement a bit, talking into his radio. I know he's running a check on me to see if I've got any convictions, or if there's a warrant out for my arrest, or if I've been in trouble with the police before. It's like I'm treated like a criminal just for existing. I search for Aimee in the crowd again. Most people must've got bored of staring and got off, because there's nowhere near as many people as there were a few minutes ago.

I finally see her standing beside one of the bins and scrolling through her phone. She locks eyes with me as the policeman comes back and I think she looks ... *embarrassed*. Not embarrassed because I'm being searched for no reason, though. It's almost like *I've* embarrassed her. *Like I'm the one who's done something wrong.*

I hear the policeman say: 'You sure? Okay ... all right!' And then he cuts his radio call.

I don't say anything about my police check coming back clean, like I knew it would, or the fact that he's even running a check on me in the first place. I just stand there and wait.

'Never been arrested,' he says. 'That's impressive! All right, you can go.'

I head back towards Aimee with his words ringing in my ears. *Never been arrested, that's impressive!* I feel him watching as I walk off, but I don't dare look back. I feel hurt and mad. He probably thinks that I'm lying and that I know more about Shaq than I'm letting on, or that my watch is actually stolen, and I just wanna get out of here. One things for sure though, he can do as many searches as he wants when he gets back to the station, but no matter how many times he runs my name through that system, it will still come back clean.

The thin police tape's been tied across the corner bit outside Next, and I take it all in for a minute. The police, the space on the ground where Shaq had been fighting for his life. People walking past and wondering what's happened. I move my hands to my head, because none of it seems real, and part of me feels like I'm stuck in some sort of messed-up dream. My head is still spinning.

'Are you all right?' Aimee asks. 'What was he asking you?

31

Did he think you had something to do with it?'

The policeman's words echo in my head, but I just shrug. 'I don't know,' I say. Even though the real answer is *probably*. Part of me is surprised Aimee's even still here. I guess I expected her to get off.

Aimee shakes her head. 'It's so awful,' she says. 'I just … I can't believe that happened.'

I don't say anything, because what am I supposed to say? I don't really even want to carry on with the date now. How can I see a kid nearly dead, then just carry on like normal? I feel hollow as Aimee links her arm through mine and ushers me away. It doesn't feel the way it did before somehow. The weight of the silence feels heavy. Everything suddenly feels heavy. I can't get Aimee's comment out of my head either, what she said about it being gang-related. I know that the only reason she said that was because of how Shaq looks. The colour of his skin, and it makes me look at her differently. I glance back towards where that girl and boy had been. Towards where Shaq lay just minutes earlier, but there's nothing there now except concrete and twisted police tape.

Aimee tries to fill the quiet by saying she looked up what had happened to see if it was on the news, and then she clearly decides to change the subject. But I ain't listening. I can't concentrate because all I can think about is that fucked-up comment that police officer made, and how scared Shaq was, and how all he kept doing was asking for his mum. What if he dies? What if he never gets to tell her how much he loves her? What if the last thing Shaq ever says is to three random strangers who didn't even know him? We walk towards the small crossroads, and I hear the sound of more sirens in the background. I kick something, with my foot.

It skids along the pavement and I stare down at the blue plastic on the floor. It's one of those wallet things that you use to keep your bus pass or something in. I bend down and pick it up, and Aimee pulls a face.

'Seriously?' she says. 'You actually pick shit up off the floor? That could be *anyone's* – you don't know where it's been.'

I shrug. 'Someone might need it,' I say, and I flip the wallet thing open. There's not much in it, just an igo bus pass and what looks like a chewed-up piece of gum, wrapped in a bit of paper, pushed into one of the clear pockets.

'Urgh,' Aimee says. 'See? That's why you don't go round picking random stuff up. That's *nasty* . . . why couldn't they have just put it in the bin?'

But I stare down at the picture on the igo card. At the thick curls that seem to be taking up most of the photo and the gold hoops. Even in the photo, it looks like she's telling me to *mind my own fucking business*.

'What is it?' Aimee asks.

'It's that girl from before,' I reply. 'The one who was trying to help that boy out. She must've dropped it when she left.'

Aimee shrugs like she couldn't care less. But I gaze at the name printed along the bottom – *Chantelle Walker* – then slide the plastic wallet into my back pocket.

5

CHANTELLE

The police had cordoned off most of the Arndale. The ground floor exits near to where Shaq had been were closed, which meant that I had to go the *long* way around. They wouldn't let anyone back in the shopping centre and all I wanted to do was find a toilet so I could clean myself up. I saw the police searching that boy while I was giving my statement and even though they'd finished questioning me long before him, I still hung back a bit. Just in case they thought he had something to do with the stabbing. Then, they let him go and he went over to his stuck-up looking girlfriend in the crowd.

I walk along, up near Shudehill Bus Station, and head to another entrance on the far side of the Arndale that they haven't closed off. I feel people staring at me as I push through a set of double doors. Probably cos I've still got some of Shaq's blood on me. But I've never really cared what people think, and I'm not about to start now. My legs feel like jelly and I head into the toilets next door to a crappy bagel place. I walk to the row of sinks beside this long mirror, and I pump soap into my hands, then hit the cold tap. For a minute, I just stand there, in the middle of these rank-smelling toilets, feeling the water running along my hands, yet not really feeling anything at all. I scrub my fingers and up my arms, then I get more soap, then even more. The tap only stays on for a few seconds, so I hit it again, then again, then *again*. I can't stop thinking about Shaq. I can't stop thinking about whether or not they'll get him to the hospital on time, if they'll be able to save him. And I can't stop thinking about him lying there. Wanting his mum *so* badly and knowing that he might not ever see her again. I feel an ache deep inside my chest. I pull off my coat, then unzip the hoodie that I'm wearing underneath. There's blood on that too. I shove it in my bag, then button my coat all the way to my neck. I was going to hang around town for a bit longer but now all I want to do is go home and see Marni and Gran.

I barge into a woman as I head out the toilets and make my way towards the bus station.

Piccadilly is rammed and I see the 101 getting ready to leave, just as I'm crossing the road. I leg it towards the bus, knocking people out the way, cos I'm not about to be waiting around for another five hundred hours on a Sunday. I get there just in time and I rummage through my pockets for my bus pass, but it ain't there. The bus driver sighs and looks around.

'One minute!' I say, and I shove my bag down on the single seat that's right near the front so that I can look properly. I pull everything out my bag, the jacket, my purse, but it still ain't there. *Fuck. I must've dropped it.* It could be anywhere ... in the toilets, or back where Shaq was. I open my purse, praying to God that I've at least got some change, enough to get home, or even halfway home, but it's empty apart from a few coppers. One woman sitting near the front tuts, like I'm holding them up on purpose, and I give her a dirty look.

'Come on, love,' the driver says. 'I haven't got all day.'

I feel my heart sink. What am I supposed to tell him? That I've got no money. That there's no way I can afford to get home without my bus pass. He sighs loudly again.

'All right!' I snap, and I carry on looking, even though I know for certain that my pass ain't there. Most bus drivers are usually pretty all right, and if they see you looking for your pass, then they just let you on. But not this one. This one is a complete knob.

'Look,' he says. 'I'm already running late, thanks to you. Either you pay your fare, or you get off.'

He stares at me, and even though I don't care what people think, it's still proper embarrassing. When you don't even have two quid to get yourself home. I look down and I hear a few people muttering the background. *This is the last thing I need.* I take a deep breath, cos I'm not about to start beefing the bus driver.

I feel embarrassed, so I lower my voice and say: 'I ain't got it. I've lost my bus pass.'

'Oh, yeah.' He snorts loudly, and I feel everyone looking at me.

'And what, you conveniently don't have any money either? Pull the other one. Get off,' he says. 'Go on. This isn't a free service!'

I feel myself go red, but I still don't move. 'I don't have any money,' I say. 'I can't get home. I live too far . . .'

'That ain't my problem,' he replies. 'Do I look like your dad? You should've thought about that before you left the house.'

'What?' I say. I look around to see if anyone else has noticed how rude this guy is being, but no one has. Tears start to prick my eyes, and not just cos I've lost my bus pass. It's cos of Shaq, cos of everything that's happened, cos of the fact that I just want to get home. The bus driver points to the double doors.

'*Off!*' he says.

And I'm suddenly angry. I've been trying to control my temper and not mouth off so much these days, but this guy is taking the piss. I snatch my bag up.

'Well, I ain't moving,' I say. 'I need to get home. Anyway, ain't you supposed to give free lifts to minors if they're stranded? Ain't that part of the law?'

He switches the engine off and I hear people behind me groan, but I still don't move.

'You can stand there all you want,' he says. 'But I'm not moving this bus until you pay or *get off*!' He pulls open the little door to his compartment then shouts towards the back of the bus. 'Ladies and gents,' he says, 'in case you're wondering what the hold-up is, you can thank this young lady right here. She's refusing to pay her fare and she won't get off the bus. Because she's a selfish so-and-so—'

'Who are you calling selfish?' I say.

'*Just get off the bus!*' I hear someone else shout, but then what? I do the same thing again? Try and get home with no money? Walking home would take me ages. I hear some footsteps storm towards me, then feel someone barge me out the way, so that they can get to the driver. I think it's just some random person at first. Then I recognize him – the boy from before, who came over to help with Shaq, then just . . . disappeared.

'I actually wanna get home before next year, y'know,' he says. He turns to the driver. 'How much is it? Her bus fare?'

'Two pound,' the driver says.

He sighs, then roots through his jacket pocket and throws some change down. 'Two pound,' he repeats. 'You're really out here, inconveniencing my life over two pound? What is wrong with you?' He kisses his teeth, then stares at me as he walks past. 'You're welcome!' he snaps, then heads towards an empty seat at the back of the bus and sits down.

I feel myself getting hot. I would've said thank you, if he'd have given me the chance.

The driver starts the engine and I think about going to sit next to this boy. The boy with plaits and Doc Martens, who tried to help earlier. I think about asking him why he ran off, and if he's okay. But when I catch his eye, he shoves his earphones in and looks away. So I pull my bag onto my shoulder and make my way up to the top deck of the bus.

I don't look at the driver or the boy who paid for me as I get off the bus. I just keep my head down and walk off. The truth is I'm embarrassed. You see, I don't care if people hate me, or if they just take one look at me and think that I'm rude or gobby. I don't even care if people think I'm a waste of space, or someone who will never amount to anything. It's the pity I can't stand. The way people look at me when I have to use all these vouchers on the self-service till in Asda, and still end up having to put something back. Not being able to afford to go to concerts, or on school trips. Whenever everyone in my year goes to Alton Towers, it's usually me and a handful of other kids that get left behind cos there's no way we'd be able to afford to go.

The worst is when teachers can't even make eye contact with you, cos they know. They know everything about your life and how the one person who was supposed to love you more than anything in the world can't even be bothered to do that. I don't want people thinking they have to be extra-nice to me, just cos of the way my life's turned out. I'm *fine*. If anything, I'll just show everyone it doesn't matter that the woman who gave birth to me isn't around. It doesn't matter that we've never had any money. I can still make something of my life. I can still go on and do something worthwhile. I don't really know what that is yet, I'm hoping I'll figure it out. But I've applied to do A-levels at this really good college not too far from me. I've picked English language and lit and history and psychology, cos they're the subjects I'm interested in the most, and the ones I get the highest marks in too. The college is proper difficult to get into, though, and I need six 5-9s in my GCSEs. That's why I've been trying so hard at school.

It's getting dark now, and I cross over the road and walk past the park towards a row of terraced houses behind this strip of grass. I've lived in Moss Side ever since I was born, but until we went to stay with Gran three years ago, we used to move around a lot. Trudy was always getting into some sort of fight with the neighbours, or we'd end up getting kicked out cos she'd spend all the money she got on herself and never pay any of the bills. Our house is right on the main road that leads to the motorway and all you ever hear is noise. Cars, buses, sirens, no matter what time of day it is. But at least me and Marni are safe. At least Gran's here to look after us. Instead of me trying to look after everyone.

I turn the key in the front door. Marni's already inside, sprawled on the carpet. She doesn't even look up when I come in, just carries on watching whatever cartoon's on the telly, resting her head in her hands. We both have different dads, and we don't look alike, not really. Marni's much darker than me and her curls are more like loose waves. Whereas mine are thick and never do what I want them to do. Marni's face is pointy and sharp, whereas mine's just round. I never get why people call it having a half-sister, though, cos there's no half about it. She's my sister. End of. She can get right on my nerves and piss me off sometimes, but I still love her. More than anything. I dump my stuff on the settee and after everything with Shaq, I just wanna rush over and hug her, but I don't.

'You done your homework?' I say, but Marni still doesn't look up. '*Marni!*' I snap.

'I've *done* ittt!' she says, and gestures towards an open

exercise book on the floor. 'Can't you see I'm trying to watch something?'

I bend down and pick the exercise book up. I stare at Marni's rushed handwriting.

'A week in the life of a Greek god,' I read aloud. 'Monday, nothing happened. Tuesday, still nothing. Wednesday, went to Asda. Thursday, nothing happened. Friday, life is *sooo* boring being a Greek god ...' I pause. 'You serious?' I say.

'What?' Marni says. 'Nothing happened, cos we never go anywhere. We never do anything ... and anyway, it's *so* dumb! How am I supposed to know what it's like be a Greek god?'

'You're supposed to use your imagination,' I say. 'Make it up. What are you even supposed to be the god of?'

Marni shrugs and moves her hair away from her face. 'I dunno. We had to invent one.' She pauses. 'The God of Nothing *Ever* Happens and My Teacher is *Sooo* Dry, and This is Dumb,' she says.

'You can't use that as a god,' I reply.

'Why?' Marni snaps. 'It's *my* homework, and my teacher *is* dry. School's dry ... *you're dry* ... and if nothing happened, how is that my fault?!'

I used to feel the same way about school as Marni. I properly hated it and I'd hardly ever go in. The amount of times I wouldn't bother with homework, either. I spent pretty much three years in 'return to learn' which is where they send you when you're too 'badly behaved' to go to your normal lessons, but they don't wanna kick you out. Then I got my Year Nine mock results back and I saw all 2s and 3s and Gran was proper

41

mad and I guess, it all just sort of hit me. About the type of future I wanted. Or didn't. And I realized that I'd much rather choose whether I wanted to go to college or not, or do a certain job or not, than *have* to do something cos it's my only option. After that, I started working proper hard, and I even got moved up in all my sets. I want the same for Marni, too. I guess that's why I'm so tough on her sometimes.

I grab the remote and switch the TV off.

'Oi!' Marni shouts. 'I was watching that! I'm telling Gran. Graaaaan!' she screams. '*Graaaann!*'

'Tell her!' I say. 'What d'you think Gran's gonna say when she finds out you ain't done your homework properly?'

Marni pauses for a minute, then she gets up and pulls at the pink leggings she's wearing. They're way too small for her, but she'd never let me throw them away.

'Fine!' she says loudly, snatching the exercise book from me. 'Why you always ruining my life?' she continues.

Marni stomps over to the small table at the far end of the living room and sits down, loudly unzipping her pencil case, and slamming each pen down on top of the glass table. I feel her glaring at me, but she picks her pen up and starts writing anyway.

I head out of the living room. I know I can be a right killjoy sometimes, but I've always been the one who's looked after Marni. I'd pick her up from school, get her dressed, make dinner, take her to the doctors when she was sick. Even when she was a baby. Trudy was always off with some guy. Or sometimes, she'd disappear for days on end and leave us with

42

no money or food in the house. I tried to keep everything hidden back then, though. Even from Gran. Maybe cos part of me was secretly hoping that one day, Trudy might change. Or maybe, cos I felt like I *had* to protect her. I had to do it, cos she was my mum. But I guess I realized, that just cos you share the same DNA and cells as someone, doesn't mean that they should be allowed to treat you badly. *It doesn't make it okay.*

I actually hated being lumbered with Marni at first, cos it meant that I couldn't do normal stuff like go to town with Leesha and my other mates, and Marni was with me so much that people thought she was my kid. Some people still do. Then, I guess, I got used to it. Not only that though, I could tell how much she needed me. I know what it's like to feel unlovable, or like no one wants you, and I never want my little sister to have to through that, so I try to give Marni all the love we never got off Trudy, plus more.

I head into our tiny kitchen and I smell chicken being cooked and plantain being fried. Gran works a double shift at Asda most days, but she always makes sure she has Sundays off, so she can go to church and cook Sunday dinner. The kitchen is proper hot and there's loads of pans bubbling away the small stove. I pull myself up onto the kitchen counter, in the space next to the boiler, and I lean my head against the wall. I still can't get my head around everything that's happened. I can't stop thinking about Shaq ... lying there, the blood, saying over and over that he wanted his mum.

Gran looks up from her frying pan. Her thick hair's slicked

back into a bun and I can see the grey starting to creep down at the front. It's weird, cos I don't think me and Marni look much like Trudy, but I can see us all in Gran.

'You're back early,' Gran says.

I suck in a sharp breath and I stare up at the patch of damp on the ceiling.

'Someone got stabbed in town,' I blurt out. 'And I saw it happen . . . well, I didn't see it or nothing like that, but I saw the boy and I tried to help, and . . .' I don't know why, but it's like it all suddenly hits me at once. Shaq. *Trudy.* Having a mum, but not really having one. I try not to think about it too much, but hearing Shaq call out for his mum like that made me realize how much it hurts that she ain't around. I guess I try to ignore it. But deep down, there's a part of me that's always wished that she would just be the type of mum that me and Marni need. Or, that I could somehow find a way to make her love us back. I feel the tears prick my eyes and Gran turns off one of the hobs.

'Oh my god,' she says, and she rushes over to me. 'What happened? Are you okay?'

I shrug. I'm used to being okay, or at least, pretending that I am. But I shake my head slowly. 'I don't think so,' I say, and I feel a tear slide down my face.

Gran wipes the tear away with her hand and she brings me in for a hug. And for the first time since I was probably about Marni's age, I sit there and let myself cry.

6

JACKSON

We're in Nando's, squashed into one of the small booths beside the window. It's still pretty busy considering most of town has been closed off, and I wonder how many people actually know what's happened. Or maybe they don't care. I can hear the familiar Nando's mash-up of Portuguese songs and I can tell that people are laughing and joking and eating around me, but I feel numb. Even though I'm sitting here with Aimee, it's like part of me is back there, on the street, with Shaq. And no matter how hard I try, I can't get his face out my head. I can't stop hearing him cry out for his mum. I can't stop feeling his fingers wrapped around mine.

I stare down at the table, and I wonder if Shaq got to the hospital in time. I keep trying to work out the law of averages

45

in my head and figure out how much of a chance he has of pulling through. I read somewhere that last year there were 375 stabbings in Manchester. And I know that there's a 27.4 % survival rate with stab and gunshot victims, because I remember reading that somewhere too. So surely there's a chance that Shaq could be in that percentage that survives? I'm half-tempted to look up the figures properly on my phone. But it's like I can't even move. Aimee's not stopped talking since we got here. I don't even know what she's banging on about because I've not been listening. Everything seems insignificant, unimportant, in comparison to what just happened.

Aimee is halfway through some story about the time she got kicked out of a chemistry lesson by a teacher we all hate, when I say: 'Do you not even care?'

Aimee looks confused. 'Huh?' she replies. 'About being kicked out my lesson?'

I shake my head. 'About Shaq!' I say. 'I don't get how you can sit here and carry on like everything's normal. Like we didn't just see someone ...' I stare down at my hands. 'What if he dies?'

I feel Aimee stiffen, then she shuffles over in her seat. 'Oh,' she says. Like I'm talking about a maths book she's left behind, or someone's birthday she's forgotten. Aimee rubs her arm.

'I mean, yeah, it was horrible,' she says. 'You hear about people getting stabbed all the time, read about it and stuff, but to *actually* see it.' She shudders and then she says, 'But, I mean, we don't know the circumstances, do we? It's not like we know the full story or anything.'

46

I stare at her and my breath catches in my throat. 'Full story?' I say, and I can feel the anger rising inside me. 'A kid was stabbed. And everyone else apart from that girl was just ... walking past him. Leaving him there to bleed out. What more do we need to know?'

She shrugs. 'I mean,' she starts again. 'He looked pretty rough, d'you know what I mean? And with boys like *that*, it's always drugs, or gangs, or something ... and I dunno, I just think that if you're gonna get involved in all that stuff, well, that's what happens.'

I stare at her and every part of me is shaking. 'Boys like what?' I snap. 'Why don't you just say what you *really* mean? Black.'

'No,' Aimee adds quickly and she starts to go red. 'That's not what I meant, Jackson, you're twisting my words. *You're* nothing like him. You don't walk around acting all ghetto ... you're from a good home, and you don't even talk ...' She pauses. 'You're *different*,' she says.

The words hit me, hard. Like I've just been punched in the stomach. *Different*. Like I'm supposed to take it as a compliment that Aimee doesn't quite see me as being Black. Or her messed-up version of what that is. I'm always being told that I don't 'act Black' or even 'sound' it at school, whatever the fuck that means. Or I have to put up with my friends' mums asking me what I 'really think about the Black Lives Matter movement', and then coming out with some bullshit like: 'But all lives matter. Trees' lives matter.' And now Aimee is saying this. I can't even look at her. I've fancied Aimee for *years* but it's like the person I thought she was and the person she actually *is* are completely different. I used to think Aimee was the prettiest girl in school, by far. But what she's saying is so ugly and all I want to do is get out of there.

I don't even say anything, I just stand up.

'What are you doing?' Aimee asks.

'I'm out,' I say. 'I ain't staying here ... I can't sit here with you, after what you just said.'

Aimee looks confused and I climb out of the booth. 'No, wait!' she says. '*Jackson!* I didn't mean it like that ... it came out wrong ... I didn't mean it that way ... I'm sorry, *okay*?!'

I feel people staring at us, but I pull my jacket on and make my way to the door. I hear Aimee shouting my name, and the next minute I feel my phone vibrate in my pocket, but I don't answer. She did mean it. She meant every word and why should I have to sit there while she plays dumb and asks me to explain exactly why what she said was so messed up? *Fuck that!* I head out into the cold and I pull my phone out. This morning, all I wanted was for Aimee to fancy me back. For her to like me and maybe even let me kiss her. And now ... I can't believe that this is how she really feels. I've had to deal with shit like this most of my life, but I guess I just never expected to hear it from Aimee.

I've got a couple of missed calls and a few messages. My mum's tried to phone me twice and so has Aimee. Harrison's sent me a load of messages on WhatsApp as well:

Did she turn up?

How's it going????

I'm praying 4 u cos I know you've got no game!

Jaxxxx?

I don't respond. I just shove my phone back in my pocket and make my way to the train station.

The front door's barely clicked shut behind me when my mum comes rushing out of the living room.

'Jackson,' she says. 'Thank god! I've been calling and calling and *calling* you. Anyone would think you don't know how to pick up your phone. What's the point in having the latest iPhone and earphones that connect to whatever it is if you aren't even going to answer? *Hmmm?*'

I take my shoes off because Mum's always going on about scuffing up her floorboards or getting the carpets in the living room dirty. I pull my jacket off and go to hang it up.

'I didn't see your calls,' I lie. Mum had tried to call me when I'd been on the train back as well, but I couldn't pick up. I can't explain it, I just felt numb. Like I knew stuff was happening around me, but I couldn't do anything except think about Shaq. Think about his red puffa jacket weaving its way through the crowds, over and over. Asking me to tell his mum he loved her.

'I was worried sick!' Mum says. 'It's all over the news ... about there being a stabbing in town and I knew you were going in, and then when I couldn't get hold of you, I started to panic, so I phoned Harrison's mum—'

'You did what?' I say and I pray to god Harrison didn't let it slip I wasn't with him. Not that my mum's funny about me going out or anything like that, but she'd start asking me all these questions about who I was going with. And *who* this Aimee was. And if I liked her. And I wasn't about to have any of those awkward conversation with her. Who wants to talk about any of that stuff with your mum? So I just said that I was going to meet Harry instead.

'Yes,' my mum continues and she purses her lips. 'That's the other thing.' And I can tell by the way she pauses that she knows I wasn't with Harrison. 'Harrison's mum,' she continues, 'said that he hadn't left his room all day. So are you going to tell me why you've suddenly become an international boy of mystery? I can't get hold of you, and then you're lying about who you're with ... you know I don't like it when you lie to me, Jackson.'

'I know,' I say. Even though I've been lying to her and my dad for time. Pretending I want the future they've already planned out for me. Pretending that I want to stay on at St Anthony's to do my A-levels, then go on to study law at uni. When really, that ain't what I want. I'm not interested in law in the slightest and I don't wanna go into medicine like my dad, either. My parents suggested it ages ago, because I've got this cousin who's training to be a barrister in London. For as long as I can remember, all my mum and dad have gone on about, is how important my education is. Especially because I'll have to work ten times harder than everyone else, once I'm out in the real world. And that I need to think 'very carefully about my future,' and make sure that I study 'proper subjects' that will give me the best start in life and allow me to get a good job, when I'm older.

I went along with saying law just to keep them off my back. I even picked it as one of my A-level options for next year. But now, I'm dreading starting sixth form in September. The truth is, I actually really love English and I don't just mean reading and essays and stuff like that. I love creative writing. That's the part I look forward to the most. I've even written a few short stories outside of class, not that I'd ever show anyone. I can't really explain it, but writing helps me make sense of things. I just wanna go to a normal college. Not a private one. I've even been looking into this one called Xaverian, where I could do English language and lit, and maybe film studies, as well. The other reason I really wanna go there though, is because they offer a creative writing enrichment class too. And I'd just be able to write, every single week!

But I can't tell my mum and dad that, not when they're paying so much for me to go to St Anthony's. Besides, I don't wanna let them down.

I shrug. 'I know,' I say, and I feel her watching me carefully. 'I just ...' I sit down on the stairs and I try to tell her that I went to meet up with some girl in my class, but I can't get the words out. And even if I could, what does it matter? It seems so unimportant, compared to Shaq. I put my head in my hands and force my eyes shut. And I just want to stay here and forget any of this happened. Maybe, if I wish hard enough, it'll all go away.

'Jackson?' my mum says, her voice softer this time.

'I was there,' I say, and I lift my head slightly to look at her.

51

'I mean, I didn't see it happen,' I continue, 'but I saw *him*, the kid who'd been stabbed, and the way everyone was just walking past ...' I shake my head. 'Like he didn't matter. Like his life wasn't even worth anyone stopping. I tried to help,' I say. 'But ...' I feel my words dry out. My mum sits next to me and she wraps her arm around my shoulder.

'Oh, Jax,' she says, and she touches the side of my face with her hand. My mum holds onto me and it makes me think about Shaq. How he might never get to see his mum again. How he might never get to hug her, like this. I feel this ache from deep inside me and I move my hand to cover my eyes.

'I felt so helpless,' I say. 'I just want him to be okay, Mum,' I croak.

And that's when I start to cry. My mum brings me in tighter, wrapping her arms around me, and kissing the top of my head. She rocks me gently and I breathe in her smell, perfume and shea butter.

'It's okay, baby,' she says. 'It's going to be okay.'

But I can't stop thinking about Shaq and if he'll make it. Part of me hurts too, because I wonder, if it had been me in Shaq's place, whether people would've just walked past me too. I don't know how long we sit there, but my mum lifts up my chin with her hand. I'm already way taller than her, so she's bent forward at an awkward angle. I can see the sadness in my mum's face.

'I'm just so glad that you're safe,' she continues. 'That poor boy ...' My mum pauses. 'I love you so much, Jackson. You know that, don't you? More than I could even begin to put into words ... I just want you to be okay. More than *okay*. I want you to thrive. I want you to go as far as you possibly can in life, do you hear me?'

I nod. I know that my mum means it, but I also know that she's saying it because of what's just happened to another young Black boy, too.

'Yeah,' I reply. Even though her definition of me going 'far,' would be staying on at St Anthony's, then doing law at uni. I don't tell my mum about that police officer and what he said, because I know it'll just make her more upset and angry. Besides, I just wanna try and forget about it. I straighten myself up.

'I love you too,' I say, and for once I don't go on about her being cheesy. My mum kisses the side of my forehead again.

'Are you *sure* you're okay?' she asks. 'I can't imagine how *awful* that must've been.'

I nod. Even though I'm not. Seeing Shaq is something that will probably stay with me for the rest of my life. I don't want to worry my mum any more, though.

'Yeah,' I say. 'I'm all right. I've just got some homework to finish.'

My mum smiles, but she doesn't look convinced. 'Okay,' she says. 'Well, dinner will be ready at six.'

I nod, then I turn and head up the stairs. In my room, I close the door behind me and I finally feel like I can breathe. I'm not being searched by the police, or in Nando's with Aimee, or on the train, surrounded by half of Manchester, or being scrutinized by my mum. It's just me. Me and my *Star Wars* posters. I sit down at my desk and open my maths book. Just for something *normal* to do. I usually can't stand algebra, and if I'm honest, I hate anything that has a 'this is right' or 'this is wrong' answer. I don't mind it so much today, though, because it means that I can distract myself by trying to work out all of these equations, instead of thinking about Shaq and everything else that happened. I do a few questions and I feel a bit better at first, but then I stare down at the numbers, and I'm just reminded of the same one I thought of earlier.

27.4%.

That's Shaq's chance of survival.

There's a sudden knock at my door that makes me jump.

'Come in!' I say, and I expect it to be my mum, making sure that I'm all right, again. My dad pushes open my bedroom door. It's kinda weird seeing him standing here, because he hardly ever comes into my room, not as much as my mum does anyway. He looks out of place. My dad clears his throat. I know he loves me, deep down, but he hardly ever says it. He doesn't really hug me or anything, either. He just goes on about exams and grades, and how I need to make sure that I'm consistently getting 8s and 9s. I got a 5 in my maths mock, it was the only one out of all my grades, but my dad still hasn't let me forget it.

'Jackson,' he says. 'Your mum told me what happened. Are you all right?'

'Yeah,' I lie. *'I'm fine!'*

My dad nods and I can tell that he doesn't really know what to say next, but he glances down at the open textbook on my desk.

'I'm glad!' he says. 'Anyway, I just came to see how you're getting on with your maths homework? You know you need to try extra hard ... make sure that you're putting the work in. Especially if you're aiming for a higher grade. There are no practice runs this time, Jackson. In a few weeks, that'll be it.'

I try not to pull a face. That's typical of my dad. I was there when another kid got stabbed, and all he cares about is whether or not my homework's done.

'Yeah, I know, Dad,' I say. 'I'm on it.'

My dad nods. 'You're a good boy, Jackson,' he says. He pauses, like he's about to say something else, and I wish that he'd just tell me that he's proud of me. That it doesn't really matter what results I get, because I'm doing my absolute best, and that's all that counts. But he doesn't. He just closes the door behind him instead. I stand up and grab my phone from the other side of the room. I need to see if Shaq's okay. I've got loads of messages from Aimee:

WTF cnt believe u just left me in Nandos!!!

Why u ignoring me???

I told u, I never meant it like that!

Jackson??

Jackson!!??

But I'm too mad to even reply right now. I open the search browser on my phone and type: *stabbing Manchester Arndale*. If my mum said it was all over the news, maybe there will at least be something about whether or not Shaq survived.

There's loads of stuff on Twitter. Mainly people asking why town has been closed off, or what was going on in the Arndale. There's loads of tweets saying there'd been a stabbing and a few photos. Most of them are blurry and far away, but there's one of Shaq running through the shopping centre. And another one, taken outside. There's loads of people in the way of the shot, but I can make out that girl, crouching down to help him.

There's a few video clips on YouTube taken from the news report. I click on one and see a reporter standing outside the Arndale. The twisted police tape is still stretched around that corner near the stone steps and there's a few people stopping and staring into the camera to see what's going on. I notice one of the fluorescent jackets of the police officer in the background and I wonder if it's the same one who ran a check on me, but the camera isn't on him for long enough.

I hear the reporter say:

'I'm outside the Arndale Shopping Centre in Greater Manchester, where earlier today a stabbing took place. Many were shocked, as it happened in broad daylight, just here, outside the Corporation Street exit. It is believed that the victim is a fourteen-year-old male, and although some passers-by did attempt first aid at the scene, he currently remains in critical condition in hospital. As you can see, there's still quite a visible police presence behind me. This is the fifteenth stabbing that's taken place in the city centre this year, and Greater Manchester Police have said that they will do all they can to crack down on knife crime.'

The video flicks back to the studio and one of the presenters starts talking about the weather and I click off the video. I guess I'd never thought about it before. How the news can go from something like a fourteen-year-old being stabbed to the *weather*. And maybe I'd never thought about it before, because I'd never seen it. Not in real life, anyway. If Shaq is in critical condition, then it means that there's a small chance he might pull through. That he might be in that twenty-seven per cent. Even though I saw how bad the wound was. I saw how much blood he'd lost. That girl trying to stop it with her T-shirt, and I suddenly remember . . .

I reach into my jeans pocket and pull out the igo card. I'd forgotten I even had it. I flip open the plastic wallet and I stare at the name: *Chantelle Walker*. I don't know why I didn't notice when I looked before, but she's really pretty. Even if she does look like she could knock you out with one punch. I open Insta, then I type her name in the search bar. It only takes me a few seconds to find her profile.

I go to the *message* button and I type out a DM.

7

MARC

I'm awake *long* before my alarm goes off, mainly cause I hate Mondays. I hate every day that I'm forced to be at this damn school, but Mondays are defo the worst. That's when the week feels like it won't ever come to an end. It's also when I have double science, and who in their right mind would enjoy that? I reach for my phone and check WhatsApp to see if there's anything from Rhys since yesterday. Still nothing. I walked around the Northern Quarter for *time* as well. At least I got to look at all the old murals and graffiti again, as well as the new ones that have popped up. I can't explain it, but it's like, being among all those grainy words and painted bricks is the only place I feel like I belong. It's kinda like being seen, without really being seen, if that makes sense? Most people don't know who half the artists are, but I could name all of them without even seeing their tags. The one of the twenty-two bees on Oldham Street that was done after the Manchester attack, that's Qubeck. The one of George Floyd on Stevenson Square is Akse. The old man with a cig hanging out his mouth is C215, and the one of the girl whose smile is being forced by these unknown hands is Axel.

Then there's loads of Noer's tag that's been graffitied all over the place. Among them are my own. The first bit of graffiti I ever did is on Tib Street, then a proper small painting of a bee on the old metal shutters of this broken down factory. Whenever I got moved somewhere else, I'd do some graffiti around there too. I spray-painted a canary escaping from its cage in Levenshulme and this little boy with wings coming out his back in Gorton. Or sometimes, I just do my tag – *Nomad*. One of the kids from my old school called me that when he found out I was in care. I've been called shit like that for most of my life. I didn't want what he said to have some sort of power over me though, so I decided to take the word and use it for myself. Besides, it makes a pretty good tag.

It sounds stupid, but painting something on a wall makes me feel like I'm leaving my mark on the world somehow. Leaving something behind that will be there long after I'm gone. Cause when you're moving from place to place and you don't have any family or even proper friends, it's so easy to feel like you don't matter. And I hate that. Seeing Shaq yesterday made me think: who would even miss me, if it'd been me? Not my social worker, or my birth parents, or Dry Eileen, that's for sure. Even the few friends I had from my old school probably wouldn't and that just made me feel even more alone.

I scroll though my messages to Rhys. He *always* does this. Ghosts me for time then messages me out of the blue. Sometimes he asks me to meet him somewhere, then keeps me hanging around for ages. Or, like yesterday, he just doesn't bother to show up. I dunno why I bother, really. Maybe it's cause when I'm with him, he makes me laugh and feel good. I can just forget everything else that's going on. And I ain't gonna lie, I like kissing him and stuff too. But then the next minute, it's like he doesn't wanna know?

I type: *Hello??? U must b dead coz that's the only excuse u have 4 not replying!!!* but then I stop myself from pressing send, cause I've already sent him five messages and I don't wanna be looking like some stalker. It hurts, though, that he doesn't care enough to even text back.

I pull myself out of bed. I was late back last night, by over an hour, but Dry Eileen didn't go off on one, or call the police. That's what they're supposed to do if you're not back after a certain time, or if you go out after your carer's told you not to. It's part of the law or something, cause technically it means you've run away. But Dry Eileen just sat me down and explained that this – me living with her – was about mutual respect, and if I was gonna be late, then I should at least call her and let her know, so that she knows I'm safe. Then she went and made me something to eat.

That was a first. I ain't used to being treated like that, to be honest. Having someone actually talk to me on a level.

Sometimes, it's worse when you're with a family that's already got kids, cause then you just feel like an outsider. Watching this family you're living with go about their normal lives that you'll never fully be part of. That's proper hard, cause it makes me think about my own mum and dad, and what things might have been like if they were different. Or, if I'd been born another person, someplace else, with parents that actually love me. How different things would be. How different I'd be. I guess I've learned that no matter how nice someone pretends to be in the beginning, it never lasts.

That's why I never see any point in trying. I don't get attached to people or places or things, cause everything can be taken from you in an instant. It's the only way to make sure you don't get hurt.

I get dressed quick-time and stare at my reflection in the mirror. I took my twists out last night, for something to do. To try and take my mind off all the thoughts I was having. About how I couldn't even make myself go over to the boy, right away. How I very nearly didn't cause of how scared I was. I never could've rushed straight over there, like the way that girl from school did. I kinda admired her for that. Even though I'd never tell her.

I pull my Afro comb through my hair and straighten my shitty clip-on school tie. I open my wardrobe and root through the pile of bin bags, and this tattered suitcase that's got my clothes in. I ain't even bothered to unpack. I know that it won't be long before Dry Eileen tells my social worker she's had enough of me and then I'll be with someone else before you know it. I find my black waterproof coat with the hood. It's too short for me and there's a rip under ones of the arms, but it's the only one I've got.

I pull it on and head downstairs. I'm always late for *everything,* it's no joke. My social worker and the teachers at my old school say that I run on 'Marc timing', which is true, but I take even longer in the mornings, cause if I'm late for school then it means I get a detention. And that means I don't have to spend break times walking around like a saddo, when everyone else is with their mates. Even though I started towards the end of Year Ten, cause I'd moved in with my other carer before Dry Eileen, I still feel like the new kid. Everyone's already got their own mates and no one bothers with me. I ain't got long left, though, thank fuck. GCSEs are in three months and I'll only have to go in for revision classes soon.

I head into the kitchen, grab my bag off the back of one of the chairs and pull my headphones out. Dry Eileen's sitting at the table. This woman is so extra. She doesn't even have to get up early, but she does, just so she can chat rubbish to me and say bye. There's no way I'd be getting up at 6.45 a.m. to talk to anyone.

I shove my earphones in, so she gets the hint.

'I'm going now,' I say.

Dry Eileen hands me the money for my bus pass and my dinner. Most of the other people I stayed with just used to leave it on the side.

'Do you want some breakfast to take with you?' Dry Eileen asks. 'I can put some toast in if you want?'

I shake my head. 'Nah, I'm all right, thanks,' I say. 'Can't really eat in the mornings.'

Dry Eileen nods. 'Okay,' she says. 'Have a good day.'

I stare at her. Sometimes I think that old people forget what it's like to even go to school.

'Yeah, that ain't gonna happen,' I say, and I put my music on shuffle. 'I'll see you later,' I add, then I head out the kitchen. Dry Eileen shouts something after me but I don't hear her properly cause of the music and I don't bother checking to see what she said either. It's probably something about me coming back on time, or letting her know if I'm gonna be late. What's the point? I know she's already written me off. The idea of having a kid like me is much better than the reality.

I'm twenty minutes late to school. I'd made sure to get off the bus two stops early and walk the extra-long way around to kill more time. Hopefully I'll get a lunchtime detention as well as one at break. I sign in at the KS4 office, then make my way to maths. The corridor's never really empty in this school, cause there's always groups of kids who are supposed to be in lessons wandering around, and some Pupil Support Manager running after them, trying to get them back to class.

I stand outside the classroom for a minute. It's hard, cause trying not to get noticed isn't as easy as you might think. It's actually pretty hard. You need to be quiet enough for people to forget that you're there, but if you're *too* quiet, then that can draw attention to you and make you stand out as well. I've learned to survive by hiding parts of myself and not letting anyone in. It ain't just about being in care and what people might say, or how differently they might treat me once they find out, though. It's about being gay too. At my old school, all my friends knew and pretty much my whole year did as well, so I never had to hide that part of myself. But I've been in placements where foster carers have said all sorts of homophobic shit before. Or I've had to live in areas where I barely left the house, cause I didn't feel safe being gay and Black.

I'm out, but coming out ain't just something that you do once, then that's it. You kinda have to do it again and again, with every new person that you meet. Give that part of yourself over to them and you never know how they're gonna react. If they're gonna be cool with it, or start with all the personal questions. Especially once they find out that you're in care as well. Or if you're gonna end up fearing for your life. Even though there were a few idiots at my old school, I felt safe. I had mates and I could just be myself. Not like that matters now, cause since I moved here none of them have even bothered to message me back.

I wait for another minute, then I take a deep breath and push open the door.

I don't make eye contact with anyone, but I can feel people staring. I mutter a sorry to my maths teacher under my breath, then I head to my seat, which is right near the front. That's the other thing about being in care. None of the teachers would ever admit it, but there's stuff they let you get away with. Like when you're rude or late. Maybe cause they feel sorry for you, I dunno. Not that I've back-chatted any of the teachers here. The only thing I've done is try to blend in. I usually sit next to this quiet girl in maths who doesn't bother to talk to me, but she's not in today, so I'm at the table on my own.

I get my book out and Mr Reed starts going on about the exams being three months away, and that just makes me switch off, cause I already know how long I've got till I'm outta here. Trust me, I've been counting down the days. I try not to die of boredom, as he goes through a question about how to work out the circumference of a circle using Pi, when the door flies open. That girl who was at the stabbing comes in. The one I paid for on the bus too. I didn't do it cause I like her or anything, especially not after she told me to mind where the fuck I was going on my first day. I just wanted to get home. And maybe, I dunno, after seeing how she tried to help that boy, part of me thought I should at least do something.

She pulls her jacket off and makes her way to her seat at the back of the class, but Mr Reed stops.

'Chantelle,' he says. 'You're late.'

'Yeah,' she replies. 'What d'you want me to do about it?'

I hear a few people laugh and Chantelle goes to sit down, but Mr Reed moves away from the whiteboard. I already know that they're gonna get into it again. Just like they always do.

She'll end up kicking off and being sent out. Or he'll call for one of the PSMs to come and remove her. That's what ends up happening most lessons, anyway.

'What, no apology?' he says. 'You just stroll into my lesson late, disrupt my class and affect everyone else's learning? And why are you late?' he continues. 'You're late *every* morning. Is it so hard to be on time?'

She turns to the girl she's sitting next to. 'Please don't let this guy start with me today, you know,' she says. ''Cos I really ain't in the mood.'

The girl smirks and Chantelle flops into her chair.

'What was that?' he says.

'Nothing,' Chantelle replies. 'I wasn't actually talking to you.' She mutters something else under her breath and the girl sniggers.

'Right!' Mr Reed snaps. 'Move. *Now!*'

'Why have I gotta move?' she says. 'I didn't do nothing.'

'You came in late and now you're back-chatting – so either you move, or I'll radio for someone to come and escort you out. The choice is yours!'

He looks around the classroom and I think, *God, if you're up there and you like me, please don't make this happen. Please don't let him come and sit this girl next to me.* But, of course, God must hate me, cause Mr Reed points in my direction and goes: 'There! Sit there, please. Where I can see you.'

I knew there was a downside to being at the front. Chantelle turns to see where he's pointing and she catches my eye. For a split-second, I see her face change. She's obviously never noticed me properly before, maybe she didn't even know I was in her class. But now I can't explain it – it's like there's something else there – maybe cause we were the only two people in this whole school who were there when that boy got stabbed.

Mr Reed clicks his fingers. '*Now*, please!' he says.

Chantelle mutters something under her breath, then she picks up her things and sits down next to me. Mr Reed carries on with the lesson, but I feel Chantelle staring at me. When I catch her eye, she looks down at her hands and says: 'Thanks, yeah? For yesterday. You didn't have to pay for me or nothing, on the bus.'

I think about telling her that I only did it cause I wanted to get myself home too. But there's something about the way she says it. Like it was more to her than just bus fare.

I shrug. 'It's fine,' I say. 'Anyway, who knows how long you would've been holding us all up for?'

She leans back in her chair and I feel her staring at me, again. 'I owe you one,' she says. 'Then after that, we're even. Okay?'

I pull a face. I don't need any favours. 'Okay,' I say, even though I don't mean it. Chantelle nods and picks up her pen, then we sit in silence for the rest of the lesson, until the bell goes.

By the time I get to second lesson, it's pretty much all round the school that the boy from yesterday – Shaq, his name is – was stabbed. I saw some girl in the year below who must've been going out with him crying in the corridor while one of her mates rubbed her back. A group of boys went over to her and I could tell they were proper upset too. I even heard some of the teachers in the hallway talking about it on my way to science. Shaq's not dead, but he's in intensive care. It's mad cause before today, I didn't even know Shaq's name, but now that's all I'm hearing. I reach science and I sit at one of the long wooden tables. This is one of the reasons I hate Mondays. This is the class where I feel the most seen.

I'm in set two for science cause I've always been all right at it, but not to the point where I'd be in set one. You'd think that being in a higher set would mean that you're around less idiots, but that definitely ain't the case. Chantelle comes in and a few people crowd around her, asking what happened with Shaq. Apparently people had recognized her from some photo that had been included in a news article online. I suddenly feel mad. Someone stopped long enough to take a photo, but didn't even try to help Shaq ...

Chantelle glances over at me, but she doesn't say anything about me being there too. She doesn't even say much about what went on. She just sits at a table at the far end of the classroom. Then loads of other kids bustle in, talking and shouting. This class is always loud, cause there's usually some idiot messing about with the Bunsen burner, or people drowning out the teacher. But Mrs Maguire is one of those teachers who couldn't control a class if her life depended on it. She looks like she's been here for about five hundred years and is just about ready to drop or retire at any minute.

Back at my old school, I'd probably be making a whole heap of noise too. Here I don't say anything. Mrs Maguire starts trying to get on with the lesson, even though only a handful of people are listening, and I feel Tyler staring at me from the other side of the class. Y'know how there's some people in life who are just absolute knobs? Who find a way to bother you, even when you're minding your own business and just want to be left alone? Tyler is one of those people. I see him out of the corner of my eye, leaning forward on his desk, then I feel something hit the back of my neck. I hear sniggering, but I don't turn around. I just wait for it to stop.

No one really bothered me in my old school, cause I at least had a group of friends there to back me if anyone said anything. But here, it's different. Something else hits me in the back of my head and I freeze. Tyler does this every Monday, but today, it's like he's really got it in for me. Like he's trying his hardest to get me to react. It's usually some shit about my shoes being too small, or the rip in my coat that I'm trying to hide, or the fact that I never seem to say anything. Even when Mrs Maguire asks me a question I just shrug, cause I'm scared that if I open my mouth, then it'll be game over and I'll suddenly become more visible.

I hear him sniggering and laughing. Something else hits my shoulder, then the back of my head, and bounces off the edge of my desk. It doesn't hurt, but it makes me jump. He's throwing screwed-up bits of paper that look like they've been chewed in his mouth, then spat out. *Ewwww!* The last thing I want is anything that's been in his mouth anywhere near me. I hear him and his mates laughing even harder, but I still don't do anything. I stare down at my desk. It ain't just that I'm scared of Tyler, it's like whenever anyone says anything to me, I just clam up. I'm scared of stuff kicking off and what might happen. I try to avoid that happening by doing nothing. I swallow hard and will the clock to move faster and the lesson to be over.

Then, I hear Tyler say: 'What the fuck is wrong with him? He's so fucking weird ... he doesn't even talk. Can you not speak or something?' he says, and he dashes something else at me. I don't move. 'Oi!' he spits. 'You fucking deaf, or what?' I still don't move or say anything. I feel myself shaking and everyone turning to look in my direction, but I carry on staring down at my desk.

I take in a sharp breath and I catch Chantelle looking in my direction. She probably thinks I'm pathetic, like everyone else does. I look away, embarrassed, then somewhere behind me, I hear Tyler say: 'How much d'you wanna bet that I can get him to turn around? Should I dash this can at him, or what?'

'Do it. Do it. Do it!' his mates start to chant and I move over in my chair. I really wanna turn around and tell Tyler to try it if he's bad, to tell him to just piss off and leave me alone, but I can't seem to move. My hands are shaking even more now and I try to think about being anywhere else. I hear more laughter from behind me and his mates egging him on, and then I hear Chantelle say: 'Oi, Tyler! Don't be such a fucking knob. I know you can't help it, cos you were obviously born that way. But for once, give it a rest.'

His mates all start cracking up and I see Tyler jump to his feet, but Chantelle barely seems bothered.

'What's it got to do with you?' he spits. 'You're always sticking your nose in where it don't belong. Was I even talking to you?'

Chantelle catches my eye and I can't quite explain it, but it's almost like she understands. But then it's gone, just as quickly as it came and part of me wonders if I'd imagined it.

'He's my mate,' Chantelle says. 'All right? So unless you want me to break your nose again, like that time in Year Eight, I suggest you leave him alone, sit your four-foot self down, and try and learn something. *Okay?*'

My eyes almost pop out my head and all his mates start cracking up. The tops of Tyler's ears go red and I hear him say: 'Nah, who d'you think you're talking to? I'll knock you out!' He turns to his mate, who's flat-out dying from laughter and says: 'She didn't break my nose, bruv, it was just bruised. She didn't break it . . .'

That only makes his friend laugh harder. From the front, I hear Mrs Maguire tell everyone to settle down, but as usual, her voice is drowned out by the noise.

'Right. Whatever makes you feel better,' Chantelle says, and then she turns back around. One of Tyler's friends is collapsed on the desk, hitting it with his fist. He lifts himself up and I see him wipe the tears away from underneath his eyes.

'Nah, I think I popped a lung,' he says. 'Four-foot, y'know . . .'

Tyler mumbles something under his breath, probably so Chantelle doesn't hear, but he sits down and doesn't so much as look in my direction. I turn and catch Chantelle's eye but she doesn't smile. She gives me this look that says, *Yeah, you're welcome.*

Then she picks up her pen and starts trying to actually do some work. But for some reason, I can't stop looking at her. She probably only called me her mate to get Tyler off my case, and so we're even now, but I liked it. Having someone call me their mate. Even if that someone was ultra-mouthy Chantelle. And even though it was only for a split-second, it was nice to have someone on my side.

8

CHANTELLE

I wait back at the end of the lesson, so that Mrs Maguire can fill out my report. I'm surprised she even knows what was going on with how noisy it was. She barely looks at me as she goes through the *behaviour, lateness* and *attendance* boxes, then scribbles a few comments. I've been on report since the beginning of term, and this time Mrs Cohen, who's also the head of KS4, says I've got to stay on it until the end of the year. Not that that makes any sense, cos by that point, I'll be getting ready to go to college. The reason I'm even on report in the first place, is cos of my English teacher, Ms Stinking Edwards. She thinks I've got a 'bad attitude,' just cos I ask genuine questions like why we only study these dry, boring texts in English that they've been doing for about a hundred years, when they could find something much more interesting and relevant? I mean, there's millions of books in the world, yet we only *ever* get given ones by dead white men. I don't think that's rude, it's something I actually wanna know! But I just get told that I'm being 'disruptive' or whatever.

Even though I never used to try in lessons, I was never, like, *that* bad. There are other kids who've done way worse and never got sent to return to learn. I just used to muck about and chat, or do the bare minimum amount of work. Sometimes I wouldn't even bother going to my lessons. I'd just run around the school with Leesha and Siobhan, trying not to get caught by one of the PSMs and sent back to class. As soon as I say anything, or I don't agree with one of the basic points that Ms Edwards is making about one of the books, I get told that I'm being 'too intimidating and aggressive'. No one else is ever 'intimidating' or 'rude' for asking a question and having an opinion. I know for a fact that if I was white, then they wouldn't be using any of those words to describe me.

I've been trying my hardest not to answer back in class like Gran told me to, though. I sit there, with my hand up for ages sometimes, and still no one ever asks me for an answer. I guess they don't care what I have to say. I know that most of my teachers, apart from Mrs Cohen, still don't expect much from me. That's why I can't wait to get out of here and go to college. I grab my report and head out of the classroom and into the corridor. There's loads of people pushing and shoving past in groups, trying to get outside, or making their way to the canteen. Out of the corner of my eye, I clock Leesha and Siobhan, waiting outside one of the classrooms. I'd been friends with Leesha and that lot since Year Seven. But when I started trying harder, I got moved up in all my sets, and away from my mates. Leesha and the rest got fed up of me blowing them off so that I could do my homework. Then Leesha started saying how stuck-up I was now, and how they didn't want to hang around with me any more, cos I clearly thought I was too good to be friends with them. It proper upset me at first, but then I got over it, cos if there's one thing I'm used to, it's being on my own. I walk past them both, and I see Leesha glance in my direction then whisper something to Siobhan. They burst out laughing, but I just shoot Leesha a dirty look and carry on.

That's another thing I've learned, how to make out like nothing bothers you, even when it does. I squeeze my way through the heaving corridor, to make my way to detention for being late. Pretty much everyone's talking about Shaq, but people still don't know if he's pulled through or not. I check online for the millionth time, but it still says the same thing, that he's in critical condition. I check Insta as well, to see if that guy Jackson has messaged back. At least I know what happened to my bus pass. He DM'd last night to see if I wanted it back. Like, *obviously!*

There's a few people lined up outside the classroom, waiting for whichever teacher's on detention duty and a few kids huddled in the corner around Damar. That's when I see him, that boy from science and the bus. He catches my eye, then looks away. I'm about to go over to him, when Damar makes a beeline for me. I don't even know how it's even possible to be as tall as Damar is, but it's like he never stops growing.

'Yo, Chantelle,' he says, and he opens up his rucksack. 'I got some Fruit Pastels for you, Kinder Buenos, Tootsie Rolls – even raided my mum's secret stash and picked up some of them Twirls.' He gestures towards the classroom door. 'Y'know you're gonna need all the help you can get for your time in there. Especially if Death Breath's on. I had him for period two, and *oh my days* ... the breath is next-level funky today!'

I pull a face. 'Can't wait!' I say.

Our school put a ban on us having sweets and chocolate and fizzy drinks to try to be healthier, but it just means that people sell them when the teachers aren't looking. I normally get my sweets off Damar cos they're cheaper than going to the shop, but I already spent the money Gran gave me on the bus to school, cos I didn't wanna tell her that I'd lost my pass.

'Oi!' some kid in Year Seven shouts. 'I thought you didn't have no Fruit Pastels?!'

'I ain't got no Fruit Pastels for *you*!' he says. 'Now get gone, before I kick you into next week.'

The Year Seven gets off and Damar turns back to me. 'Haroon showed me that picture in geography, the one from the news report ... you were there, innit? Yesterday, you tried to help Shaq?'

I swallow hard, I know the picture Damar's talking about. I saw it this morning, after loads of people sent me Snaps, asking me what happened, and if it was definitely me with Shaq? I wasn't named or anything like that, but I may as well have been.

I sneak a glance at that boy again and I think of Shaq crying for his mum, while everyone else just walked past . . .

'Yeah,' I say and I gesture towards the boy from science. 'We both were.'

Damar's eyes widen. 'Shit!' he says. 'My older brother's friends with Shaq's brother. It's just mad, like . . . he's just a kid. But I guess it happens, innit.' He pauses. 'My little cousin in Birmingham got killed and he was just eleven. It's like, if you make it to twenty you're doing well.' Damar shakes his head and I stare down at the floor.

'You heard anything?' I ask. 'About Shaq.'

'Nah,' Damar says. 'The last I heard he was still the same. My brother said they've got him hooked up to all these wires and shit. Apparently his mum ain't left, she ain't been home since yesterday. She doesn't wanna leave him in case something happens . . .'

Damar pauses and I catch that boy's eye again. In case Shaq dies, that's what he means. And somehow, that makes it worse.

I swallow hard. 'Will you let me know?' I say. 'What happens?'

'Yeah,' Damar replies. 'Course!' Then he lifts his cap up to run a hand through his hair. 'Anyway,' he continues. 'What d'you want? One packet? Two?'

It catches me off guard for a minute, cos it feels weird, going from talking about someone being stabbed to how many packets of sweets I want, but I shake my head anyway.

'Not today,' I say. 'I ain't got no money.'

Damar shakes his head. 'Don't worry about it,' he says.

'These are on the house. After what you did, it's the least I can do ...' He tosses me a packet of Fruit Pastels, then turns to the boy.

'Yours too!' he says, then he throws another packet in his direction. The boy catches them with one hand.

'Thanks!' the boy says and Damar shrugs.

'It's cool,' Damar says. 'Who knows how much worse Shaq could've been, if you two hadn't stepped in. You make a good team!'

I catch the boy's eye again. Maybe Shaq would've been much worse if we hadn't stopped. But a small part of me still feels like I didn't do enough. Then Yohan from my form comes over and pushes me out the way.

'D'you mind?' I snap, but he just ignores me.

'Yo, Damar,' he says. 'Can I get a Mars and Tootsie Roll? Actually, what other sweets you got?' Damar turns and unzips his rucksack, then Yohan peers in. 'How much for the Skittles?' he says. 'Is that a lemon sherbet? Nah, actually, how much for the Mars and the Skittles?'

'They're one pound each,' Damar cuts in. 'But you're taking the piss, so I'm adding 50p interest for being long.'

'What, you the Royal Bank of Scotland now?' Yohan says, but he hands Damar the money, anyway.

'Nah, I'm the Royal Bank of Damar, and if you hold me up again like this, you're banned. Y'hear me? I'm a busy guy. Got places to go, people to see ...'

Yohan looks like he's about to say something back, but one of Damar's mates who's on watch at the other end of the corridor shouts: 'Yo, D! PSM coming. He's coming *now*.' Damar zips up his bag quick-time.

'Almost making me get caught!' he says to Yohan. 'I'll catch you in a bit, Chantelle,' he shouts to me. Then he disappears into the crowd. I see a PSM looking to see where Damar got to, but he's already long gone.

I go over to the boy from science, shoving a Fruit Pastel in my mouth.

'You shouldn't let Tyler treat you like that, y'know,' I say. 'You need to stand up for yourself, say something. That's the only way people like that will ever leave you alone. *Trust me.*'

He shrugs. 'That might work for you,' he says. 'But it ain't that simple for everyone else. Anyway,' he continues quietly, 'I thought if I ignored him, he'd just get bored ...'

I snort. 'Yeah, right,' I say. 'If there's one thing Tyler never gets bored of, it's being an absolute knob.'

The boy smiles. 'I can see that now,' he says. And I check my phone again.

'What lessons you got next?' I ask.

'Err, double PE,' he replies. 'Why?'

'Well, we all know that PE is the most pointless lesson on the planet. So you can either go there and run around outside in this heat for two hours. Or you can come to town with me and get my bus pass back.'

'And what about detention?' he asks.

I shrug. 'Well, technically I shouldn't even have to be here. I take my little sister to school, that's why I'm *always* late. And I've told Mr Reed that loads of times, but he still gives me detention. So … am I even doing anything wrong?' I pull my chapstick out my pocket and I spot a teacher coming towards us in the distance. Damar was right, it is Death Breath. I know that if I want to get out of here I need to get a move on quick, before he reaches the classroom.

'It's up to you!' I say. 'But what else are you gonna do? Hang around school on your lonesome all day?'

He doesn't say anything at first and I try to act like I'm not bothered either way, but I'm secretly hoping he'll come. I dunno why. Maybe it's cos part of me feels sorry for him. Especially, after seeing how he was just trying to get his head down when Tyler was bothering him, and I know *exactly* what that can be like. But also, he was there when Shaq got stabbed. This boy, and that guy Jackson, who I barely know, are the only two people in the world right now who fully understand what it's like to see something like that. Who might actually get whatever it is I'm feeling right now. The boy glances back at the classroom but he still doesn't move.

'Suit yourself!' I say. I'm walking off and thinking I'm probably gonna have to go to town on my own, when he says: 'All *right*, I'll come!'

I smirk, but I try not to show him how pleased I am that he actually said yes.

'Good choice,' I say, then I grab the sleeve of his blazer. 'Come on, we need to get outta here, quick.'

We push our way through the crowds in the corridor and head out into the playground. It's so full that if we hurry, we'll be able to climb over the metal gate at the far end of the field without anyone noticing. We get to the large metal gate, then I throw my school bag over first and pull myself up.

'What's your name, anyway?' I ask, as I jump down onto the pavement on the other side of the gate.

'Marc,' he replies. 'My name's Marc.'

9

JACKSON

I stand awkwardly inside the Greggs where we agreed to meet, and I feel Chantelle staring at me. I watch as she whispers something to the boy she's with, before she gets up and makes her way towards me. We're not supposed to leave school at lunch unless we've got a pass, but it seemed like Chantelle wanted her bus pass back pretty urgently, and I needed to get out of school, anyway. I was sick of listening to Aimee going around telling everyone how she was at the stabbing and saw it all happen and how traumatized she is by it all. I heard her tell Harrison that if she'd left the Arndale a few minutes earlier, she probably would've got caught up in some 'gang crossfire' and she couldn't sleep because she'd been having nightmares. She left out what she'd said to me Nando's, and the fact that she didn't even want to go over and help.

That was on top of everyone asking me what happened all morning, and if it was true I'd tried to help. Even Harrison was at it, asking if it was true I'd been caught up in some 'Moss Side gang fight'. Said he wished he'd been there to see it. No one asked about Shaq, or seemed to care what happened to him. It was all: *Poor Aimee, for seeing something so awful; poor Aimee, who must've been so frightened.* Never mind the fourteen-year-old Black boy, who'd been left to die on that street corner. I couldn't take any more. So I got off at dinner and didn't tell anyone where I was going.

Chantelle sighs loudly and she moves her thick curls away from her face. 'You got it, then?' she says. 'Or did you just come to stand here and take in the ambiance of Greggs?'

She raises her eyebrows and I almost stutter. Her friend starts laughing and I realize that I've seen him before. He was there, at the stabbing too ... Chantelle gestures as if to say, *Well?*

'I've got it!' I say, and for some reason my voice comes out small and shaky. I pull her bus pass out of my blazer pocket. I don't know why, but she kinda makes me nervous. I hold the pass out to her and she takes it off me with a forced smile.

'Thanks,' she says. 'I appreciate it, yeah?' She pauses for a minute, and I see her staring at my uniform. 'You go St Anthony's?' she asks, and something in her voice changes.

I shrug. 'Yeah,' I reply. I clock the uniform that she and her friend are wearing. It's for one of the local academies. One of the worst ones at that. I'm hardly surprised, considering the last time I saw her she was shoving a stolen jacket back into her bag. You'd be lucky if you left that school with one GCSE, let alone eleven. Chantelle gives me a funny look and I feel like she's judging me, just because I obviously go to a decent school and my parents have money. Her mate who's sitting at one of the tables turns his head.

'What's St Anthony's?' he asks, screwing up his paper bag and throwing it into a nearby bin.

Chantelle widens her eyes. 'What? Ain't you heard of it?' she says. 'It's this posh school – I'm talking five-grand-a-term posh. The uniform costs more than my entire wardrobe, and they take you skiing and all sorts.' She pauses. 'We're lucky if we get to go Alton Towers, never mind skiing in god knows where.'

Her friend pretends to pass out. 'Five grand for one school term?' he wheezes. 'D'you know what I could buy with that!' He stares at me. 'You even been into a Greggs before? Ain't this too poor for you?'

I feel my cheeks colouring. I don't tell them that it isn't even that much money to us. That I was almost gonna go to another school which cost double that, but Harrison decided to go to St Anthony's because it has a better sports team or something, and we've been mates for forever, so I wanted to go with him. We're not the richest family at school, we don't own a yacht or have another house abroad like some people do, but we ain't the poorest either.

''Course I've been into a Greggs,' I say.

The boy stares at me, then he shakes his head and carries on muttering 'five grand' under his breath. 'Anyway,' he says, standing up, 'I need something else to eat, cos that pasty didn't even touch the sides.' He turns to Chantelle. 'Especially after you had me running down the corridor and climbing over school gates, like some real-life prison break . . .'

I snort. 'I'm surprised they didn't just let you walk out!' I say. It slips out, without me even meaning it to and Chantelle give me a dirty look.

'And what's that supposed to mean?' she snaps.

'Nothing!' I say, quickly. Although she probably knows full well what I mean. A school that crap probably doesn't care if you walk out or not. It's one of the worst schools in Manchester. Everyone knows that. All I keep thinking about is how Chantelle hid that stolen jacket when the police turned up and I'm annoyed that she's the one trying to make *me* feel different. Especially when I went out of my way to bring her bus pass back! I don't know what I was hoping for before I got here. Maybe that there would be some kind of connection between us, after what we shared yesterday. But I wish I hadn't bothered now.

Chantelle pulls her jacket on, then she stands up.

'Guess I was right, then,' she says. I feel a bit offended, but I don't have chance to ask her what she means by that, because she continues. 'You, my friend, think you're better than everyone else, cos you go to that posh school. Probably always get what you want, cos Mummy and Daddy pay for it. Are boring as fuck and have never had to go without anything your entire life.' She shrugs. 'Am I right?' Her friend comes back, shoving another pasty into his mouth.

84

'Chantelle ...' he mumbles, through a mouth full of food, but she shrugs.

I'm suddenly angry. Chantelle barely knows me and she's making all these assumptions, just because of the school I go to. She did it the moment she saw my blazer. Although, I guess I can't be too mad, because I just did exactly the same to her. I open my mouth to say something back, but I can't, because she's right. My mum and dad do pay for everything ... the latest phone, trainers, even my watch. I've never had to go without anything. *Ever.* And most of my friends would probably say I'm boring as well, because I've never been in trouble. I've never even had a detention. I'm always home when I'm supposed to be and Harrison takes the piss because I like listening to my mum's old CDs and watching *Star Wars*, and working out things like the law of averages in any given situation, or how probability works. It's weird because even though I'm not especially cool, I'm still popular. I still have loads of friends and people seem to like me.

Chantelle shoves her hands into her pockets 'See?' she says.

Even if she is right, I don't want her to know it. 'You don't know the first thing about me,' I say.

Chantelle smirks and glances over her shoulder towards the woman behind the counter.

'I'm a pretty good judge of character,' she says, as she pulls her bag over her shoulder and walks over to the long fridge.

Her friend finishes his pasty. 'Are we going now or what?' he says. 'D'you know how depressing this place is?'

Chantelle runs her hand along the bottles of drinks, then the next minute – it all happens so fast – she reaches out, grabs a few of the bottles and swipes something else from one of the metal baskets.

'Eh!' the woman from behind the counter yells. 'Eh, I saw that! I'm calling security ...'

'Now we can go!' Chantelle shouts, legging it towards the door.

Her friend almost trips up, jumping off the stool and grabbing his stuff off the table. Chantelle's already out the door, and her mate isn't far behind her. I don't do anything for a minute, then the woman comes from behind the counter, and I don't think, I just run. I know that if security does come, then they'll see we were all together and think that I was in on it too. And I'm not about to get into trouble for this. We run out of the Greggs and into the shopping centre, which is even busier now because everyone's coming out on their lunch break. My heart starts beating proper fast and Chantelle's already down by one of the far exits. I don't even know how she can run this fast.

'*Hurry up!*' she shouts to me and her mate.

We knock into people who are trying to move out our way, and out of the corner of my eye, I catch a flash of the red jackets that belong to the security guards. I don't know if they've been called for us, or if they're just walking about anyway, but I'm not about to find out. I speed ahead, barely keeping up with Chantelle. We've not even been running that long and I've already got a stitch. I heave open one of the doors and I hear her friend, breathing and panting heavily behind me. I head out of the shopping centre and the cold air from outside hits me in the face, as I run across the road and head towards a side street.

Chantelle's already waiting there, beside this old building. Leaning against the wall next to this boarded-up window. I double over with my hands on my knees, trying to catch my breath and sucking in air.

'Where's Marc?' she asks, but I'm so out of breath all I can do is pant and point back towards the Arndale. I straighten up and wipe away some of the sweat from my forehead.

'What's wrong with you?' I snap, but I'm still out of breath. 'You can't just go and rob something then get off. You could've got us *all* into trouble? You think I want to get in trouble for shoplifting?'

I want to add that if my mum found out, my life wouldn't even be worth living. She'd kill me. More than kill me. And I can't even imagine what my dad would say. Chantelle opens her mouth like she's going to say something back, but then I see Marc, heading towards us. He's got his coat shoved under his arm and he looks pissed. He's moving his mouth about ten to the dozen before he even reaches us and Chantelle gives me a sideways glance.

'Oops,' she says. 'He don't look too pleased.'

'Of course I ain't too pleased!' Marc snaps. 'What kind of foolishness are you getting me into? If I wanted to go running around all over the place, d'you not think I would've stayed in school and gone to my actual PE lesson?' He pauses to pull on his jacket. 'Some of us,' he continues, 'ain't Usain Bolt like you two ... and another thing, not only am I all hot and sweaty, but I dropped my good-good Afro comb.' He turns to Chantelle. 'You owe me a new one!'

87

'*All right!*' Chantelle says. 'I'll get you a new comb. I'm sorry!'

But Marc just kisses his teeth.

Chantelle tries to wrap her arm around him. 'It was a bit of fun, that's all and anyway ...' She pauses and pulls one of the bottles out of her bag. 'Ain't you thirsty after all that running? Don't you want a nice, cold, drink of Coke?'

Marc snatches the bottle from her. 'Who steals for fun? And don't think you're forgiven,' he says, opening it and taking a swig. Chantelle turns and offers one of the other bottles to me. 'Jackson?' she says.

My mouth's so dry, and I've only got the dregs from a nearly finished bottle of water in my bag, but I shake my head. I'd down that in a minute, but I don't want to, because I know where it came from. I know that it's stupid because it's only a drink, but it still feels wrong, somehow.

I shake my head. 'Nah, I'm all right, thanks,' I say.

Chantelle shrugs. 'Suit yourself!' she says, then she opens the bottle and takes a gulp. We stand there for a minute and it feels a bit awkward, then Chantelle shoves the bottle into her bag. She turns and starts to walk slowly down the side street that we're on, and Marc mouths, *Oh, she crazy*, to me behind her back. Then he follows her too, but I still don't move. My lunch hour is gonna be up soon, and then I've got double history – with Aimee. I should move, but it's like I'm rooted to the spot. I don't want to go back to school and listen to Aimee going on about how traumatized she is. I don't want people to keep asking me about what happened.

And it's like these two people, who I barely even know, are

the only ones who might possibly understand what I'm feeling right now. How I can't stop replaying what happened in my mind. I can't stop thinking about Shaq's hand wrapped around mine, or the sound of his breathing, or his voice saying: *'I don't wanna die. Will you tell my mum I love her?'* Over and over again. And a small part of me wants to talk about it. Wants to be near them, because of that.

Chantelle and Marc stop bickering, then at the far end of the alleyway she turns to look at me.

'Jackson,' she shouts. 'You coming with us, or what?'

And for the first time ever, I do the most un-Jackson thing in my *entire* life – I follow them.

10

MARC

We walk along one of the back alleyways that's full of rubbish and proper stinks, before we come out into the Northern Quarter. Jackson barely says anything. Chantelle's moaning on about something or the other, but I can tell she ain't got no clue where to go, so I lead the way. It's nowhere near as busy here as it is in town and it feels good to be near all the murals and metal shutters covered in spray paint. I stare at the graffiti as we walk, to see if anything new has popped up since yesterday. I'm still pissed at Chantelle and not just cause she made me lose my good Afro comb running outta Greggs like a loon, but cause she could've got me into some serious shit too. If we'd been caught and the police were called, I would've been in so much trouble with Emma and Dry Eileen. No one would even care that I didn't actually take anything.

I've already had enough run-ins with the police to know that I don't want no more. They're always the ones who come out and bring me back, whenever I've tried to run away. Even if the carer was proper horrible, they'd just put me in the back of the car and tell me how I'm 'wasting police time.' When I got caught spray-painting that mural in Levenshulme, the police officer called me a hooligan, and said I'd be in prison by the time I was eighteen. I know he wasn't just saying it cause I'm Black either, it's cause I'm in care, too. People don't expect you to do anything decent with your life when you come from a background like mine. I've always felt so different cause of it, so I don't go around broadcasting my situation.

Especially to people I barely know.

I try to keep it hidden from the other kids in all the schools I've been at, but it's hard to fully keep it a secret, cause I'm always being dragged out my lesson for a meeting with someone who's got a bait lanyard on. It's also embarrassing when one of your carers turns up to parents evening cause it's obvious that you ain't related. And I can't just stay over at a mate's house like most other kids do, cause my social worker needs to go round there first, and they've gotta be police checked. Then when people find out, they start asking me all this shit they've got no business asking – about my parents, or what the reason is for me ending up in care. Or they start hassling me, or stop talking to me altogether. The worst, though, is when the other kids are only mates with you out of pity. I can't explain it, but it's like, as soon as they find out, they don't even see me as Marc any more. They just see me as a kid in care.

And I'm more than that.

Way more.

We walk along, past this big multi-storey car park, that's covered in even more graffiti, then Chantelle says: 'Where exactly are we going? We've been walking for *ages*!'

I give her a funny look. 'Erm, you're the reason we had to go legging it out of Greggs in the first place!' I say.

'True!' Chantelle says, then she shrugs and pulls a doughnut out of the paper bag in her hand. 'Soz about that,' she says. She takes a bite as we carry on down the road. I point towards a closed-off bit up ahead, where the street gets wider and there's all these bollards in place. I don't know why they've cordoned this part off, but it's been like this for ages, and there's hardly ever anyone about. I clock a few of my tags on different parts of one of the walls. This was one of the first places I practised it, cause I knew there'd be no one about, and that I'd be less likely to get caught. There's a few concrete road blocks running partway across the road and Chantelle plonks herself down on one of these and stuffs the rest of the doughnut in her mouth. I sit next to her and Jackson looks like he doesn't quite know what to do for a moment, but then he perches himself on the end.

I come here a lot, when I need some space. Or when I've run away from certain placements, but I ain't about to tell Chantelle or Jackson that. Chantelle elbows me, then holds out the paper bag in my direction.

92

'Want one?' she asks, but before I can even answer she adds. 'Only one, though, cos the rest are for my sister.'

I stick my hand into the bag. 'Yeah, I do!' I say. 'It's the least you can give me, after making me lose my comb!'

Chantelle rolls her eyes. 'I ain't never gonna hear the end of this, am I?'

'No!' I reply and I pull a doughnut out. I take a bite, then Chantelle turns to Jackson who's looking around at the beaten-down walls, like he doesn't really know what to do with himself. I can't tell if he's reading the graffiti, or if he just wants somewhere to look, but he seems proper awkward.

'Jackson?' Chantelle says, and he shakes his head.

'Nah, I'm all right,' he says, but then his stomach rumbles proper loudly and he looks embarrassed. Chantelle smirks and I try not to laugh.

'Just take one!' Chantelle says. 'You're obviously hungry!' This time, he mumbles a quiet 'thanks' to Chantelle and pulls a doughnut out as well. We sit there, all three of us, on this closed-off road and it's like there's so much we all want to say, but no one knows how to start. The air feels heavy, like there's this huge weight, hanging over all of us. I only started talking to Chantelle today and I don't know Jackson from Adam, but even though I still feel a bit weird around them, cause they're strangers and none of us know the first thing about each other's lives, it's like there's something else there too. Somehow, there's this ... connection between us, cause we were all there, yesterday. I stare down at the floor.

'I can't stop thinking about him,' Jackson blurts out suddenly.

It takes me by surprise, but I'm relieved that someone's finally said something. It kinda feels like that weight's been lifted, almost.

'I keep replaying what happened,' Jackson continues. 'Over and over. I couldn't sleep last night, cause I just kept seeing him on the floor like that. What if . . .' Jackson pauses. 'What if he ends up dying? We wouldn't have just seen some kid get stabbed, we would've seen him murdered. Right in front of us. Like it was nothing.' He puts his head in his hands. 'The last thing he said to me was to tell his mum that he loved her. I don't even know who she is. I don't even know where he lives. What if he never gets to tell her that himself?'

Jackson sneaks us a glance and I can't help but feel guilty. I was there, at the tram stop and I saw it all. The guys come running out the Arndale Centre, the knife. I saw it happen and I still couldn't do nothing. I couldn't make myself run over to him. Not like Chantelle did, or Jackson. I swallow hard and I try to block out his cries and the screams of everyone around us. All I did was phone the ambulance again. I should've done more. I should've been less of a coward. Chantelle shoves her hands into her pockets.

'I know,' she says quietly. 'Someone at school said he's in critical condition. I don't know what that means . . . but he could still be okay. People survive being stabbed. Like, you hear about it all the time. It does happen!'

'Yeah,' Jackson says and he straightens himself up. 'Depending on how bad it is. Like, there was this study that was carried out, where 27.4% survived – but that was for gunshot

94

and stab wounds combined, and it doesn't take into account the level of trauma, cause there's two different types, and we don't know what type Shaq is. But if you think about it in combination with the law of averages, and how likely you are to see someone get stabbed, and them surviving, well, there's still a chance that he could be okay—'

Jackson pauses and I dunno if it's cause he's noticed that me and Chantelle are both staring at him, but he trails off.

Chantelle pulls a face. 'What?' she says, confused. 'You looked up percentages of people dying from stab wounds?'

Jackson shifts over on the road block. I can tell that Chantelle thinks it's weird, but she doesn't say anything else. Maybe cause she can tell how upset Jackson is. I don't think it's weird, but I'm not about to say that, either. I used to look up percentages and statistics as well. Mainly of kids in care, cause I wanted to know what happens to them. What their futures are like. What might end up happening to me. But I hated the stuff that I saw, so I stopped looking.

Jackson stares down at his hands. 'Stuff like that . . . helps me make sense of it. And I don't know what else we're supposed to do. Are we just meant to wait?'

Chantelle's face softens. 'I guess so,' she says, then she turns to look at the boarded-up buildings covered in graffiti, around us. 'I hope we did enough,' she says finally, and her words hang in the air. No one else says anything, we all just sit there. In the middle of this closed-off road, surrounded by concrete and graffiti, hoping that Shaq will be okay.

11

CHANTELLE

I had a couple of missed calls from Gran while I was out, which I knew were probably to do with me walking out of class, cos Marc had a phone call from home about not turning up to his lessons and had to get off pretty quickly. I wasn't about to rush back just so I could get an earful, though, so I stayed in town for a bit longer. Then, I told Jackson to have a nice life, and went and caught my bus. Cos let's face it, it's hardly like we're gonna see each other again. Especially now I've got my bus pass back. Jackson couldn't be more different to me and Marc if he tried. If I'm honest, I was surprised that he even came along with us in the end, and that he was so open about how he felt too. I didn't expect that at all, and it made me think that I probably judged him a bit too quickly when we first met in Greggs. He's really good-looking as well, but I'm hardly gonna tell him that!

I push open my front door and I'm barely through it when Marni comes rushing towards me.

'Ooooh, you're in trouble,' she hisses, then she pushes past me and heads into the living room. I follow her in, then toss the squashed bag of doughnuts towards her.

'Here,' I say. 'Not like you deserve 'em! Didn't even get a hello!'

Marni catches the bag and her face lights up. 'You got me jam doughnuts?' she says. 'You're the best sister *ever*!'

'Yeah, yeah,' I reply. 'I know!'

I head out and wonder if I can make a quick dash up to my room before Gran clocks I'm home, but it's too late. She comes out the kitchen and I can tell by the look on her face that she's about to give me what for.

'Hi, Gran,' I say.

'Don't "hi, Gran" me, Chantelle!' she says. 'Would you like to explain why I've had the school phoning me up at work to tell me you've got no afternoon marks?'

I bite my tongue. I know there's no point in trying to lie and say that school got it wrong or something like that, cos she already knows. And if there's one thing that Gran hates more than the backchat or the skiving, it's when I lie to her. Besides, I already know that I'm in for a fifteen-hour lecture, so there's no point in me making it worse.

I shrug. 'I went to get my bus pass back,' I say. 'And before you say anything, I never told you cos I knew you'd just go on about me not looking after stuff. But I dropped it in town yesterday – and it's just double PE and geography. Like, PE doesn't even count towards my final results and missing *one* geography lesson is hardly gonna make a difference—'

'That's not the point!' my gran snaps. 'After everything we've been through with you and that school. Look how far you've come, how hard you've been trying. I don't want you to start with this nonsense all over again!'

'I'm *not*!' I reply. 'You've seen my report – you know I've been fine for ages. I just went to get my bus pass, and I didn't see the point in going back. That's *all*.'

'And you couldn't pick up the phone?' Gran says.

I don't say anything and Gran rubs her temples. I feel bad. She's not as old as most people's grandparents cos she had my mum proper young, and she didn't really have much choice with me and Marni. We got lumbered with her cos there was no one else to look after us. When I lived with Trudy, no one really cared what I did. No one bothered to check on me, or pulled me up if I got into trouble. So, moving in with Gran took some getting used to. Sometimes, I can't actually believe that Gran and Trudy are related. They're so ... different.

'You can't just go walking out!' Gran says. 'Whether you "see the point" in something or not – that's not how life works. You're so close to getting your GCSEs, Chantelle, and I don't want you to throw it all away. I don't want you to be like me!'

That last part takes me by surprise and Gran doesn't look half as pissed as she first did. She almost looks sad. She pauses and moves a hand to her forehead. 'I know things haven't been easy for you, or Marni,' she continues. And I know that she's talking about Trudy now. 'But you can't use that as an excuse. I left school pregnant at fifteen, with nothing. I could barely read or write. I don't want the same for you. I want you to have whatever type of future you want. For you to go on to university, if that's what you want to do. Education gives you choices.' Gran pauses and touches the side of my face with her hand. 'I don't regret having your mum,' she says. 'But I wish I'd stayed in school. You've got the chance to go so far, and do so much – don't throw it away.'

All the anger is gone from Gran's face now. I know that she only goes on at me cos she cares. It's weird, cos I don't think I ever felt that from Trudy. With Trudy, I only ever felt like burden.

'I'm sorry,' I say. 'I won't do it again. I promise!'

'I know you won't,' Gran replies. 'Because if you do, you'll be grounded until you finish college, you hear?'

'All *right*!' I say and I fully know that she means every word.

I head upstairs and push open my bedroom door. Me and Marni share a room, which can be proper fucking annoying sometimes, especially when I want my own space, but Gran's house is tiny and she only has two rooms. And I suppose that as irritating as Marni can be, I'm just glad that we're somewhere together.

I grab my copy of *Great Expectations* off the windowsill and I climb onto my bed. We've got a practice exam question in English tomorrow and I really wanna make sure that I get a good mark. Especially cos it's with Ms Stinking Edwards. I've been revising proper hard since I found out about it two weeks ago, and I've highlighted so much of the book that the pages are more or less all yellow. I wouldn't say I love the book or anything like that, but it's *way* more interesting than I thought it would be. Ms Edwards is always banging on about the description, but I couldn't give a toss about any of that. It's all the stuff about the law and Magwitch's trial and the unfairness of it all that I care about the most. It makes me so mad. The way that Magwitch's fate is already decided, just cos of who he is.

I carefully go through the plan I've made, drafting out a few more points to support the quotes I've chosen and I'm just about to move on to the conclusion, when my phone vibrates in my pocket. I've got two notifications. Jackson's followed me and he's sent me a DM as well. I'm kinda surprised, cos now I've got my pass back, I thought that would be it. His account's private, so I request to follow him back, then go to my messages. He's sent me a link to a story from a news website.

Manchester Gang Stabbing: Boy, 14, dies after being knifed in broad daylight,

12

JACKSON

I can see that Chantelle's read the message, but she hasn't replied yet. I didn't think I'd ever speak to her again, but after I found that article, she was the first person I thought of messaging. They'd included a mugshot of Shaq in the news story, but it was like whoever wrote it deliberately picked the one picture where he looked angry. Where he isn't smiling. In the photo, Shaq's got a bruise under his left eye, so it makes you think that he probably got it fighting. Or that he's as violent as the headline is trying to suggest. He looks much older in it, as well. Not like the fourteen-year-old kid he actually was. Not how he looked when I saw him that day. *Scared and alone.* Crying out for his mum, with tears and snot streaming down his face.

There's a few grainy photographs taken from the CCTV

footage from inside the Arndale Centre, as well. You can just about make out the smudge of Shaq's jacket, and the group of boys with their faces covered, who are chasing him. The caption underneath it says:

Moments before thugs close in on rival gang member. Shaqeel Townsend was banned from Manchester Arndale for criminal damage and aggravated behaviour. Teen is believed to have close connections to the Chillingham Close Gang.

Even if that was true, about Shaq being banned, what the fuck does that have to do with him being murdered?

Of course, Aimee WhatsApp'd me the article as well:

> See!! Told u I was right about him!!

> Can we just forget all this now & go back 2 normal???

I can't believe that I ever liked her in the first place now. She's tried to WhatsApp call me a couple of times, but I've just ignored her. I guess a small part of me was hoping that she'd realize why I was so upset by what she'd said on our date. I was even willing to give her the benefit of the doubt because people say stupid things sometimes, but the way she's been about it at school has just pissed me off even more. I wasted three years fancying her and this is what she's really like.

As soon as I saw Shaq's surname in that news report, I looked him up on Insta right away. The Shaq on Instagram and the Shaq in the article were like two different people. His profile is public and full of loads of pictures of him with his mates, playing football and one where it looked like he was coaching some younger kids. There was a post he'd uploaded on Mother's Day last year, with loads of pictures of him and his mum and what looked like his older brother, and a caption saying how much he loved her, how she'd been both his parents. Did he get to say goodbye to his brother and his mum? Did he get to tell her that he loved her, like he'd asked me to do? The journalist could've picked *any* of the photos from his profile, but instead they chose that mugshot. I don't even know where they found it. They didn't mention Shaq's football career or the bright future he could've had. It's the way they talk about Shaq in the article that makes me so angry and upset, though, because it's like he's not even a victim. Instead, he's someone to be feared. And it's like he somehow deserved to die because he was just another Black boy from Moss Side.

The more news reports and Tweets and comments I read, about Shaq being this thug who'd got into fights in the Arndale, who was carrying a knife as well, the more furious I felt. A few people on Twitter had posted a link to a music video on YouTube. Shaq was in the background with a few of his mates. It looked like the video had been filmed on an estate or something like that. His mate mentioned something about breaking someone's jaw in one of the lyrics and all the RTs had comments like:

We're really supposed to believe that he was the victim??
Look at him in this video!!

103

> Bunch of council estate thugs, might as well just leave them
> 2 it and let them kill each other!

The mugshot of Shaq with the bruise under his eye had been shared so many times as well, with people saying:

> Well, he looks like a nice lad. LOL!

I just couldn't take any more, so I stopped reading and searched for him on Facebook instead. All the posts from Shaq's friends and family, the people who actually knew him, were about how kind and funny and talented he was. How he looked out for the younger kids on the estate, and how the older kids looked out for him too. And even though I didn't know him, I could tell that all the photos shared on Facebook and Instagram were who Shaq really was. Not this violent criminal they were making him out to be.

I saw a post from a girl on Facebook, who said that the reason he'd ended up being stabbed was because one of the guys thought he was someone else. It was mistaken identity. Shaq was in the wrong place at the wrong time, and because of that he was dead. I still can't get my head around it. How shit like this can just happen. How someone could just stab another kid, then leave them to die.

I pick up my algebra book and I try to remember what I've just read, but nothing's sinking in. It makes me mad that the media and everyone else are creating this whole different narrative about Shaq, about who he was, and *what* he was, and there's nothing he can do about it. He can't even prove them wrong . . . and I want to do something. I don't know what, but I know I have to do something. I throw my book down and I put my head in my hands to try and stop it from spinning. I'm sitting at my desk, in my room. There's a knock at my door and my mum does that pointless mum thing where she comes in without waiting for a reply. She's carrying a pile of washing and some clean school blazers.

'Hey, sweetheart,' she says. 'How was school?'

I shrug. Harrison told me that the teacher had asked where I was, and even though I never told Harrison I was going to meet Chantelle in town, he'd covered for me and said I was ill. Which is probably why no one phoned home.

'It was fine,' I lie. 'Same old.'

Mum looks at me for a minute, and I almost think she's clocked that I'm lying, but then she shakes out my clothes and heads over to my wardrobe. The silence makes me uncomfortable. Almost like if I don't keep her talking, she'll suddenly suss me out and know that I skipped school for the first time in my life. And she'd really loose her shit. Especially if she found out I was with a girl who'd gone on a robbing spree in Greggs too.

'How was your day?' I ask.

Mum stares at me for a minute, then she shakes out a pair of trousers and makes her way to my wardrobe. 'It was *fine*,' she says. 'The usual. Lots of boring departmental meetings, blah-blah-blah. But since when were you ever interested in my day?' My mum's a senior lecturer at one of the big unis about an hour away from us. She teaches psychology, which is probably why she's always trying to psychoanalyze me. And my dad's a medical consultant, which is probably why they're both always on at me about getting a 'proper job' and taking 'sensible subjects' that will give me the best start in life. She's right, though. I never normally ask about her day.

I shrug. 'I'm always interested,' I reply. 'I just don't always show it!'

Mum narrows her eyes. 'Okay, who are you and what have you done with my son?' she says. 'Because this boy right here is not him!'

I pull a face. 'You're full of jokes, innit, Mum?' I reply.

Mum shoots me a smile, then she hangs my blazers in the wardrobe, and comes over to me. 'Where else do you think you get your sense of humour from?' she says. 'Because lord knows it isn't from your dad. Haven't known him to crack a joke in years!' Mum peers over my shoulder. 'Glad to see you're working hard, though. I used to hate algebra, all those numbers and sums, Pi this, Pi that.' Mum shudders. 'I still don't know what Pi means ... give me a calculator any day. You, on the other hand –' she pauses – 'are my little genius!'

'Yeah, not so much when it comes to maths!' I mumble.

Mum moves a hand to my face and I can tell she's going to start getting all emotional. She's been doing this a lot lately.

I shake my head. 'Ohhhh, Mum, don't be starting with this!'

'I'm sorry,' she says, 'It's just ... I can't believe that in a few months' time, you'll be in sixth form. Feels like only yesterday I was changing your nappies, taking you to baby group ... you'll be at university before you know it. Working, getting called to the Bar ...' Mum wipes some tears away from her face and I shake my head.

'Mum, chill out!' I say. 'I've not even left school! Don't be wishing my life away.'

'I know,' she says. 'It's just you're growing up so fast!' I pull a face. Sometimes I wish I had a brother or sister, then maybe Mum wouldn't get so worked up about stuff like this all the time. Maybe she and my dad would put less pressure on me too. I know that if I turned around and told them I don't want any of the stuff that they've planned out for me, or that I really want to do creative writing at uni, they'd be angry and disappointed. Or they wouldn't understand. Studying creative writing or even film studies at college goes against everything my mum and dad have told me my education should be. It's not about doing what I love, it's about doing what will give me the best start in life.

Mum straightens herself up. 'Okay,' she says. 'No more tears, *I promise.*' And I raise my eyebrow, because we both know that ain't gonna happen.

Mum laughs. *'Okay!'* she says. 'Maybe, I can't promise for sure ... but I won't cry when I'm around you, how about that?'

'Deal!' I say. We share a smile but it hurts, because it makes me think about Shaq, and how he'll never get to have daft conversations like this with his mum again.

'That boy,' I blurt out. 'The one who got stabbed yesterday in town. He died.'

My mum moves a hand to her mouth. 'Oh, Jackson,' she says,

and I see this look of deep sadness spread across her face. Mum wraps her arms around me and I hold onto her tight. And all I can think about is the way that people looked at Shaq when he was lying on the floor. The way they walked past him when he was crying for help.

'Do you want to talk about it?' she asks.

But I shake my head. 'Nah, I'm all right,' I say. '*Promise!*'

Even though I'm not all right and I know Mum means well, there's only two people in the world who I'd want to talk about it with. Who would fully understand, because they were there too.

Mum pulls away. 'If you're sure?' she says gently. 'You know I'm always here for you, Jackson?' She continues. 'Whatever it is, you know you can always talk to me, right?'

I nod. 'Yeah,' I say. 'Thanks, Mum.'

Mum stands up and heads to the door. 'Dinner will be ready in twenty,' she says, and then she's gone. My phone vibrates and I see Harrison's sent me that article as well.

> Aimee was right! Jokes that u almost got caught in some gang crossfire!!!

I don't reply.

13

MARC

I could probably get to school faster if I crawled there, never mind walked. Dry Eileen is driving me in her clapped-out Ford and blasting some equally dry old people's song on the radio. She called me while I was out with Chantelle and Jackson, then when I got back she gave me the *longest* lecture, talking about if I'm staying with her I need to make sure I don't skip any more lessons, and how she'd also be driving me to school every morning as well, cause my form tutor filled her in about me always being late. I didn't bother telling her that the only reason I'm late is cause I don't have any friends. I don't expect her to understand, not when she looks like she went to school in the Stone Age. Although, I guess now Chantelle could be sort of classed as my mate. It felt good hanging out with her and

Jackson yesterday, and even though it wasn't for long and bits of it felt proper awkward cause it was like no one really knew what to say, it kinda helped. Being around the people who were there when Shaq was ... murdered.

Chantelle followed me on Insta last night and sent me the article. I barely knew Shaq, but it made me so angry and sad. He was just a kid. He was the victim. But that article and all the Tweets and comments made him out to be some sort of animal.

People who look like me and Shaq, we're never seen as what we are – *kids*. We're never even seen as being human. It made me want to do something to just let off some steam. So I shoved four bottles of spray paint into my bag before we left for school. Now, I rest my bag on my knee and I'm regretting the fact I'll have to lug the paint around with me all day, cause my bag already weighs a ton.

There's all sorts of junk in Dry Eileen's car – sweet wrappers, old walking boots, you name it. And I try to hide my disgust at the fact that it looks like she ain't cleaned it in years. Centuries, even. Dry Eileen pulls into the car park at the back of the cinema and arcade complex near my school. I'm half an hour early. I've never been this early for *anything* in my entire life and I don't know what she expects me to do to kill time.

'Right,' Dry Eileen says. 'I've told the school to ring me if you go disappearing again. But I really hope that won't be the case. I've asked your form teacher to let me know if you're late as well!'

I pull a face. School already feels like prison and Dry Eileen is making it a million times worse. 'I won't!' I say. 'That's the

110

last time!' Even though I don't mean it. That's the other thing I hate. When you first go to a placement, it's all, *We just want you to be comfortable, it's your home too! Blah-blah-blah.* The next minute, there's all these rules they suddenly expect you to follow. If there's one thing I hate it's when people try and tell me what to do. Even though I've lived in different places, I haven't had to answer to anyone for most of my life, and I sure as hell ain't about to start now. Dry Eileen can drive to school at the end of the day if she wants but if I leave before she can catch me, what can she really do?

I pull down the folding mirror on the passenger side and I pat at my 'fro. Dry Eileen rushed me out the door before I was barely awake and I could kill Chantelle all over again for making me lose my comb. I pull a face, then snap the mirror closed and grab my school bag, just as Dry Eileen says: 'Remember to come straight home today!'

'All *right*!' I say.

I'm about to open the door when Dry Eileen goes: 'Hang on a minute,' and I think, *Here we go again!* But she doesn't start with another lecture, like she did last night. 'I can't imagine how hard it's been . . . coming to live here. Leaving your old school behind, and your friends . . . but if you want to see them, you can invite them round anytime. I really want this placement to work, Marc, and as soon as I know that you're going to school on time, that you're not skipping lessons, then I'll ease up. Once you show me that you're sticking to your end of the deal, then you can go out. But for this week, I want you straight home. Is that fair?'

I shrug. Dry Eileen doesn't sound mad or anything. I've had carers lock me in the house to stop me from going out, even though you ain't supposed to do that. And once, when I lived with this couple, the guy came to pick me up from Cadets, where I didn't even want to be, and he stood there and screamed and shouted in my face. In front of everyone. Dry Eileen just talks to me in a normal way. I know, though, that as soon as she gets tired of me, I'll see the other side of Dry Eileen. Just like I have with all the others. Or she'll just send me packing without a second thought. I'm telling you, you can't trust no adults!

'Suppose,' I say, and I get out the car.

I mutter a 'thanks,' under my breath, then the Ford makes the loudest sound as it drives off and I'm glad that no one's here to see that. I think about hanging around outside the arcade and the cinema, just to kill some time. When I hear someone in the distance shout my name, I don't need to turn around to know who it is. Chantelle's big gob could probably be heard from space. Chantelle walks towards me and she definitely ain't in any hurry.

'I ain't got all day!' I shout, even though we're probably the only two kids in this early.

'What?' Chantelle shouts back. 'What did you say?'

I don't bother replying, cause the only person you'd actually be able to hear from this distance is Chantelle, anyway. I lean against this metal railing while I wait for her, and, oh my days, does she take her time. Chantelle smiles when she reaches me and tosses her thick curls over her shoulder.

'Could you be any slower?' I say. 'You could've run!'

Chantelle pulls a face. 'Erm, I don't run for no reason,' she says. 'The only time you'll ever catch me running is if I'm being chased by someone, or something. Other than that, it ain't happening.'

I roll my eyes. 'Okay,' I say, with a grin. We walk towards the school gates and for the first time since I started at this school, it feels good to have someone to walk in with. We head into the playground, which is still pretty dead, and Chantelle stuffs her hands into her jacket pockets.

'How much trouble did you get into yesterday? I thought I'd got away with it at first, but then my gran was ringing out my phone, not long after you left. Should've known! Were your mum and dad proper mad?'

I pause. It always feels weird whenever I hear someone say those words – *mum and dad*. They're just words, but whenever I hear them, I feel both empty and hurt, cause it reminds me of what I don't have. I shrug and try to make out that it's just a normal question. Like those words mean the same to me as they do to everyone else.

'Yeah, kind of,' I say quickly. 'I did get the *longest* lecture, though. And I'm grounded!'

Chantelle looks like she feels bad for a minute. 'Yeah, soz about that,' she says. 'That was my fault for telling you to come. If it makes you feel any better, my gran went in on me too! And then she started getting upset and saying how she just wants what's best for me which made me feel worse, cos at least if she's just shouting for ages then I can just switch off and pretend that I'm listening to her.'

We head into the main school building and I feel this hurt creeping up inside me. I feel like telling Chantelle how lucky she is to have her gran, even if she did give her a lecture. I don't, though, cause then she might figure out that I actually have no one.

'Anyway, you didn't just get me into trouble,' I say. 'You made me lose my Afro comb as well!'

'I'll get you another one!' Chantelle says. 'I just ain't had chance, yet.'

I pull a face, cause her getting me one another time ain't gonna help me now, and lord knows I need it. I'm just glad that Rhys ain't here to see me looking like this. I sent him another WhatsApp last night as well, but even though he's seen it, he still hasn't bothered to reply. I must've checked my phone about fifty million times before I went to bed. But still ... nothing.

We walk up the stairs and along the corridor to where our form rooms are. Me and Chantelle ain't in the same form, but all the Year Eleven ones are in the languages block. There's a few more people about and I can tell that the news about Shaq is all round school. It was all over the internet and on the news last night. The few kids that are in look proper upset. I turn to say something to Chantelle, but I don't know what. I feel Chantelle stop and I follow her gaze to the row of lockers at the far end of the corridor. There's a small group of kids huddled beside one of them. A few people stick something on one of the lockers, then get off. It must be Shaq's, I realize. Chantelle heads towards it and I follow her.

'I can't believe he's dead,' she says quietly. 'I know it sounds stupid, but I really thought, hoped, that he'd be . . .' She shakes her head. 'How's it even fair?' she says, and I can tell how mad she is. 'That a group of guys – some fucking strangers Shaq never even met – get to just change his whole future like that?' I can see that she's trying her hardest to hold back tears. I know what she means. It ain't fair that there's things out of your control that change your life so massively, but there's nothing you can do. I know it ain't quite the same, cause Shaq's dead and I'm here, but that's how I've always felt about my own life. It's always been decided by other people. *My* future is always in someone else's hands . . .

Up close, I can see that Shaq's locker is covered in all these Post-its. Pale blue, and green and fluorescent yellow, with stuff scribbled on them. Someone's drawn a massive number 10 on a sheet of paper and stuck it right in the middle of his locker. I stare at it and I must look proper confused, cause Chantelle says: 'He was the same number as Rashford. People even called him the next Rashford, the papers didn't write anything about that, though!' Chantelle roots around in her coat pocket for a pen, then she pulls out one of her school books and rips a page from it. 'If Shaq was white and from one of those posh areas, all those news reports would've been about his "promising football career" and what a tragedy his death was. But cos he's a Black kid from Moss Side, he had to be in a gang, cos what else would he be doing?' Chantelle scribbles, *RIP Shaq xxx* onto the piece of paper, then she holds it out to me.

'D'you wanna write something?' she asks.

'Yeah,' I say. I dunno what to say at first, cause I feel sad that he's dead, but it's not as if I knew him, so it feels weird. I write: *RIP Shaq,* then I draw a little football and hand the paper back to Chantelle. She glances at the paper, and nods.

'That's a good drawing, that,' she says, then she wedges the paper into the gap between Shaq's locker and someone else's. We stand there for a minute and a few PSMs walk past, saying stuff about how sad it is, how much of a waste it is. I hear one of them mention that video. The music video that Shaq was in that people had been sharing on Twitter to try and say he was some kind of criminal. And all the things that had been written about Shaq being banned from the Arndale Centre. Whatever. None of that's got anything to do with him being murdered.

'I just wish there was something we could do,' I say.

Chantelle nods. 'Same,' she says.

I don't say the next bit to Chantelle, but part of me wishes all over again that I'd done something sooner. That I'd called an ambulance right away, or I dunno ... tried to stop it as soon as I could tell it was about to kick off, but I was too scared. I never wanna stand up for myself or get involved in shit, cause of the thought of what might happen. Of things getting violent. I just freeze. I used to see my dad hit my mum. And when he wasn't hitting her, he'd hit me. I still hear my mum screaming, like it was yesterday and not twelve years ago. My face must've gone funny cause Chantelle tugs at my sleeve.

'Hey,' she says. 'You all right?'

'Yeah,' I lie. It's a lot. I suddenly realize how busy the corridor is getting. More people start to come and write notes and stick them to Shaq's locker. I notice that a few of the Post-its have fallen to the floor already and it makes me sad, cause I think that in a few weeks, some cleaner or a teacher will take it all down. All of the words about Shaq. All of the messages about who he really was, and how loved he was, will just end up in the bin. And he needs something more permanent. He *deserves* something more permanent. Then, it hits me. I'm gonna paint a mural for Shaq, after school. I was just gonna go and graffiti some random shit, to let all my frustration out, cause if I don't, I feel like I might explode. But seeing Shaq's locker tribute and thinking about all that crap online and in the papers makes me want to do more. And I don't care if Dry Eileen kicks me out, or if she tells Emma, or if she grounds me for the rest of the year, cause it's something I *have* to do.

I hear more people saying Shaq's name and see a couple of girls in the year below crying. The first bell goes, but me and Chantelle don't move. It's like we're both rooted to the spot. Chantelle opens her mouth like she's about to say something, but Mr Reed comes strolling past.

'Ms Walker, Mr Okoye, get a move on. Form. *Now*!' He snaps. 'Come on, you've got assembly!'

Chantelle pulls a face. 'I wonder if they boss you about this much in college?' she says, but we head along the corridor anyway. We *never* have assembly on a Tuesday. It's gotta be about Shaq.

14

MARC

The whole school's crammed into the assembly hall. I sit on a row next to Chantelle. Everyone's talking proper loudly while we wait for our head teacher, Mr Frances, to start. I clock Tyler with his form group, sitting a few rows in front, he catches my eye, but he just looks away and doesn't crack up laughing with his mates, like he usually would. I notice Damar on the other side of the hall, sitting with his head in his hands. There's loads of people in the year below that are crying and even some of the teachers look proper upset. You can tell by the way they're huddled in small groups, shaking their heads and wiping underneath their eyes. Most of the PSMs are here too.

I can't stop thinking about Shaq, or seeing it all happen in town that day, so I scan the hall for something to take my mind off it. I clock this boy sitting a few rows back, with the rest of the Year Tens. I've never even noticed him before, but he's sitting next to the girl who'd been going out with Shaq, and I can tell that he's trying his hardest to hold back tears. I feel proper bad for him, cause him and Shaq must've been pretty close. It's like everyone around me is hurting. Everyone is grieving.

I look away and I slide down in my chair. I feel this weird mix of emotions – sadness, anger, pain. And I'm just glad that I'm with Chantelle, that I paid for her on the bus that day, and that Mr Reed decided to sit her next to me in maths. Cause it helps having someone here who knows exactly what you're going through. Who's probably replaying that day over and over in their head as well. Chantelle must notice that something's up, cause she says, 'Hey, I never asked you. What school were you at before this one?

It feels odd, someone asking such a mundane question, right before we're about to have an assembly about a kid that's been murdered, but at the same time, it feels good to kind of talk about something normal, to take my mind off how fucking awful and sad it is, even if it's only for a minute.

'Harper Green,' I say. 'You know it?'

'Yeah!' Chantelle replies. 'That's *faaar*, though. What, did you just move round here or something?'

I pause and I try to think about what to say. If I tell her that I moved here, then she might start asking me why, and before I know it, I'll have to come up with something. *Say something, man*, I think, and I'm relieved when Mr Frances comes to the front of the hall, so I don't have to reply.

119

There's no picture of Shaq on display or anything, like I thought there might be. Everyone has to stand up whenever he does an assembly, then sit back down when he tells us to, which I think is pretty extra to be honest, but we all get to our feet.

'Good morning, Roundthorn Academy,' Mr Frances says. And I hear the words: '*Good morning, Mr Frances,*' echoing around me.

'As most of you are probably aware,' he continues. 'Shaqeel – Shaq – Townsend who was in Year Ten, was stabbed on Sunday afternoon and taken into hospital. It's with great sadness that I have to let you all know that Shaqeel died in hospital yesterday evening. Staff and students alike would agree that Shaqeel was a much-loved member of this school and he will be deeply missed. If anyone's struggling, I want you to know that my office door is always open—'

'Yeah, right,' I hear Chantelle mumble under her breath.

'—and there will be drop-in counselling sessions available to anyone who needs it. Make sure you go and see Ms Brooks in student services. I know that this will be huge shock to many of you, but I also know that the next three months are probably the most important three months of your lives. They will determine the rest of your future. Something that, sadly, Shaq will never have. We're going to do everything we can to support you through your GCSEs. We're aware that knife crime is also a growing issue, so we will be conducting random bag checks.'

A few murmurs echo around me and I can't help but think – what that will even do? Is it supposed to make us feel safe? Shaq wasn't even stabbed in school.

'I'd like us all,' Mr Frances continues, 'to have a minute's silence for Shaq.'

Normally, when we've had to do that in assembly for other things that have happened and stuff, most people do it, but there's always a few kids who mess about, and try to make each other laugh and stuff like that. But not this time. I see everyone's heads go down and a few people close their eyes. I watch as all the teachers and the PSMs do the same. I don't move for a second, not cause I don't want to or nothing like that, but cause I can't. I look around at how sad everyone is, and I suddenly feel this pain, deep inside me. I think about all the Post-its on Shaq's locker and how it was already getting so full and we haven't even got to period one yet. And I feel for Shaq, but also it makes me think that if it'd been me, my locker would've stayed exactly the same. Cause no one will miss me and when I leave this world – I'll just be gone, and that's it.

15

CHANTELLE

We all pile out of assembly and everyone's much quieter than they usually are. I can tell something's up with Marc cos he hardly says a word as we push our way through the hallway, but I think that it's probably just cos of Shaq. I've got double English now, which is *definitely* my worst lesson. Not cos I hate it, but obviously cos I have Ms Blame-Everything-on-Chantelle Edwards for two hours. Even if she doesn't pick the best books, it's the way she teaches them that makes it *way* worse. There's been a few times when we've had to listen to her read for more or less the whole lesson and people have just fallen asleep in the class. KO'd right on the desk. I actually like when we do the essays, though. When we have a choice of questions we can pick from and we can talk about the themes we notice in the book and stuff. I like to just figure things out my own way. I don't like to be told that this is what the author meant when they wrote whatever it was. I like to think about what they meant for myself. No one ever cares about what I have to say in class, so with essays it's my chance to be heard. Even if that does sound stupid!

'If you get out before me, meet me outside class at break, all right?' I say to Marc as we head down the English corridor.

'Okay,' he says. 'Although Greenwood likes to take his time letting us out. I'll see you in a bit!' he says, and then he disappears into one of the classrooms. I can hear the noise from out here and Greenwood's already started screaming at people to behave, even though the lesson's literally only just started. That's the one thing I don't miss about being in the bottom set.

I push open the classroom door. Ms Edwards has had it in for me from day one. Even before I used to play up to be honest. Y'know when you can tell that some teachers just don't like you? Even now, after I've been working hard for the past two years, I can tell she wishes I wasn't in her class. She's tried to get me moved to a lower set loads of times, cause of my 'challenging behaviour'. Whenever I ask something, or finish my work before everyone else and have nothing else to do, so start talking or whatever, she always goes on about how 'disruptive' I'm being, or how I've got a 'serious attitude problem'. I wouldn't even mind, but there's people in the class who do *way* worse, and don't get anywhere near as much stick as me.

The desks are set up in exam style, ready for us to do this practice essay question, and I take my seat. Even though it's not the real thing, I've been getting proper nervous about all these practice exam questions and revision classes. Cos in three months, that'll be it. I'll only have one shot at my GCSEs and I really wanna get good grades. My form teacher, Mr Sharpe, said that I should have a 'back-up plan' cos of how difficult Xaverian is to get into. In other words, he doesn't think I'm capable. But I don't have a back-up plan, cos Xaverian's the only college I wanna go to.

Ms Edwards writes the start and finish time underneath the essay question on the board.

'Okay, Year Eleven,' she says.' Get your books out, please. There's paper on your desks. Just a reminder that this is exam conditions. If you finish before the time is up, make sure to read over your work. You have an hour, starting from now.' I pull my book out my bag and I look at the essay question, one last time. Then, I take a deep breath, pick up my pen and start to write.

I'm finished before most people in the class and I actually feel pretty good. I read over my essay for the second time, just to make sure I ain't missed anything important out. I tried proper hard with this and I even tried to choose my own quotes, instead of the ones Ms Edwards told us to use in class. Holly and Jessica must've finished too, cos they start doing that thing where they try whispering to each other from across the room. But it's so loud, they may as well be talking. I can hear them and I know for sure that Ms Edwards can too, cos I see her glance in their direction. She doesn't say anything, though, and I know that if it was me, then it would be a completely different story!

I notice that Ms Edwards has spelled a word wrong on the whiteboard and I've got nothing else to do but stare at the mistake, so I put my head down on the desk instead and wait for the rest of the time to go by.

Someone's phone goes off in the back somewhere and Ms Edwards turns to me.

'Whoever's phone that is,' she says, although she's clearly talking to me, cos she's staring right in my direction, 'you shouldn't have it on you in school. And as a reminder, it's supposed be exam conditions! If it goes off again, I'll be confiscating it!'

I kiss my teeth. Why do teachers *always* do that? Make out like they're addressing the whole class when they are clearly talking about one person in particular. It's like, if you're going to make a comment, at least do it with your whole chest. Part of me wants to ask Ms Edwards why she's always coming for me. Why I'm *always* the one to get the blame whenever anyone talks or laughs or breathes. But I just stay with my head on the desk.

'Is there something you want to say, Chantelle?' she says, and I try to keep my cool.

There's lots of things I want to say, to be honest, but my gran and Mrs Cohen have already told me that I need to control my mouth. Especially where Ms Edwards is concerned.

'No,' I say, and I can't help it, but the next bit just comes out. 'Is there something you want to ask me?'

People in the class start to snigger and Yohan has some sort of coughing fit, to try and hide the fact that he's actually laughing.

Ms Edwards stares at me. 'It's one thing to answer back,' she

125

says. 'But to do it in the middle of a practice exam question! I'll be having a word with Mrs Cohen ... Year Eleven,' she snaps. 'You've still got fifteen minutes, so if you've finished, I suggest you read over your answer, *in silence*!'

Ms Edwards goes back to what she's doing and I roll my eyes so hard. The phone goes off *again,* and this time, Ms Edwards doesn't even try and act like she doesn't know whose it is. This time, she marches right over to me and holds out her hand.

'Right,' she says. 'Chantelle, give it here. Hand it over!'

I stare at her empty hand. 'Hand what over?' I reply. 'I don't know what you're coming over here for ...'

A few people start sniggering and Yohan goes: 'Yo, Ms Edwards got told!' which only annoys her even more.

I obviously know that she's talking about my phone, but I *always* have it on silent when I'm in school for this reason. And I'm not about to hand it over when it wasn't even mine that went off in the first place. Ms Edwards sighs loudly, in a *here we go again* type of way, like I'm the one who's in the wrong. I know that I really can't afford to get into any more trouble, especially since I skipped school the other day, but I'm not backing down. It's the principle.

'Your *phone*!' Ms Edwards snaps and by the way she's staring at me, I can tell she's going to go off on one. 'I already told you,' she continues, 'that if I heard it again, I would be confiscating it. So, hand me your phone *now*, and you can come and collect it at the end of the day. Either that, or you can go to the Key Stage Four office.'

'I ain't giving you my phone!' I say.

I hear more laughter and I feel everyone staring at me. I'm proper mad that whoever's phone it actually is, is just sitting there laughing while I get into trouble. 'Why do I *always* get the blame?' I continue. 'D'you not think that you should find out whose phone it actually is first before you start blaming me?' I gesture towards the back of the class. 'It was clearly,' I say, turning back around in my seat, 'coming from that direction.'

'*Get out!*' Ms Edwards says.

'What?' I reply.

She storms over to her desk and starts writing something down furiously on my report card.

'You're disrupting my lesson yet again,' she says. 'Refusing to follow school policy, breaking the rules, being aggressive. The list goes on . . . Go and see Mrs Cohen, and you can explain to her exactly why I've asked you to leave my class. I'll be phoning home too.'

Normally, there'd be an *'ohhhhh'* at that, but people are still kinda quiet cos we're supposed to be in exam conditions, which somehow makes it worse. I know if I wanted to, I could make things even more difficult for Ms Edwards. I could refuse to leave, but I already know that she'll radio for a PSM to come and escort me out if I do. Besides, I don't wanna be in this stinking classroom with her. I shove my things into my bag and Ms Edwards comes back and hands me my report card. I can see that she's already circled the boxes that say: *'aggressive and intimidating behaviour,'; 'refusal to comply with school policy after several warning attempts,'; 'swearing'.*

'When did I swear?' I say.

'You swore when you sucked your teeth at me.'

'Nah, that ain't swearing, miss!' Yohan says.

'I'm giving you a warning, Yohan!' Ms Edwards replies.

I shoot Ms Edwards a dirty look, then I take my report off her and make my way to the door. I don't even care if she phones home, now. I'm sick of this woman. I'm sick of being blamed for things I didn't do.

'By the way,' I say, before I head out the door, 'you spelled *ambiguous* wrong. Maybe you should put more energy into doing your job correctly instead of coming for me.'

The whole class erupts with laughter and I slam out. I head out of the humanities block and make my way along the corridor. I see two PSMs but before they have a chance to ask me why I'm out my lesson, I say: 'I'm going to the Key Stage Four office!' I feel them watching me to make sure that I'm actually going where I said I was. I bet Jackson doesn't have to put up with this crap in his thirty-grand-a-year school. I bet no one's telling him to have a 'back-up plan' just cos he wants to go to a decent college.

I push open the door to the Key Stage Four office. Mrs Cohen's chair is empty and the only other person here is this woman who signs us in if we're late or phones home if we're ill.

'D'you know where Mrs Cohen is?' I ask the woman.

'She's with a student,' she says. 'She should be back in a minute.'

I pull over one of the computer chairs by Mrs Cohen's desk, then I sit down and pull my phone out. I know that she won't take it off me if she sees me with it. There's only a handful of teachers who actually like me in this school and Mrs Cohen is one of them. I don't know how, but Mrs Cohen just has a way of talking to me that calms me down. She doesn't patronize me or anything like that and even when I used to muck about or miss lessons, it's like Mrs Cohen still saw something in me. It's like she's always seen me as bright and clever, even when no one else did.

I open Instagram while I wait and I see that Jackson's sent me another DM. He's sent me two screenshots, with:

Have you seen this!???

I stare down at the screenshots. They're of two different news stories from the same paper, written by the same journalist, published an hour apart. One of them is about Shaq's stabbing and the other is about a white teenager who was stabbed in Edinburgh.

Mother's heartbreak as teen is killed in unprovoked attack

Then:

Manchester stabbing: hooded gang fight turns violent

I don't even need to read on to know which one's about Shaq. Two teenagers have been murdered, yet only one of them is seen as a victim. Only one of the attacks is 'unprovoked'. I stare down at the words they use to describe the other teenager. The article is all about this great future he could've had, and how what happened was a truly awful tragedy. Shaq's article talks about how 'scared' everyone who was out shopping was; how passers-by feared for their lives, how Shaq was already known to the Arndale security staff; and how this was the fifth gang incident to happen in town this year. There's nothing about how loved Shaq was, or the bright future he could've had. Or even how heartbroken *his* mum, and *his* family must be. I think about all the notes on Shaq's locker and how upset everyone was in assembly. I feel sick and angry. I hate that the world is making him out to be something that he's not.

I'm about to reply to Jackson when Mrs Cohen comes in. I click off Insta and put my phone away.

'Chantelle,' she says. 'To what do I owe the pleasure? And I'll pretend I don't see those,' she says, pointing to my ears. 'Or *that*,' she says, gesturing at my phone.

I move my hair, so that my earrings are fully covered and put my phone away. Maybe she's not so strict on uniform cos she knows I'll be leaving soon.

'See what?' I say.

Mrs Cohen shakes her head, but she's smiling. 'Funny,' she says. 'But you know if any other member of staff sees those, they'll be taken off you?'

'Yeah, I know,' I say

Mrs Cohen pauses and glances down at her watch. 'Well, I'm guessing,' she continues, 'since it's Tuesday period one, you're supposed to be in English?'

I slump down in my chair. 'Yeah,' I say. 'I swear I fucking hate that Ms Edwards—'

'*Language!*' Mrs Cohen interrupts.

'Sorry,' I say. 'But I do! She kicked me out, yet again, over something I didn't even do. Someone's phone went off, and she tried to say it was mine ...'

Mrs Cohen sighs. 'Did she fill in your report?' she asks.

I nod and pull the crumpled piece of paper out my pocket.

'She's made it out like it was much worse on there,' I say. I watch as Mrs Cohen scans it quickly.

'*Not only did Chantelle refuse to follow rules, when asked to work in exam conditions,*' Mrs Cohen reads out, '*but, she quickly became disruptive and confrontational. Chantelle hasn't complied with the school policy on mobile phones, and after giving Chantelle several warnings, she responded in an aggressive and intimidating manner ...*'

There it is. What they always say about me. That I'm 'aggressive,' or 'intimidating,' or 'confrontational,' just for speaking out. Mrs Cohen pauses and even though she's always careful about what she says about other teachers to me, I can tell that she thinks Ms Edwards is an absolute knob too.

'I didn't swear!' I add. And I know that Mrs Cohen believes me. I'm always honest with her, no matter how bad I think it is. That's the deal I made with her, a long time ago.

'I just kissed my teeth,' I say. 'How is that a level five in aggressive behaviour? It's nowhere near the same thing. And I ain't being funny,' I continue, 'but Ms Edwards is a big woman. How are you intimidated by a sixteen-year-old girl? If you're that scared of teenagers, go and get another job. I dunno, go and work in a post office. Get a job selling soap.' I slump back in my

131

chair. 'It wasn't even my phone that went off. She's gonna ring my gran and I'm gonna be in trouble *again*.' I stare down into my lap. 'My gran already said that if I get into any more trouble, then I'll be grounded! And I already feel proper bad about . . .'

I pause. But of course, Mrs Cohen knows *everything*!

'Skipping class yesterday?' she asks and I can tell she looks proper disappointed. Somehow, it's almost as bad as my gran going off on me.

'I had to get my bus pass back!' I say.

'Okay,' Mrs Cohen continues, but she doesn't seem pissed. 'Yesterday's gone now so there's not much we can do about that, but I *really* don't want to hear that you're skipping lessons again, Chantelle. Not after how far you've come. You're this close,' she says, and she pinches a small bit of air between her fingers, 'to getting your GCSEs. I want you to leave here with all 9s and 10s, do you hear me?'

'Yeah,' I say.

I move my hands to my head. I feel myself getting worked up. Not just cos of Ms Edwards going off on one, but cos of Shaq and all that stuff about him in the papers, and school. All everyone keeps talking about is how important these last few months are and how once we leave here we'll be out in the 'real world'. I hate this school so much sometimes, but the truth is, I'm actually pretty scared of leaving. This is all I've known for ages and what if I don't figure out what I'm supposed to do with my life? I've been trying really hard in my classes and that, but what if I'm just not good enough? Like everyone else seems to think. I sink down further in my chair and I don't wanna look at Mrs Cohen, cos I don't want her to see how upset I am.

Mrs Cohen's face softens and she moves a hand to touch my arm. 'Are you okay?' she says. 'I was down to pay you a visit during period one anyway, because your gran told me what happened in town. She said that you were there, that you tried to help Shaq?'

I nod and I don't even realize I'm crying until I feel the tears streaming down my cheeks. I'm more mad at myself than anything cos I've *never* cried in school. Not even when I got smacked in the face with a football, or Leesha and Siobhan sacked me off. Or things were really bad at home. But if I'm gonna cry in front of anyone, I'm glad it's Mrs Cohen.

'I'm all right,' I say, and I wipe my face with my sleeve. 'Didn't do much use, though, did it?' I say. 'It's not like I saved his life.'

Mrs Cohen looks proper sad. 'Chantelle,' she says. 'Do you know how brave it was that you went over and helped him in the first place? You can't be expected to save someone – you're just a child. But I know for certain that what you did, would have made Shaq feel so much less alone. And I know that it would have meant a lot to his family.' Mrs Cohen pauses. 'Did you hear what Mr Frances said this morning about counselling?'

'Yeah,' I say. 'I'm all right, though. I think.'

Mrs Cohen nods and I don't know if it's cos she feels bad for me, cos I saw Shaq like that, but she says: 'I'll phone your gran at lunch and let her know what happened with Ms Edwards, okay? And I'll have a word with Ms Edwards as well. But promise me, Chantelle, no more skipping class, okay?'

'I won't! I say. 'I promise!'

'Okay,' Mrs Cohen smiles. 'When's your induction evening, for college?'

'Couple of weeks,' I say.

'You looking forward to it?' she asks.

I shrug. 'I think so,' I say. The truth is, I am and I'm not. I've picked the subjects I think I wanna do, but I'm not even sure about psychology any more. To be honest, I'd forgotten all about this open evening until Mrs Cohen brought it up.

'I know you'll love it,' she says.

The bell goes and I stand up. 'Thanks, miss,' I say. 'I'm glad there's at least one decent teacher in this whole place.'

Mrs Cohen laughs. 'I'll take that as a compliment, shall I?' she says.

'Yeah, you should!' I say, as I make my way to the door. 'Cos it's the only one you'll ever get!'

The rest of the morning drags like no one's business. But it's lunch now, and I sit in the canteen with Marc and empty a load of cheese on my chips. He's already heard me going on about how much I can't stand Ms Edwards for the first half hour and even I'm sick of talking about her.

'I can't believe that!' he says.

'I swear,' I say. 'If I actually end up grounded cos of that woman, I'm gonna switch!'

I swallow a forkful of food and in the distance, I see Damar making his way around the dinner hall without any of the PSMs or teachers noticing. That's another thing I don't get about this school, they put a ban on sweets and chocolate, but they serve pizza and chips for dinner? It feels weird inside the dinner hall, cos even though it seems like any other lunchtime, you can tell that everyone's still upset over Shaq. Damar comes over to us, and he sits down on one of the spare chairs at our table. But even Damar ain't cracking as many jokes as he usually would.

'Yes, Chantelle!' he says. He reaches out to give me a fist bump, then he leans over the table, and does the same to Marc. Damar's so lanky that his legs seem to take up most of the space beneath the tiny plastic table. I notice he's got a cap on and I don't know how he's managed to get away with wearing it in school.

'It feels weird,' he says. 'Don't it? Like, knowing Shaq's ...' He shakes his head. 'And what was all that about this morning?' he continues. 'Mr Frances saying he's going to do random bag checks. He ain't rooting through my bag. Shaq wasn't even stabbed in school!'

'I know,' I say. 'That's what I said!'

Damar pauses. 'It's mad, my brother said how his mum and brother and that really thought he was gonna pull through. But then they had to switch the life support machine off. Like, imagine having to make that decision.' Damar shudders. 'They saw that picture of you with Shaq, and I told them about you,' he says. 'That you go to my school and that.' He points to Marc. 'And you as well. I told her that you both tried to help him. His mum said it gives her faith that there's at least some humanity left in this world.'

I put my fork down and I think of Jackson. 'There was

another guy there with us, who tried to help, as well. He doesn't go to this school or nothing, but he was there, with Shaq ... he was the one talking to him and stuff.'

Damar nods and none of us say anything for a minute. I catch Marc's eye and I'm suddenly glad he's here with me. Not just cos I've actually got someone to sit with and chat or moan about Ms Edwards to for once. But cos being around him and knowing that he was there too ... I can't explain it, but it makes me feel better. Like I'm not just going through this thing on my own, which is how I've felt for most of my life.

Mr Reed walks past and Damar ducks down and tries to hide.

'Don't let him see me!' he says. 'He'll try and take my cap off me!'

'What's with the cap, anyway?' I say, and I go to pull it off, but he moves his head to the side so quickly, I'm surprised he doesn't get whiplash.

'*Don't,* man!' he says. 'My hair's only half-done, I'm waiting for my sister to finish the rest. Can you believe she sent me to school with only half my head in cane rows?'

I look at Marc and we both burst out laughing. It feels weird to laugh, especially considering everything today, but it feels good too.

'She's taking the piss!' Marc says.

'Yeah, I *know*!' Damar replies. 'I told her, if anyone rips this hat off, it's game over. Anyway,' he continues. 'D'you lot want anything? Fruit Pastels, Tootsie Rolls, Chocolate? Not on the house this time, though, man's got a business to run!'

'Nah, I'm good,' I say.

'No, thanks,' Marc replies.

Damar pulls a face, but he doesn't rush off like he normally does. Instead, he pulls out his phone and flicks to his photo gallery. He still doesn't sit all the way up, in case a teacher sees him, but he leans over the table.

'Yo, have you seen this?' he says, and he pulls a picture up on his phone. 'It's this guy who does all these murals around Manchester. Nomad, or wherever his name is. Have you seen 'em? There's bare in the Northern Quarter and in Levenshulme as well. Even if he didn't use his tag tho, I'd still know it was him, cos he always does this shadowy bit on the right, like this,' he says, pointing to the mural.

The Manchester bee has been graffitied onto some metal shutters. Even though it's been done with spray paint or whatever, it looks proper real, almost like it could be a photograph. Yet, there's this explosion of colour behind it, covering the entire shutter, so you can't even see the rusty metal any more. I know what he means about the shadowy bit too, it's only subtle, but it's definitely there. I take Damar's phone so I can get a closer look.

'That's amazing!' I say.

'There's more,' Damar replies. 'Just click through. But swipe *left!* Swipe *left*!' he shouts.

'Don't worry,' I say. 'Don't wanna be looking at none of your dodgy photos!'

I go through all the pictures and I don't know how it's possible, but each one is better than the last. Even when it's just words on an abandoned building, or this Nomad tag. I can't explain it, but it's something about the fact that they're in places that I recognize, or on normal street corners. I've never been to an art gallery or nothing like that, cos I don't really understand it and if I'm honest, I've always felt like that stuff ain't for people like me. But this feels like it is. Like it's something I can actually relate to and connect with.

'No one knows who he is, though!' Damar says. 'Like, you try to search for him online and nothing comes up.'

'Errr, what makes you think it's a guy?' I say. 'Could be a female graffiti artist?'

'Could be!' Damar says. 'Whoever did it though, they're proper good!'

I stare down at the last mural, not too far from Princess Road. It's a mural of a kid with angel wings coming out of his back. But there are all these other colours and mini paintings inside the silhouette.

'Whoa,' I say. 'That one's amazing!'

'I know,' Damar nods. 'It's my favourite!'

I hand Marc the phone, so he can see it too. He nods and he flicks through the photos a bit, but he doesn't really say much. He just mumbles something about them being all right, then hands the phone back to Damar.

Damar pulls his rucksack onto his back. 'Right,' he says, and he stands up. 'I'm out! Got my lunch round to do. I'll catch youse in a bit!'

'Bye!' me and Marc both say.

He's about to leave, when a Year Seven comes over and asks about buying a Tootsie Roll. Damar drops the Tootsie Roll into the kid's bag, and has just put the money in his pocket when a PSM comes marching over.

'Damar!' he shouts. 'Come with me! *Now!*' Damar looks at me, as if to say, *Shiiiit!* And the PSM turns and heads off, expecting Damar to follow. I see Damar quickly swap his bag with someone in the year below without the PSM noticing. Then he slumps off to the other side of the dining hall and disappears.

'If they search his bag and find out that he switched it, he's gonna get into *so much* trouble,' I say to Marc.

Marc shakes his head. 'The extraness of this school!' he says. He opens his mouth like he's about to say something else, then suddenly stops. I notice that Parveen, who was going out with Shaq, has made her way over to us along with a few of his mates. I'm kinda surprised to see her in school, I dunno why. I guess I just assumed she wouldn't be here. I almost don't recognize her with her hair scraped back and no make-up on. She's obviously been crying – her eyes are all red and puffy.

'Chantelle?' Parveen says and her voice cracks. 'I just wanted to say thanks to you both, y'know, for what you did with Shaq? I saw that picture and then Damar told me that you were both there.' She moves a hand to her face, to wipe away some of her tears. 'I'm just glad he had people around him,' she continues. 'That he wasn't on his own . . .'

I swallow hard. 'It's all right,' I say, but I wish I could say more. That I knew what to tell her, to make it hurt less. I guess nothing I say can do that. It feels even worse seeing Parveen and Shaq's friends, the people who were closest to him. Cos I can see how devastated they all are. They'll probably never get over losing Shaq. One of Shaq's mates, Kade, sits down on the edge of the table and nods at me and Marc.

'We tried to speak to Mr Frances,' Kade says. 'To ask him to do something for Shaq, innit. Like, we asked if we could do some kind of vigil at school, cos of how many friends Shaq had here, and y'know what he said?'

'What?' I say.

Kade shakes his head. 'That it ain't appropriate.' He moves his fingers in air quotes and I feel my mouth fall open. Marc looks exactly the same as me and I can tell that he's just as angry.

'Like what the fuck?' Kade continues. 'They didn't mind shouting about Shaq every ten minutes when it was to do with his football stuff, but now that he's dead . . .' He pauses. 'I swear, I wanted to bang man out. He started saying all this shit about how he'd had some parents on the phone over all that stuff they put in the paper and he actually said, "Put yourself in my shoes, we don't want to upset the parents. And if we have this vigil, there might be some kind of trouble."'

'What the fuck?!' Marc says.

'I know!' Kade nods. 'It ain't about upsetting someone's parents,' Kade continues. 'It's about Shaq . . . I'm sick of all the shit they're saying about him online. That ain't who Shaq is. Shaq deserves more than a dusty assembly with a one-minute silence.'

'You shouldn't let Frances stop you,' I say.

Kade nods. 'We ain't,' he replies. 'We're doing one on the estate. We've already spoken to Shaq's brother and that. It's tomorrow. We wanted to come over and invite you both.'

I nod. 'Thanks,' I say and I notice Marc has gone quieter than before.

Kade gets up. 'I just wish there was something else we could do.' He sighs. 'It's always the same fucking thing. Y'know why Shaq got kicked out the Arndale that time? Cause some fucking security guard started following us round the Apple shop. Like I'm gonna just turn around and put some MacBook in my back pocket. Shaq asked him what his problem was. Then the security guard started getting rude, manhandled Shaq out, said he was being aggressive, then banned us both! That's why I only ever roll with Samsungs now!'

Parveen shakes her head and even though she still looks upset, a small smile spreads across her face. 'You're an idiot, y'know that?' she says.

'What are the police doing about the guys who stabbed him?' I ask. 'Have they arrested anyone?'

The colour drains from Parveen's face. 'Nothing,' she says. 'No one saw their faces, all they got was some blurry CCTV. They said they're not taking their enquiries any further. She pauses. 'I guess another gang stabbing is hardly a priority.'

We all fall silent for a minute, not knowing what to say, but feeling the weight and the unfairness of it all. Kade rubs underneath his eye and the bell for the end of lunch goes. Sometimes I get so angry at the world and I really want to do something, but I think, I'm just one kid. One sixteen-year-old, from a council estate in Moss Side. What can I do?

'Anyway,' Parveen says. 'I'll see you both at the vigil, yeah?'

'Yeah,' me and Marc both reply.

'I'll catch youse in a bit,' Kade says and he nods at me, and I see him checking Marc out. Kade gives Marc a smile, and Marc mumbles a bye, but he seems to have gone shy all of a sudden, then Parveen and Shaq's friends disappear.

'Errr,' I say. 'You and Kade?'

'What about him?' Marc replies.

'Hello!' I say. 'He was proper checking you out, even I could see that!'

Marc pauses for a minute, and then he says: 'I'd never even seen him till assembly this morning. He *is* cute, though. Was he really checking me out?'

'Oh yeah,' I say, as we make our way to afternoon registration, and I see this grin spread across Marc's face. I'm thinking about all those notes on Shaq's locker as me and Marc make our way along the corridor, and who Shaq actually was, compared to who everyone else is making him out to be. We should be celebrating his life, not having to justify it.

Then I pull my phone out and send a message to Jackson on Instagram:

Some of Shaq's friends are organizing a vigil 4 him 2mrw. Me & Marc r going. D u wanna come?

16

JACKSON

'Yh, I'll come!' I type to Chantelle, then I click off Insta.

I'm sitting at one of the tables in the canteen, with Harrison and the rest of my mates. Only I'm not getting involved with whatever it is they're talking about. I'm staring at my history book and pretending to be revising for the mock test we've got after lunch, when the truth is I've been looking at the same page for the last twenty minutes. I don't want anyone to notice I'm being quiet and ask me what's wrong, but all I can think about are those two newspaper articles, and the completely different way they spoke about Shaq.

I've never really thought much about how everyone else at St Anthony's sees me, to be honest. Even though there's only, like, five Black students in the whole of the school. But ever since Aimee came out with all that stuff in Nando's, and the way Shaq's stabbing was reported, it's made me wonder what people really think about me. *That I'm violent and dangerous too?*

Harrison is doing some TikTok Doritos challenge and getting Elliot to film it on his phone, and I see Aimee come in. It's only been two days since we went on that date, but I can hardly look at her. It seems like she's finally got the hint and she's stopped trying to talk to me. She catches my eye now, then looks quickly away. She sits on one of the tables closest to us and I stare down at the page again. I hear someone asking her about what happened again, and I look up from my book. Aimee's sitting there, telling everyone her version. She seems like she's enjoying it. How can she not care that someone is *dead*? I can't believe I used to like her.

There's loads of people in my year crowded around. Aimee flicks her hair over one shoulder, and says: 'It was honestly terrifying. Like, I've never been that scared in my *entire life*. My dad doesn't even want me going to town any more. You should've seen him – apparently, he had a knife on him too. If I'd have come out the Arndale a few minutes later, I probably would've got caught in the middle of it all ...' Aimee moves a hand to her mouth, like she's trying to hold back tears. The whole thing just makes me want to fucking laugh.

'I keep having nightmares,' she finishes, and her friend wraps her arm around her. Shaq was murdered, which she barely even seemed bothered about at the time, and now she's making it all about her.

I shake my head, and I say: 'Unbelievable! You should get a BAFTA for that performance!'

I feel Harrison and my other mates turn to look at me. Everyone seems to go quiet. Aimee shifts in her seat and wraps her arms around herself. I can't sit here, listening to this shit. I grab my books and throw them into my bag.

'Someone was murdered!' I say. 'A *kid* was murdered, and the way you're going around talking about it . . . Can't you give it a rest?'

'He was in a gang, Jackson!' Aimee snaps. 'It would've happened sooner or later.'

'Wow,' I say. 'What did I *ever* see in you? He wasn't in a fucking gang, Aimee. Maybe you should get your facts straight before you go running your mouth!'

I think about telling her that even if Shaq was in a gang, it doesn't mean he deserved to die. But I know there's no point in wasting my breath. I shake my head and I pass her on my way out of the canteen. I'm barely near her, but I see her flinch like I was about to hit her or something. I head into the corridor and I feel sick. I just want to get out of here. I hear Harrison shouting after me, but I don't stop. The corridors are massive, but everything suddenly feels like it's closing in on me.

I stop near one of the long benches outside a classroom, and I sit down, and put my head in my hands.

'Jackson,' Harrison says, as he reaches me, and sits down on the bench. 'You all right? I'm worried about you, man. You've been acting so weird the past couple of days.'

I straighten myself up and look at Harrison. 'Have you not

heard the bullshit she's coming out with?' I say. 'And then look at this!' I show him the two screenshots of the newspaper articles. Maybe I expect more, because we've been mates for ages, but I suppose we've never really had these conversations before. They've never really come up. Harry just stares at the screen blankly.

'He wasn't in a gang,' I say. 'What they're saying – it's rubbish.'

Harrison pulls a face. 'Oh, come on,' he says. 'The papers wouldn't say it if it wasn't true. Besides, d'you really expect me to believe that he was from that estate and not involved in anything?'

'Why?' I say. ''Cause he's Black? What if that had been me?'

'Whoa,' Harrison says, and he puts his hands out in front of him. 'I don't mean that. *That boy* was clearly from a rough area. It's got nothing to do with him being Black. You're nothing like him, Jackson. You're completely different.'

The bell goes and I can hardly move for a minute because I feel like all the air's been knocked right out of me. Harrison doesn't even realize what he's said. He's been my closest friend for years, yet he thinks I'm nothing like Shaq. And the way he said it, like it's a compliment. Like I should be pleased that he doesn't *really* see me as Black. The corridor starts to get busy, and if Harrison notices how upset and angry I am, he chooses to ignore it, because he starts talking about some video on TikTok instead. Somehow, I get to my lesson and I sit down. But all I can hear is Harrison's voice in my head, over and over. *You're nothing like him, Jackson. You're completely different.*

We're sitting in the McDonald's opposite Piccadilly Gardens. Me, Harrison and the rest of my mates. I wasn't really in the mood to go to McDonald's, especially not after today, but I had to come into town anyway to catch my train home, and Sam and Elliot wouldn't let it slide. I think a small part of me, just wanted things to go back to normal, with me and Harrison too.

It's crowded inside McDonald's because this is where everyone from school usually goes. Harrison, Sam and Elliot are ordering, and I said I'd save a table. The truth is, I wanted a minute to myself. To look up Shaq's mum again. As soon as I found Shaq's Facebook, I searched for his mum as well. I found her straight away – Pamela Townsend. I knew it was her because she'd put a public status up about how heartbroken she was to have lost Shaq. Plus, I recognized her from Shaq's Insta and Facebook posts well. I must've tried to type a message out to her a million times. To let her know that I was with Shaq, to pass on the message I promised I would. But each time I deleted it, because it doesn't feel like something you can just say over Messenger. That's why I wanna go to Shaq's vigil. I need to tell her what Shaq said. I owe Shaq that.

It's stuffy and hot inside and I stare out the window overlooking the gardens. There's loads of police about, more than I've seen in *ages*, and I know that all this is because of Shaq. They'd already started saying that there was going to be more of a police presence in the city centre and they'd be carrying out more stop and searches, like it wasn't already bad enough.

Harrison comes over and puts a McFlurry in front of me.

'Eh, Jackson,' he says. 'I know you wanted the Oreo one, but they only had Smarties left.'

'It's all right,' I say, and I pull it towards me.

The Smarties one is definitely the deadest flavour out of them all, but I take it anyway. Everyone starts laughing about this party we all went to on Saturday, and how Sam threw up over this girl he fancies, but I don't say anything. I don't even try to laugh along like I normally would. I can't believe that on Saturday, all I was bothered about was how late my mum would let me stay at this party and if Aimee would turn up for our date on Sunday and now ... I guess I'm trying to act like nothing's changed, but it has. It feels like I've slipped into a different world. A different universe, where all the things that used to matter just don't any more.

Harrison stares at me for a minute and he says, 'You're being proper quiet, Jax, are you sure you're okay?'

'Yeah,' I say. 'I'm just not feeling too well, that's all.'

Harrison nods. 'I'm sorry,' he says. 'You know I didn't mean anything by what I said before? You know, I didn't mean nothing like that ...'

I shove a spoonful of ice cream in my mouth. 'I know,' I say, and I want to believe him.

'I know what's wrong with him,' Sam says. 'He's nursing a broken heart, cause Aimee pied him off!'

I shake my head. That's another lie that Aimee's going around telling everyone. That she'd pied me off, not the fact I'd walked out on her in the middle of our date. I can't even be bothered to correct it.

'Hardly!' I say.

Harrison drapes an arm around my shoulders. 'She was punching anyway,' he says. 'Don't worry, there's plenty more fish in the sea. And if not –' he picks up my McFlurry – 'this'll never let you down. And if it does, I'll be here to dry your tears.' Harrison gets me into a loose headlock and rubs his knuckles on the top of my head. 'No matter what!' he says.

I manoeuvre my way out of the headlock and push him off. '*Move,* man,' I say, but I can't help laughing.

I push open the double doors of the McDonald's and take my phone out. Chantelle's sent another message and I catch myself smiling. I'd tagged a video of Harrison in my Insta stories of him trying to cram a whole Big Mac in his mouth. Harrison is *always* doing stupid stuff like that and asking me to film him. I see that Chantelle's replied to my story with:

Me and Marc r in town 2! Come meet us!!

I hear Harrison inviting everyone back to his to play games on his PS5. I'm not really a massive PS fan. I normally just sit there and watch, or have one go then get ribbed to death because I always lose. But, yesterday, being around Chantelle and Marc felt … right. *Easy,* almost. Like I don't have to pretend to be okay, or make out I'm not upset, because Chantelle and Marc are too. They understand. I don't have to defend Shaq, or put up with people talking about him like his life meant nothing. I can just feel what I'm feeling. Be myself. Not just that, though,

I kinda liked spending time with them as well. Chantelle's actually pretty cool and Marc's funny!

I reply to Chantelle's message:

Where r u???

17

CHANTELLE

I'd asked Marc if he wanted to come to town with me after school. I wasn't sure if he was gonna say yes, especially as I'd already got him into trouble with his parents or whatever, but he said he would, and that he didn't like being told what to do, so wasn't about to rush back home. Which is definitely something I can relate to! I was glad he agreed to come – it's been nice hanging round with him. Since Leesha and Siobhan sacked me off, I haven't had anyone properly to hang around with. And I don't mean just tagging on to someone's table at dinner, or chatting to Damar when he's not doing the break rounds. I mean having someone who waits for me after class. With Marc, we just click ... I'm not gonna lie, it's helped, being around someone who was there that day too. I know Jackson doesn't have that, so when I saw that he was in town, I didn't really think. I just invited him to come and meet us.

I tell Jackson where we are and Marc makes a face as he looks around. We're sitting in this small milkshake place off one of the main roads. It's only tiny, cos not many people sit in really, and me and Marc are crammed onto this small table. He keeps looking around at all the empty cartons that have been left, then he folds his arms across his chest.

Marc stares at me. 'When was the last time this place was cleaned?' he says, and he nudges an empty waffle box off the side with his elbow.

'I dunno,' I say. 'Anyway, it ain't even that bad ...'

Marc's eyes widen. I've realized that Marc ain't as quiet as I first thought. He's funny and sharp. Which kinda surprised me to be honest.

'This place is *nasty*, man,' Marc says. 'I can't believe you dragged me in here. Y'know if I catch something and die, I'm coming back and haunting *you* until you're old and grey. Even when you're in your old people's home, rocking away in your chair, thinking, *Has Marc left me yet?* No! I'll still be there. Haunting you, *for ever.*'

I shake my head. 'I can fully believe that you would actually do that! Just drink your milkshake ...' I add. 'You ain't gonna keel over in Shakeaway!'

'I wouldn't be so sure,' he says.

I roll my eyes and drink some of mine, just to make a point. It does look pretty grimy here, but they do the best milkshakes ever. Marc takes in a deep breath, then he rolls up his sleeves and clasps his hands together in front of him.

'What are you doing?' I say.

Marc closes his eyes. 'Let me just call on Jesus,' he begins. 'The ancestors, anyone up there who is willing to help.'

'Oh, Christ!' I say, and I take another sip of my drink. 'You really doing this?'

Marc turns his head. '*Shhhhh!*' he snaps. 'Can't you see I'm trying to have a moment here?' And he closes his eyes again. 'Jesus,' he continues loudly, and at this point, I'm glad there's no one else around. 'I know I haven't been the most well behaved lately. Or ever. I know that I don't read the Bible and that I cuss too much, but please don't let this milkshake be the death of me. Don't let my sweet life end here. *Amen.*'

I raise my eyebrows. 'You done?' I ask.

Marc unclasps his hands. 'I'm done!' he says. He picks up his milkshake. He takes his time sniffing the top, and moving the straw around, and lifting it up to his nose. And just being that bit extra for a bit longer. Then he leans forward and takes a sip.

'Well?' I say, as Marc goes silent.

'Nah,' he replies, and his eyes widen. 'This milkshake's banging!'

'Told you!' I say. 'I used to come here with my gran. But now, I dunno . . . I guess she's too busy working.'

Marc pauses for a minute. 'D'you live with your gran?' he asks.

'Yeah,' I reply. 'It's all right really. I mean, she'd go mad if I ever brought a boy round and she can be proper strict sometimes, but . . . I like it. When I lived with Tru— my mum, it was nothing like this.' The part about Trudy just slips out, without me meaning it to. Maybe it's cos I feel comfortable around Marc now. I suddenly feel embarrassed and I glance at him, cos I wonder if he's gonna be looking at me the way my old friends used to, when they found out that Trudy doesn't have anything to do with me and Marni. Like there was something wrong with me cos my mum wasn't around. Or they'd say: 'Well, it's your mum, innit? You'll work it out.'

But family ain't always like that.

I expect Marc to look at me that way too, but he doesn't.

'Do you not see her, then?' he asks.

'No,' I say. 'Haven't seen her for like three years now.' I shrug, like he's just asked me a normal question. But the truth is, whenever anyone asks me about Trudy, it's like an old wound, opening up again . . .

'What happened?' he asks. 'Or you can tell me to mind my own business, if you don't wanna talk about it.'

I pause. Even though I try not to think about it, or show how much it bothers me around Marni and Gran, it still hurts. Maybe it always will in some way. It's not like they teach you this in school. How to cope when both your parents aren't around. When they don't want you. When they probably never did. I don't mind Marc asking me about it, though, cos it doesn't feel like he's asking it to be nosy. It feels like he's asking cos he genuinely cares, and it's kinda nice to talk about it with someone for once, instead of pretending I'm fine all the time.

I shrug. 'We used to live with her,' I say. 'Me and my sister, but it's like even then I was always the one looking after Marni. Y'know how when you're little and that, your parents always say nice things to you and stuff? About how pretty you are, or how clever you are, or how you can go on and do whatever the fuck it is you want to do?' I pause. 'Well, she never said none of that to me. It was all about how much I ruined her life, or how stupid I was ... and she'd go off with some guy she'd just met and leave me and Marni on our own. Sometimes with no food. And when she cleared off three years ago, she just dumped us at Gran's and said she didn't wanna do it any more and Gran could do it now, cos she'd had enough.'

I have to stop myself then. It's been ages since I thought about that day and I feel all these emotions flooding back. Not just the pain, but feeling like I'll never be good enough, no matter what I do. I feel like that about school sometimes, too. I suck in a deep breath and I try not to cry. Then I pick up my milkshake and shrug, to try and make out like I'm okay, but I can tell that Marc ain't convinced. He stares down at his hands for a minute and I see a look of sadness flash across his face. It's not just sadness, though – it's almost like he understands. Like he really gets it. I wonder if I've blurted too much out, but then Marc picks at the label on his cup and says: 'I know what that's like.'

He looks like he's about to say something else for a minute when the door to the milkshake place flies open and Jackson walks in.

'Hey,' Jackson says.

'Hey!' Marc replies.

'Hi,' I say, but I can't help wondering what he was about to tell me before Jackson came in.

18

JACKSON

For some reason, I feel a bit nervous heading to the milkshake place. But as soon as I walk in and see Chantelle and Marc, the nerves disappear. Chantelle smiles at me and I have to look away for a minute, because I'm caught off guard. It's only the third time I've seen her and we've only spoken to each other properly once, but I don't know. I guess I didn't really clock just how pretty she was before. We've been talking a bit over Instagram too, and the more I speak to her, the more I realize I judged her too quickly and I actually like her. She's smart and knows her own mind, and she's easy to talk to as well. The milkshake place is grim, that's for sure. There's an old menu peeling off one of the back walls and it looks like it hasn't been decorated or even cleaned since the eighties. I clear my throat and Marc moves over, so that there's a space between him and Chantelle.

'Grab a chair,' Marc says. 'And you might as well get your milkshake while you're up there. Don't worry, it ain't as bad as this place looks.'

I nod. 'All right,' I say, and I make my way over to the counter to order. When I head back to Chantelle and Marc, she's already dragged another stool over.

'Thought I'd save you the hassle!' Chantelle says. I smile, and I shove my bag on the table.

'Thanks,' I say, as I sit down.

Marc shuffles his stool over to make more space, and for the first time all day, I just feel at ease. Sat here, with the two of them. Chantelle stares at me for a minute, and I don't know how she can tell that something's up, but she says: 'What's wrong with you?'

I pause. I don't know where to start with everything that happened today. Harrison, the way Aimee was carrying on, wanting to talk to Shaq's mum … then on top of that, I don't get why they haven't caught Shaq's killers yet. Why it's taking them so long? My head feels like it's about to explode.

'I keep looking up Shaq's mum,' I blurt out. 'On Facebook and stuff. I've been close to messaging her so many times, to tell her that I was there and let her know what Shaq said to me … y'know, about letting her know he loved her? But each time, I chicken out. It doesn't really feel like something you just say in a message.'

Marc nods. 'Maybe you can talk to her at the vigil?' he says.

'Maybe we all should.' He pauses. 'I mean, I dunno if it'll make a difference, cos it's not like we can change what happened or nothing, but it might help?'

'Yeah,' Chantelle says. 'I think you're right.' She turns to me. 'They wouldn't do anything at school except for some poxy assembly. They said it wasn't appropriate or some crap. That's why his girlfriend and his mates are organizing it themselves. Something that celebrates the Shaq everyone knew, and not all that shit in the papers . . .' She shakes her head. I notice this weird look come across Marc's face, then he shifts over in his chair and takes a sip of his drink. Chantelle doesn't seem to clock it, though.

'I'll definitely be there!' I say.

Everyone goes quiet for a minute, but it doesn't feel awkward this time. In a weird way, it feels good to be figuring all this out, with two people who I know are going through the exact same thing. Marc straightens himself up.

'So, Jackson,' Marc says. 'You got a pool in your house and that? Cos if you do, I'm selling Chantelle out!'

'Yeah, thanks for that!' Chantelle says. 'I'll remember this!'

'Nah,' I shrug. 'No pool. It's just a . . . *normal* house.'

Chantelle raises an eyebrow. 'I doubt it's "normal",' she says. 'You can't go to St Anthony's and live in a normal house.' She doesn't say it in a rude way or nothing. Not like she did when we first met up that time in Greggs, but I feel embarrassed again. I hope Chantelle doesn't thinks I'm some stuck-up idiot. Part of me is surprised that I even care about what she thinks, and I'm not even sure why I do either . . .

'I'm willing to look past that!' Marc says. 'When we getting an invite? Ooh, you seen *The Real Housewives of Atlanta*?'

I shake my head. 'Nah,' I say. 'My mum watches it sometimes. Even though she pretends she doesn't!'

Marc pulls a face. 'Not even *New York*?' he continues. 'Or *Orange County*?'

'Nope,' I say. 'None of them.'

'What *do* you watch, then?' he presses.

I shrug. I feel on the spot and I hate being the centre of attention. I feel Chantelle looking at me too.

'I dunno. *Star Wars*,' I say.

'Wow!' Marc responds quickly. 'I take it a back. There's no hope for our friendship. I don't care what type of mansion you live in. I tried watching *Star Wars* once, and it was so dry, oh my god! Like, who even is the guy with the pointed ears and what's his deal? My man is mis-er-able—'

I widen my eyes and I swear I almost have a full-on heart attack. 'That's *Star Trek*!' I shout, a bit too loudly. 'It's not even the same show ... it's not even the same universe. They're *completely* different!'

Marc and Chantelle stare at me.

'I mean,' Marc shrugs. 'They're both set in space. They both have spaceships. How much more similar can you get? That's *practically* the same show.'

I groan and put my head in my hands. I think about going through all the detailed reasons why *Star Wars* and *Star Trek* are not the same. Or even listing the *Star Wars* films in order – from the best to the downright disappointing. Though from the way that Chantelle and Marc are looking at me, I know that it'll be lost on them. Chantelle shakes her head, but I notice that she's smiling.

'*What?*' I say.

'You're such a nerd,' she replies, and I can't work out if she's saying it in a bad way, or not. But I find myself hoping it's the good way.

'Yeah, yeah,' I say. 'Nerd and proud! Anyway, you two just don't know a classic when you see one!'

'Okay,' Chantelle says, and she shakes her head again.

'I mean, we'll allow it this time,' Marc says and he nudges me gently. 'But I ain't joking about that invite!'

Chantelle smiles and she shoots me this glance that I can't quite make out. And then it's gone, just as quickly as it came.

We ended up spending *hours in* that place. Drinking more milkshakes, laughing and talking, and not just about Shaq either. It's the happiest I've felt since before everything happened. Marc got a message and left pretty early because there was somewhere he needed to be. I'm walking with Chantelle back to the bus station, so that she can catch the bus home, before I get my train. I feel awkward again and I don't know what to say. My mind keeps racing with things I could ask her, or stuff I could talk about, but for some reason, I can't get the words out. I clear my throat as we turn down one of the back streets and I'm about to force myself to say … *something*, just to fill the silence, when Chantelle turns to me.

'What else was up with you before?' she asks. 'I don't just

mean you thinking about Shaq's mum and that. I dunno, I could tell that something was wrong as soon as you sat down. Even after we spoke about the vigil ...' She pauses. 'It's like something was still up. I dunno if you realize, but you give *everything* away with your face. You'd be a rubbish liar, y'know that?'

I'm glad Chantelle's not staring at me, so she can't see how awkward I look. That's another thing that surprises me about her. She's perceptive. Even though I had a good time with her and Marc, I guess that somewhere, in the back of my mind, I was still thinking about all the stuff with Shaq, and what Aimee and Harrison had said, too.

'Yeah, I know,' I say. 'I'm just glad school didn't phone home the other day, otherwise, my mum definitely would've caught me out. I probably would've caved and confessed under the pressure.' I pause. 'It's embarrassing!'

'Oh, I dunno,' Chantelle shrugs. 'I think it's kinda sweet. Shows you're genuine.'

I stop in my tracks. *'Wow!'* I say. 'Was that actually a compliment?'

'Oh, ha ha,' Chantelle replies. 'I can be nice, y'know ... Anyway,' she continues, 'are you gonna keep avoiding the question, or are you actually gonna tell me what's up? She raises her eyebrow and I can't help smiling.

'Jeez,' I say. 'You could at least give me chance to try and shoot you down with my too-cool-for-school comebacks.' I do these two shooting motions with my hands and I don't even know why I'm doing them. But it's already too late by the time

I've realized how much of a fool I'm making of myself. I lower my hands and Chantelle shakes her head.

'Don't ever do that again,' she says. 'And who says "too cool for school"? What are you, fifty?'

I pull a face and I wish that the ground would swallow me whole. Or that the universe would at least let me rewind a bit, so I could go back a few seconds, and not come out with something so lame. *Too cool for school* – that's what my mum says!

'*Jackson!*' Chantelle snaps. 'Am I gonna have to ask you again or what?'

We head down the street that leads to the bus station and I can see the station in the distance. Packed out with people waiting to go home or somewhere else.

I shrug. 'I don't know,' I say. 'It's everything, I guess. Me wanting to message Shaq's mum is true, but it's like since that day, I don't really understand anything any more. Like, how people can just walk past a kid crying for help on the street? If you, me and Marc hadn't stopped, would anyone else have helped him? And everyone at school, my mates and stuff, are just talking about Shaq like he doesn't matter. Like, if he didn't end up dead that day, then it would've happened sooner or later.' I pause. I don't mean to blurt all this out, but it's like everything I've been bottling up the past three days is finally coming out. 'And even that day,' I continue. 'When I went to help Shaq, I got searched.'

I guess that's another thing I've tried to forget. How I went over to help and was treated like a criminal.

'I know,' Chantelle says. 'That's why I waited. I didn't wanna get off in case something happened. In case, they tried to blame you, or ...' She trails off, and I know that she means in case I ended up arrested, or hurt, or dead.

I'm surprised because I didn't even realize that she'd noticed and the fact she stayed to make sure that I was all right just makes me like her even more.

Now that I've said all that stuff, though, I just wanna get the rest of it off my chest.

'D'you know what that police officer said to me as well?'

'What?' Chantelle replies.

'That he's impressed, cause I've never been arrested.'

'That's so fucked up!' Chantelle says, and even though I can hear the anger in her voice, she doesn't seem surprised.

'I've been getting searched since I was twelve,' I continue. 'So it ain't like it's new to me, and I've had all the comments you can imagine by now, but ...' I pause. 'I don't know. I just worry that one day I'm gonna explode. That I'm just not going to be able to take it any more, cause why should I? Why should I have to just take it all the time?

It messes you up, being constantly told over and over again that you don't matter. Seeing pictures and videos of people who look like you being murdered. Being told that you're a criminal, or that you're dangerous. And sometimes I just don't know what to do. I don't know how to handle it all.

Chantelle stares at me, then she goes: 'D'you know what my gran says?'

'What?' I reply.

'That sometimes, the best form of resistance, the best form of protest is for you to do well. To succeed and live the best life you possibly can. Thriving and being here is a form of resistance. But I know it's hard,' she continues. 'When you constantly feel like you're being pushed back down. That's what I keep thinking about Shaq. He was gonna go on and do so much, but look at the story that's being told about him.' She pauses. 'At school, I'm always being told that I'm "too much". That I'm too loud, or confrontational, or that I'm aggressive. And sometimes, I feel like my voice just doesn't count for anything. That no one cares what I think . . .'

Chantelle trails off and neither of us says anything for a minute. Part of me wants to ask her how we're supposed to do it. Exist in a world that constantly tries to dehumanize you. That constantly makes you feel worthless. But I doubt she'd know the answer either. We're standing in the middle of this concrete island that runs through the middle of all the different bus shelters. And even though I'm still hurt and upset, I'm glad that I've at least been able to get it all off my chest. That I've got someone to talk to.

'I dunno if anyone else would've stopped to help Shaq,' Chantelle continues. 'And I know we didn't save his life, but at least we tried.'

'Yeah,' I say, and I really hope, in some small way, that the three of us made a difference. That we helped Shaq feel less scared, or afraid, or alone. Chantelle shoves her hands into her jacket pockets. There's loads of groups of people about, but they all seem to fade into the background. And I'm glad that I met up with her and Marc today.

There's this awkward silence again, so I nudge Chantelle with

165

my elbow. 'By the way,' I say. 'I care what you think. Even if to you I'm just some lame *Star Wars* geek.'

She laughs and moves her hair over her shoulder. She catches my eye, and even though it's so dimly lit at the bus station, I can't stop staring at her and thinking again how pretty she is. More than pretty, I realize. *Beautiful*. I have to look away, because I don't want her to think I'm some sort of weirdo. Chantelle smiles, and says: 'Maybe you're more than a lame *Star Wars* geek.' Then she pauses and I think I catch that look again, the same one she gave me in the milkshake place. She pulls the zip up on her jacket and gestures to the other side of the bus station.

'I'm gonna go get my bus,' she says.

'All right,' I say. 'Bye.'

'See ya,' she says, and then she heads off.

19

MARC

I cross over the road and head down one of the side streets that leads onto Shaq's estate. I didn't really wanna leave Chantelle and Jackson, cause it was cool, just laughing and joking in that milkshake place. Plus, Chantelle had surprised me when she started telling me about all that stuff with her mum. I guess I just assumed that both her parents were around, and even though it's different, cause she still has her gran and her sister and stuff, it made me feel like there was something else we had in common. Having parents that are still alive and stuff but at the same time aren't part of your life. Chantelle was making out like she wasn't bothered, but I could see it in her eyes. I was about to tell her how I know what it's like to feel unwanted and let down by the people who are supposed to love you the most, cause I've spent most of my life in care, but then Jackson walked in. And I guess I just chickened out.

I cut across this bit of grass and I heave my rucksack onto my other shoulder. It's bare heavy and I can't believe I've actually managed to carry it around with me the whole day. I usually like to go somewhere I'm gonna graffiti a few times first so I can scope the place out, but I ain't had time to that. I wanna make sure it's done before Shaq's vigil tomorrow. It's late enough that the estate's empty, but there's still a bit of light so I'll be able to see what I'm doing. I walk down one street of the estate, looking for any spaces, a stretch of wall, or the side bit of someone's house, but there's nothing. Everything's either too small or I'd have to climb into someone's garden to do it on the side of their house and I don't wanna do that.

I reach what must be the middle of the estate cause it widens out into this U-shape and I'm suddenly annoyed cause I still can't find anywhere. Then I end up on this road I must've missed and that's when I see it. All the flowers and cards spilling out on the pavement outside this house. That's where Shaq lived, and his family are inside, hurting and upset. And I know I wanna find somewhere on this road. I walk past Shaq's house and I hear sirens somewhere in the distance. I keep going until I reach this other entrance to the estate, at the far end of the street. And as I get closer, I spot this massive wall. My heart starts pounding. It's *perfect*! It's on the side of someone's house, but it's not in a garden or anything cause it's on the corner and the street name is at the top. There's a street lamp across the road as well, which means that I'll be able to see what I'm doing even more.

I double-check the coast is clear, then I dump my bag on the floor and pull out the cans of paint. I take my phone and go to this photo that I screen-grabbed from Shaq's Insta. And even though I know it won't change what happened that day and even though none of us could save him, I hope this is a way for me to do something good. For me to show who Shaq was and how much he mattered, even if the rest of the world is trying to make out that he didn't. I shake the can and suck in a deep breath, then I press my finger down on the nozzle, and spray the first line on that brick wall.

When I get back, I already know that Dry Eileen's going to kick off. If she hasn't already, she'll probably be straight on the phone to Emma, telling her she wants me gone. *Good.* I'd rather she kicked me out sooner than pretend she wants me around. I'm proper starving cause I ain't had anything since the milkshakes earlier. I turn my key in the door and I'm praying Dry Eileen's already gone up to bed. But of course that ain't the case. All the lights are on and she rushes into the hallway when she hears me come in and she don't look happy. She's got her phone pressed to her ear and she says: 'Oh, he's just come back, Emma. No worries, I'll speak to you tomorrow!' before she cuts the call. I was right, didn't take her long to get onto my social worker. My stomach's proper rumbling but I don't wanna hang around and have another lecture, so I turn to go straight upstairs.

'Erm, hang on a minute!' Dry Eileen says. 'Where've you been? D'you know what time it is? I've been calling and calling you. Why is your phone switched off?'

'My battery died,' I lie. I knew she'd be belling me out like there's no tomorrow, so I switched it off as soon as I left school. I don't even know what time it is, but it must be late, cause she looks proper tired.

'I was this close,' she says, 'to calling the police and reporting you missing! I've been on the phone to Emma all evening, she's tried calling you too. You can't just go disappearing like that, without letting anyone know where you are! What if something had happened to you?' Dry Eileen pauses and I feel like telling her that if something did happen to me, then I'd be all right. I'd survive. I'd manage, just like I've been doing my whole life.

I shrug.

'I thought we'd had a bit of a breakthrough this morning,' she says, and she genuinely looks upset. 'Look, Marc,' she continues. 'I can't force you to come back if you decide to go off like that again. But the only thing I ask is that you at least call or text me to let me know that you're safe. *Okay?*'

I stare at her. Dry Eileen seems more bothered about the fact something could've happened to me than me coming back late. I don't really know what to think. Or if Dry Eileen even means it, but she says it like she does. I've never had that before.

'Okay,' I say finally, and I think I mean it this time too. Maybe it's cause she's not screaming or shouting, or trying to tell me that I can't go out. I turn to go upstairs and even though I'm starving, I don't ask if there's any food. I don't want to push my luck.

Then Dry Eileen says, 'Are you hungry? I made you some dinner. It won't take me long to heat it up!'

For the first time ever, I could hug her, but I ain't about to show her that.

'Yeah,' I say. 'I guess I could eat!'

20

CHANTELLE

All last night, I found myself thinking about Jackson and how there's more to him than I first thought. I guess when we first met, I just thought he was this stuck-up snob, but the more I talk to him, the more I realize that he's sweet and thoughtful. I felt a bit weird around him yesterday, cos I kept wondering what he thinks of me. Which ain't like me at all, cos I don't normally give a toss what other people think. But with Jackson ... I dunno. I kept glancing at him and thinking how cute he is. I get to form late and I've barely sat down when Ms Edwards comes storming in. I don't have her until period three so I don't know why she's here. Already ruining my morning with her miserable face.

'Chantelle, there's your mate!' Yohan says. 'What does she want, anyway?'

I shrug. 'Dunno,' I reply. Then Ms Edwards goes: 'Can I have a word with Chantelle, please, sir?'

The whole class starts with all the, '*Oooooooh, Chantelle's in trouble!*' And I roll my eyes. I hear Mr Sharpe telling everyone to be quiet, and I stand up.

'Bring your stuff!' Ms Edwards says, and the class gets louder again. I grab my coat and bag. Ms Edwards only ever sees me when she wants to get on my case. How can I be in trouble already, when I've only just got in? I haven't even stepped foot in her classroom yet. I don't say anything, but I follow Ms Edwards. At first I think we're just gonna have a chat outside my form room. And that maybe it's something to do with me being kicked out of class yesterday, but she walks straight down the corridor.

'What's this about?' I ask as I follow her, but she doesn't even look at me.

'This way,' she says. 'We'll talk about it when we get there.'

I kiss my teeth. I know that Gran told me to keep my head down, but it's like it just happens involuntarily around her.

'Less of the attitude,' she snaps. 'You're already in enough trouble!'

I don't say anything else and I swear it takes every ounce of strength in my body not to tell Ms Edwards about herself. But I know that if I do that, it'll be a million more behaviour points. We take a left through a set of double doors near the science corridor and go into the KS4 office. Mrs Cohen and Mr Povey, the deputy head, are there. I pause and my heart almost stops in my chest.

'What's going on?' I say. 'What's this even about?'

Mrs Cohen smiles sadly. 'Chantelle, sit down, please,' she says, and I slump down in one of the chairs they've brought out. I look at all of them and I fold my arms across my chest. I hate it when teachers do this. When they ambush you and wait ages to tell you what's going on.

'Is someone going to tell me why I'm here?' I say.

Of course, Ms Edwards is the first one to open her gob. I'd rather anyone *except* her told me what was going on. She pulls something out of a file on her lap and shows it to me. It's the English essay that I did in class, yesterday.

I shrug. 'Yeah, that's my essay,' I say. 'I don't get it.'

Ms Edwards shakes her head the way she always does, in this *Chantelle's being a troublemaker again* kind of way

'I started marking this last night,' Ms Edwards says. 'And it's really very good, probably one of the best essays I've ever read – it's articulate, detailed, insightful . . .'

I stare at her blankly. I studied proper hard for this, so I should hope so. But surely, they didn't arrange this meeting just to tell me how good they think I am at English?

'It's far too sophisticated for a sixteen-year-old,' she continues.

'What?' I reply, and then it clicks. Ms Edwards doesn't believe I wrote it. She thinks I cheated.

'Ms Edwards just has some questions,' Mrs Cohen interrupts. 'No one's accusing anyone at this point.' I glance at Mrs Cohen and she smiles at me. She's still the only person at this school who's ever on my side.

'What are you trying to say?' I ask Ms Edwards.

'We take plagiarism very seriously here, Chantelle,' Mr Povey butts in. 'We don't condone cheating of any sort, even in mock exams, and if this was your real GCSE paper and it was sent off to the exam board then you would be in serious trouble. It would be an instant disqualification. Not only that, the school would be in trouble too.'

I turn to Ms Edwards. I'm so angry. Cos my essay is 'articulate' and 'insightful', she's accusing me of cheating? I worked really *fucking* hard, but it's like they've already decided I'm guilty. I can feel the rage and hurt rising inside me. Why is it so much easier to believe that I cheated, rather than accept the fact I actually wrote a good essay?

'I've had enough of this!' I snap. 'You're accusing me of cheating cos you couldn't possibly believe that someone like me could write an essay like that? Why is that?' I ask, but no one responds. 'If it was Jessica or Holly who handed it in, would you be saying the same thing? That it's "too articulate" for them?'

Ms Edwards looks uncomfortable and her face flushes. 'This isn't about them, Chantelle,' she says. 'And I know what you're getting at by that comment, but this isn't about race either.'

I shake my head. It's *always* about race, whether or not she realizes it. Whether or not she wants to admit it. I'm so mad I feel like crying. Especially cos I felt so proud of what I'd written

175

in class yesterday. But I'm not about to do it in this office, and *definitely not* in front of them.

'How was I supposed to have cheated anyway?' I say 'You were in the class the whole time!'

'You had your phone out,' Ms Edwards replies. 'It went off several times, then you refused to hand it over.'

My blood is boiling now. 'It weren't mine!' I shout. 'I told you yesterday that it wasn't even my phone that went off. Did you see it in my hand? *No!*'

'Chantelle,' Mr Povey interrupts, and he puts his hands out, like he's trying to calm me down. But I've got a right to be angry, e*specially* now.

'The thing to do, going forward,' Mr Povey continues, 'is to just be completely honest. If someone helped you, if you copied it from somewhere online, or bought it, then just tell us so we know how to progress with this.'

I can't believe what I'm hearing. The thought of buying an essay online is so ridiculous I want to laugh. We hardly have enough money as it is – there's no way I'd waste my money buying an essay online. Not when I can do it myself. I fold my arms more tightly across my chest, but I still can't look at them. It hurts to know that even after how much I've been trying, *this* is what they really think of me. *This* is all they think I'm capable of.

'I did it!' I say, and my voice catches in my throat. But I know that now is not the time to just sit here and take it. 'I wrote it myself,' I continue, and I make sure that I look Ms Edwards in the eye. 'Have you tried typing bits of my essay out online? Cos if you actually did that, you'd see that fuck all comes up—'

'*Chantelle!*' Mr Povey interrupts. 'That's enough swearing.'

'Well,' I say. 'Have you? I wouldn't even mind, but all this, and it ain't even a real exam. It doesn't even count towards my final grade!'

'That's not the point,' Mr Povey snaps. 'We take a strong stance on cheating, whether that's in a mock exam or a real one, you know that. Besides,' he continues. 'You've applied to do your A-levels at Xaverian and we're providing you with a reference. Something like this could jeopardise your place.'

That hits me hard. I never even thought of that. 'That's not fair!' I say, and I turn to Ms Edwards again. 'Have you tried searching for it online? *Well?*'

'I have,' Ms Edwards says.' And I couldn't find anything, but that doesn't mean you didn't copy it from somewhere. I've compared it to your previous essays, the ones you handed in last year and the year before that, and this one is far better than anything you've ever written—'

'That's cos I really tried!' I say, but only Mrs Cohen looks like she believes me.

'We'll be looking into this properly,' Ms Edwards says. 'And we *will* get to the bottom of it.'

I've never wanted to dash someone out of the KS4 window more in my entire life. It's my word against hers. How can I possibly fight this? I can feel my eyes stinging. I bite down hard, on the inside of my cheek, to remind myself not to do it. I look at Mrs Cohen and I know that she can't say much, but I can see the anger in her face.

'Hang on a minute,' Mrs Cohen says. 'If Chantelle said she wrote it, then she did. What proof do you have? She's a bright, intelligent student.'

Ms Edwards still doesn't look at me. Neither does Mr Povey. All I want is for people to see me the way that Mrs Cohen does. The way my gran does. For people to see me for who I really am.

'Chantelle,' Mr Povey says. 'You've given us no other choice, we're going to have to suspend you for a couple of days while we investigate this. I'll escort you down to isolation and you'll have to stay there until we can get your grandma on the phone and get her permission to send you home. Okay? This is your last chance – is there anything you want to say?'

The words hit me, hard. Part of me wants to scream and shout and tell him and Ms Flipping Edwards to do one, but I can't get the words out. Mr Povey starts saying something about me 'having to deal with the consequences of my actions,' and how this school is 'preparing me for the real world,' but this school hasn't prepared me for shit. I'm so upset and angry, cos all I can think about is my college place, and what might happen if they don't end up believing me in the end.

I can feel the tears coming now and I grab my stuff. I ain't staying here a second longer.

'Fuck this,' I say, and I storm out.

I hear Mr Povey shouting after me and saying something about behaviour points and how he's going to radio for a PSM, but I just need to get out of this place. If he thinks I'm going to isolation as well, he's got another thing coming! I hear Mrs Cohen's voice.

'*Chantelle!*' she says. 'Just come back in the office. Just for a minute, I know you didn't cheat ... I know you wrote it ...'

'*No!*' I say, but the words don't come out anywhere near as angry as I mean them to, and this time I can't stop the tears coming. 'I ain't going back in there! What's the point? I'm sick of it! I'm sick of *her,* always treating me like I've done something wrong. I'm fucking tired!' Then I walk off, the tears falling even quicker as I head down the stairs.

21

CHANTELLE

I move the pillow away from my face. I went straight up to my room and cried when I got home. It was like I couldn't stop. I don't know if all of it was cos of Ms Edwards and school, or if it was just *everything* coming out at once – school; thinking about what might happen with my college place if Ms Edwards and that idiot still don't believe me; Shaq.

I dunno if I feel better now, or just tired, but I know I don't want to spend any more time upset. Cos sometimes you just have to get on with things. Gran has her double shift until late this evening. She's texted me to say that school phoned and we'll talk when she gets back, and Marni's going to her mate's house after school, so I'm on my own for a bit, which I'm kinda glad about.

I climb down the ladder of my bunkbed and reach for my phone. I've got loads of WhatsApp messages from Marc, complaining he's got no one to hang around with in school and asking where I was at break and dinner? I don't respond. I'll tell him when I see him, and anyway, I don't want to think about Ms Fucking Edwards right now. I know that Gran wouldn't have been happy when school told her I'd been suspended and that I'd walked out, but I know she'll believe me about the essay. I know she'll have my back. I go to the bathroom and I stare at my face in the mirror. It's blotchy and red and my eyes look like they're disappearing into their sockets. I splash some cold water on my face, then I go back to my room and put some make-up on, trying to hide some of the redness. I scrape my curls back into a bun. Shaq's vigil's on the other side of the estate, so it will take, like, ten minutes to get there, if that. I told Marc and Jackson I'd meet them at the bus stop beside my house. I bet Jackson's never even stepped foot in Moss Side before – never mind on an estate.

I rummage through my drawers looking for something to wear, but I can't really concentrate. I'm nervous about the vigil. It feels good to be involved in something positive for Shaq, but I don't know how I'll feel when I see his family. And I think Jackson's right about us going to speak to his mum, but what do we say? What if we just end up upsetting her? Even though Parveen invited us, it's not like any of us knew Shaq. I still can't get my head around it. The fact that I saw Shaq get stabbed ... *killed*. And now I'm about to go to a vigil for him. I pull on a pair of jeans and a vest top, then I grab my jacket and leave the house.

I'm already running late. My phone buzzes in my pocket and I know it's probably Jackson or Marc telling me they're here.

It's proper warm outside and I already regret putting my jacket on. I spot Marc and Jackson in the distance, waiting by the bus stop. I have this fluttery feeling in my stomach, as I make my way towards them. Me and Jackson were messaging more last night, sending each other voice notes and stuff. Some of them were about Shaq and the vigil, but mostly it was just daft things, what we both like doing and stuff. I'm still just trying to get my head around the fact I like him, though, cos it's all so new. Not that I'd ever tell him how I feel or anything. I don't want to make myself look stupid. Besides, I saw him with a girl that day in town, so he's probably going out with her.

'Hey!' I say as I reach them both. Jackson smiles. He looks even cuter when he smiles. It's like his whole face lights up and this one dimple appears on the right side of his cheek. I wonder if my face is still blotchy and red from all the crying. Marc throws his arms around me and gives me a hug, and Jackson looks awkward, like he doesn't know if he should hug me too.

Then Marc goes: 'What happened to you? I waited for you, outside your English class, but Yohan said that Ms Edwards dragged you out of form in the morning. Why?'

I gesture in the direction we need to walk in. 'Urgh,' I say, as we head down the road. 'Don't even get me started on *her*! I got suspended today and d'you know the reason? Cos I wrote a good essay and no one believed that I was the one who actually wrote it.'

'*What?*' Marc says.

I see Jackson's eyes widen. 'They can't do that!' he says and he sounds genuinely shocked.

'Well, they can, and they have!' I reply. 'So ...'

'Can't you complain, or ... get someone to go in, or I don't know ... how is that even fair?' Jackson looks annoyed, more than I expected him to be, which is nice, but I just shrug. I'm not about to tell them both how long I've spent crying over this, or how much it's upset me.

'Life ain't always fair, is it?' I say. 'I guess they'll realize when they try and search for it online or whatever it is they're gonna do, and they find fuck all.' I go quiet, cos I really don't wanna talk about it any more, then Marc goes: 'Nah, d'you want me to rush Ms Edwards, cause I will, you know? Just say the word.'

I smile, and even though being accused like that still hurts, it feels good to have Marc and Jackson on my side.

'I'm good!' I say. 'Thanks. It'll all get sorted out.' And I just hope that's true, cos I don't want this to get in the way of my college place, like Mr Povey said. We walk along the street past a row of shops: a newsagents, a Caribbean takeaway, an internet café. No one says anything as we get to the other side of the estate.

We cut across this massive grassy bit opposite the estate, then Jackson says: 'I still can't believe we're doing this, that we even saw someone ...' He shakes his head. And it's like I can see it all again. Shaq's face, trying to stop the bleeding, shouting for someone to help. Marc swallows hard and I notice he's gone proper quiet so I grab hold of his arm.

183

'Hey,' I say. 'You all right?'

Marc nods. 'Yeah,' he replies, though he clearly ain't. I link my arm through Marc's and glance at Jackson. He looks pretty upset too, and as we get closer he starts saying something about the difference between *Star Wars* and *Star Trek,* but I know he's only going on about it cos he's trying to fill the silence. If he started going on about this any other time, I would've told him to shut up. But in a weird way, it's kinda comforting to have Jackson talking about something completely different.

When we get onto the estate, it's already packed. I mean, the only time I've ever seen it this rammed is in the summer during Carnival. I recognize quite a few people from school and we ain't even reached Shaq's house yet. It's even warmer now and I feel proper sticky. I pull my jacket off. Jackson glances at me then looks away quickly when I catch him. I stuff my jacket under my arm. Then Marc goes: 'I ain't gonna lie, Jax. You just explained *all* that and I still don't have a clue.' He pauses. 'There's so many people here.'

'I know!' I say. 'I bet this ain't even everyone, either!'

Both sides of the street, as well as the road leading down to where Shaq's house must be, are rammed. There's groups of people standing about and loads of cars parked up with their windows wound down. The stretch of grass opposite is full of people sitting down, drinking and laughing, or talking to their mates. I can hear music blasting from a little bit further down, where everyone is gathered, and even though we're all here for such a sad reason, it feels ... joyful. Like one big party. Which is fitting for Shaq. It's nice to have something so uplifting after all the crap that's been in the media, and it's as if the whole of Moss Side – no, Manchester – has come out to celebrate Shaq.

I scan the crowds to see if I can spot Damar or Parveen, but there's so many people that I can't really tell. I turn to walk in the direction people seem to be heading in, then I notice a massive group of people gathered by the side of this house. I clock a few of Shaq's football mates, all wearing shirts with *Shaq 10* on the back and I notice that Jackson and Marc haven't moved. It's like Jackson's rooted to the spot. I can't work out what they're both looking at, at first. And then I see it.

On the brick wall on the side of this house on the corner of the estate, there's a massive mural of Shaq. It must be by the same person who's done all the other ones around Manchester that Damar showed me and Marc, cos the style's the same and I recognize the Nomad tag in the corner. Even though it's spray-painted, Shaq's face looks more like him than any of the photos and pictures the papers have used. It takes up the whole of the wall. Shaq's got the biggest grin on his face and his eyes look like they're brimming with laughter. The way that they used to look in school. Two doves have been spray-painted either side of him, as well as the outline of a football pitch in the background and the number 10. He doesn't look dangerous or frightening, he just looks like what he was. *A boy.* Someone's graffitied the words: *RIP Shaq* in big letters, with a crown above his name. There's loads of flowers and stuff on the pavement in front of the wall and so many cards and photographs and United shirts too. It's perfect.

'*Wow!*' Jackson says. 'That's incredible!' And we're all just a bit speechless for a minute as we take it in.

'Do you think he knew?' Jackson adds, quietly. 'Do you think he knew when we found him that this was it? I just keep thinking about how scared he must've been . . .'

Jackson trails off. He doesn't need to finish. I'd wondered the same. Would there be stuff that I'd regret not having done, or said, if that was me? Would I have wanted my mum as well? Would I have wished I could've told her that I loved her?

'I don't know,' I say to Jackson. 'But at least we tried. At least we tried to do *something,* instead of just walking past.'

Jackson hesitates. 'It's just . . . the fact that all it takes is *one thing.* One moment, one action, and your whole world can end up – *you* can end up – and it's, like, you can work all that stuff out in physics. You can calculate what makes a moment, or when it's going to come and how big the magnitude of it will be, when it's all laid out in front of you on an exam paper, but you can't do that with life.'

I pause. I guess I've always known that life can be fucking shit sometimes, but I've never really thought about that stuff. How one moment can change your life *for ever.* Good or bad. If I hadn't been walking out of Next at that exact time, would I have even seen Shaq? If I hadn't stopped to help him, would he have died sooner? And would I be standing here, right now, with Jackson and Marc?

I reach my hand out and touch Jackson's arm. I don't really know what to say, so I go: 'Come on! Maybe we should go that way, where everyone's heading.'

186

Jackson nods and we turn to follow the crowds, when I hear someone shout my name. I dunno who it is at first, and then I see Damar, towering over everyone else, weaving his way through the groups of people. He's wearing a black T-shirt with Shaq's face printed on the front and the number 10 printed on the back.

'Yes, Chantelle!' he says, and he holds his fist out for me to bump it. He does the same to Marc and gives Jackson a nod. 'That looks proper sick, don't it?' He points to the mural. 'It's the same person who's done the other ones, cos look at the tag! Must've took about fifty million pictures on my phone.' He shakes his head. 'Can't get over how much it looks like Shaq! When his mum saw it, she started crying, y'know? Just burst into tears, cos she said it was like having a piece of him back.'

'I can see why,' I say. 'It's amazing!'

Jackson nods his head in agreement and Marc looks awkward. The other half of Damar's hair's cane-rowed now too and come to think of it, I ain't seen him about since he got pulled by one of the PSMs for selling sweets.

'What happened yesterday?' I say. 'After break?'

'Mate,' Damar says, and he kisses his teeth. 'Check it, yeah. Y'know how I got pulled into the office by that PSM? She saw me selling to that Year Seven, innit, but obviously, I weren't about to admit to nothing. So, she was giving it all, *I saw you with my own eyes. Open your bag, Damar. I want to see what's in it!* And obviously I switched bags, so I was like, cool. Knock yourself out, innit. And when I opened it and she looked inside, she found nothing, bruv. Just empty space and a few books. So then she started saying, *I saw you give someone some sweets,*

Damar. So I said, *I think you're seeing things, miss. You might need to go and get yourself some new glasses.*'

I burst out laughing. 'You didn't?' I say.

'Damn straight I did!' he replies. 'You should've seen how she tried to manhandle me into that office. Then she was all like, *Whose bag is this, Damar?* So, I go, *It's mine, why?* And then she starts pulling out all the books and shaking them, and she pulls out this one exercise book, and is like, *Since when do you do French? Since when is your name Abdi?* Anyway, long story short, she went and called Mrs Cohen, got my mum in and I've been suspended. I can't go prom or nothing. Can't believe I've been suspended for selling a bit of chocolate.' Damar shrugs.

'*A week*?' I say. 'And they're banning you from prom?'

Damar shrugs like he ain't bothered, but I can tell that he is. 'Yeah,' he says. 'Already got my suit and everything, y'know. It wouldn't be so bad, but my mum is making me do the most amount of housework. They're taking the piss, though, cos that Ryan Taylor smashes up a classroom and tells Mr Reed to fuck off, and he still gets to go prom!' He shakes his head. 'They did the same with my brother, y'know? He kept getting suspended over foolishness, then they chucked him out in Year Ten. Didn't even get to sit his GCSEs.'

I shake my head. I'm so mad and I try not to think of Ms Edwards again, especially as I'd managed to push her out my mind for a bit.

'Well, if it makes you feel any better, I've been suspended as well cos Ms Edwards thinks I cheated on my English essay.'

'You *serious*?' Damar says. 'That Ms Edwards is something

else,' he continues. 'She should not be working with kids. Gave my brother hell as well, y'know? She was teaching back when he was there, still had that *same* dusty haircut as well. Hasn't even changed it up since the eighties. What even is that – a short back and sides?'

I laugh. 'I don't even know!' I say. I'm smiling, but I feel so hurt and angry and I can tell that Damar does too. Someone in the crowd shouts Damar's name.

'Yo, I've gotta go!' Damar says. 'Let me know what happens, yeah? I'll try and catch you in a bit!'

'Bye,' me and Marc both say, and then Damar disappears.

Jackson's staring at me, like he can't believe what he's just heard, and it makes me think he *definitely* doesn't have to deal with any of this shit at St Anthony's. People are walking past us and there's music blasting from further down the estate. I see more of Shaq's mates wearing those T-shirts with his face on and I spot Parveen and Kade, but they're gone before I even get a chance to try and shout them.

'I think it's this way,' I say, as we follow the crowds and music further into the estate.

22

JACKSON

We head down the street past the houses and the music gets louder. As we get closer, I realize that someone's plugged one of those massive speakers in and it's resting against an opened window. There's people dancing and drinking and singing along to the lyrics. We reach this part of the street that snakes around into a U-shape and there's another bit of grass in the middle. It's nothing like where I live. All the houses are packed proper closely together and a few of the windows have metal bars on them.

We reach this bit where everyone's gathered in a circle on the grass and then I see it to our right, Shaq's house. I know it's his because there's even more flowers outside and there's four inflatable balloons tied to the fence, which spell out Shaq's name. My heart quickens and I scan the small group of people, to see if I can spot Shaq's brother or his mum. I see his brother, Fabio, nodding his head along to the music. I recognize him from Shaq's Insta. He must be in his twenties or something and it's weird because he's the double of Shaq and looking at him is like seeing how Shaq would've looked when he was older. *If he'd made it past fourteen.* He's wearing one of those T-shirts with Shaq's face on it too. I freeze and Chantelle notices: 'What's the matter?'

But I can't take my eyes off Fabio, because it must mean that Shaq's mum is close by too.

'There's Shaq's brother,' I say and I scan the faces that walk past. 'Where d'you think his mum is? D'you think we should knock on the door? Or should we just talk to his brother instead?'

Chantelle and Marc scan the crowds. 'I don't even know what she looks like!' Chantelle says. I don't tell her that I could describe her with my eyes closed, because of the number of times I've flicked through her pictures on Facebook, but I know that'll probably make me sound like some sort of weirdo. I turn my head, and then I see her. She's making her way over to Fabio.

'That's her!' I say.

Fabio wraps his arms around his mum and kisses her forehead as she cries into his chest. He says something to her, but she barely seems to respond. She just carries on crying. I think about that day. How he asked for her, told me to tell her he loved her ... *I need* to speak to her. I need to do it for Shaq. I turn to Chantelle and Marc.

'I'm going to speak to her,' I say.

191

'Hang on,' Marc says. 'We're coming with you!' And before I know what I'm doing, or I get too scared and chicken out of it, we make our way towards them. Fabio's still got his arms around his mum, like he's too frightened to let go and I see him lean down and wipe away her tears with his hand. I feel nervous. I mean, we're just three random strangers. What are we even doing here? I push all that aside, because of the promise I made to Shaq. I'm glad that Marc and Chantelle are with me, that I'm not doing this on my own. I suck in a sharp breath when I reach her.

'Pam— I mean, Ms Townsend?' I say, and I feel my voice shake. *Great start, Jackson. She really doesn't need to know that you've stalked her so much you know her first name!* I clear my throat and try to take a breath, to start again. His mum turns to me and I can see how tired and weary she is. Fabio is staring, probably wondering who the hell I am. My throat's dry. I've thought about this moment a million times. I even tried to memorize one of the messages I'd typed out in the notes section of my phone. But now I'm here, looking at the two people who loved Shaq the most, I can't even get the words out. How am I supposed to begin? How do I start to tell her that we were there that day? The day she probably wishes she could go back in time and change. I wonder if it was a stupid idea to come, and if I should've just sent her a message after all, but Marc gives me a nudge. And Chantelle smiles. They've both got my back.

'You don't know us or anything!' I blurt out. 'But these two went to school with Shaq – they're in the year above – and . . . I didn't know him.' I pause. 'But we were there when it— We tried to help, and we stayed with him till the ambulance came …' I trail off. 'I thought you'd want to know that Shaq asked for you. He told me to tell you he loved you. I promised him I would.'

My throat clamps up then, and I go quiet. I feel Marc rub my shoulder and suddenly I can't stop shaking. There's so much I want to tell her – how sorry I am, how I desperately wanted him to pull through. But I can't get any more words out. I see all of these emotions flash across her face. Sadness, hurt, anger, and I think I see relief.

'You're the ones who were with him?' she says and she moves a hand to her chest. 'When we got to the hospital,' she continues, 'he was unconscious, so we never got to say goodbye. I kept thinking, if only I'd been able to talk to him one last time. Just to let him know how proud I was. How lucky I feel to have been his mum.' She moves her hand to wipe tears from her cheeks. 'Since that day, all I've been able to think is how wicked and cruel the world can be, how *awful* the people in it are. For someone to just do that, take my Shaq's life without so much as a second thought … But to know that there were people with him.' She pauses. 'That you three tried to help. It's given me hope. It's got me through.' She looks at me and Chantelle and Marc.

'*Thank you,*' she says. 'All of you.'

Fabio nods. 'Yeah,' he says. 'Parveen told us what you lot did. It means a lot that you came. If there's ever anything I can do, just let me know. *I mean it!*'

I nod, even though he doesn't need to owe any of us.

'What's happening with the investigation?' I ask. 'Have the police found who did it and stuff?'

193

Fabio lets out a laugh, but not in a rude way. 'Have they fuck!' he says. 'There ain't enough evidence, apparently. The guys who did it were all ballied up, so there was nothing on CCTV. That's it. They'll give it a few weeks, then they'll close their line of enquiry.' He wipes some sweat away from his forehead. 'They don't care,' he continues. 'Why would they? You've probably seen the bullshit they've been writing in the papers. They ain't gonna waste their money and resources on another kid from Moss Side who got stabbed.' He shrugs. 'Shaq might not matter to the rest of the world, but he mattered to us. And tonight we're gonna celebrate him the way he would've wanted us to!' He pauses. 'Do you three want a drink?' He turns towards their house. 'Yo, Stacey!' he shouts to a girl who's heading into their house. 'Can you bring three drinks out?' She nods and disappears. Then he pulls out a roll-up and lights up.

'Whoever did that mural, it's like they've properly captured Shaq. *That* was my brother,' he says, breathing out some smoke.

He's right. Shaq's mural's like nothing I've *ever* seen before. And even though I barely knew Shaq, it's exactly how he looked on his Facebook and Insta photos. I can see why his mother said that it was like having a piece of him back.

I nod. 'It's unbelievable,' I reply. 'We saw it when we first got here.'

Seeing the mural and all the people here somehow makes me madder than ever, to think about all the crap that the papers are saying. Did they even bother to interview his parents, or the people who actually loved Shaq? The girl called Stacey comes back and hands us all a drink.

194

'You ready, babe?' she says to Fabio. 'I think we should do the balloons now.'

He nods, then flicks his cig away. 'We're gonna let some balloons off on the grass over there,' he says. 'I'll catch youse in a bit, yeah? Enjoy yourselves!' he adds, and then he turns and heads off with Stacey and his mum.

Marc shakes his head. 'That's it?!' he says. 'His killers get to walk free?'

'Looks like it,' Chantelle replies.

We don't say anything for a minute, we just stand there, thinking about the weight of it all. How Shaq's family will never get justice. How Shaq's been turned into something that he's not. Marc lifts his cup to take a sip of his drink, and he starts to cough.

'*Woi!*' he splutters. 'You can smell the alcohol from here! How much did they put in this thing?'

Marc takes another gulp and Chantelle moves the cup to her mouth. 'There alcohol in it?' she says and she takes a sip. Chantelle splutters too.

'Oh my god, this is strong!' she says. 'My mouth is on fire!'

Marc shakes his head and Chantelle takes another sip, but I just stare down into the cup.

'Erm, it won't kill you!' Chantelle says.

'Nah,' I reply. 'But my mum will if she so much as catches a whiff of this stuff on me. And trust me, nothing gets past her.'

Chantelle rolls her eyes and I think, there I go, embarrassing myself again. We follow Shaq's mum and brother to a patch of grass.

There's loads of people standing around Shaq's mum and Fabio, and they're all holding balloons. The guy who came over to talk to Chantelle and Marc is there too. They join Shaq's family on the grass and someone behind us cuts the music. There's loads of people crammed around us, standing in the middle of the road, and all over the pavement. And in the other houses around Shaq's, there's people standing in their front gardens. All I can see around me are a sea of white balloons and T-shirts with Shaq's face on.

Fabio clears his throat. 'I just wanna say thanks for coming,' he says. 'Whether you knew Shaq well, whether you were his best mate his neighbour, or you just passed him on the street – the one thing about my brother was that he just seemed to have an effect on anyone he came in contact with. You only needed to speak to him for two minutes before he'd have you cracking up. And he had the biggest, loudest, most infectious laugh I've ever heard. I swear you could hear him all the way from the other side of the estate. Ain't that right, Mum?'

A few people around us laugh.

'*Uhm-hmm,*' his mum says.

'He was the life and soul of any party,' Fabio continues. 'And if there was food, best believe his plate would be piled up higher than him, and he'd be going back for seconds, thirds, fourths, fifths . . .' His voice breaks a little here. 'But the thing I loved most about Shaq was his big heart. How kind he was. How caring he was. How much he loved me, and his mum, and this place – where he was from. So, I want us all to turn up and celebrate, the way that he would've wanted us to!'

There's cheers and clapping and a few people who are parked up in their cars beep their horns. Fabio makes his way back over to his mum and he puts his arm around her again

'To Shaq!' he says, and the same words echo all around us. Fabio and Shaq's mum let go of their balloons, then everyone else does the same. There's a girl standing with them crying and I wonder if that's Shaq's girlfriend. She lets go of her balloon too, then there's more clapping and cheering. I stare up at the balloons, floating up out of the estate and into the sky. It's kind of breathtaking and beautiful and special. Someone puts the music back on. This time it's even louder. People start dancing and singing, and Marc and Chantelle start dancing along in time to the beat. I stand there awkwardly for a minute, then Chantelle nudges me.

'Don't be so boring!' she says and she shoots me a grin. I'm worried about making a fool of myself because I can't dance for shit. But there's so much joy and laughter and the air almost feels electric, so I think *fuck it*. I bop along as well and it's still hot and sticky but none of that matters because everyone's having a good time, celebrating Shaq. I can't help thinking how glad I am that we came, because it's almost like we're part of something. Right here, on this estate. Someone knocks into me and I spill a bit of my drink on Marc. He wipes at his T-shirt but he doesn't seem to mind too much. He just carries on dancing. I see some guy standing on a nearby wall, singing along to the music and filming it all on his phone, and I think I hear police sirens but that could be the music, it's hard to tell.

Chantelle catches my eye again and I have a sudden mad thought that I should tell her that I like her. Not right now, but maybe when we get out of here? The next minute, someone shoves me from somewhere inside the crowd. I lurch forward and I grab onto Marc's elbow, and a few people fall to the floor. I hear shouting and screaming. The music stops and the screaming gets louder.

23

MARC

I freeze in the middle of the crowd.

'What was that?' Jackson says. He's trying to see what's going on, but there's too many people about. I feel the mood change and it's that feeling again. The same one I got that day in town. The one that tells me something bad's about to happen. My whole body starts to shake and I look around, trying to find a way out. I need to get outta here! The screaming and shouting gets louder and I crane my head to look at the road leading through the estate. Loads of police vans have turned up and I can hear more sirens screeching towards us in the distance. I dunno why there needs to be so many. There's loads of them and they've got on riot gear as well. *For what?* To shut down someone's vigil? I see one of them arguing with Shaq's brother and I feel the anger and panic rising in the crowd. I hear someone say: 'Nah, what the fuck are the police doing here? Who called them?' I suddenly realize how packed into the crowd we are and my whole body starts to shake. I can't even think straight. I'm hot and I'm trembling and I feel the sweat running down my face. I'm struggling to breathe properly and I shove Chantelle and Jackson.

'We need to go!' I say. 'We need to get out of here, *now*!' I turn to push them in the direction we first came, but the words are barely out of my mouth when I hear more shouting. This time, it's louder and angrier. And I realize it's Shaq's brother, Fabio.

'What the fuck?' he's shouting, and I see Stacey next to him. 'Why you coming over here troubling us when we ain't even done nothing? Where's the trouble, eh? We're having a vigil for my *dead* brother. That's all we're doing! Where's all this energy when it comes to finding his killers? Don't you have nothing better to do than to come and harass me, all the fucking time—'

More police officers go over to Fabio and I hear dogs as well. I push through the crowd and Chantelle and Jackson are behind me. I can hear my heart pounding in my ears and I manage to get to an opening. The next minute, there's a high-pitched scream. Stacey's shouting at the police. I turn to look and see that they're restraining Fabio. They've got his face pressed down into the concrete and his hands are twisted and cuffed behind his back. I hear him shouting at them to let him go, and that they're hurting him, but they just press has face down harder and tell him to 'stop being so aggressive'.

Some guys come over and start kicking off, telling them to

let Fabio go. And I see Damar filming it on his phone. One of the officers tries to stop Damar, but Damar tells him to fuck off. There's more people now, shouting and trying to help and I hear Shaq's brother say he can't breathe.

The next minute, it's chaos.

They drag Fabio into one of the vans, even though he's yelling that they're hurting his arm. One of his other friends is being restrained against the bonnet of a car, and two more officers are trying to drag Damar off. People start pushing and running in all different directions and I see some people throwing punches at the police too. I hear the noise of the dogs and Chantelle shouts: '*Move!*'

My legs have turned to jelly. I try to run, but I feel weak cause it just reminds me of being at home when I was a kid. Of all the times the police got called to my house. Of seeing my dad hitting my mum. More people push past me and I lose Chantelle and Jackson in the crowd and hear someone say that they're blocking everyone in, but my head is spinning and I can't think straight. I see a policeman whacking one of Shaq's mates with the metal truncheon thing and I scan the crowd, searching for Chantelle and Jackson. I can't tell if it's sweat or tears running down my face, and I can't find a way out of the estate. Someone knocks into me and my phone goes flying. I hear a crack and I reach down and pick it up.

I feel the blood pumping hard in my ears and everywhere I look, there seems to be more and more police, or someone being restrained or hit. I can't move. It's like I'm frozen to the spot, just stuck in the middle of it all. I'm alone, like I always am.

Everywhere seems to spin again and I think I hear Chantelle and Jackson. I keep telling myself to run, but it's like my whole body has shut down. Just like it used to do at home, with my dad. I'm trembling and it's like I'm struggling to breathe. Gasping for air. I see the blur of a uniform and hear someone far off, telling me to get out the way. I hear the words, 'I won't tell you again,' but I can't stop shaking.

I put a hand out to try and say that I can't move, that it's all too much. That I need help, and that's when I feel it. A burning, right in my eyes. I yell out in agony and try to move a hand to my face, but my eyes and my face feel like they're on fire. There's tears streaming down my face and I can't see a thing. I scream in pain. It's like nothing I've ever felt before. Then I feel steady arms either side of me, supporting me, helping me through the crowd.

24

MARC

My eyes won't stop streaming and my vision's still blurry.
There's sweat pouring down my face and neck and I'm still
proper hot.

'Can't believe they fucking pepper-sprayed you!' Chantelle
says. 'Here, come over to the sink. You're proper burning up . . .'
I can just about make out her hand wafting in front of me, like
she's trying to cool me down, but it don't make any difference.
I feel myself wheezing and even my nose and mouth are on fire
too. It reminds me of the time I accidentally burned myself with
boiling water, only it's all over my face and it's a million times
worse. I hear the sound of the running tap and Chantelle brings
me over to the sink.

'Put your head under there!' she says and I feel the cold

water hit my face. It makes me feel instantly better and the stinging eases, but it still fucking hurts. Chantelle fills a cup with water and she pours it over my eyes. I reach a hand up to touch my eyes, cause they're still burning and raw and she moves them down.

'Don't rub them!' she says. 'You'll make it worse! One of my mates got pepper-sprayed at Carnival a few years back. It should ease off in a bit.'

I stay there with the water running down on me for a bit longer and she's right, it ain't as painful as it was, but it still stings. My chest feels tight. I start to cough and Chantelle fills up a glass again and hands it to me to drink.

'Here!' she says.

'Thanks,' I say, and I knock it back. My throat and my mouth feel raw. I'm about to ask where Jackson is, when I see him standing awkwardly in the corner. He looks proper worried.

'Are you okay?' he asks. I nod, even though my eyes are still sore. Chantelle's kitchen's only tiny and it feels crowded and stuffy with the three of us in there.

'We'll go in the living room,' Chantelle says. 'It's cooler in there.'

Me and Jackson follow her in and she opens all the windows. I sit in the chair next to one and the breeze cools me down. I'm still shaking.

'We're lucky we managed to get out when we did!' Chantelle says. 'They cornered everyone in! I really hope Shaq's brother's okay, and Damar . . .'

'They cornered everyone in?' I say, and my voice cracks with the anger and unfairness of it. How can they do that? There's no point in me even asking, cause I already know the answer. We don't matter. They do it cause they can. I look at Chantelle and Jackson. I really thought they'd left me. That I'd been left on my own, like what normally happens. I shake my head and I start to cry.

'Hey, hey!' Jackson says and he gets up from the sofa and squeezes himself on the arm of the chair. 'Is it still hurting?' he asks. 'Should we call an ambulance?'

I shake my head. 'Nah,' I say. 'It ain't that. It still stings but . . . I thought youse left!'

Chantelle stares at me. 'Why would we do that?' she says. 'We're your friends!'

Jackson nods and the tears come down even more. I ain't never really had friends like this before. The mates I had in my old school would get off and leave me if we were meeting up in town and I was later than I said I was going to be. My nose starts to run and I wipe it with the back of my hand.

'I don't even know what happened,' I say quietly. 'I knew I needed to get outta there, I just froze. That's what happened that day with Shaq too. I can't explain it, but just being there, while all that was happening with the police. It reminded me of . . .' I pause and I can't look at either of them for a minute. 'They got called to my house loads of times when I was little, cause there was always fighting at home . . . and one time, y'know what they said? That they'd be amazed if I made it out of here alive. *I was five.*' I think it just reminded me of all that. And I guess seeing everyone celebrate Shaq made

205

me think, who do *I* have? Who would celebrate me when I'm gone?'

I ain't used to opening up to people like this, but it feels kind of a relief to get it out.

'I'm sorry you went through all that,' Jackson says. 'I can't even imagine what that was like, but of course people will celebrate you. Your family will—'

I go quiet. Then at last I say, 'I don't have any family,' I say. 'I'm in care.' I sneak a glance at them. It feels good to finally say it, even though I'm not sure why I've told them and a small part of me is still scared. But they don't look at me weird, or like they feel sorry for me. Or start asking me all these questions about what happened.

Chantelle smiles. 'You've got *us*,' she says. 'And, anyway, family ain't always about blood. You make your own family. At least, that's what I think, anyway.'

And I suddenly know exactly why I told them, and I'm glad.

25

CHANTELLE

We wait with Marc for his carer to come and pick him up. I was a bit surprised when he said about being in care, but it explains why he looked like he understood when I told him all that stuff about Trudy. I knew better than to start asking questions and all of that, though, cos I know what it's like when people ask you about your family stuff. Marc had to put his SIM in my phone and call Irene, or whatever her name is, cos his phone was wrecked after dropping it at the vigil. A car pulls up on one of the side streets.

'That's her!' Marc says. 'I need to go before she decides to come out and bore you both with her life story!'

I stare towards the car. I dunno what I was expecting, but it's definitely not the woman in the driver's seat. She looks about fifty. She unbuckles her seat belt, like she's about to get out the car but Marc doesn't give her a chance. He throws one arm around me and the other around Jackson, then brings us in for a quick hug, before heading over to her.

'I'll catch youse later,' he says, and he pulls his school bag onto his back. 'And if you need me, I dunno, send me a smoke signal or something . . .'

'I'll message you on Insta!' I say. 'But get your phone sorted!'

Marc waves goodbye, then he climbs in the car and slams the door. I watch as Marc's carer drives off, and I try to see if she looks angry or not, but it's hard to tell. Then it's just me and Jackson. I just want to carry on spending more time around him and I feel myself blush.

'You gotta rush off?' I say. 'Or . . .'

'Nah,' he says. A bit too quickly. 'I can hang around. My trains are every hour after six anyway, so I've got time to kill.'

I raise an eyebrow.

'No, not like that!' he says. 'I just meant I don't have to rush off.' He looks embarrassed and I shake my head. He's still proper cute, even when he looks all awkward. I never in a million years thought I would've invited Jackson into my house. Not when it's probably tiny compared to the massive one he lives in, but after Marc got pepper-sprayed, we just needed to wash it out. So I guess it's too late now. We go back inside and I peel my jacket off and throw it onto one of the nearby chairs. 'D'you want an ice lolly?' I ask. 'I'm getting one.'

'Sure,' he replies. 'Thanks!'

I disappear into the kitchen and grab two ice lollies out the freezer and I feel myself getting proper nervous, again. I've never been alone with a boy in the house, before. Gran would go mad if she came home and found Jackson here, but I don't have to worry about that right now. When I come back into the living room, Jackson's looking at some of the photos that are around the living room and I suddenly cringe. The last thing I need is Jackson seeing me when I was little, in some frilly, polka-dot dress. There's an old photo of Trudy holding me when I was just a baby.

Jackson points towards the photo.

'Is that your mum?' he asks.

'Yeah,' I say and I throw an ice lolly in his direction. '*Catch!*'

Jackson moves both his hands up to try and catch it, but he just grabs thin air instead. The lolly bounces off him, then falls to the floor. And he looks proper embarrassed. Jackson reaches down and picks it up, but even that makes me like him even more.

I shake my head. 'How could you miss that?' I say. 'I was *this* close, Jackson, *this* close!' I add and I move my hands out to show the distance. I slump down on the settee and he doesn't look at me as he makes his way over to sit next to me. I unwrap my ice lolly cos it's still proper hot and stuffy.

'Yeah, well,' Jackson says. 'Maybe you need to work on your throwing skills! Throw it better next time and I might catch it . . .'

I scoff. 'More like you have no co-ordination!' I say.

'I mean,' Jackson says and he clears his throat, 'my dance moves earlier would've proved that to you!'

I catch his eye and we both laugh and I get this weird feeling. Sometimes, I feel like there might be something between us. Like, I swear Jackson was checking me out at one point this evening. But then I dunno if I've imagined it all. I nibble along the edge of my ice lolly and Jackson gestures towards the photo of me and Trudy.

'I don't think I've ever heard you talk about your mum,' he says. 'Just your gran and sister.'

I shrug. 'Don't see her,' I reply, and weirdly, I don't feel embarrassed saying this to him. If it hadn't been for Shaq, I probably never would've spoken to someone like Jackson, who goes to this posh school in the middle of nowhere, never mind fancy him. I dunno what it is, but he's so easy to talk to. Even if his life is so different to mine.

'Awww, shit. I'm sorry,' he says, and he looks like he feels bad for asking. 'I didn't mean to – that must be hard.'

I shrug. 'Sometimes it is, sometimes it isn't. Like, there are days where I go over everything in my head and think about what it was like before everything went wrong and she was around … and I think I miss that. Or maybe it's the *idea* of having a mum that I miss. She turns up every now and then, probably to make herself feel better, and when she does …' I shrug. 'It's weird cos I know that I loved her once and I probably should love her now, but I just feel … nothing.' I glance at Jackson. 'I know that sounds bad, but I dunno. She just feels like a stranger to me. She doesn't know the first thing about me. What music I like, what I wanna do with my life, what college I wanna go to. It's hard, when you feel like your own parents don't want you. Cos it makes it feel like it's you. Like you did something wrong just by being here ...'

I glance at Jackson and I suddenly wonder if I've said too much. Been too honest. But he ain't looking at me funny or anything like that.

'What about your dad?' he asks.

I shrug. 'Never met him,' I say. 'But at least with that, you can't miss what you've never had. I'm just glad I've got my sister and my gran.' I pause. 'What about you? D'you get on with your mum and dad?' I ask.

Jackson finishes his ice lolly and puts his wrapper down on the table

'Yeah,' he says, and he looks like he feels proper guilty for saying it.

'You don't have to look at me like that,' I say. 'You get on with your parents, mine are shit. It's fine! That's just the way it is.' I suddenly realize how close we're sitting and Jackson must notice too, cos he shifts over on the settee, so there's a bit of space between us.

'I get on well with my mum and stuff,' he says. 'We're proper tight. But with my dad, it's like ...' He scratches his neck. 'Whatever I do, no matter how much I try, it's *never* good enough, y'know? It's like he always expects more. Or he just wants to push me into doing what he thinks is best for me. The subjects I should take, the future he thinks I should have. I didn't even get a choice about whether or not I wanted to stay on at St Anthony's after my GCSEs. He just told me that I was. Sorry,' he says, and he looks embarrassed again. 'I know it sounds like nothing.'

I pause. 'It ain't nothing' I say. 'It's your future! Like, do you wanna stay at St Anthony's? What do you wanna do after school and stuff?'

He goes quiet again. 'Nah,' he says. 'I don't wanna stay on at St Anthony's. I've picked to do English Language and Lit and A-level law. But . . .' Jackson looks embarrassed and he can't look at me for a minute. 'Don't laugh,' he says. 'My friends took the piss when I told them this, but the thing I love most about English is the creative writing part. Like, I love writing stories and stuff. It's just something I've always done. I really wanna go to Xaverian, because they do a creative writing enrichment class, and film studies too.'

He glances at me. 'I've applied to go there!' I say. 'And why would I laugh?' I continue. 'No offence, but your friends don't sound that great to me if they laugh when you tell them what's important to you.' I shrug. 'If that's what you wanna do, then you should just do it.'

'I suppose,' he says. 'I'm not sure how my parents would react to that, though. They're always banging on about me studying sensible subjects and getting a "proper" job. He hesitates.'No way have you applied to Xaverian as well, though? What are you going to do?'

Jackson turns to me and I suddenly feel embarrassed. 'I'm doing A-levels,' I say. 'I'm doing English as well actually, and I've put down sociology, but I'm not so sure. I just don't know what I'm supposed to do after that, y'know? Like, I know I wanna make something of my life and go on to uni and stuff, but I just don't know what I wanna do.'

'You'll figure it out! 'Jackson says. 'You're too smart not to.'

I feel myself blush. 'You're all right, for an embarrassing nerd, y'know that?' I say. 'Even if you do dance like someone's grandad.'

'*Wow!*' Jackson replies, but he's laughing. 'Your insults are actually gonna finish me off one day. Just so you know!'

I smile and I feel myself blush, again. 'I'm only messing!' I say, and I can't look him in the eye when I ask, 'Who's that girl you were with that day in town? You going out with her?'

'Aimee?!' Jackson says. '*No way!!* I can't stand her!'

Relief floods through me and I feel happy, but I try not to show it too much, cos I still don't know if he likes me back?

'Why?' Jackson asks.

'No reason!' I say, quickly, then: 'I like being around you, though.'

'Even though I'm a massive geek?' Jackson teases.

'Yeah,' I say. 'I think it's kinda cute . . .'

I feel myself flush. Jackson stares at me for a minute and he's almost looking at me like he wants to kiss me, and I want him to. He clears his throat and moves over on the settee.

'Same,' he says. 'I like being around you too.' And he's grinning way harder than he should be when he says the next bit: 'What? So you think I'm cute?'

I can't look him in the eye. 'You know you are, Jackson!' I say.

26

MARC

For most of the journey home, which took another five hundred hours, cause of how slow she drives, Dry Eileen didn't say much. Normally, she'd start chatting away about something or the other, but I didn't really feel like talking and I think she could tell. I appreciated that. I squished myself against the passenger door, and closed my eyes the whole way back. I was tired from everything that had happened and my eyes were still stinging a bit too. It felt good telling Jackson and Chantelle about me being in care, almost like a weight had been lifted. I kept thinking about what Chantelle had said, about making your own family. I guess I've never really looked at it that way before.

Now that I'm in the car, my head feels like it's about to

explode. It felt good seeing the mural and how much it meant to everyone. Especially to Shaq's brother and mum, cause that's all I ever wanna do. Make a difference with my art, y'know? But when I saw Shaq's mum, I dunno ... it made me think about my own mum and dad. Sometimes I feel like I've lived a thousand lives. I've seen so many things and stayed in so many different places. And even though I try not to think about my parents or all the rest of it most of the time, bits and pieces still come up. I hear my mum's screams or my dad shouting, or I get a flashback of my dad with his hands around my mum's neck. Or I remember how my mum would run into my room and pull me out of bed, so she could hide behind me. Like I was some sort of human shield.

Maybe that's why I don't ever trust any grown-ups, cause if your own parents are supposed to protect you and look after you, and they can't do that, how are you supposed to trust some random person? I'm exhausted from everything and I feel a tear slide down my cheek, but I don't want Dry Eileen to see that I'm crying, so I wipe it away, quick-time. The car pulls up and we get out, but I still don't look at her.

'Marc?' she says, as we head into the living room. 'Are you okay? Have you been drinking?'

Shiiiit!! It can't be those two sips of punch I had, even if they were proper strong. Then I remember that Jackson and his clumsy self spilled his drink all over me. I don't dare tell Dry Eileen I've had some punch, cause I know that she'll kick off for sure, and she'll probably tell my social worker. And that would be a *whole* other lecture.

'Nah!' I say. 'I swear! I was at this vigil for some boy from school, and someone spilled their drink over me, then the police came, and it proper kicked off ... one of them pepper-sprayed me, and I dropped my phone and everything. But I ain't been drinking. I promise!'

I don't know if she can tell that I'm lying about not drinking, but she doesn't look pissed, like I expect her to.

'Oh my god,' she says, and she moves a hand to her mouth. 'Are you okay? Are your eyes still hurting? Do you need to get checked out?'

She sounds proper worried and she doesn't ask me what I was doing wrong to get pepper-sprayed in the first place, which most of my other carers probably would've done. I feel kinda bad for not coming clean about the drink, but I've had to lie about stuff my whole life. Keep secrets for people, make out that things really aren't as bad as they seem, even when they are. But after Shaq, I dunno, I don't wanna just survive, any more. I don't just wanna move from place to place and do what I can to get by. I wanna be happy.

'I'm all right,' I say. 'My friend put water on them. They just feel a bit sore now.'

Dry Eileen pauses. 'Is that the boy I read about in the paper?' she asks. 'The one who was stabbed outside the Arndale on Sunday?'

'Yeah,' I reply, and I dunno why I say the next bit, but it just comes out. 'I was there. I saw it all happen.' I look down at my hands and Dry Eileen goes quiet.

'Oh, *Marc*,' Dry Eileen says at last, and she genuinely looks

216

like she's bothered. 'Why didn't you say something? I can't imagine how frightening that must have been . . .'

I shrug. I want to tell her that it was and it wasn't. I was scared, but it's like I've been that way my whole life. Dry Eileen looks at me and I wonder if she's thinking about my file. That's the other thing I can't stand, how people know everything about your life. All of the things that have happened to you and you don't get any say.

'You know you can come to me about anything,' she says. 'I mean it. Maybe talking to someone might help? I'm a good listener.' She pauses. 'I've got an old phone somewhere you can have,' she says. 'Let me go and dig it out. You can use it for now, until we get a new one sorted.'

I stare at her.

No one's ever said they'll buy me something. It's like I've had the same clothes for years. The same trainers and shoes and tracksuit bottoms. Nothing I've ever had has just been mine. Part of me wonders if I heard Dry Eileen right.

'What did you say?' I ask, just to check.

'You can use my old one for now, until we get you a new one sorted,' she replies.

I stare at her and for a minute I don't know what to do. I don't know, how to feel about it. I just shrug and pick up my school bag.

'Thanks,' I say. 'I'm going upstairs, yeah?'

I lie on my bed, in my tiny box room and I swear, I've never been more bored in my *entire* life. No phone, no music, no nothing. Just me, staring at the same dry four walls. I can't even message Chantelle or Jackson or send them some funny video from TikTok ... I try not to think about Shaq, or the people who brought me into this world, or all the other things that have been spinning in my head. But it's hard when you ain't got nothing else to do.

I hear a knock on my door and I pull myself up. 'Come in!' I say.

Dry Eileen comes in and she sits down on the edge of my bed. 'Here,' she says, and she hands me an old Samsung. It's nowhere near the ancient brick I'd imagined it would be, so I can at least put some music on there and download WhatsApp.

'How about we go and get your new phone next weekend?' she says. Part of me wonders if she's taking the piss, but she seems pretty serious. Although if there's one thing I've learned about adults, it's that they say loads of shit they don't mean, cause they think that it's what you want to hear.

I nod. 'Okay!' I say.

Dry Eileen smiles and she glances around the room. My wardrobe door's open and she clocks the bin bags stacked up inside and spilling out of it. There's a few more piled on the floor beside it. Dry Eileen furrows her brow, then she gestures towards the bags.

'Are they your clothes?' she asks, even though she knows full well that they are, cause she helped me cart them up here the day I moved in.

I shrug. 'Yeah,' I say.

Dry Eileen goes quiet for a minute and I can tell that she's thinking about what to say. 'You can unpack, you know,' she says. 'You don't have to leave all your stuff like that.'

I move down further on the bed, but I don't say anything. I want to tell her that it makes everything easier, that way. It means that I won't have to go through all the effort of having to pack everything back up again when she finally decides that she doesn't want me around.

'Don't see the point,' I say.

'Look, Marc,' Dry Eileen starts. 'I know it's going to take a while for you to trust me ... and that's okay. I don't expect it to happen overnight. I know these things take time. But hopefully the longer you're here, you'll see that I do want this to work, and that you can have a home here.' She pauses. 'If you want to keep your clothes in those bags, that's fine, I'd never force you to do anything you're not comfortable with ... but how about you start by hanging one thing up? Just *one*. It might make the room feel more like you own, then.'

I pause. I can't work out if it's stupid or not, what she's asking me to do. But I guess if I hang one thing up it ain't gonna be that hard to pack away, when the time comes. And maybe if I do it, it'll get her off my case.

'Okay,' I say.

Dry Eileen gives me a small smile and she gets up. 'Tea will be ready in half an hour,' she says. She pauses, like she's going to say something else. But she doesn't, she just turns and heads out. I put my SIM in Dry Eileen's phone and all these messages come up. There's a few from Dry Eileen, some Insta notifications from Jackson and Chantelle and a WhatsApp from Rhys. I stare at his message:

Hey, wot u up 2??

I ain't heard from him in four days. Usually, I'd message him back right away. But maybe it's being at Shaq's vigil and thinking about how short life is, maybe I don't want to waste it on someone who doesn't make me feel good. Maybe I'm worth more than that.

I delete it and Rhys' number. Then I go on Insta and reply to Jackson and Chantelle.

I put the phone down and look around the room. At the white walls and wooden furniture and the small TV crammed in the corner. I get up and walk over to one of the ripped bin bags. I bend down and pull out this old grey hoodie. I can't even remember who gave it to me. Which carer. Or which one of their kids it belonged to, before it was given to me. The cuffs are frayed and one of the plastic toggle things from the bottom of the drawstring has popped off.

I don't know what's gonna happen tomorrow, or next week, or next month. I've got no idea when I'll get *that* visit from my social worker to tell me that I'm being moved again. But I slide the hoodie onto a metal hanger and shove it inside the wardrobe.

27

JACKSON

I get off at the train station that's a short walk from my house. I ended up staying at Chantelle's for ages, just talking about anything and everything with her. The more we talked, the less awkward it felt. I've never been able to talk this easily with a girl before. I didn't even realize how long it'd been until it started to get proper dark. I couldn't stop thinking about what she'd said, about me being cute and knowing it. *Ha!* I can't tell if she actually fancies me, or if it she just said it as a joke. But there were definitely moments when I swear I felt like Chantelle might like me too and that it wasn't just all in my head. The whole way home I've thought about telling her how I feel. I must've typed out and deleted a WhatsApp message fifty million times, but I was too scared to send it. What if I tell her how much I like her and it makes things weird and she doesn't wanna be friends any more? But what if she does like me and I don't do anything? Then it'll just be *another* thing I don't have the courage to say. Like telling my mum and dad I don't want to stay on at St Anthony's and that I really want to pursue creative writing. Even do it at uni.

Where I live couldn't be more different to where Chantelle and Shaq are from. It's always just been home to me, but as I walk away from the station and through the town centre, it fully hits me how different it is. My area, with the massive Waitrose, boutiques and coffee shops; the Rolex shop and the Aston Martin car place. No wonder Chantelle and Marc thought I was stuck up when they found out what school I go to.

I head away from the town centre and walk past my old primary school, then take a left. It's pretty dark now, but I don't mind. I'm used to coming home when it's like this. Nothing ever happens round here anyway. There's loads of big, detached houses either side of me, with huge driveways that have at least three cars in them, and loads of electric security gates. The road starts to curve around a corner and there's less houses and more trees and grass, and the path gets a bit narrower.

I feel my phone vibrate in my pocket. I'm already hoping that it's Chantelle, before I even unlock my screen and see her name come up. She's written:

Get home safe, u geek! x

I stare at the *x*. She's never put an *x* at the end of any of our messages before. Does that mean something? I should just stop

222

messing around and tell her I like her. Not just that I think she's pretty or whatever ... but that she's strong and clever too, and when I'm with her I can just be myself. I'm not about to start saying all this in a message, in case I come off like a proper creep, but I feel myself grinning as I head down the road and I'm glad that there's no one else about to see me looking like a right fool.

I start to type out another message, then I delete it. Then I decide I'll message her when I get in. That way, I can properly work out what to say. I shove my phone back in my pocket but her message makes me feel good, y'know? And I just wanna hurry up and get back. I'm so busy thinking about Chantelle and that *x* that I barely notice the group of guys on the same side of the path. There must be about five or six of them, not much older than me, all white.

I walk straight into one of them and I stumble a bit. They're all laughing and joking but they go quiet when I knock into the boy closest to me. There's something about the way they're staring at me that makes me want to get out of there, quick.

'Sorry,' I mumble, as I duck past them.

I'm barely three steps away, when I hear one of them shout: 'Watch where you're fucking going,' and then *that* word.

It echoes all around me in the dark. On and on and on. And I feel like I've just been punched in the gut, but I don't turn around, I don't say anything. The first time I was called *that* word was when I was walking home from primary school. I must've been about seven. Some guy in his car hurled it out the window at me, and told me to go back to where I came from. I

223

didn't really understand, but it scared me and I cried the whole way home. And now all I know is that I need to get the fuck out of here. Something about how quiet they are, the way they've all fallen silent, puts me on edge. It's like I can feel their hatred, their anger at me filling the space between us.

I swallow hard and I try to push down the fear that's rising up inside me. I tell myself to keep walking, even though every part of me, every cell and muscle is starting to shake. My breath gets quicker and I feel my heart slam into my chest. My legs feel like they can barely hold the weight of my body, it's like they're not even made from flesh and bone any more. I want to run, but I'm scared that if I do it now they'll come running after me.

I quicken my pace and stare at the main road that runs off the bottom of this one. I see a few cars go past, and I try to concentrate on that. On getting to the end of this street. On the message I'm gonna send Chantelle when I get back. Anything to distract me . . . to take me away from being here. I tell myself that once I reach the corner, once I get to the bottom of this road and I'm out of sight, I'll be safe. Then I can run. I'm very nearly at the end of the street. I can see the traffic and the flicker of dim lights, getting closer up ahead, and I hear it again.

That word.

This time, it's louder. Full of more venom and anger and hate. I don't wait, I start to run. I feel the blood pumping through my ears and all I can hear is my breath. Shallow and sharp. I glance over my shoulder for the first time, and I see them all running towards me. Then the next minute, one of them grabs hold of me from behind and someone else comes in front and punches me in the stomach. I double over in pain and I'm knocked to the floor. My school bag goes flying and I feel a hard kick in my ribs. I yell out and I try to crawl away, but someone's shoe connects with my face. I feel something give, then warm liquid gushing down my face. I try to get up, but I'm punched back down.

I feel the concrete hard and cold against my cheek, and all I can do is move my hands up to cover my head. There's too many of them. I start to cry, begging them to stop through blood and snot and tears. But my words just disappear. I'm crying harder now, and one of them says *that* word again. I roll onto my back and even though my vision is blurry, I catch a flash of something that looks like a knife. I think about Shaq. How he was left in the street to bleed out and die. How he cried for his mum. And I don't want that to happen to me. I don't wanna die. *Not now, not like this.* If I don't fight back, I don't know what will happen.

Someone punches me again and my fingertips brush across something smooth on the ground. I don't know what it is, but I grab hold of it, and somehow I manage to pull myself up. Everything is still blurry and one of them is shouting something, but I don't know what he's saying, because there's this ringing in my ears. The guy I bumped into goes for me again, and I punch and fight with every ounce of strength that I have. *I fight to live. I fight not to die.* I don't know what happens, but my hand hits his face, then he staggers backwards. I notice that he's on the floor and a few of his friends have gone over to see if he's all right. Everything seems to happen in this proper fast blur. I notice a small space in the group, and I make a run for it, leaving my bag behind. A few chase after me, but I run hard and fast.

'When we catch you you're fucking dead, y'hear?' one of them shouts.

But I just keep my arms moving and my legs pumping. And even though everywhere hurts, and I feel a shooting pain in the side of my stomach, and my lungs feel like they're about to collapse, I keep going.

And all I can think is that I can't stop. I can't stop running till I get home.

28

JACKSON

I can barely breathe by the time I'm banging on the door and the windows of my house, praying for my mum or dad to hurry up and open it. I can hardly stand. I'm pretty sure I lost the guys who were chasing me pretty quickly, but it still feels like there's someone behind me. Like they could appear, any minute . . . I knock even louder.

What if they somehow find out where I live and come looking for me? My hands won't stop trembling. All I can hear is the pounding of my heart in my ears. And then I get this image, a flash of one of the guys on the floor. I don't know how badly I hurt him. I just needed to get out of there. I just needed to get away.

I ring the doorbell, then I lift up the letterbox and try to shout for my mum, but it's like the words are stuck in the back of my throat. I knock *again* and *again*, and I start to cry. I feel the tears and the snot running down my face and all I can think is, *Please, someone, just open the door.*

'All right, all right!' I hear my mum say. 'What have I told you about forgetting your keys—'

My mum opens the door and her face falls when she sees me. She must've been about to get in the bath, because her hair's wrapped up, and piled on top of her head.

'Oh my god,' she says, and she moves a hand to her mouth. 'Jackson, what happened? *What happened?*'

I'm crying even harder now, but I still can't get any words out. I move both my hands to my face and I close my eyes. The way I used to when I was a kid and I knew I was about to get into trouble. I can't move, I just stand there. Crying and shaking and wishing that I could make it all go away. My breath feels tight and sharp. I can't stop replaying what happened. Hearing *that* word. That look in their eyes. Someone kicking me hard in the face.

'*Mum* …' I manage to get out, but it sounds quiet. *Faint*. It reminds me of the way Shaq said it that day. My mum steps out onto our porch and she puts an arm around me and ushers me inside. Everything around me is blurry and my head's starting to spin. My breathing gets louder and faster. I'm trying to suck in air, but it's like there isn't enough of it. My mum leads me over to the stairs.

'It's okay, baby,' she says. 'Jackson, *I'm here.* Just breathe, okay? Just breathe … do it with me. Come on.'

My mum starts to take long, deep breaths and I do it with her. The tears are streaming down my face. I copy her for a few minutes and then my head stops spinning and my breathing starts to return to normal, but I still can't speak. I don't know where to start. I wipe the tears with the sleeve of my blazer, and my dad comes out of his study. His eyes widen when he sees me and he runs over to me and my mum.

'What happened?' he asks. 'Jackson, what's going on?'

Both him and my mum are looking at me and all I can think is I thought I was going to die, but I might have hurt somebody. I might have done some serious damage. I put my head in my hands and I feel my body shaking again. My mum leans in closer to me and rests her head against mine.

'I'm sorry,' I say, and the words kinda shock me. I don't know why it's those ones that come out of my mouth, but they do. Maybe it's because I never meant to hurt anyone, I didn't even want to fight in the first place, I was just trying to get away. Or maybe it's just because I expect my dad to be mad and disappointed, like he always is.

'What have you got to be sorry about?' my mum asks. 'Talk to us, Jax,' she says, and she lifts my head in her hands. 'What happened? Who did this to you, sweetheart? Was it someone at school?' I shake my head then she wipes some of the tears away from my face with her hand. 'Come on,' she says, and she gestures towards the living room. 'Let's go in there.'

My mum stands up and I hear her tell my dad to go and get the first-aid kit. I hold onto her as she leads me into the living room. If I didn't do anything, if I didn't fight back, would I be here now? Or would I have just been left in the street, like Shaq? My mum sits me on the settee and I wince at the shooting pain in my ribs. Now that I've stopped running, now that some of the shock has gone, it's like all I can feel is the pain. I've never seen my mum look this worried. She sits next to me and she holds my hand.

'Jackson, please,' she says. 'What—'

'I dunno,' I interrupt and I shake my head. I still can't make sense of it. I still can't believe that it happened. 'I was coming home,' I say, and I hear my voice crack. 'And there were these guys, I don't know how many, maybe four or five. But I bumped into one of them by mistake, and he called me a ...' I wipe some more tears away with the back of my hand. 'I kept thinking that if I made it to the end of the road, then I'd be all right. That once I got there and round the corner, I'd be fine ... I didn't wanna fight, but I was so scared, Mum. I thought they were gonna kill me. What else was I supposed to do?'

I cry harder and my mum pulls me into her and wraps her arms around me. She kisses the side of my head and I know she's crying too. I can hear the muffled sobs and I can tell by the way that her body shakes. My mum holds me even tighter.

'You did the right thing,' she says. 'D'you hear? I'm so glad that you did fight, because we don't know what would've happened if ...' She sucks in a breath. 'We don't know how far they would've gone,' she continues. 'All it takes is one punch and you ... you could've been dead.' I hear the fear in my mum's voice and she kisses the side of my head again. 'I'm just glad you're *okay*,' she says. 'Thank god.'

I see the tears roll down my mum's face and this time, I wipe them away. I turn and realize that my dad's there too. He's heard everything. And he doesn't look mad or even disappointed. There's an expression in his eyes I've never seen before. It's a mixture of sadness and anger. He comes over to us and gives my mum the first-aid kit, then he reaches down and puts his hand on my shoulder. I can't remember the last time he did he something like this. The last time he hugged me, or even checked that I was *okay*. It feels weird and I can tell he's a bit uncomfortable too.

He shakes his head. 'We have to call the police,' he says. 'We have to report it. We can't let those *cowards* get away with this.'

I nod, even though I just want to forget. I want to forget that any of this ever happened and go to bed. I don't understand how one minute everything can be fine – more than fine, even. I was walking home feeling on top of the world. Thinking about Chantelle and her message and what I was gonna say back, then the next minute …

My mum clips open the first-aid kit and douses some cotton wool in TCP. Out of the corner of my eye, I see my dad pacing up and down the living rom.

'This might sting a bit,' my mum says softly, as she dabs at the cuts the cuts on my face. My face feels like it's on fire and I wince in pain, but she's so gentle, it's like she's barely touching me. She wipes up most of the blood, then she blows lightly onto the cuts, to try and cool the stinging. I don't even know if it works, but that's what she used to do when I was younger. I shuffle over and I feel that shooting pain in my side again. I grimace and let out a yell.

'We might have to take you to the hospital,' Mum says. 'To get you checked out.' She turns to my dad. 'Let's take him there first, then we can call the police.' My mum fixes her gaze back on mine. 'Let's have a look, sweetheart,' she says, and she rolls up the bottom of my school shirt. My mum gasps. There's a massive bruise all the way down my side that spreads from my ribs to my stomach.

'Oh my god,' she says, and she rummages back through the first-aid kit.

My dad stops pacing, then he comes back over to us and crouches down next to me.

'Can you remember what they looked like?' he asks. 'Build, height, anything like that? Would you be able to recognize their faces if you saw them again?'

My head is throbbing and I suddenly feel *so* tired. I just want to go to bed. 'I . . . I don't know,' I say.

I try to think back, but it all happened so quickly and it was dark. There was the one I bumped into, but all I could tell was that maybe they were around the same age as me. I try to think of faces or anything like that, but I can't. Nothing seems to slot into place. The only thing I can remember is their eyes. *Cold and hard and full of hate* . . .

I shake my head and my dad looks annoyed. 'Sorry,' I say.

'You must remember something!' he snaps, and I can tell he's frustrated. 'Think, Jackson,' he says. 'This is important. How old were they? Were they boys or men? What were they wearing? Did you hear anyone mention any names, or nicknames, anything like that?'

'I—' I start, but it's all still a blur in my mind.

'*Derek!*' my mum interrupts. 'This isn't helping right now. Can't you see that he's in a state? Do me a favour and get Jackson some water, so I can at least give him these painkillers. And while you're at it,' she continues, scooping up the bloodied balls of cotton wool and shoving them into his hand, 'put these in the bin!'

I know my dad wants to carry on pressing me about what happened, but I guess even he knows when to listen to my mum. My dad takes the balls of cotton wool from her, then heads out of the living room. I breathe a sigh of relief. How am I supposed to tell the police anything, if I can't even remember what they look like? What chance would they have of catching them?

My mum strokes the side of my face.

'I know your dad can come off as being a bit harsh sometimes,' she says. 'But he's just worried about you, Jax.' She pauses. 'He is right, though. We can't let them get away with this. Once we've got you checked out and you feel up to it, we'll write down everything you remember, *okay*? So that we have as much detail as possible when we go to the police.'

My mum gives me a small smile.

'Okay,' I say.

She gives me another hug, then straightens herself up and wipes underneath her eyes. I suddenly feel this rush of emotion. I've always got on with my mum, but I never fully realized how lucky I am. Maybe it's mixture of thinking I might never see her again, or hearing Chantelle talking about her mum before, but I say: 'I love you, you know.'

My mum looks taken aback, because I say it out of nowhere, but then she smiles.

'I know you do,' she says. 'And me and your dad love you more than you could ever know. You're our whole world, Jackson. You're our light and our hope.'

My mum's getting proper emotional again, I can see fresh tears in her eyes. I lean my head back against the settee.

'Mum, that was *bare* soppy!' I say and she pulls a face.

'Oh, please,' she replies. 'I'll be as soppy as I want to in *my* own house.' She pauses. 'I'll make you something to eat,' she says. 'I bet you're hungry ... and I don't know where your dad's got to. Is he getting water out the fridge, or has he gone to dig a well?'

I laugh and even though everywhere still hurts, it feels like there's some sort of normal again. I can't help wishing that I'd done things differently. Maybe if I had, none of this would've happened. If I'd gone straight home from school. Or left Shaq's vigil earlier. Or spent less time at Chantelle's. If I'd caught an earlier train and walked the long way home ...

There's a knock at the door and I hear voices. My mum's about to head out of the living room, when my dad comes in. And the first thing I think is that he's not even got the glass of water, but then I clock them. The two policemen behind him. I sit up, worried that he went ahead and called them anyway, especially when I told him that I couldn't remember much about what the boys looked like. My mum folds her arms across her chest and she looks pissed. She shoots my dad a look that says, *I'm about to kill you for not speaking to me about this first*, but there's something about his expression that makes my stomach drop. My dad looks just as confused, like he can't work out why they're here either. I see one of them staring around our living room and the colour drains from my mum's face.

'What's going on?' she says. 'Did someone tell you what happened?'

One of the police officers, this young-looking one with dark hair, steps forward.

'Jackson Campbell?' he says.

'Yeah?' I reply, but the words come out dry and hollow.

And what he says next knocks the wind right out of me.

'I'm arresting you on suspicion of section twenty assault. You do not have to say anything, but it may harm your defence if you do not mention when questioned something which you later rely on in court. Anything you do say may be given in evidence.'

It takes me a few minutes to process what's happening. To make sense of what he's just said. *They're arresting me?* I hear my mum gasp. My dad just stands there. But he looks mad. Furious.

My head starts to spin. This has to be some sort of mistake. I stand up. I know my mum and dad are saying stuff, because I can see their mouths moving. I can see my mum's hands moving frantically in front of her face, like she's trying to explain. But all I can hear is this high-pitched ringing in my ears. All I can make sense of are these distorted bits of speech. It feels like I'm being held underwater, trying to make sense of what's going on above me, while my breath is just slipping away ...

And then it hits me. All at once.

'This is some sort of mistake!' my mum shouts. 'Jackson was *attacked* ... Look at his face. *Look at it!* They followed him. Chased him. This is ridiculous—'

'It isn't, I'm afraid,' the police officer cuts in, and he doesn't even seem bothered. If anything, he sounds bored. 'It's quite a serious matter, Mrs Campbell,' he continues. 'The victim in question has been severely hurt. He's currently in hospital, due to the extent of his injuries. It seems like your son used a weapon.'

My heart stops.

Victim? I get called *that* word and attacked, yet it's one of those guys who's the victim? And I never had a weapon ... then I remember, whatever it was I picked up off the ground to try and protect myself with. *And now he's in hospital?* I don't even know what I did, but I never meant to hurt anyone that badly. I just wanted to get away.

He holds up my school bag, which has been put into one of those clear evidence bags that you only ever see on TV.

'Is this yours?' he asks.

'Yeah,' I reply.

'You've got the wrong person,' my dad interrupts and I can tell that he's doing his best to try and keep his anger under control. 'It's those cowards you should be arresting,' he says. '*Not my son!* Jackson was trying to get away ... what was he supposed to do? Just do nothing, while he was being attacked?'

I hear my dad arguing with the police officer. I feel numb. How badly did I hurt this guy, for the police to get involved?

The other police officer comes over. She looks like she's in her early twenties and she gives me a slight smile, which is more than the other officer's done. I can already tell that he thinks I'm guilty. But even though this one is pretending to be nice, deep down she probably thinks the same thing. It's like I'm outside of myself, watching this happen to someone else.

'Can you confirm your date of birth for me, please, Jackson?' she says.

I hear my voice come from somewhere inside my chest and I know I'm talking, that I'm answering her back, but the words barely register.

'Okay,' she says. 'Because you're a minor, you're going to need an appropriate adult with you at the station. We can't question you without one present.'

I look at my mum.

'I'll go!' my dad says, before my mum gets chance to open her mouth.

And I don't know why, but I can't meet his gaze. I feel the shame creeping up inside me. Even though I don't know what else I could've done in that moment to get away. *To survive.* All my life, I've been told how to do things right. How to act, because when people look at me, they don't just see one Black boy, they see *all* Black boys. How to behave when I get stopped and searched. How to co-operate and do everything I can, not to end up in a police cell and now, look … look, where it's got me.

'Are these the clothes you had on when the incident took place?' the officer asks.

'Yeah,' I reply.

'Okay,' she continues. 'We need to take those into evidence as well, so you'll have to get changed before we take you to the station, if that's okay? And I'm going to have to come with you.'

I don't know why she asks me if it's okay, like I have a choice. Like I can turn around and tell her that I don't wanna get changed, or go the station, or have her follow me up to my room. But I just nod.

'He's not going to run off!' my mum says. 'And what are you doing about the other people? The ones who attacked my son,' she continues. 'He didn't start any of this . . .'

'Mrs Campbell,' she interrupts, 'I'm just doing my job.' And I can't help thinking of Harrison. How that's exactly what he says, whenever I get stopped and searched. If he was at Shaq's vigil today and he saw the way the police were holding Fabio down, or the way they'd barricaded everyone in on the estate, he'd probably say the same thing. *They're just doing their job. The UK is nothing like America and police brutality isn't an issue, it isn't even a thing, over here . . .*

I head out of the living room and the female police officer follows me. I can still hear my mum and dad arguing with the other police officer as I head up the stairs, but I know it's no use. It's not like they're suddenly gonna change their minds. I go into my room, but she doesn't come in with me, just waits on the other side of the door.

I take off my uniform and my school shoes and pull on a T-shirt and a pair of jeans, then come out and hand the stuff I was wearing to the police officer. She dumps them inside another of those clear evidence bags. I want to ask if the other guy's okay. And what exactly happened to him. But will it make me look guilty? I'm not sure how I'm supposed to feel either. Should I feel bad for hurting him, if he attacked me first? If they all did? If he wanted to hurt me?

When I come downstairs, my dad's waiting with his coat on and I can tell that my mum is holding back tears.

'Come on, Jackson,' the male police officer says and he pulls some handcuffs out.

'Is that really necessary?' my dad says. 'He's just a *child*.' But the officer cuffs me anyway.

I'm not 'just a child' to them. I'm not even the victim in their eyes. I'm some dangerous, violent criminal. Just like Shaq was. The handcuffs feel tight and cold against my skin and they're heavier than I expect them to be. I can see the tears falling slowly down my mum's face now. And I feel so scared, so frightened about what's gonna happen.

My mum turns to me. 'Just tell them the truth, baby,' she says. '*Okay?* Tell them the truth about everything you can remember, and it will all be all right!' But her voice doesn't match the words coming out of her mouth. I can hear the fear creeping its way through the space around us.

'Okay,' I say, but the words come out quiet.

The police lead me outside and I don't know what I expected. Maybe a normal police car? But there's a massive van. They brought this big police van to arrest *me*. Some of the neighbours are looking and I feel even worse now. I sneak a glance at my mum who's standing at the bottom of the path, like she's letting me know that she's still here. Just like she did on my first day of primary school when I didn't want to leave her and go to class. Then I climb into the back of the van with my dad. I sit on this bench thing and the door slams shut. It's dark inside and only the tiniest bit of light comes through the windows on the back doors. I suck in deep breaths and I look down at my hands as the van starts to move.

That's when I start to cry. Big, retching tears as I lean into my dad. He wraps his arms around me tightly. Like he's trying to hug all the fear and pain away.

'It's okay, son,' he says, and he holds me tighter in the dark. 'I've got you.'

29

JACKSON

When we get to the police station, everything goes by in this blur. They take my fingerprints and a mouth swab, then they take my phone off me too. Now me and my dad are in the holding cell. I can't believe that just a few hours ago I was sitting chatting to Chantelle, and the only thing I was worried about was what I was gonna say when I messaged her back. I sit on the hard bed with my head in my hands and I stare at the floor. It's grotty and covered in scuff marks and I wonder how many people have been in this police cell before me.

My dad's sitting next to me, but we don't speak. I move my hand to rub underneath my eye and my hands are trembling. *What if I end up in prison? What if they don't believe my side of the story?* I try to push all those thoughts to the back of my mind. My mum has to be right: if I just tell the truth, everything should be okay. If I tell them what happened, they'll understand that it was a mistake . . . that I was only trying to protect myself. *To get away.*

I turn to my dad for the first time since they put us in here.

My dad usually has the strongest presence of anyone I know. Like, he can walk into a room without even saying anything and everyone knows he's there. My mum says that was one of the things she liked about him. His confidence and his kind heart, but here in this police cell, he just looks so . . . small. *Scared.*

'Dad,' I start and my voice cracks. 'I never meant to hurt anyone. I—'

He shakes his head. 'Don't you dare apologize,' he says, and his voice is stern. 'Do you hear me, Jackson?' he says, and he looks me firmly in the eye. 'What other choice did you have? Were you just supposed to let them attack you and do nothing?' My dad shakes his head. 'Let me tell you now,' he continues, 'I'd much rather be sitting in this police cell with you than going to identify your body in the morgue. Even if it is absolutely ridiculous that you're here.'

I nod. He is right. What other choice *did* I have? I think he's going to say something else, but then the cell door opens and I'm told that they're ready to do my interview.

We walk down this long corridor and go into one of the interview rooms. I've seen stuff like this on TV millions of times, in films and Netflix shows, but I never thought *I'd* be sitting in one of these small, dingy rooms. I don't know what it is about this place, but it's like there's hardly any air, and they've purposely blocked out all the natural light. There's two plastic chairs on one side of the table and on the other, there's the female police officer from before and this older guy. I already know that he's super high-up, just by looking at him. Just by the way he seems to fill the space.

His face is red and blotchy and there's specks of grey in his bushy moustache. I feel him staring at me closely and then at my dad, and something about the way his eyes seem to pass over me, then move to my dad makes me feel *proper* uncomfortable. I can tell that he thinks I'm guilty. That I'm the one in the wrong. I can see the flicker of it on his face. I try to think about what my mum said, about telling the truth. That as long as I do that, then it will all be all right. And I try to remember all the things my mum and dad have told me before – *speak clearly, don't use slang, don't get angry, make sure you speak in proper sentences.* And it suddenly makes me mad, that I have to do all this just to get by in this world. I take a breath.

'Jackson,' the police officer says, barely looking at me. Like I'm not even worth being seen. 'I'm Chief Inspector Greenwood,' he says. 'And this,' he continues, gesturing to the female police officer, 'is Sergeant Wilson.'

'Hello,' I say. I try to make my voice sound bold and clear, but the word catches in my throat. I feel my dad gently squeeze my shoulder. Greenwood gestures towards the chairs and I sit down on one of them and my dad sits on the other.

'Right, Jackson,' he says. 'We're going to ask you a few questions about the incident that took place at twenty hundred hours. There might be a few things that we'll ask you to clarify for the sake of the tape, such as when we ask you to say "yes" instead of nodding your head.' Greenwood pauses. 'And who is this with you?' he asks.

'I'm his dad,' I hear my dad say. His voice sounds calmer, bolder, than mine, though I can tell he's worried. Maybe because he knows that all of this is out of his control.

'All right,' Greenwood continues. 'I'm going to press record on the tape now, you'll hear a long beep for a couple of seconds, then once that's stopped, the interview will begin. Okay?'

'Okay,' I say. Greenwood reaches over and clicks two buttons on the tape recorder that's resting on the table and the high-pitched noise fills the room. The panic starts to rise and I feel my body shake as I try to remember all the details, what exactly happened, what I might have hit that guy with. My throat feels dry and I want to ask them for a glass of water, but I don't want them to think I'm being difficult. And maybe the sooner I get this interview done, the sooner I can just go home. I turn to my dad, and he gives me a reassuring smile.

'This interview is being recorded at Hawthorn Road Police Station in Manchester,' Greenwood says. 'It's Wednesday the twenty-third of April and it's exactly twenty-one hundred hours. I'm Detective Inspector Jed Greenwood, five-five-one-two-zero, and the other police officer present is ...'

'Sarah Wilson,' the policewoman says. 'Seven-nine-zero-zero-three.'

'Jackson,' Greenwood says and I try to slow my breathing, to keep my hands still. 'For the sake of the tape, can you state your full name?'

I swallow hard. 'Jackson Michael Campbell,' I reply, and my voice trembles.

'And your date of birth?'

'Seventeenth of September, two thousand and six.'

'And the other person present is?'

'Derek Campbell,' my dad says calmly. 'Appropriate adult.'

I glance over at Greenwood, but he still doesn't look at me. He's got all these different papers spread out in front of him and he moves over in his chair.

'For the benefit of the tape,' he says again. 'This interview is about the incident that took place on Fairclough Road, at twenty hundred hours, this evening, between yourself and a Mr Oliver Hayes. The victim is currently in hospital being treated for severe facial injuries.'

I stare down at my hands, trembling in my lap. I don't know why, but hearing the boy's name aloud makes everything seem more real. Like, this definitely isn't some bad dream I'll suddenly wake up from. All I was trying to do was get away. By the way Greenwood says it, I already know that he's on this Oliver's side. I can tell by the way he uses that word for him – *victim*. Even though I'm the one who was attacked. Even though I didn't wanna fight. Even though there were so many of them and only one of me.

'Did you know Oliver before the incident took place? Had you been in any kind of contact with him?' Greenwood asks me.

'No,' I say. 'I'd never seen him before.'

'In your own words, Jackson,' he says. 'Can you tell us what happened?'

I suck in some of the stale air and I glance at the marks on the table. Faint rings left from coffee cups, scuffs, marks. I don't want to think about it, I really don't want to go back there. To have to go through it all. I feel my dad lean forward in his chair. I sneak a look at him and he gives me a nod.

'I was walking home from the station,' I start, and even though my voice is trembling, I'm glad to just be able to get some words out.

'What station?' Greenwood says.

'Mead's Cross,' I reply. 'I got off there and I was walking home. I cut though the town centre and I was heading down Fairclough Road, and that's when I bumped into one of them—'

'One of who?'

'One . . . one of the guys. I think it must've been Oliver, I don't know. I said sorry, and I walked past and that's when he . . .' I pause. 'That's when he called me a . . . he told me to watch where I was going and called me the n-word,' I blurt out. I glance at my dad. He reaches a hand over and presses it down on top of mine, then he gives me a gentle squeeze.

'I'm sorry,' Greenwood says. 'What exactly did he say? What word? We need you to be as specific as possible, Jackson.'

I feel my dad's hand stiffen. Greenwood knows exactly what I'm talking about, what other word could I mean? I don't wanna say it, I don't wanna have to repeat what they said to me.

'For the benefit of the tape,' Greenwood says. 'Can you repeat what exactly was said?'

My dad's hand presses down even more firmly on top of mine

and I tell them. I swear, I feel my dad flinch when I say it, but he doesn't let go of my hand. He just holds on even tighter.

'That must've made you angry,' Greenwood says. 'Furious, even.'

'Yeah,' I say. 'I mean . . . no, I was just more scared and upset.'

'So, let me get this straight,' Greenwood says. 'You're walking home from the station, when you come across Oliver. You accidentally bump into him, he tells you to "watch where you're going" and calls you a . . .' I can't believe how smoothly the word rolls off his tongue. 'And you're not even a little bit mad? So then what did you do? Did you confront Oliver?'

'*No!*' I say. I don't get why he's trying to twist my words. Like I had some sort of reason for doing what I did. 'I-I was just scared and I wanted to get out of there.'

Greenwood leans back in his chair and he stares at me. Right at me. It's the first time he's looked at me this hard the whole time I've been in here. And I wonder what he's thinking. Is he enjoying this? What would it be like if my dad wasn't here with me? How would this all go down?

'Okay,' Greenwood says. 'Then what happened? What did you do?'

I swallow hard and I try to remember everything I can, without going back there. Without finding myself on that road again. I suddenly feel aware of everyone in the room. Not just my dad, but Greenwood and this other officer too. I just want to get out of there, I want to run out of this stuffy room with no windows and no air. But if I do that, I know I'll look guilty.

I put my head in my hands and I close my eyes. 'I was scared,' I say. 'I was scared something was gonna happen, so I walked off. I tried to walk away down that road—'

'Fairclough Road?' he asks me.

'Yeah,' I say. 'I was walking as quick as I could. I didn't wanna run, cause . . . I thought that if I did, if I started to run, they'd chase after me. So I was waiting until I got to the end of the road, and around the corner. And then one of them shouted *that* word at me again. And something told me to run, that's when I tried to get away, but they all ran after me. Someone punched me in the stomach and knocked me to the ground – I think it was Oliver. And more people were kicking and punching me and I just wanted to get away . . .' I pause and I realize there's tears streaming down my face again. I wipe them away with the back of my hand. No one asks me if it's too much, if I wanna stop, if want a break, or some water, or even a tissue. They just carry on.

I wipe some snot away, on the sleeve of my hoodie.

'And then what happened?' Greenwood asks

'I thought I was gonna die,' I say and I feel more tears running down my face. 'I thought one of them had a knife and I just picked something off the ground, to try and get away. I didn't even know what it was, I just picked it up, and I managed to get up, and . . .'

Greenwood puts one of those clear evidence bags down on the table. It's got a number written on it and I can see now in the bright light of the interview room, that it's part of a broken bottle.

'For the benefit of the tape,' Greenwood says again – I'm already sick of hearing that phrase – 'I'm now showing Jackson item number three, five, zero, D, R. Which was the weapon that was used to inflict harm on the victim. It's part of a broken bottle that was uncovered at the scene of the crime. Jackson, do you recognize this?'

'No,' I say, and I'm not lying. I just picked it up, grabbed it out of fear. Greenwood raises his eyebrows and I don't want to look like I'm lying either, because I know that that will only make things worse.

'I mean, I don't recognize it,' I say. 'Cause I didn't get a look, I just grabbed it. But thinking about it, I don't know . . .' I pause. 'I guess it felt like glass.'

Greenwood pushes the bag towards me. 'Can you show us how you held it?' he asks. 'How exactly did you pick it up?

How am I even supposed to remember? I look at my dad and he gives me a small nod. My hands are trembling and I pick up the broken piece of bottle in the evidence bag. I suddenly panic that if I don't remember *exactly* how I held it, *exactly* how I picked it up, then they'll somehow know. And then I might get accused of lying. Or they might make out that I'm trying to mislead them or whatever. I wrap my fingers around the piece of glass inside the bag and I try to remember. I was holding it onto it tightly, because I was so scared and I remember pressing the edge of it, hard, into my palm. I turn my fist over, in the way I remember hitting Oliver. I'm not even looking at what I'm doing really, I'm just moving my hand through the logistics of it, trying to remember exactly what I did.

I pause, holding my hand out in front of me. 'Like this,' I say. 'I held it like this.'

Greenwood stares at me and that's when I look down. I see my fist clenched tightly around the broken bottle and a jagged bit of glass, sticking out between my knuckles. I feel sick. The way I'm holding it doesn't look good. I didn't even mean to grab it like that . . . I didn't think. It was like fear and panic took over. Surely the police know that it was self-defence? They know how many of them there were against me. They know that Oliver called me *that* word, and that I've got injuries too. That I tried to run away. Shouldn't it all be okay?

The room suddenly feels eerily silent, then I hear Greenwood say: 'Just to clarify, Jackson's clenching the piece of glass in his fist and the jagged bits of it are sticking out of his knuckles. Almost like a weapon.'

A weapon.

And just like that, I know that nothing is ever going to be okay again.

30

CHANTELLE

I keep checking my phone. I must have looked at it about a million times, wondering why Jackson hasn't messaged me back. I know he's seen my text, and that he started writing something back, cos the little bubble thing came up right away. But then he went quiet and that was almost four hours ago. He hasn't replied to Marc's messages in the group chat either. What if I read into things wrong? Even if he isn't going out with that Aimee or whatever her name is, it doesn't mean that he actually likes me back. Maybe he's not replying to the group messages cos I've made things awkward. I turn over in bed. I think about sending another message, but I don't wanna look desperate, and what's the point if he already ain't replied to the first one?

Marni's fast asleep in the bottom bunk and I hear the key turn in the door downstairs and Gran come in. I don't move, though, cos I really can't be bothered to have the conversation about me being suspended right now. I can't sleep either, thinking about Jackson and today and what I'm going to do with my life. I reach for my college prospectus that's on the windowsill. I'm going to a taster day next week which I'm excited about, but I still don't know what I'm supposed to do after college. I flick through the pages of the subjects I've picked and I stare at this little box underneath them that tells you what you can study at uni and the type of jobs you can go into. Teaching, counselling, marketing, but I don't wanna do any of those things.

I could see how much Jackson loves writing when he spoke about it earlier and I want to find something that I'm passionate about, too. I suppose that all this stuff with Shaq and the unfairness of it all, has made me realize that I don't just want a good future and to do well. I want to make a difference somehow, too. Or at least try. I carry on flicking through the prospectus and I just hope that Jackson's right. That whatever it is I'm meant to do with my life, I'll figure it out.

31

JACKSON

It's almost 11.30 p.m. by the time the interview's finished and I'm finally allowed to leave the station. I'm tired. Tired and empty from having to go over and over and over everything that happened. My throat's proper dry and I've not eaten since lunchtime, so I'm proper hungry too. Me and my dad wait outside the station for my mum to come and pick us up and I'm just glad to be out of there. To be outside, breathing in the fresh air. I told the truth, but Greenwood kept trying to twist my words. My dad had to butt in a few times. Greenwood asked if I intended to hurt Oliver. Said I must have at least wanted to a little bit, if I held the bottle like that. Said I must have been angry. The thing is, I never wanted to hurt anyone, but I knew that if I didn't fight back, if I didn't do something, then they would end up hurting me.

And when you're in that position, where you have to save yourself or do nothing, what else are you supposed to do? My dad got angry and told them it was self-defence, but he was asked to stay quiet for the rest of the interview. Then, before we left the station, I was told I was being charged. They were charging me with section twenty assault – *wounding with intent* – and I'd get a letter to tell me when my court date would be. And all the while, I still couldn't get my head around it. I didn't start any of this, yet I'm the one being charged and arrested. They handed me this charge sheet before we left and I just kept thinking how crazy it all was. Like with Shaq. How one moment, one instant, can change your whole world *for ever.*

Now we're waiting on one of the side streets that's a short walk away from the police station. I just want to crawl into bed, and crash out, and pretend like none of this ever happened.

My dad turns to me. 'I'm so sorry you had to go through that,' he says, and he moves a hand to squeeze my shoulder again. 'It makes me so angry that we live in a world where even when our lives are in danger and we have to protect ourselves, we're still punished. We're still seen as criminals. But we'll fight this, Jackson,' he says, and I hear the determination in his voice. 'We'll get a decent lawyer, we'll fight this every step of the way ... so when it does go to court, there's *no way* you'll end up being convicted for this. For defending yourself when those racists attacked you!'

I'm suddenly grateful for my dad, the fact that he's here

now, and that we've got the money to be able to afford a decent lawyer. But it makes me think about the people who can't. All the people who end up in that holding cell, who have to go to court with no money, or have no one decent to represent them. What chance do they have?

I'm shivering now, because even though it was warm earlier on, the temperature's suddenly dropped and my hoodie just ain't cutting it. My dad takes off his coat and he wraps it around me.

'Your mum should be here soon,' he says. There's so much I want to say. I wanna thank him for everything today. I don't know how I would've got through that interview without him.

'Dad,' I start, but then my mum's car pulls up, and he gestures towards it.

'Come on,' my dad says.

My mum's blasting some old nineties slow jam and she turns the music down as we climb in. My dad never listens to anything when he's driving – he might have the news on every now and then. But my mum's car is almost like being inside some sort of rave. I climb into the back and my dad gets into the passenger seat. He leans over and gives her a quick kiss on the lips. My mum and dad have been together since school, which is mad, when you think about it. And no matter what happens, my parents *always* have each other's backs.

My mum turns around and smiles at me. 'You hungry?' she says. 'I got you some food.'

She points to a paper takeaway bag on the floor, the smell of pepper steak wafts through the car, but now I'm finally sitting down, and I'm away from the station, I just want to close my eyes. I rest my head back and let them shut. My mum and dad's voices drift in and out around me. I hear my mum ask my dad, 'What exactly happened? Then I hear her say: '*What?* So Jackson was the one attacked and he ends up being charged?' I can hear the anger in her voice. 'You know this wouldn't be happening if it was the other way around. If Jackson was some posh white kid, and it was a group of Black boys who'd chased him down.'

'I know. I *know*!' my dad says, and I can hear the helplessness in his voice. 'But what can we do? We'll just have to wait until it goes to court. No one in their right mind would convict him for defending himself!'

I hear my mum breathe out slowly. 'You'd hope not,' she says and she lowers her voice. 'But you know the statistics, miscarriages of justice happen *all* the time ... we'll have to get the best lawyer we can find. I'll make sure I'll get some good character references together ... I can't believe we're having to do this. That we have to prove *what kind of person* our baby is ... The sheer fucking nerve of them calling the police in the first place, after they attacked Jax—'

I can hear my mum getting upset and my dad says something to her in a quieter voice. I don't know what, but it seems to calm her down. I zone in and out of their conversation the rest of the way home. Surely my dad's right, and no one in their right mind would convict me? But what if he's not? The thought of a trial, of having to go to court and relive everything, terrifies me.

I feel the car stop and I open my eyes, then get out and follow my mum and dad into the house. It's only been a few hours, but it feels like a hundred years have passed. Being with Chantelle and Marc was a lifetime ago. I go to walk up the stairs and my mum holds up the paper bag.

'D'you not want something to eat, sweetheart?' she asks. 'I got your favourite – fried dumpling and pepper steak.'

The nicest Caribbean takeaway is over an hour away, so my mum only usually goes there on special occasions. Like birthdays, or good exam results. I nod my head and I go into the living room. I her my mum plating everything up, then she comes through and hands it to me. She doesn't tell me to sit at the table like she usually would. I'm so hungry that I eat everything in no time, barely coming up for air. But it's like there's this bitter taste in my mouth that no amount of good food can get rid of. When I'm done, I turn to my mum.

'I'm gonna go to bed, yeah?' I say.

My mum gives me a small smile and my dad nods from the other side of the room. Then, my mum brings me in for a hug.

'We love you, Jackson,' she says, and she stands there, holding onto me. 'We're gonna get through this, okay?'

'Okay,' I say. 'I love you too.'

Then I pull away. I don't bother to switch the light on when I go into my room. Or get changed. I just climb into bed and lie there, staring up into the dark.

32

CHANTELLE

I wake up to Marni kicking me from underneath my bunk. I don't even know what time it is, but I'm still suspended, so there's no way I'm getting up early if I don't have to. I groan and turn over, but Marni kicks me again, moving the mattress upwards.

'Channi,' she says. 'Wake up! Wake up!'

I'm still so tired. I didn't sleep much last night. I kept waking up and checking my phone, to see if Jackson had replied. But even though he'd read my message, nothing. I never should've put that *x* at the end. Marni kicks me again, but this time it's proper hard and I feel it right between my shoulder blades.

I reach my hand down and try to grab hold of her foot, but all I touch is air.

'*Oi!*' I snap, as she kicks me again and starts to laugh.

'Ha, you missed!' she says. 'You need to get up! You're gonna be late for school. And ain't you forgetting something? *Chantelle?*'

She gives me one final kick and I sigh loudly, then pull the covers back. I love my sister, but I swear she does test me sometimes. I climb down from the top bunk and I rub underneath my eyes. Marni's already wearing her school uniform and Gran's plaited her hair into two French braids. She's wearing a massive pink badge that says, *I am 10 today!* in silver writing. I made sure I wrapped her present and everything last night.

I shrug. 'I'm not going in,' I say. 'And I'm not sure what I'm supposed to be forgetting. It's just any other Thursday . . .'

Marni scowls at me and for a minute I can't work out if she wants to kick me again, or if she's going to burst into tears. Her lip quivers so I wrap my arms around her and bring her in for a hug.

'Of course I ain't forgotten what day it is!' I say, and I hold onto her tighter and give her a load of kisses. 'Happy birthday!'

'*Ger-off!*' she says, even though she's smiling, and I finally let her go. I dunno what it is, maybe it was being at Shaq's vigil yesterday and seeing how . . . *broken* his mum and his brother were, but it made me think about Marni. Shaq was only four years older than her and I *never* want anything to happen to my little sister. I want her to know how loved she is. How much I love her. Waaaay more than Trudy could ever love her. So much it hurts sometimes. I used to think that it was just Marni who needed me, but I think I need her just as much. I get up and I make my way over to the chest of drawers, then I root around inside and pull something out. I hide it behind my back and turn to Marni.

'I've got something for you!' I say.

Her face lights up. 'What? I don't have to wait till after school? What is it? What is it?'

I hand her her present and she rips it open. It's the jacket that I stole from Next.

'Do you like it?' I ask.

'*I love it!*' she says, and she throws her arms around me. 'Thank you! Can I wear it now?'

I nod. Marni pulls the jacket on, then she turns to me and throws her arms around me again.

'*Thank-you-thank-you-thank-you!*' she says.

'It's all right,' I say.

She stares at me for a minute. 'Why ain't you going in?' she asks. 'Are you sick? You don't look sick to me. Does Gran know?'

'I've been suspended,' I say.

Marni pulls her face. '*Why?*' she says, and she puts a hand on her hip. 'Gran said you've got to stop getting into trouble! What did you do?'

'It wasn't my fault!' I snap, and I don't even want to think about Ms Fucking Edwards, let alone try and explain it to Marni. She picks her book bag up again and grabs her coat from the back of the door.

'Really?' she says. 'I'm not sure if I believe that!'

I pull a face. 'I'm not sure I like how rude you're getting with age,' I say, and I push her out the door. Marni looks at me like she's about to say something else, then Gran shouts for her from the hallway and Marni goes rushing down the stairs. I guess I can't put off having this conversation with Gran any longer. I head downstairs and Gran's already got her Asda uniform on.

'Chantelle said she's not going in!' Marni says, shoving an arm through her coat.

'Carry on,' I say to Marni, 'and you won't be getting your other present later.'

Marni's face drops. 'I've got something else?' she says. 'I'm sorry!'

'Yeah,' I say. 'I bet you are!' I turn to Gran.

'It's all right,' Gran says. 'We'll talk about this properly when I'm back. Mrs Cohen phoned me again this morning ... we've got to go in for your meeting on Monday.' She pauses. 'I can't believe she's accusing you of cheating!'

Marni's eyes widen in shock.

'Yeah,' I say. 'I told her to type my essay in online, if she was *so* convinced I'd copied it, and she said that nothing had come up, but they'd be "investigating it properly".' I kiss my teeth. 'I swear,' I say. 'It's such *bullshit*. She's always looking for any excuse to get me into trouble, or kicked out ...'

'Orrrrr!' Marni starts. 'Chantelle swore—'

'*Marni!*' Gran snaps. 'Go and get some breakfast!' Marni slumps off towards the kitchen and I see her pull a face behind Gran's back. I bite down hard on the inside of my cheek. I don't know if Gran got rid of Marni so she could have a go at me, but I really don't wanna get worked up over Ms Edwards again. I've already wasted enough tears on her. It makes me mad, though, how you can try to do everything right, and it still doesn't stop people from thinking the worst about you.

Look at Shaq. It's so much easier for people to believe he was involved in some sort of gang, and his death was somehow his fault, rather than the fact he was a victim. And it's so much easier for Ms Edwards to believe I cheated on that essay, rather than accept the fact that I wrote it myself, and that I'm actually smart enough to get a decent grade.

Maybe that's another reason why I started to try harder in school. Not just for myself, but to prove Ms Edwards and anyone else at that school who thinks the same as her wrong. I bite down harder on the inside of my cheek. Knowing how quickly they suspended Daymar or kicked his brother out, when there's people in that school who have done *way worse,* I know Ms Edwards is gonna go all out with this shit. Maybe if I lived in a posh area like Jackson and went to a school like St Anthony's, I wouldn't have to deal with this kind of stuff.

'You know I've been trying, though,' I say and it comes out quieter than I mean it to. 'Like, I've been trying so hard not to answer back like you told me, but Ms Edwards is *always* on my case.' I shrug. 'It's like it's never enough ... no one at school apart from Mrs Cohen thinks I'm gonna amount to anything and ...' I pause. 'Even though I know deep down that I wanna make something of my life, sometimes a small part of me thinks, what if they're right?'

The next part comes out even quieter and I see Gran's face soften.

She comes over to me and lifts my chin. 'Chantelle,' she says, looking me in the eye. 'Let me tell you now, there are people like Ms Edwards who you're going to come up against time and time again throughout your life. People who've already made their minds up about you, because of who you are and where you're from and the colour of your skin. But you don't listen to them, you hear me? That Ms Edwards isn't right, neither is anyone else who tries to make out that you're nothing. They don't know you. You're smart and brave and talented, and I know you've got that fight in you, because all the women have it in this family ...' She pauses. 'So don't you dare let the likes of her – or anyone else, for that matter – stop you from having the future that you want. Okay?'

I nod. 'Okay,' I say. I fling my arms around Gran. I can feel the tears pricking my eyes. No one's ever believed in me as much as Gran. Gran kisses my forehead and I know she's right. I want to be able to have a good life. I want to be able to do something important, something that matters. Not just that, I want to set an example for Marni. So at least she knows that if her sister can go and do something, she can too, and that she doesn't have to play into what other people expect her to be.

I pull away from Gran and Marni comes back out the kitchen with some toast. Gran grabs her bag off the side. 'And don't you worry,' she says, 'I'll bring that sour-faced Ms Edwards down a peg or two. No one's accusing my granddaughter of cheating!'

I smirk. 'Well, I feel for any teacher who has to cross you,' I say. 'Not her, though.'

Gran glances at her watch. 'Right, we've got to go!' she says. 'Marni, come on!' Gran glances at me. 'Did school give you some work?' she asks, as she ushers Marni towards the door.

'Yeah, they did,' I say. 'And don't worry, I'm on it!'

Gran smiles. 'All right,' she says. 'I'll catch you later!'

'Bye,' I say. 'Bye, Marni,' I shout.

'Bye, you bighead!' she shouts from by the door, then the next minute they're gone. I dunno what I'm supposed to do, if I'm off school for the whole week. I go upstairs and check my phone. There's still nothing from Jackson, but I've got two missed calls from a number I don't recognize. I go to Insta and see that I've got five missed video calls and three messages from Jackson, and I don't even think, I just call him back.

I stand outside Jackson's house. I couldn't believe what had happened when he told me. I still don't think it's sunk in, if I'm honest.

Jackson's house is massive. His front porch is probably bigger than my hallway. I've never seen anything like it. I knew he was posh but this actually takes the piss. I wonder what he really thought about being at mine yesterday. Even his front garden's huge and I haven't seen the inside of his house yet!

I take a deep breath and I ring the doorbell. I move my hair over my shoulder and I feel my heart start to beat proper fast as I hear someone unlocking the door. Jackson opens it. There's a few cuts on his face and underneath his eye looks swollen.

Maybe it's seeing him standing there like that, with the cuts and bruises on his face, but I dunno what comes over me. I don't even think, I just throw my arms around him. It must catch him off guard, cos he stumbles a bit, but he hugs me back.

'Ouch!' he says, and he winces as he holds onto his side.

'Oh, I'm sorry!' I say and I let go and suddenly feel embarrassed. Then he closes the door, and I see a smile spread across his face and it makes me feel nervous all over again.

'It's all right,' he says, although he grimaces in pain as he walks towards the stairs. 'It doesn't hurt anywhere near as much as it did yesterday. My mum took me to the hospital first thing to get checked out and they gave me some proper strong painkillers. I swear I just feel high . . .'

I shake my head. 'I mean, that's a first!' I say. 'You, getting high.'

'I know, right?' he says.

Jackson smiles but he looks sad. Sad and frightened. He rubs underneath his eye. I try to think of something to say, but I can't stop staring around his house. My mouth must be fully open as well, cos he gives me a weird look. I can't help it. I've never known anyone who lives anywhere like this. Everything looks new and shiny and expensive.

'Errr, this is insane!' I say. 'You could fit five of my gran's house inside here.'

Jackson rubs underneath his eye again. 'Errr, you have to take your shoes off if that's okay?' he says. 'My mum'll go mad if there's any marks on the floor . . .'

I shrug and I pull my trainers off. His house seems so

quiet. Mine's always so loud, even though it's only me and Marni and Gran.

'Where are your mum and dad?' I ask.

He shrugs. 'They're at work,' he says. 'My mum was gonna take today off, but I told her to go in. I just need a bit of space, y'know? She's already asked me if I'm all right about fifty million times this morning.'

'Well, I promise I won't ask you that once!' I say.

Jackson smirks. 'I knew I could rely on you,' he says.

We're standing so close. Jackson glances down at my mouth, then moves a bit away.

I put my hand in my jacket pocket and pull out a packet of Haribo. 'Thought these would cheer you up!' I say. 'But just so you know, I'm having half!'

He smiles and takes the packet. 'Thanks,' he says. 'Come on, we'll go upstairs!'

We go up the stairs and I can't stop looking around his house and noticing how posh it is, how big it is, how much space there is ... I've never even had my own room. One time, when we were living in this really grotty flat close to the park, me, Trudy and Marni were all in one room. Part of me always wonders how different mine and Marni's life might be, if we'd had other things. A better mum, more money, if I was able to go to a better school.

Jackson pushes his bedroom door open. He sits down on his bed and I dunno what to do at first. If I should sit down next to him, or if I should sit on the chair beside his desk ... or the big bean bag thing that he's got on the floor. I sit on the bed, but I make sure that there's a big space between us, cos I don't want it to feel weird.

Jackson opens the packet of Haribo, but he doesn't take any. He just stares down at his hands, then he pulls one of the squidgy eggs out the packet and says: 'I swear, when I was on the floor, in the dark … I thought …' He hesitates. 'I honestly thought I was gonna die. That I wouldn't see anyone again – my mum, my dad, no one. I've never … I've never been so scared in my entire life.'

I move closer to him and I see a tear slide down his face. He looks embarrassed that he's crying in front of me, then he shrugs and wipes underneath his eye with the back of his hand.

'And last night,' he says, 'I was so tired, but I couldn't sleep. I just kept thinking about it over and over. Thinking that's how Shaq must have felt. Frightened, cause he knew that his life had just been taken away and there was nothing he could do about it. Even today, I wanted to go to the shop, just to get a drink, but …' He pauses. 'I'm too scared to even leave the house, in case I run into one of them. It's *stupid*!'

I'm sitting so close to Jackson now that our knees our touching and I'm so mad that he has to go through this. And on top of that, he's the one who got arrested. It's so fucked up!

I shake my head. 'I'm not surprised,' I say. 'It ain't stupid, though! It's normal to feel this way after what happened … I'm just glad you're okay. That you fought back, cos what if you hadn't? What if you hadn't picked up that piece of glass? It could've easily been a different story.'

The words sit heavy between us.

Just imagining, what if. . . I try to concentrate on the fact he's here now. Jackson puts the Haribo in his mouth. He doesn't say anything for a minute, he just sits there, chewing silently. Then he turns to me and says: 'I know.'

His voice is so quiet, that I have to strain to hear it. He puts his head in his hands and he can't look at me, as he says the next bit.

'Why do I still feel so guilty, though? It's like I know they were in the wrong. That they wanted to hurt me, that they're fucking racists, but . . .' He pauses. 'I keep thinking that maybe I should've done things differently. Not fought back so much . . . or picked that bit of glass up off the floor.' He shrugs. 'It doesn't even make sense, but I just . . . I *never* meant to hurt anyone. I never meant for it to get like this . . .' He trails off.

I shake my head. 'You feel guilty cos you're a decent human being,' I say. 'That's why. D'you think they're sitting around feeling bad about attacking you and calling the police? There's no way!' I shrug. 'I don't get what else you were supposed to do. How else were you supposed to act? I pause. 'You don't know how far they would've gone . . . You could've ended up dead!' My voice cracks at the last bit and I feel all the emotions rising up inside me again. I don't mean to get upset in front of him, but I can't help this weird mix of emotions. It's like this deep sadness and hurt and anger, then on top of that: fear. Fear that I could've lost Jackson. That I might never have seen him again and it just makes me want to make the most of being with him. It makes me want to tell him how much I like him. I move my hair away from my face and Jackson turns to me.

'That's what my mum keeps saying,' he says. 'And I'm trying

to remember that, I really am. It's just *mad* that my two choices were to either do nothing and risk being beaten to a pulp or to defend myself and go through all this.' He pauses. 'What if I'm found guilty? What if I end up with a conviction, or I have to go to prison? I can't go to prison . . .' he finishes.

His face crumples and I move over and put my arm around him. Surely he wouldn't be found guilty for this? I feel my whole body shake with anger.

'I know it don't feel like it,' I say. 'But you're lucky you have money. That your parents can afford to get you a decent barrister, or whatever. Surely, though, there's *no way* anyone in their right mind would find you guilty for trying to defend yourself!'

Jackson hesitates. 'I hope not,' he says.

We fall silent, cos we both know that it wouldn't be impossible. Jackson might have money, but he's still Black. He'll still be painted as the criminal, and they'll still try and make out that he's violent and dangerous, like they've done with Shaq.

'It's just crazy,' Jackson says, 'how before, my future was in my parents' hands, how they were the ones deciding everything and now, it's like, it's in the hands of something and someone *way* bigger than that. Something that my mum and dad can't even control. A bunch of strangers get to decide the type of person that I am. They get to decide the rest of my life.'

I go quiet, cos I'm not sure what to say.

'When's the court date?' I ask finally.

He shrugs. 'I dunno. I'm on bail at the minute, I'm just

waiting for the hearing in a few weeks, so they can confirm the charges. But after that, I'm not sure how long it'll take. It could take weeks or months even, before there's an actual trial. They said they'd write to us once they have the dates and stuff. It's all still sinking in, if I'm honest ...'

'I'm not surprised,' I say.

Jackson turns to me and I suddenly realize just how close we're sitting. How close our faces are. I don't move away. I catch him glance down at my mouth again. I swallow hard and my heart starts to beat proper fast. 'I'm just really glad that you're all right,' I say.

Jackson smiles and his grin seems to cover his entire face. It's the first time he's smiled like that since I got here. 'I didn't think you cared,' he teases, and he pokes me in the ribs. I grab hold of his hand to stop him from poking me again and my fingers wrap around his. Our faces are centimetres apart now and Jackson's looking at me like he wants to kiss me. I want it too.

'Maybe I do,' I reply.

Jackson pauses for a minute, like he ain't quite sure what to say. Our lips are nearly touching and all I can feel is my heart beating hard and fast in my chest. Jackson moves a hand to touch the side of my face, then he leans in and kisses me. I feel these butterflies in my stomach again and my heart is going a million miles a minute, then I move my hands up to his chest and I kiss him right back.

33

MARC

I'm waiting outside school for Dry Eileen to come and pick me up. I might not trust her one hundred per cent yet, but she's actually not as bad as I first thought. I don't even complain about the old-people songs she plays in the car any more. She said that she's taking me somewhere after school today, though she won't tell me where. It's supposed to be a sort of surprise. Which is why I didn't go to see Jackson with Chantelle. I'd have much rather made sure that Jackson's all right and checked out his massive house, but Dry Eileen was so excited that I felt kinda bad. I get a message from Dry Eileen saying that she's gonna be a couple of minutes late cause of traffic and I lean against the metal fence. More like she's gonna be late cause of how slow she drives!

It's been proper boring without Chantelle in school this week, but I've actually started talking to a few people in class. Some of Shaq's mates walk past me and I clock Kade with them. I haven't really seen him around since that day in the canteen and I can't stop thinking about what Chantelle said, about him checking me out. Shaq's mates nod but when Kade sees me, he hangs back. I can't believe I never noticed him in school before, cause he's proper fit.

'Hey,' Kade says, and he leans against the fence next to me. 'It's Marc, innit?' he says.

'Yeah,' I reply. I suddenly feel shy and Kade gives me a grin. One of his friends shouts: 'Kade, man, you coming or what?'

'I'll catch up in a minute!' he shouts. 'I'll meet you at the bus stop – two secs!'

His friends head off and Kade turns back to me. He nudges me with his elbow.

'Yo, I heard you got pepper-sprayed,' he says. 'At the vigil – you okay? That shit hurts, man. They proper fucked up Fabio's arm, y'know. It got dislocated from its socket . . .' He shudders. 'Did you lot get cordoned in as well?' he says. 'Or did you manage to get away?'

'Nah,' I say. 'We managed to get away. Don't ask me how, I don't even remember. All I know, is that my eyes were proper stinging.' I pause. 'What about you?'

'*Me?*' Kade says, and he flashes me a smile. 'I'm the fastest in my year. Probably the whole school, to be honest, so when I tell you I was gone, I was *gone*! Had one of them police dogs chasing me as well, but I cut down all those back streets in the estate. Had to jump over some massive fence thing . . .'

I laugh. 'At least you got away!'

'Yeah!' Kade replies. He stares at me for a minute and I swear, he's *definitely* checking me out. It feels kinda good to be noticed, even though I've tried to be invisible for so long. Kade looks proper awkward for a minute, and then he goes: 'So, errrr, like, you seeing anyone and that? Or ...'

I almost choke. It takes me by surprise, but after Rhys, it's refreshing to be around someone who actually shows me that they're interested.

'Nah,' I say. 'I mean, no.'

Kade smiles. 'I'm glad,' he replies. He looks like he's gonna say something else, but then his friends start shouting him from the other end of the road.

'I better go,' Kade says. 'They're gonna cuss me even more if I don't hurry up. But ... I just wanted to check that you're all right?'

'I am,' I say. 'Thanks.'

'I'll see you around, yeah?' Kade replies.

'Yeah,' I say. 'See you around.' Kade smiles and heads off, and I almost have to pick my jaw up off the floor. Did that just happen? Kade flirting with me and coming to check that I was okay? I pull my phone out to message Chantelle, but then Dry Eileen pulls up. I'm glad she didn't come about two seconds ago, cause I know she'd have a million and one questions about who my friend was. I climb in the car.

'Hey,' I say.

'Hi,' Dry Eileen replies. 'How was school?'

I shrug. 'Same old, same old,' I respond. 'Are we getting

273

going or what?' I wanna add *cause it will take another five hours to get to wherever we're going at your snail's pace*, but I bite my tongue. I can tell that she's trying to make an effort and I don't wanna be rude or nothing.

Dry Eileen nods. 'I have a feeling you'll like it!' she says.

Dry Eileen parks up and I wanna ask her if she's taking the piss, cause out of *all* the places in the whole of Manchester – the Trafford Centre, Nando's, town, the cinema – I was not expecting this. I stare at her as I climb out the car.

'My surprise is ... Asda?' I say and I'm proud of the fact that I'm not cussing as hard as I would've done a few weeks ago. 'Why would I really like it in Asda?' I ask. 'D'you not know teenagers?'

Dry Eileen smiles. 'This is just where we're parking,' she says. 'Come on!' She gestures for me to follow her and we cut across the car park. I've been past this Asda a million times on the way into town and I know that there's literally nothing else around here. We come out the car park and turn onto a narrow street.

'Where are we going?' I say and I suddenly hope she ain't taking me to see one of her dusty friends.

'You'll see!' Dry Eileen says, and she grins. We reach the bottom of the street and then there's some sort of path that leads up towards some old, boarded up flats. They're proper high and made of grey concrete and they curve round into this big semicircle, only part of the flats have been demolished. They look weird, especially compared to all the other new buildings that are around. We cut through what would've been the courtyard in front of the flats and Dry Eileen says: 'You ever been here?'

'No!' I say. 'And I don't ever wanna come again. What is this place?'

Dry Eileen laughs. 'I noticed some of your sketches in the bin,' she says. 'Of the mural, of that boy who went to your school. What was his name?'

'Shaq,' I say

'Shaq,' she replies, and I don't ask why her nosy self was even looking in the bin.

'I've seen the mural on his estate,' she says. 'I went to go and look at it up close, but I had no idea that was you.' I'm kinda pissed that Dry Eileen knows that I'm the one behind the mural and probably all the other ones where my tag is too. I kinda like the fact that no one knows it's me. Besides, if I was gonna tell anyone, then Dry Eileen would be the last person on that list. I shove my hands in my pockets and I expect her to start giving me a lecture about criminal damage, or how I should be concentrating more on school work instead of graffiti-ing everywhere, but she says: 'You're so talented, Marc, that's why I thought you'd like it here!'

I stare at her. Some of my other carers had noticed me doodling and stuff, but no one has ever paid attention to what I was doing. If anything, I'd get told to stop being lazy and do my homework.

'Come again?' I say

'Seriously,' she replies. 'Look, let me show you ...' She

takes me along, beneath this concrete underpass and out near this other half-demolished block and that's when I realize. Everywhere, all the boarded-up flats at the bottom, the balconies and this old skateboard ramp, is covered in graffiti. I thought I'd seen everything in the Northern Quarter, but this is something else. I recognize a few of the tags, but there's loads that I don't. Everywhere I look, there's more murals and colours and words and I don't mean to say it out loud, but I hear myself go: 'Whoa!'

Even the balconies way up, I'm talking seven floors high, are covered in graffiti. There's hardly any grey concrete left on this side of the flats. It's just colour and colour and even more of it, reaching up towards the sky. I'm kinda speechless cause of how incredible it looks, but also cause none of my carers have ever done anything like this for me before.

I can't even stop myself, cause just being here makes me feel alive, and I go: 'That one there's kELzO, you can tell it's him without even looking at his tag, just by the way he does his Zs ... and that one up there, on that balcony, at the top, that's Aksi. He did Marcus Rashford's mural.'

Dry Eileen doesn't look bored, or like she's in any rush to go. She actually looks interested as I point out all the different murals and bits of graffiti. And I think, maybe, she ain't so dry after all. Maybe she's just Eileen.

34

JACKSON

It's been a few days since Chantelle was here, and we've messaged almost every night, or talked on the phone. My mum's letting me use hers, because the police still have mine and apparently I can't get it back until after the case. That makes me mad. Not that I've got anything to hide, but still. And not only that, but the pictures of that Oliver guy have been posted online too. He put it on Instagram and named me too, even though I'm sure that with the case and everything, he shouldn't be doing that. He goes to one of the other private schools in my area and I'd only seen it because Harrison sent it to me. His face had been hurt proper bad from where I'd cut him with the glass and it said that he'd needed a skin graft.

Seeing the photo made me feel sick and guilty all over again.

Harrison sent it to me on Snap and asked if it was true. I didn't respond. When I phoned him and told him I'd been arrested, there was just this silence that stretched out between us. He didn't ask if I was okay. He just asked what I'd done. And when I'd told him, he'd said maybe I'd gone too far. Then it felt weird and I hung up. I guess after all this time, after how long we'd been friends, I sort of expected Harrison to understand. To know that I'd never do anything like that on purpose. It's probably all around school by now too, especially as my mum had to call the head teacher and let him know why she'd kept me off yesterday.

I'm standing in the hallway, waiting for my mum to drive me to school and I feel sick. I really don't want to go. I don't want everyone looking at me, or asking me what happened. A few guys in my year have joked about having the police come up to them when they've been in the park drinking before, but this isn't some police officer telling me I shouldn't be underage drinking. It's my whole life. *My whole future.* Getting arrested, sitting in the dark in the back of that van, then on that hard bed in that tiny police cell, is something I'll never forget.

I try to take some deep breaths. My heart is beating proper quickly in my chest. Ever since that day, I've not been able to leave the house. Even to go to the shops, or the end of my road. When I've tried to push myself, it all gets too much. It's like the weight of everything comes crashing down on me, and I can't even open the door. It's not even the fact that *they* could be out there. And a few of Oliver's mates had said that I'd picked the wrong person to mess with, and told me they were going to make sure that I needed a skin graft too. It's *everything*. It's like the world never scared me before and now it terrifies me.

At least when I'm at home, I can try to shut it all out.

My mum comes into the hallway, pulling her coat on. 'You ready, Jax?' she asks.

I nod. Even though the last thing I want right now is to be around crowds of people. I pull on the sleeves of my blazer. It's a bit too short, but it's the only spare one I had at home. I swallow, hard. It's like nothing really belongs to me any more. Not the clothes they took off me, or my shoes. Not even my future. It's like everything I have – or *am* – can just be taken from me.

My mum brushes some fluff off my shoulder. 'I suppose this is what happens when you get your dad's height and don't stop growing . . .' She reaches a hand up and rests it on the side of my face.

'Yeah,' I say. 'I guess so.' I try to smile, but my voice is quiet and I hardly recognize it. I just feel so worthless and insignificant. And the only time I can forget about all this, even for a little bit, is when I'm talking to Chantelle and Marc. Especially Chantelle. My mum pulls me in for a hug.

My eye's not as bad as it was and my cuts are starting to heal, but they're still there. *They're still a reminder of what happened.* Along with the flashbacks I get when I close my eyes. I hold onto my mum and I don't want to let go, but she straightens herself up, and grabs her keys from beside the door.

'Come on,' she says, and I follow her out.

I get into the car, and then it's like everything happens on autopilot. My mum starts the engine and I feel the car move. I know that she's talking because I see her mouth moving, I can see that she's nodding at me and giving me an encouraging smile, but the words don't really connect. Nothing sinks in. All I keep thinking is how much I don't want to get out the car. How I don't want to face it all. My hands start to shake again as my mum pulls into the school car park and I feel this knot in the pit of my stomach. I want to ask her to turn the car around. To drive me home.

'You okay?' she asks. I try to push everything aside and I nod.

'I'll be here to pick you up at three forty-five, and then we'll go and meet the barrister, okay? Your dad's going to meet us there.' She pauses. 'She's a really good one, Jackson. And we're going to do everything in our power to fight this. I've spoken to Louise and she's already said she'll give you a character reference for the trial, as well.'

I nod. 'Okay,' I say. 'Thanks.'

Louise is a magistrate Mum knows, and as soon as all this happened, Mum said that it couldn't hurt to have a reference from her. My mum moves in and she kisses me on the forehead, again. I swallow hard and grab hold of my school bag. I can feel my heart pounding in my ears, but I don't wanna tell her that I'm too scared to get out the car. Not when she's already cut her hours back at work, so that she can drive me to school and pick me up every day. So that she can come to all these meetings with the solicitor that we're gonna have.

'Love you!' she says.

'Love you too,' I reply, as I unbuckle my seat belt and get out of the car.

My whole body shakes as I walk through the car park and up to the main school building. First period's already started, but Mum arranged with the head teacher for me to go in later, so that I could avoid the crowds. I've got chemistry first. I make my way down the empty corridor and I try to focus on my breathing, I try to tell myself that I'm all right. That I'm as safe here as I am at home, but it doesn't seem to help.

All I feel is this deep dread. Like my whole world is breaking apart around me, and there's nothing anyone – not me, or my mum, or my dad, or even the best barrister out there – can do about it. I push open the door and I walk into the classroom. I feel the room go quiet. I feel them all looking as I make my way to my seat.

My chemistry teacher glances at me but he doesn't say anything, just carries on with the lesson, and that somehow makes everything worse. Normally, when I'd walk into class, people would shout or cheer. Or Harrison would call me over. Today, there's none of that. I go over to my usual table where Harrison and the rest of my mates are, but he doesn't give me a massive grin, or try to talk to me. He just averts his eyes, the same way that everyone else is doing.

I wonder if they all think the same as the police. That I'm guilty. I pull my chemistry book out my bag and I feel eyes on me from across the other side of the room. I see Aimee whisper something to her friend. I turn away, because it all feels so much. I just wish that I never came back. That I'd stayed off school and just came in to sit my exams. Or even better, that I could just disappear . . .

My teacher carries on, droning on about the exams, and how we all need to make sure we're prepared. And Harrison doesn't even ask if I'm all right. He doesn't even look in my direction. I move over. I'm so angry and hurt. Harrison is supposed to be my best friend but he's looking at me like he doesn't even know me. I feel the anger rising up inside me.

'Why you being like this?' I say. 'Harry?'

Harrison finally looks at me and shakes his head. 'Don't you dare fucking talk to me after what you've done,' he says. And he turns away.

The bell for second period goes and I grab my stuff. I couldn't concentrate the whole lesson. *Don't you dare fucking talk to me after what you've done.* What *I've* done.

Everyone starts to filter out of the classroom but Harrison doesn't wait for me, he just heads out into the corridor with a few of our other mates. I see people staring and whispering and I shove my way through the crowds.

'Yo, Harrison,' I shout '*Harrison!*'

He doesn't turn around. I run to catch up with him and my head is racing. Out of everyone, I thought he'd at least be the first person to check if I was okay. And I know that he was funny with me and said all that stuff on the phone, but he's supposed to be my mate. Harrison's the person I've known the longest.

We've been friends since primary school! I grab hold of him, then he stops and pull his arm away. He turns to face me and the way he looks at me makes my stomach sink. Like I'm some sort of criminal.

My throat tightens and I feel myself struggling to get the words out, but I try anyway. 'Yo, Harrison,' I say and I'm not even hurt any more, I'm just angry. 'What was all that about? What do you mean, what *I've* done?'

Harrison stares at me and shakes his head again and I feel everyone else looking at me too. By the way they're whispering and moving away, I can tell that they all think I'm in the wrong. That they all think what I did was bad.

'Look, Jackson,' Harrison says. 'I ain't gonna make a big thing of this, but how can you just walk in here? Like you aren't even bothered? Have you not seen what you've done to that guy?' He looks away. 'I thought I knew you, but how could you do that? How could you go that far?'

I stare at him. A week ago, Harrison's words would've crushed me. The sad thing is, they don't even come as that much of a surprise any more.

'How can you even say that?' I shout, and I don't even care that people are staring now, I'm just so mad. 'You're supposed to be my mate!' I continue. 'Do you have any fucking idea what it's like, to have a gang of people attack you? Do you even know how scared I was?' I shake my head. 'What would you have done in my situation?' I say. 'Go on, tell me ... *tell me*!'

Harrison stares at me. 'You've changed, man,' he says. 'Ever since you met those other friends, since the stabbing – I don't fucking know you any more. I don't know what you're … capable of.'

My eyes start to sting. Out of everything he's ever said, that hurts the most. Harrison will never get it. He'll never understand, because he'll never have to fear for his life the way I do, just because of the colour of my skin. I feel the shame and guilt creeping up inside me again. It's that same guilt and shame I felt when I was arrested. That same shame I feel every time I get stopped by the police, or someone crosses the road to avoid me.

'Just stay away from me, Jackson, all right?' he says finally, and then he's gone. The bell for the start of second period goes and people trickle off. I'm left alone in the corridor.

I sit down on one of the benches and I put my head in my hands. Because if my own friend thinks that, what chance do I have when I'm up in court?

My mum's waiting in the spot she said she'd be. I don't tell her what happened with Harrison, because I don't want to give her *another* thing to worry about. If I just keep my head down, then I'll be able to get through the last few months of school. I can't stop thinking about what Harrison said, though. How I've changed since I've met Chantelle and Marc. How I've changed since Shaq's stabbing. The truth is, I have. I can feel it. I've grown up. I was sheltered before, but now I know what the world's really like.

My mum hands me something out the glove compartment when I get in the car.

'Here,' she says. 'I found my old work phone. You can use this one till you get yours back, that way you don't have to waste *my* minutes on whoever this mystery girl you've been calling up at night is.'

I suddenly feel proper embarrassed. How do mums know *everything*? Like, how did she even know it was girl I'd been speaking to?

'I never said I was talking to a girl,' I say, as I take the phone from her.

My mum gives me a look then she turns out of the school car park.

'Oh, please,' she says. 'You really think I was born this big? You barely spoke to anyone on the phone before, then last night it's for hours on end, and you're grinning from ear to ear.' She pauses. 'It's the first time I've seen a smile on your face since . . .'

I swallow. There used to be so many things that made me smile. So many stupid things that made me laugh. Now, all I feel is lost and confused. Me and Chantelle is the only thing that makes any sense. It's not like we're even boyfriend or girlfriend, or anything. But I want to be. It feels too soon for me to start asking her all that, though. I see my mum sneaking glances and smirking at me and I shake my head. I've never really spoken to her about girls I like and I ain't about to start now.

'What?' I say.

'Nothing,' my mum replies. 'It's just, you know, me and your dad were the age you are now when we first met. To be honest, I never would've even looked twice at him.'

She smiles. 'He used to have this *really* bad ... I'm talking *awful*—'

I groan. I've heard this story a million times. About how my dad had this off-key jerry curl perm back in the day and my mum very nearly didn't go out with him, but then Dad was super-funny and she was willing to overlook the perm and *blah-blah-blah*.

'Mum,' I say. 'Allow it, please. D'you know how many times I've heard this story?'

'*Okay,*' she says. 'I'm just saying ... she could be the one, that's all. Most people thought that me and your dad wouldn't last, that we'd break up after college or whatever. But here we are. Just don't be making me no one's grandma yet,' she says and she side-eyes me. 'I'm too young and I like my freedom and you have sixth form and university to go to ...'

I slide down in my chair. 'Can you just drop it?' I say and I move my hand to my face. I don't want her to start giving me one of those You Need to Make Sure You're Being Careful talks, when I'm stuck in a car with her, and when me and Chantelle haven't even done anything like that yet. When I haven't even done anything like that, with *anyone*. I want to tell my mum that I might not even get to college or uni. It depends what happens with court and how serious the charges end up being.

'Okay,' my mum says. 'Consider it dropped.' And she does a mic drop action with her hand.

'*Wow*!' I say, and I shake my head. I definitely get all the cringey embarrassing stuff from my mum. It's nice to see her smiling, though, and I can tell that she's pleased to have something normal to talk about. Something that isn't to do with the police, or solicitors, or my case, or getting some kind of character reference together.

But when we reach one of the car parks in the city centre, Mum's not smiling any more. We get out and make our way down the millions of concrete steps and along the street to the solicitor's office. It's in the part of town that's a short walk away from the courts, with all of these big glass buildings and offices with stone pillars outside.

I don't have time to wonder which one it's going to be, because my dad is already there, waiting outside. I stop as we reach a set of double doors.

'Come on, love,' my mum says, and then we go in.

35

JACKSON

We sit in this fancy reception area while we wait for the solicitor to come through. I'm not sure how much this is costing my mum and dad, but judging by the inside it's not going to be cheap. A woman with dark hair who looks about the same age as my mum comes over to us. She's holding a stack of files in her arms and she gives me a warm smile.

'Mr and Mrs Campbell,' she says, and she holds out a hand. 'I'm Sian, hi.' My mum and dad shake her hand then she turns to me. 'Hello,' she says. 'You must be Jackson.'

'Hi,' I reply. I shake her hand and she gives me a little nod, then she ushers us into one of the meeting rooms. There's a large wooden table in the middle of it. Sian gestures for us to sit down. I take a seat in the middle and my mum and dad are on either side of me. My mum must be able to tell that I'm nervous because she reaches over and takes hold of my hand. I wouldn't normally be caught dead holding my mum's hand, especially not in public, but it feels comforting today. To know that whatever happens, my mum and my dad will be with me every step of the way.

'Can I get you a drink?' Sian asks. 'Tea? Coffee? Water?

'No, thanks,' I hear my mum and dad say, and I shake my head.

Sian nods and opens her files. 'Okay, I guess we'll get started, then,' she continues. 'I've got the police interview transcripts here, Jackson,' she says. 'And I do have some photos of the injuries that the young man who is pressing charges sustained. What I'm going to have to get you to do, though, I'm afraid, is go through everything again. We'll read through the transcript and make sure that nothing was missed out, that there's nothing you were coerced or misled into saying.' She pauses. 'Your initial hearing is in a few weeks, so what that means is that they'll just confirm the charges and let you know the dates of the trial. Okay?'

'Okay,' I say, but it feels weird that Sian is saying all this stuff to me. I'm still just a kid. *Sixteen.* I should be worrying about my exams, or what's happening with me and Chantelle, or Harrison beating me on some PlayStation game. My head is spinning from it all, and out of the corner of my eye, I see my dad writing some notes in his pad. My mum doesn't let go of my hand, she just holds it tighter. I'm glad.

Sian pauses. 'Jackson,' she says, and she looks me right in the eye. 'I want you to know that I'm going to do everything in my power to make sure you're found not guilty. I've handled *a lot* of self-defence cases, but I do need to need to make sure you're aware of the risks ...'

I feel my mum stiffen. 'What risks?' she says and her voice goes up at the end.

Sian smiles, and I can tell that she's trying to be as positive as she can. 'Self-defence,' she continues, 'is still such a grey area of the law. There are so many different factors that are taken into account when we're dealing with something like this. Such as the situation, and how high or imminent the threat of danger was—'

'Jackson was attacked,' my mum says defensively. 'By at least four boys, that's a pretty imminent threat.'

'I know, I *know*!' Sian says. 'And I'm not saying that he's in the wrong ... in fact, I don't know what else Jackson could've done. But the law around self-defence is quite tricky, like I said. You're allowed to defend yourself with "reasonable force". So we have to prove that Jackson was defending himself, reasonably.'

My mum shakes her head and I see my dad clench his jaw.

'But what's reasonable?' my dad says. 'When your life is in danger? When it's just you against a whole bunch of people ... When you're scared, you don't think about any of that. The only thing you're thinking is how to do whatever it is you can to get away—'

'I know!' Sian says. 'And I agree with you. But I wouldn't be doing my job if I didn't tell you the risks. There is a chance that even though Jackson was attacked, and it was five of those boys against him, because of the injuries that Oliver sustained, he could still be found guilty.'

I feel myself stiffen and my mum sucks in a sharp breath. I've been worrying about this for days, but hearing Sian say it makes me feel like I might not even have a chance. I can see the anger building on my dad's face. Not because of Sian, but because of all this. Even with a solicitor as good as Sian, I could still be found guilty. Even after trying to run away, and telling the truth, I could still end up being punished, just for defending myself. I hear my dad going on about how unjust this all is and Sian nods along with him, but I know that no amount of arguing is going to change the law.

'What happens if I'm found guilty?' I blurt out.

The room goes quiet for a minute and my mum and dad share a look.

I hear my mum say: 'Baby, that's not gonna happen. Sian was just telling us about the risks.'

But how can she be sure? How can she know for certain that I'll get let off?

'I need to know,' I say.

Sian nods. 'Well, you've got no other offences,' she says. 'So the lighter end of the scale would be a fine, community service and a conviction. And the harsher end could be a custodial sentence.'

Sian's words hang in the air and I feel my mum's hand go limp. But I needed to know. At least now I'm prepared. I know my mum and dad are only trying to protect me but it's better that I know the truth. I take a shaky breath. Out of the corner of my eye, I see my dad put his head in his hands. He looks like he's tired from carrying the weight of it all and hearing Sian tell him that I could get a prison sentence out loud has finally broken him. I sit there as it all sinks in. That, maybe, for the rest of a life, I'll have to tick the box that says: *Do you have any previous convictions? Please declare here.* And someone will see that and think I'm a criminal. They'll judge me but they'll only see part of the story. The fear creeps up inside me, but I try not to let my mum and dad see just how scared I am.

I just nod. 'All right,' I say.

36

CHANTELLE

I stare down at the news article on my phone. I'm waiting for Gran to hurry up so that we can go into school for my meeting with Ms Edwards, Mrs Cohen *and* Mr Povey. I've had so many of these meetings that I already know what to expect. There's the whole speech about how disappointed they are in my behaviour, then they ask me how I think we can move forward. Like, I don't fucking know. I usually just say something about trying harder so that I can get out of there and back into my lessons. But there's *no way* I'm saying that today. Not when it's Ms Edwards in the wrong and the only way we could 'move forward' would be if she pissed off out of that school for good.

I glance back down at Damar's Snap. He's sent me two links

to news reports of what happened at Shaq's vigil. Damar's video has gone viral, but it weren't the only one. Kade and Parveen and some of Shaq's other mates posted videos online of the police officers holding down Shaq's brother and twisting up his arm. And someone else managed to get a video of one of the police dogs attacking a kid. He only looked about ten. And loads of people were talking about how Marc had been pepper-sprayed. But none of the stories said anything about the police turning up to Shaq's vigil for no reason. That they'd interrupted a community grieving. They didn't say anything about the way they'd pushed Shaq's brother to the ground, how they'd kettled everyone in on the estate *for no reason.* And Damar told me that when they'd finally let Shaq's brother go, after keeping him at the station all night, they'd twisted up his arm so badly they'd dislocated his shoulder. And even though he kept telling them that he was in pain, they made him wait and they didn't send anyone to go and look at him, or give him painkillers, or anything like that. They just kept in that cell for hours and then, at like, some stupid time in the morning, they just let him go.

But the headlines, on the newspaper articles say:

Moss Side Madness: Police step in to control violent crowd!

And:

Gang violence breaks out at stabbed teen's vigil!

They include the same photo of Shaq. The one where he ain't smiling. Where he looks way older than fourteen and has that bruise underneath his eye. And they both go on to say the same thing, how Shaq was in a gang, how the crowd needed controlling. How Moss Side has always been known for being 'violent'. For being where some of the most notorious gangs come from. I didn't think it was even possible, but the way they talk about Shaq is worse than the other articles. Cos it's like they're somehow blaming him for triggering all of this. I feel sick. I think of Shaq's mum and his brother and the mural. And all the people who were out on the estate to celebrate him.

Part of me wants to scream. I send them to Marc and Jackson in the group chat and I'm just about to message Damar back, when Gran comes into the living room. I check the time: *11.40 a.m.* Me and Marc said we'd go round to Jackson's after school. Gran grabs her coat and her bag off the side, and I know that she's stressed, cos she's already chain-smoked three cigarettes.

'You ready?' she asks and I pull myself up from the settee.

'Whatever you do,' I tell her, '*please* don't start cussing Ms Edwards like last time. I swear, I thought I was gonna have to break up a fight.'

And I ain't even lying when I say that. The last time we went to one of these meetings, Gran started off talking in her posh phone voice, then as soon Ms Edwards was getting all uppity, Gran went *in*. And I am talking full-on putting her in her place. Not gonna lie, though, I can't say that it wasn't good to see.

Gran looks at me sternly. 'Oh, don't exaggerate,' she says, and then, 'But I will if she comes with that stinking attitude again ... I can't keep taking time off work, though, Chantelle.'

'I know!' I say, and I feel bad, cos I didn't want Gran to have to take any more time off, either. We've already had to sit through one meeting about me supposedly cheating, so I don't know why they make you do this 'phase you back in' one, after you've been suspended. As if I need 'phasing back' into a school I've been at for five years.

We head towards the door and I just hope that this meeting is as painless and quick as possible.

We sit in the reception area and I send Jackson a message. I haven't said anything to Marc about me and Jackson. I've just tried to be normal in the group chat. I don't wanna make things awkward between the three of us. Not that I think Marc would mind, but I dunno, no one wants to feel like a third wheel, do they? And it might just be nothing. I mean, I know we've kissed, but it might be nothing more than that. Jackson might regret it and, like, whatever it is between us might just end. I can't help it, but I think about Jackson all the time. How much I like him, even when he's going on about all that boring *Star Wars* stuff. How much he makes me laugh, what's going to happen when we both start college, if he'll ask me to be his girlfriend ...

I slide down further in my seat and I can tell that Gran is getting proper impatient, then I see Mrs Cohen come through into the reception area. We follow her into one of the stuffy meeting rooms and Ms Edwards and Mr Povey are already in there. We sit down and Ms Edwards says, 'Hello,' to my gran, but she barely looks at me. I don't say anything, I just keep my mouth shut.

They start going on about the school policy and me jeopardizing my own future so close to my GCSEs, *blah-blah-blah*. I zone back in again when I hear someone say my name.

'Chantelle,' Mr Povey starts and I turn to look at him. 'Now, I know we had a meeting about this last week and we are still looking into this. I like to see all phase back meetings as a chance for fresh start, a clean slate. So, I'm just going to take this opportunity to ask one last time if there's anything you'd like to own up to.'

I stare at him. I still can't believe this. I *still* can't believe they don't think I wrote it, even when they obviously haven't found any proof. I look at Gran and I can see that she's trying her hardest to stay calm.

'No,' I say, and I wanna tell him that the only thing I've reflected on is just how shit this school and most of the teachers are, but I have a feeling that won't go down too well.

'You obviously ain't found any proof,' I say. 'I'm not gonna say I cheated when I clearly didn't.' I know that it's just a practice essay or whatever, and that I'll be gone in three months, but I want to clear my name. Besides, I don't wanna give them any excuse to put this on my reference. 'Set me another essay, then,' I continue. 'And you'll see that I did it myself!'

I can tell that no one except my gran and Mrs Cohen believes me, and I see Ms Edwards suck in her cheeks. And then it really does take every ounce of self-control not to go off about how she's always picking on me. I suck in a deep breath.

'Okay,' Mr Povey says. 'Well, that's definitely an option. As I said, we're still looking into this, but we don't want you to miss out on any more school. Especially not when you have your revision classes coming up, and all of your exams.' He pauses. 'I've had a long think about all of this, and because of this *incident*, along with disrupting your peers in a practice exam, and the rest of your behaviour points ... we've decided that, unfortunately, we won't be allowing you to go to the end of year prom.'

I glance at Mrs Cohen and I can see that she's pissed. That she's obviously not happy with their decision. I'm not bothered about going to their dry prom. I hate this school and I didn't plan on going, anyway. It's the principle, though. The fact that they've taken it away from me, and I don't even get a say. I feel more angry than anything.

'What?' Gran says. 'You can't do that! You can't punish Chantelle for something she hasn't done!' She turns to Ms Edwards. 'You've been on my Chantelle's back since day one,' she scoffs. 'What proof do you have that she's cheated?'

I can hear Mr Povey trying to calm Gran down and Ms Edwards saying that she'd compared it to my previous work, not just the essays that I've done this year, but the ones I submitted in Year Nine and Ten, as well – 'the language was too sophisticated,' 'the points were too advanced'. I wish that I could advance Ms Edwards out of this flipping meeting room. I hate that I'm being punished for something I didn't do and even though it's on a much smaller scale, it makes me think of Jackson. I stand up and I just wanna get out of this stuffy room.

'Gran it's all right,' I say. Then I turn to Ms Edwards and Mr Povey. 'I never wanted to go to your shit fucking prom, anyway!' I snap, and I slam out.

'Nah, they did what?' Marc says, when I fill him and Jackson in. We're both round Jackson's, cos even though he's been trying not to let us know just how much of a problem it is, I know that apart from going to school and to the solicitor's, he still ain't really left the house. I tried to get him to come and meet me at the milkshake place in town, but he said he didn't want to go anywhere on his own. And I weren't about to force him either. Marc's sprawled out between us on Jackson's bed and it's the first time we've all been together since me and Jackson kissed. I keep catching Jackson sneaking glances at me, but Marc doesn't seem to notice.

I shrug. 'Yeah,' I say. 'They told me that cos of my behaviour and everything else I'm not allowed to go.'

'Well, I ain't going either, then!' he says. 'You think I'm going prom when they won't let you go? I'm taking a stand ... I'm boycotting that shit!'

'Thanks,' I say, and then I reach over and grab some strawberry laces from the opened packet that's resting beside his head. 'But, like, who would you have gone with, anyway? You literally don't talk to anyone in school.'

Marc reaches over and grabs one of the laces, too. 'Erm, I

have other friends,' he says. 'You've been suspended for three days, you know! A lot can change ...'

Marc wraps one of the laces around his hand, then lowers it into his mouth.

I raise my eyebrows. 'Really?' I say, but I'm pleased.

'Yeah,' he replies, taking another bite. 'I actually do! I've been talking to Parveen and Kade ... actually made some friends in my other classes too.' He points one of the laces in my direction.

'I'm glad to hear it,' I say, with a grin.

'I'm still boycotting it, though,' Marc says. 'No one treats my bestie like that. That's my sacrifice for you!'

'Awww,' I say, and I reach over and put my arm around him. 'I appreciate you too!' I reply, but Marc screws up his face and pushes me away.

'I'm *trying* to eat!' he says, though he's smiling. 'Go and bother Jackson!' I know that Marc doesn't mean it in that way, but me and Jackson glance at each other, then quickly look away. And I realize that Jackson's barely said a word since we got here. Even when I told him what happened with Ms Edwards, I know he was listening cos he was nodding along, but he barely responded. Marc must notice it at the same time I do. He pulls himself up and moves over to Jackson.

Marc nudges him gently. 'Yo, Jax,' he says, and he holds the packet of laces towards him. 'You all right?' Jackson doesn't take any of the sweets off Marc, he just puts his head in his hands and shrugs, like that's all he can do. He shakes his head slowly, but he doesn't look at me or Marc.

'Nah,' he says. 'I just . . . I *hate* it!' he blurts out. 'Not knowing what's gonna happen . . . I wish I knew whether I'm gonna be found guilty or not. So I could at least prepare for the worst, y'know? So that if I am gonna be sent to prison or whatever, I can at least try to get my head around it. I just feel like my whole world's spinning out of control. Like, everything's moving a million miles a minute, then on top of that . . .' He pauses. 'D'you know how hard things are at school? No one even talks to me. Whenever I walk into class, it goes quiet. People either move away from me . . . or they say stuff. I just want it all to be over!' he finishes.

My stomach sinks. Me and Marc made a pact before we came over not to talk about it, cos of how upset Jackson's been. I was hoping that we could take his mind off all this court stuff, even if it was only for a little bit. I look at Marc and he shuffles in closer and puts an arm around Jackson.

'I know,' Marc says. 'Like, I can't even imagine what all this has been like for you, how hard it all is . . . but whatever happens, me and Chan will be here for you. *No matter what!*' Marc pauses. 'Those people who've been saying stuff, who can't see you ain't done anything wrong. They were never really your mates in the first place. Real mates don't do that.'

Jackson looks sad, but he nods. 'Yeah,' he says. 'I've been trying to tell myself that too. It's just Harrison, my other friend, I've known him for most my life . . . I can't believe he thinks I'd do something like this deliberately. But I guess it's not always about how long you've known someone, it's about how they treat you.'

I'd never really thought about it like that before, but Jackson's right. It is about how people treat you. And with Jackson and Marc, it feels like I've found the only two people in the world who actually get me. Who I don't have to pretend with and who actually seem to like me for who I am. And finding friends like that, I dunno. It feels special.

'That's true!' Marc says. 'Although you make me feel dumb, man. Especially when you start talking about how this bit of science is linked to that bit in *Star Wars*, or whatever ...'

Marc shudders and I see a smile spread across Jackson's face. Jackson reaches out and grabs one of the laces out of the packet Marc's holding, and even though Jackson still looks sad, he looks miles better than he did when we first got here.

'Wow,' Jackson says and he chews on the end of one of the laces. 'You actually got it right this time!'

Marc pulls a face. 'Listen,' he says. 'I told Eileen that you're *always* banging on about them films and she made me sit and watch one ... and was it as bad as I thought? No. Do I regret wasting two hours of my life? Yeah. I don't even know what happened, some bald alien died—'

Jackson opens his mouth and I already know that he's about to start explaining the ins and outs of *every* film.

'Don't get him started!' I say, then Jackson closes his mouth.

'Whatever,' he says. 'You two just don't—'

'*Know a true classic when you see one!*' me and Marc say at the same time. Jackson shakes his head, but he's smiling at least, and I reach over and grab another one of the laces.

'That's a classic I'm okay with not knowing about!' I say. I chew on the end of one of the laces and Jackson goes quiet.

'Hey,' he says. 'There's no way I'm gonna be going to my prom either. That's the last thing I wanna do, especially after ... so, what if we did something together? Like, I dunno, our own version of something, or just hung out?' He pauses. 'Depending on what happens, it might be the last time we all get to hang out properly.'

The words sit heavy between us. Me and Marc both know what Jackson really means. That if he's found guilty and ends up with a harsher sentence, then he could be sent to prison. And then, that really will be the last time we all get to hang out. Prison would be tough enough on anyone, but there's *no way* that Jackson, with his big house, his sheltered life and all his money, would be built for it.

I try not to look too upset, cos I don't wanna worry Jackson and I move my hair over my shoulder. 'I think that's a great idea!' I say. 'But even if ... like, whatever happens. If it's the worst-case scenario, Marc's right. We'll be there and we'll come and see you, and, yeah ...' I trail off cos I don't know what else to say. But I wanna tell Jackson how much I like him. How I don't just want it to be a one-off kiss that happened between us. How I want us to be properly together, but I can't say all of that now. Not in front of Marc, anyway. And would it even be fair to Jax, if he's got all this other stuff to worry about?

I swallow, hard. 'I really don't think it'll come to that,' I say, and I want it *so* badly to be true, with every ounce of my being. 'Like, ain't that why the law's in place? When you're up in court and they hear what happened, there's no way ...'

'I hope so,' Jackson says.

'And if you want us to be there, when you're in court,' Marc says. 'We'll come, innit, Chantelle?'

I nod. 'Yeah,' I say. 'Like, we'll be there every day, if you want us to.'

Jackson smiles and he looks so torn. Like it's the happiest he's ever been and the saddest.

'Thanks,' he says. 'And I mean it, but I think it's something I need to do on my own . . . and my mum and dad will be there.'

Me and Marc nod and Jackson rubs underneath his eye.

'I've never had friends like you guys before,' he says finally.

'Same!' Marc says.

I don't say anything, cos even though it feels good that Jackson's said that, part of me feels disappointed. I don't *just* wanna be friends. I force a smile and Marc wraps his arm around Jackson again.

'Awwww, bring it in!' he says. 'Give me some love!'

Marc and Jackson hug, then Marc stretches out a hand and grabs the edge of my sleeve. 'Chantelle,' he says. 'We're having a moment, you better get yourself over here!'

I glance at Jackson and I suddenly feel shy and awkward, but Marc grabs my arm and yanks me towards them, so I give in.

'We can't have a group hug without the whole group!' he says.

'All *right*!' I snap and I wrap my arms around them both. I feel a bit embarrassed as my arm touches Jackson's. Then Jackson gives me a smile and it feels good to hold onto him and Marc. I think of Shaq. How he brought us together and how I'll probably never forget that day, *ever,* cos of how awful it was. Yet somehow, it brought me, Jackson and Marc together. The two people I can't imagine not knowing. And I don't understand it, really. The world and life, and how one minute, it makes you feel so frightened and angry and scared. Then the next it's filled with moments like this. Moments where you're around people who make you feel loved, and happy and alive.

37

MARC

I left Jackson's a bit earlier than Chantelle cause I've got a meeting with my social worker at Eileen's. I didn't wanna say anything about it, cause I could tell that Jackson was proper upset about the trial and all that stuff. Everything with Eileen had been good, especially since she took me to see those flats in Hulme. After that day, it was like something shifted between us. She'd ask me about different graffiti artists and she even bought me some new spray paints, cause a few of my cans had run out. She even sat and went through college applications with me, and helped me out with my personal statement too. I've started spending less time in my room and doing the things she actually asked if I wanted to do when I first got there. Like watching telly with her downstairs, and yesterday we went out for pizza. And I didn't just do it cause I felt like I had to. I was actually starting to enjoy spending time with her and stuff.

But when I found out that I had this meeting with Emma, it made my heart sink cause I know this means I'm being moved again. Maybe it's my own fault for letting my guard down a bit. I suppose I should've known that it was only a matter of time. I just hope that wherever they send me to next ain't too far away, so that I'll at least still get to see Jackson and Chantelle.

I turn my key in the door and I can already hear voices coming from the living room. I hear laughing and talking. I push open the living-room door and Emma and Eileen go quiet. Emma's holding a cup of coffee and she's got a few files on the settee next to her. The scene looks exactly the same as it usually does, only instead of some other random carer sitting there, this time it's Eileen. I suddenly feel proper angry and hurt and just ... let down cause it's come out of nowhere and completely taken me by surprise. All the times Eileen told me that she wanted to make this work, that she wanted us to have some sort of relationship or whatever, and for me to see this as my home – it was clearly just a lie. And what about her asking me what I wanted to do after school and stuff like that? I guess that even though I knew she would probably end up letting me down, a small part of me wanted to believe that she wouldn't.

Emma smiles at me. 'Hi, Marc,' she says. 'You ready for a chat?'

I shrug. 'Suppose so,' I say, and I make my way over to one of the other chairs beside the settee. Eileen stands up but she doesn't even look at me and I wonder if it's cause she feels guilty. Carers normally can't look you in the eye once they've handed their notice in.

'I'll make myself scarce,' Eileen says, but I don't reply. I've been off with her all day. Just so I can distance myself. Eileen heads out of the living room and closes the door and I sit myself down. I shove my hands into my jacket pockets. I don't bother to take it off. There's no point. I normally just leg it out and walk around for hours when I'm told I'm going, anyway. As if I'd want to stick around somewhere, after I've just been told that they don't want me. I dunno where I'll go. Maybe to Chantelle's . . .

'So,' Emma says, and she pulls a notebook out. 'I hear you've actually been going into school every day and you're on time, as well?'

'Yeah,' I say, and I lean back in the chair.

'That's *so* good, Marc!' she says. 'It's amazing! I'm so pleased to hear that you've been trying. And you've been looking into college applications too, Eileen said?'

'Yeah,' I say. 'I've been looking into doing art and design.'

Emma nods. Eileen even helped me out with the application, cause there was some stuff I didn't get. Now, though, I just wonder if that was another thing she did to try and make herself feel better about chucking me out. I wait for Emma to hurry up with the small talk, so she can just get to the real reason she's here.

'How are you getting on?' she asks. 'Eileen said that you've been settling in fine. Have there been any issues, or anything like that? Is there anything I should know about?'

308

I pause. 'Nah,' I say. 'Not really. I've been getting on all right.'

Emma starts going through the usual questions, if I've been sticking to my curfew, how Eileen's been, and all of that. She asks me about school and the new friends I've made, and the whole time, I just wait for it to come. I wait for her to stop taking notes and press the lock screen on her iPad. I wait for her to look at me and ask how I *honestly* think it's going. And I wait for her to tell me that I'm being moved. That my carer's given her notice and I'll be going to some other placement with someone else, wherever, in Manchester. And that I 'really need to try this time', but she doesn't.

She slips her iPad and the files by her side into her bag and she stands up. I stare at her, cos I don't get what's happening. I don't understand why she's doing it this way, instead of telling me like she usually does. Unless she's just gonna drop it as she's just about to head out the door.

'Wait!' I say, as Emma walks towards the kitchen to find Eileen. 'Is that it? I say. 'What about the rest? You ain't even told me where I'm going . . . You can't just come here and not say shit, not even let me know where I'm being moved to . . . or was you just gonna tell me on the day? When I'm in the car with ya?'

It wouldn't be the first time that's happened. Not with Emma, though, with some other social worker I had before her, or it might have been the one before that. I don't even remember her name. I hate how adults lie to you. How they never tell you the truth and treat you like you're stupid . . . Like you can't see through whatever it is they're doing, to try and pretend that everything's okay.

I just wanna get out of here now. Maybe if I pack a bag, I can just go and stay with Chantelle? Instead of being moved to someplace else. I don't think she'd mind and it just means that I wouldn't have to go through *all this* again. I dunno why I thought this time would be different.

'I might as well go now!' I snap. 'Seeing as you ain't telling me nothing!' Eileen must hear me kicking off, cos she comes out the kitchen and she looks proper confused. I'm about to turn and head up the stairs, when she says,

'What's going on? Marc? What's all the shouting about?'

I stare at her. 'Why won't you tell me where I'm being moved to?' I ask.

Eileen's face crumples, then she and Emma share a look. I don't get it, all the secret looks, why no one ever tells you what's going on! It ain't like I can't handle it, I've already been through enough.

'Is that what you thought this was about?' Emma asks. 'That I'd come to tell you I'd found another placement?'

'Yeah,' I say. 'Ain't that the reason you're here?' Emma gives me a sad smile and she shakes her head. I glance at Eileen and I can't work out exactly what the look is they're both giving me, but I suddenly feel like I got it wrong.

Emma lets out a small sigh. 'It was just a normal check-in, a normal review, Marc,' she says. 'Unless there's something else we need to talk about? But from what I hear you've been getting on really well. You seem settled, you've been going to school on time, and apart from a few initial hiccups, you've not missed your curfew or anything like that.'

I stand there and I can't believe what I'm hearing. I didn't even realize I was doing that stuff. I mean, I only started going to school on time cause I actually had someone to hang around with. But come to think of it, Chantelle's been suspended since Wednesday, and I've still been going to class, I've still been getting my head down and that. I didn't really clock that I'd actually been sticking to my curfew, though. Come to think of it, I ain't been back late once. I dunno if it's to do with Eileen, or if it's to do with Chantelle and Jackson. *Or Shaq.* I guess seeing Shaq's life end like that made me think about my own future. And how I don't want it taken out of my own hands. Shaq doesn't have a choice and neither does Jackson now, and for once I want to have some kind of control. For once, I want to try and have some kind of say over my own life.

I turn to Eileen. 'You're not getting rid of me?' I say.

'No,' she says. 'Not unless you want to go?' I suddenly get this massive flood of relief, and it feels weird, cause for once I'm actually glad that I ain't being moved. And I almost want to reach over and hug Eileen, but then I catch myself.

'Nah,' I shrug. 'It's all right here. I kinda like it.'

Eileen raises her eyebrows, and I swear she looks like she's about to keel over and die of shock. 'Blimey,' she says. 'Was that actually a compliment? Did I hear that right?'

I shake my head. This woman is the unfunniest person I've ever met, but I kinda like that about her. 'Maybe,' I say. 'You still need to work on your cooking, though, and whichever old people music it is you're always blasting in the car.'

Eileen rolls her eyes playfully, and I feel ... *glad.* That for once, I was wrong about all of this. Emma smiles and she hands her empty mug to Eileen.

'I'd better get off now,' she says. 'Marc, I'll see you later! Make sure you carry on the way you're going ...'

'Bye,' I say, and I head into the kitchen, as Eileen shows her out. I grab a box of cereal out the cupboard and pour some into a bowl. I'm already starving and there's no way I can sit here and wait till six o'clock. I sit down at the table and I'm partway through shoving some cereal in my gob when Eileen comes in. I used to just take my snacks and eat upstairs, cause there was no way I wanted to sit and chat to her. But now I don't mind it so much. Eileen pulls a chair out and she takes a seat next to me.

'I'm sorry,' she says. 'I didn't mean to worry you. I should've been clearer on what exactly the meeting was about. I just thought you knew that it was a normal check-in.'

I put my spoon down but I don't look at Eileen. 'It ain't your fault,' I shrug. 'I did think it was a normal meeting, but usually, I dunno ... this is when I'm told I'm being moved on.'

I finish my cereal and I lean back in the chair. I still ain't even taken my jacket off. Cause part of me was so convinced that after Emma broke the news, I'd be out of there. I'd never tell anyone this, but for as long as I can remember, I've felt like I've had some sort of ticking time bomb hanging over my head. That's the only way I can describe it. Like I'm always waiting for the day the minutes finally count down, and everything around me just turns to shit. I'm always waiting for my whole life and world, to just ... *explode*.

But with Eileen, there ain't really been none of that.

'I was going to ask you, actually,' Eileen says. 'And you don't have to answer this now, you can go away and have a think and if the answer's no, then that's perfectly fine too, but I wondered if you wanted to stay here, for the next two years. Until you're eighteen?'

Eileen gives me a small smile and I can't quite believe what she's just said. I almost think about asking her to repeat it, just to make sure. But she *definitely* said that. This rush of emotion comes over me, like I'm happy and scared and also excited. I also feel sad. Cause no one's ever asked me that before. I bite down hard on the inside of my cheek, cause I don't wanna start crying, but I don't even need to think.

'Yeah,' I say. 'I'd *really* like that!'

38

JACKSON

The days and the weeks go past and I try to get as ready as I can for the trial. Not just preparing myself for what might happen, but going over and over my statement as well. My mum drops me off and picks me up from school every day. A few people say stuff, about wanting me to get what I deserve and hoping I'm found guilty, or, how they knew I was 'like this' all along. Of course, Aimee's been going round shouting about this the loudest, saying shit like: 'Remember when Jackson almost hit me in front of everyone in the dinner hall?' Even Sam and Elliot have been joining in with that, too. Harry almost looks like he doesn't know what to believe, but when I see him around school, he just turns and looks the other way. Which is somehow worse.

I try to ignore it all, and hide in the toilets at break and at lunch. If I didn't have Marc and Chantelle, I don't know what I'd do. I concentrate on studying for my exams and I'm glad when we don't have to go into school any more and I can revise at home. We had the initial hearing in court a week ago and Sian told me that the police had decided to lower the charges, which means that I could end up with a lesser sentence, but it also means that I won't have a jury, which was what she'd been hoping for. She said that if a jury heard my story, she'd be sure that I wouldn't be found guilty, because they would see that I had no other choice.

Going in front of magistrates is slightly different. I've spent the past few days being coached by Sian. Going over my statement and being told how to talk in court; what to say and how to address the magistrates. I need to make eye contact, so I don't look guilty, but I also need to be myself, so that they don't misinterpret my eye contact as being *too* overly confident. I need to look smart, but also to make sure that I still look like a boy, so that when the magistrates see me tomorrow, they know I'm still a kid. My dad told me ages ago that when you're Black and you're a boy, you're always aged up. You never really get treated like a kid, because as soon as you're old enough, you're treated like a grown man. *A threat.* I guess I never really thought about it before.

Until all this court stuff.

Until everything with Shaq. How he was just fourteen, but the pictures they used in all those news reports made him look much older.

I'm in my room with Chantelle – she came round straight

315

after her revision class. My mum and dad are still in work. We're on my bed and it's the first time it's just been me and her since we kissed. Marc's gone somewhere with his carer and it's nice to be alone with just Chantelle, even if I don't fully know what's going on between us. We're sitting so close and I can't stop thinking about kissing her again.

'You feeling okay about tomorrow?' she asks.

I swallow hard. I've been dreading this day since they first told us the court date, I just kept wishing that it would never come. But also the not-knowing is just as bad. I just want it to be over with and to be found innocent, so that I can get on with my life. Or I've been hoping that I'd wake up and realize that this was some sort of messed-up nightmare. That the police would call and tell us that this had all been some sort of mistake, and that the guy who attacked *me* had decided to drop the charges. But I'm quickly finding out that's not how the world works. At least not for people like me.

I shake my head. 'Not really,' I say, and part me still can't believe that this is somehow my life. One minute, I'm a normal sixteen-year-old boy, and the next I'm this ... *criminal*. That's how people will see me, anyway. If I end up in prison, or with a conviction, people are gonna judge me for it. Maybe I would've been quick to judge someone for having a conviction before too. Now I know how easy it can be to end up with one.

'I've been over and over my statement, *so* many times, and even though I probably know it off by heart, it still feels like I haven't done enough.' I pause. 'And I don't know how I'm supposed to just switch from that to revising for maths. I don't even know if I'll be going to sixth form. And what happens after that? If I get found guilty, will I be able to get a job? It's gonna be there for the *rest* of my life.'

All the money my mum and dad spent on making sure I have a decent education, so I could have the best start in life, it could all be ... a waste, if I end up with a criminal record.

'You don't know what's going to happen,' Chantelle says. 'You're talking like you already know the outcome.' She pauses. 'And if it does come to that, people still get jobs with convictions, Jackson. I'm not saying that it ain't hard, or, like, these things don't have repercussions, cos I know they do. It's just, whatever happens at court, whatever the outcome, you've gotta keep fighting. You can't give up!'

I nod. Maybe I am talking like I already know what the outcome will be. There's already been so many reports online and in the paper making me out to be some sort of thug. Just like they did with Shaq. Some of the parents at school have even complained. Everyone else thinks I'm guilty, so is it stupid of me to think that I'll be proved innocent? Even though it's hard, I know that Chantelle's right. I can't give up. Whatever happens, I have to fight it in my own way. I suddenly don't wanna talk about all this. I just wanna enjoy being here, right now, with Chantelle. There's so much stuff I'm not certain of, but the one thing I am certain of is how I feel about her.

I suck in a deep breath. 'Can we talk about something else?' I say.

Chantelle moves in closer to me. 'Sure,' she says. 'What d'you wanna talk about? If you say *Star Wars*, though, I am out!'

I laugh, but I can't look at her. She's so beautiful that every time I'm near her, I can never quite look her in the eye.

'Nah,' I say, and all of a sudden I feel proper shy. 'I've just been thinking about what you said, that time at yours. About me living my life for me. And if I get found not guilty, then I *definitely* want to go to Xaverian and really pursue creative writing. I know it doesn't change everything, but it at least gives me some kind of power. Some kind of control, over my own life . . .' I pause. 'I'm gonna tell them that I'm not staying on at St Anthony's.'

Chantelle looks surprised, but then she smiles. 'I'm really glad!' she says. 'It takes guts to go for what you want in life.'

'What if they don't understand?' I say. 'Or they just think it's some stupid hobby, or get mad?'

'Well, maybe, you should show them?' she says. 'That might help them to understand. Have they ever read any of your work?'

'*No way!*' I say. Even the thought of my mum and dad reading one of my short stories makes me feel sick. 'I've never really shown anyone,' I add. 'I mean, apart from my English teacher, but that's it. And even then, there's loads of stuff I write that's just for me.'

Chantelle smiles. 'Give it a think,' she says. 'It can't hurt, can it?'

'Suppose,' I say, but I can't imagine my dad ever being proud of some story I've written.

'I just don't want to let them down,' I say quietly.

'They love you, Jackson,' Chantelle replies. 'They might be a bit annoyed or whatever at first, but they'll get over it. Especially when they see how much it means to you!'

'I hope so,' I say, but deep down, I know that she's probably right.

When I think about leaving St Anthony's and choosing subjects I actually like, it makes me feel ... good. And excited about some sort of possible future, even if there's all this uncertainty and doubt hanging over me.

Being with Chantelle makes me feel that way too. I move her hair away from her face.

'You're so beautiful,' I say.

Chantelle blushes and for once it's almost like she doesn't know what to say. I want to tell her that when I'm not thinking about court and all of that stuff, all I can think about is *her*. But I don't wanna come on too strong. It's weird, though, because we may have ended up meeting by chance, but I can't imagine my life without her in it now. I can't imagine not knowing her or Marc.

'Chantelle,' I start. 'I really like you, y'know,' but she doesn't let me finish. She leans in and kisses me. Chantelle moves a hand up to my neck and I don't think about the trial, or Harrison, or Shaq. I don't even think about tomorrow, or the next day, or the day after that. I just close my eyes and kiss her back.

I tried revising some more after Chantelle left, but no matter how hard I tried, nothing would sink in. It's 9.40 p.m. and all I can think about is what's going to happen tomorrow. What's going to happen to the rest of my life? I hear a gentle knock on my bedroom door and I shout for whoever it is to come in. I expect it to be my mum because she's already checked on me a thousand times today. But it isn't. It's my dad. I can't remember the last time he came in my room. He looks so out of place. He stares around for a minute like he doesn't quite know what to do, then he comes and sits at the end of my bed. He carries on looking around my room at all the film posters and everything, like he's taking it all in.

'Dad?' I say, and he smiles sadly but he doesn't say anything. I wonder if I should tell him about not wanting to continue at St Anthony's, but it doesn't feel like the right time.

'Jackson,' he says finally. 'I know I've been hard on you growing up, that I've been tough, or not there for you as much as your mum.' He pauses. 'But I guess, in my own way, I was trying to prepare you for *this*. How hard and unfair the world can be, especially to people who look like us. My dad was like that with me because he went through so much ... and I'm not saying that I've gone about being a dad in the right way, but all I've ever wanted is what's best for you, Jackson.' My dad shrugs. 'I want you to have the best life, so that you can see that you're not just put on this world to survive. To not end up in prison, or dead. I want you to thrive, that's why I've always pushed you. I'm sorry if sometimes I've pushed you too hard.'

My dad sneaks a look at me and I can see the guilt on his face. For the first time in forever, it kind of makes sense. Why he's always been this way. It was his way of looking out for me.

Of trying to protect me.

'Even with everything we have,' my dad says, 'I couldn't stop this from happening.'

My dad looks so broken and I feel so angry and sad that someone else has done this and he thinks he hasn't done enough.

'It's not your fault!' I say.

My dad pauses and he stares down at his hands. 'I'm sorry for the way I've gone about things,' he says. 'But I do love you, Jackson. Very, very much.'

I lean in and give him a hug. It feels weird at first, because we've not hugged like this in ages. But the awkwardness soon disappears and I'm just so glad that he's here.

I swallow and I hold back the tears. 'I love you too,' I say.

39

JACKSON

I do the buttons up on my shirt, then pull my jacket on and look at myself in the mirror. I still look the same, like, I've not really changed or anything, but it's almost like I don't recognize myself. I can smell breakfast being cooked downstairs and my phone pings with a few messages. They're from Chantelle and Marc, wishing me luck and telling me to let them know how it goes. A small part of me hoped to see something from Harrison. I don't know why, cause it's not like he even knows the dates I'm in court. But maybe it's because we'd been friends for so long. How can that count for nothing? I put my phone in my pocket and I make my way downstairs.

My mum and dad are sitting at the table in the dining room. Dad's in one of his best suits and my mum's in this

322

black dress that she only ever wears for important events. Dad's got a cup of coffee in front of him, which I can see he's barely touched. They both look up when I come through the door.

'Morning, baby,' my mum says, and she gets up and walks over to me. She starts to straighten my tie. No matter how many times I tried this morning, I couldn't get it right. Once she's finished, she moves a hand to touch the side of my face and I can see the sadness and worry in her eyes. My dad's reading the paper, but he's sort of staring at the same spot on the page, so I don't even know if he's actually reading it.

'Right, let me get you some breakfast,' my mum says. 'I've made saltfish fritters and plantain. You need something to start the day right. God knows how long we'll be there.'

She disappears into the kitchen and I sit down at the table. I don't tell her that I feel sick with nerves and that the last thing I want to do is eat.

My dad puts his paper down and he reaches over and gives my hand a squeeze.

'You know your mum loves to cook when she's stressed,' he says. 'She was almost going to start preparing a full-on meal, but I had to stop her ...'

I force a smile. All I feel right now is dread. My mum puts a plate in front of me. It's piled high with food, which normally would be gone in seconds. I pick up my fork and I force myself to eat because I don't wanna upset my mum, but my stomach is churning and I feel light-headed from not sleeping properly last night. I can't stop thinking about what's going to happen

323

today. If all the time Sian's spent coaching me, talking me through what I need to say, will be enough. My mum makes small talk to fill the silence but my head won't stop spinning. I swallow another mouthful of food, but it doesn't seem to taste of anything. I put my head in my hands and I try to take deep breaths. I breathe in slowly and concentrate on counting.

After a minute, my mum reaches over and rubs my shoulder, telling me it's time to go.

We walk along the concrete pavement, up towards the Magistrates' Court and I feel my stomach sink with each step. We've been here before – I had to go inside for the hearing – but it feels different today. The building seems more intimidating. It seems bigger than I remember and I stare up at the large bronze crest as we make our way through the double doors. My mum links her arm through mine and gives my arm a gentle squeeze.

'Are you okay?' she asks, and I nod, even though every part of me wants to turn and run away. To not face whatever outcome it's gonna be. My breath speeds up again and I feel really hot. My suit sticks to me and everything seems to happen in this sort of blur. We go through the metal detectors and get searched. I feel like everything that Sian has told me, everything that she's prepared me for, has just … *gone*. I don't know if I'll be able to get the words out once I'm inside or if I'll be able to explain it all properly.

Sian's waiting for us beside one of the big lifts, at the far end of this long corridor. She smiles when she sees us. 'Hello,' she says. 'Hey, Jackson, are you feeling okay?'

I nod again.

'Okay,' Sian says, as she presses the button for the lift. 'I've booked us a meeting room, so we'll just sit down and have a chat before we have to go in, does that sound all right?'

'Yeah,' I reply, but the words catch in my throat.

A few more people get in and I see my mum shift over to make room. She reaches down and holds onto my dad's hand and then the lift doors close. I feel like the walls are closing in on me and I'm relieved when the lift stops and I can finally get out. I suck in some air and I look around the court waiting room. I wonder how many people are here because of something they've actually done wrong, and how many people are here because they're in a similar situation to me. I guess I'd always thought that if you ended up in court, it was because you'd done something really wrong. I feel stupid for thinking that now.

We go into a small meeting room and Sian sits opposite me. I notice my mum is still holding my dad's hand. She doesn't let go, not even when they sit down.

'Right, Jackson,' Sian says, and she goes through some papers on the desk. 'Now, when they ask to see you, you just need to tell the truth, okay? Explain everything that happened and how you tried to run away, like the way that you told me, just like we practised. Everything you were feeling at the time, the fear, how you didn't want to fight. The fact they all chased after you ... they're going to question you over the bit of glass you picked up. All you need to tell them is what you told me. That you picked it up as a last resort, you weren't sure what it was, but you needed to protect yourself.' She pauses. 'They are going to try their hardest to make it look like you were the aggressor. That you were the one who started all of this, even though there's only one of you. The young man who was hurt – Oliver – will be giving evidence via video link—'

'*What?*' my mum says. 'Video link? Like Jackson's the one he needs to be scared of . . .'

'I know,' Sian says, holding up a hand. 'But it helps them paint the picture of Jackson that they're trying to prove. That he was the one who started all this. I wish I could let you know the definite outcome, but I can't. I'm going to fight my absolute hardest though, okay?'

'Okay,' I say.

'Are you ready?' Sian asks.

I nod. 'Yeah,' I say, although deep down, I know that I'll never be ready for whatever happens in that room to determine the rest of my life.

40

CHANTELLE

I kept checking my phone during my revision session to see if Jackson had messaged, but he hasn't said anything since he told me that he was about to go in and give evidence. I hope so badly that Jackson's found not guilty. It's break time now, and me and Marc are sitting outside on one of the benches. There's only, like, two more weeks of revision, then that's it. We'll sit our exams and then we're leaving. It feels proper good and exciting to know that I won't be stuck at this school any more. That I won't have to constantly put up with Ms Edwards, or some other teacher who won't get off my case. But it's still a bit scary, cos even though I hate this stupid school, it's all I know. It all feels like it's come so fast.

The good thing is that me and Marc have applied to

Xaverian and Jackson is thinking of going there too. So at least if I *do* get in, we'll be there together. I proper enjoyed the taster day I had a few weeks ago, as well. The building was proper nice and it seems like they actually treat you like an adult, too. No return to learn, or PSMs. The teachers seemed proper inspiring, too. I've been thinking a lot about what I want to do with my life, and all this stuff with Ms Edwards, and Jackson and Shaq, and the unfairness of it all, has made me realize that I want to do law. I want to be a solicitor. I won't be able to change all the messed-up things about this world, but I can at least try to make a difference, in some small way. Just like I did that day with Shaq. I check my phone again, even though I just checked it about two seconds ago, but I still ain't got any new messages.

'Still nothing?' Marc asks.

'No,' I reply.

I shove my phone in my pocket and I pick up my history textbook. I glance down at the page, at all the columns and highlighted bits, but nothing sinks in, cos all I can think about is Jackson.

'What happens if he's found guilty?' Marc says.

I put my head in my hands, cos I just wanna know if Jackson's *okay*. I still ain't told Marc that me and Jackson are kinda together now. Maybe cos we're still just figuring things out and it feels kinda private and precious at the moment. But I will do, at some point . . .

I put my arm around Marc. 'We'll just have to be there for him,' I say. 'As best we can.'

Marc rests his head on my shoulder and I look around the playground. Everyone's going about their normal lives. Messing about, or chatting in big groups, or trying to revise ... everyone's getting on with *normal* stuff. The stuff you're supposed to get on with when you're at school. And, meanwhile, Jackson's in court, having someone else decide the rest of his life.

I rub underneath my eye and I know it's selfish but I feel this pain, deep in my chest. If Jackson is found guilty, what does that mean for me and him? If he's sent away, what happens then? I turn to Marc and am about to ask if he thinks I should just phone Jackson, when Mrs Cohen comes over. She's proper red in the face, like she's just been running.

'Chantelle,' she says. 'I've been looking *all over* for you. Will you come with me a sec?'

Marc looks at me. 'What have you done now?' he mumbles.

'No clue!' I say, as I get up off the bench and I follow Mrs Cohen across the playground.

'What's this about?' I ask, as we head into the main school building.

'You'll see,' she says, and we go into an empty classroom.

My face drops when I see Ms Edwards is there, and I almost walk straight back out. I have to stop myself from asking Mrs Cohen why she's trying to ruin my day by making me breathe in the same air as this woman, but she just closes the door behind us. I redid another version of the essay like I said I would and it was even better than the first one, Mrs Cohen told me. So Ms Stupid Edwards and Mr Povey didn't have a leg to stand on, and it won't be going on my college reference, either! Ms Edwards doesn't make eye contact with me and I can't believe my break was interrupted for this.

Mrs Cohen perches on one of the tables. 'Ms Edwards has something to say,' she says. I stare at them both blankly, and I see Ms Edwards go red.

She clears her throat. 'We, erm, did a thorough investigation of your essay, and we couldn't find anything online to suggest that you'd cheated or had some help. The essay that you re-did was just as good as the first one. Better, even. So, I apologize for making the accusation.'

I stare at her. It's barely an apology, to be honest. It looks like it's killing her to get the words out and they're just empty and hollow. Like she's just saying it for the sake of it, cos she knows she has to. I know she wouldn't even be apologizing if Mrs Cohen hadn't brought us together. I just look at Ms Edwards and I don't accept her apology, or even say that it's all right, cos it's not. And why should I have to accept it? I just fold my arms across my chest.

Ms Edwards makes some sort of excuse about having to cover a Year Nine class, then leaves.

I look at Mrs Cohen. She doesn't say it out loud, but I know that she's thinking the *exact* same thing as me about Ms Edwards – *what an absolute knob.*

'Well, she *obviously* didn't mean it,' I say. 'But it was worth it, just to see her sweat.'

A smile creeps up on Mrs Cohen's lips. 'I'm so sorry you had to go through all of that,' she says. 'I was pushing for them to let you go to prom *ages* ago, but now they've realized that they were wrong all along, they've said you can go!'

I shake my head. Even if a small part of me did wanna go to prom – which I don't! – it's the principle of it all. Besides, I'd much rather do something with Jackson and Marc, like we've planned.

'Nah,' I say. 'I'm good!'

Mrs Cohen nods. 'Can't say I blame you,' she says, and I don't know why, maybe it's knowing that soon, I won't ever see her again. Or cos she's one of the few people here who actually ever believed in me, but I throw my arms around her and give her a hug. It takes her by surprise but she hugs me back.

'Thanks,' I say, then I feel a bit awkward and pull away. 'Thanks for, like, giving me a chance when no one else would! For actually believing in me.'

Mrs Cohen smiles and she's got tears in her eyes. 'You don't have to thank me, Chantelle,' she says. 'I'm proud of you, you know, and everything you've overcome. You're going to go *so* far.'

I pull a face. It feels good to hear someone say it, but I still doubt myself, sometimes.

'I'm actually thinking of changing my A-level options,' I say. 'I've looked into it and you can do it in the first two weeks.' I pause. 'That's if I get in.'

Mrs Cohen smiles. 'Oh, yeah?' she says. 'What are you thinking of doing?

'Law,' I say. I look at Mrs Cohen but she doesn't laugh or tell me that I'm being 'too ambitious' or that I should have a 'back-up plan', she just says: 'I think you'll make a wonderful lawyer!'

'Really?' I reply, but it feels good to hear her say that. 'Cos I'm still so nervous about doing it. Like, what if I'm not smart or good enough?'

Mrs Cohen smiles. 'Nerves are a good thing,' she says. 'They show you care! That it matters to you. This probably won't be the last time that you doubt yourself, but don't ever forget how far you've come and what you're capable of. Everything you've achieved, it's all you!' She gestures towards the door. 'Now clear off,' she says. 'I want a break too, you know!'

'*Rude!*' I reply, then I wave and head out the door.

When I get back to Marc, he's sprawled on the bench, textbook resting open on his face, to shield himself from the sun. I pick it up.

'Been revising hard without me?' I say.

Marc grins. 'Ermm, you never heard that saying two heads are better than one?'

'Nah,' I say, as I sit down next to him. Then, I suddenly remember. I grab my bag and pull an Afro comb out.

'I got you this!' I say, as I hold it out to him. 'And before you ask, I bought it!' I actually did as well. All the stuff that's happened over the past few months, has made me realize that I don't wanna do any of that crap any more. I want to try and make the right choices as much as I can, from now on.

'*Wow,*' Marc says. 'You really took an *age* to get me that back! Good job I weren't relying on it or nothing!' he says, pointing to the Afro comb that's already in his hair.

332

'Well, you've got a spare now!' I say. Marc takes it and puts the second comb in his fro as well. 'Right,' he says, turning a page of the textbook. 'Back to the Cold War!'

I smile, and even though I'm still worried about Jackson and the future and what will happen after here, I feel a little bit lighter.

41

JACKSON

By the time I come out of court, my throat is hoarse and I feel like I've got no tears left. I'm exhausted from having to go over everything and I just want to go home and sleep. I couldn't look at my mum or dad while I was answering Sian's questions, because they just kept crying throughout. I made sure that I spoke clearly and looked at the magistrates like Sian said, but it was weird, having to explain to three people who couldn't be more different to me – really posh, old and white – just how scared I was. Just how much I thought my life was in danger. Even if they did 'try' to put themselves in my shoes, to see it from my point of view, they'll never know what it's like. Not really.

Them just knowing what my mum and dad do for a living, that my mum has managed to get a character reference from one of her magistrate friends, makes a difference. If it was Shaq, or his brother, or Marc, up in court, how would they be seen? We're standing in the large waiting area, outside the gallery. Sian rubs my shoulder and I take small sips of water from the plastic cup my dad has just handed me.

'You did so well, Jackson,' Sian says. 'We'll have to wait and see what they say tomorrow,' Sian continues, 'when the verdict comes in. It'll be more waiting around, I'm afraid, but I'm *so* proud at how well you've done.'

My mum forces a small smile and wipes her eyes. 'Me too,' she says, and she brings me in for a hug. I hold onto her and wonder what I'd be doing now if all this hadn't happened. I'd probably be in McDonald's with Harrison and the rest of my mates, or round Harrison's trying to revise.

It feels weird, people telling me how proud they are, because I haven't really done anything to be proud of. I just told the truth to a bunch of strangers who don't know the first thing about me. I pull away from my mum and my dad rubs my shoulder.

'I'll see you tomorrow,' Sian says. 'Try and get an early night. It's been a long day!'

When we get in, I just want to go to sleep. Chantelle and Marc have messaged me loads and Chantelle's tried to call me too. But I don't really want to talk. I send a message to the group chat and let them know that I'll find out tomorrow, then I get changed and climb into bed. I open Insta and I search for Harrison. I stare at his latest posts. There's pictures of him hanging out with Aimee, and one where he's face-palming the desk, with a pile of books next to him with the hashtags #fml #revision #cntwait4ittobeover #lifeisfuckinghard.

I stare at the picture and it makes me so upset. Harrison really doesn't have a clue. I search for some of my other mates, and it's just more of the same. Photos of people revising, Insta stories of people getting ready for exams.

It's like everyone's preparing for this future that I might not have. I click off my phone because I don't wanna look at it any more and there's a knock at my door.

'Come in!' I say.

My mum and dad come in together, which they never do.

'I brought you some camomile tea,' Mum says. 'I thought it might help you sleep.'

I take the mug from her. 'Thanks,' I say, and I take a sip and try not to gag. It's like drinking cat wee. My mum and dad sit on the edge of my bed. No one says anything for a minute and I don't know if it's because of all the posts I saw on Instagram, or if it's because I don't know what's going to happen tomorrow or if it's just because I don't want them to waste any more money paying for my place at St Anthony's, but I blurt out: 'I don't wanna stay on at school. I don't wanna go to the sixth form there.'

My mum and dad look a bit shocked, probably because for them it's come from nowhere, but it feels good to finally get the words out, and now I've said it, I can't stop.

'Like, I know you both want the best for me,' I say. 'But if I do get off without a sentence ... being at St Anthony's won't make me happy. Going on to do law won't make me happy. I've never really wanted that. I just didn't want to disappoint you. And now . . .' I shrug. 'I want to live my life for myself,' I finish quietly and I sneak a glance at both of them. I expect them to kick off, for my mum to say that St Anthony's is the best thing for me, or for my dad to start going on about the career and life that I should have, but they don't. My mum nods and she moves a hand to my face.

'Oh, Jax,' she says. 'You could never disappoint us.' She leans in and kisses the top of my forehead. 'We just want you to do well and be happy. So, if you don't want to stay at St Anthony's, that's okay.' She pauses. 'I do still think you need to go to college and get an education, though!'

'Yeah,' I say. My dad still doesn't say anything and I sneak a glance in his direction.

'Dad?' I say and I feel my heart beating faster.

'What is it you're thinking of doing?' he asks.

'I really love writing,' I say.

'Writing?' he replies, but he doesn't seem too pleased. I knew he wouldn't understand, but for the first time ever, I really want him to. I want them both to realize just how much writing means to me. Not just that, though, it's something that I'm actually good at, that I get my highest marks in. I think about what Chantelle said and I stand up and make my way over to my desk. Maybe, before, I would've been too scared to show them a story that I'd written, but even though I'm nervous, the fear doesn't feel as strong.

I pull a crumpled piece of paper out of one of my books and hand it to my dad.

'It's kinda long, so I don't expect you to read it all,' I say. 'But, like, I wrote this story for English and I got a ten ...' My dad stares down at the piece of paper and I see my mum reading over his shoulder, too. I can't look at them because I suddenly feel really self-conscious, but I'm desperate to get my point across.

'Writing's the only thing I *really* want to do,' I continue. 'It's something I'd want to do at uni as well. And I don't know what job I can get at the end of it, or anything like that, but it's the only thing I enjoy. I'd still be taking English Language and Lit for my A-levels, but I want to do film studies too. And I want to go to a normal college. I want to go to Xaverian actually, because they offer this creative writing enrichment class and ...'

My dad puts a hand out and I fall silent. 'This is really good, Jackson,' he says, and for the first time in ages, relief floods through me.

'You think so?' I say, and my mum nods.

'It's amazing,' my dad says. 'Maybe I'll never fully get this whole doing a creative degree thing, but I can see how strongly you feel about it, and I can see how gifted you are.' He smiles. 'You're growing up,' he says. 'So fast ... but your mum's right, we do just want you to be happy, and if you don't want to go to St Anthony's, then that's okay. We'll support you.'

All these emotions come flooding through me. This is the happiest I've felt all day. My dad's never even said that I'm gifted at anything before. I throw my arms around him.

'Thanks,' I say. My dad holds onto me tightly. 'Can I take this?' he says, holding my story out. 'So I can finish reading it?'

'Course,' I say.

My mum leans in and kisses the side of my head. 'We're so proud of you,' she says, and then she stands up. 'Anyway,' she continues, 'you'd better get some sleep. It's a big day tomorrow.' I nod and my mum and my dad make their way to the other side of the room.

'Night, Jax,' they say.

'Night,' I reply.

My mum switches off the light and I know that whatever happens at court tomorrow, whatever it is they decide, I'm glad I told my mum and dad that. That I've finally been able to tell them what I want and that my dad actually seems interested, too. I close my eyes and I try to go to sleep, but as soon as my head hits the pillow, my mind races. It's like all I hear is their footsteps, and *that* word, then the sound of the van door being slammed over and over. I'm not sure if I believe in God, or anything like that, but right then I put my hands together and I pray. I pray with everything I have that it will all be okay.

In the morning, there's lots of waiting around, like Sian said. We sit in the waiting area again and it feels like we're there for hours, until finally Sian comes over to us and says: 'They're ready for you to go in now, Jackson.'

We walk into the room and I stand in the same spot I stood yesterday: inside this stand at the side of the court room. I glance over to my mum and dad and they give me a reassuring smile. Then I turn towards the magistrates. I feel my hands trembling and I pray that everything will be put right. Because surely being a good person and not wanting to hurt anybody, never setting out to cause any harm, is enough? One of the magistrates with this blue dicky bow speaks to me and he reminds me a bit of my head teacher.

'Jackson Campbell,' he says. 'We've spent a while deliberating the outcome of this case. With the evidence that has been presented, we do accept that you were the victim of a pre-meditated attack, and that you were acting in self-defence. However, the law of self-defence requires that you defend yourself with "reasonable force" and in this case, we believe that you defended yourself too much. That it wasn't reasonable.'

I glance at my mum and dad and see the colour drain from my mum's face.

'Therefore,' he continues, 'we find you guilty of section twenty assault. But, as this is your first charge and you've proven to be of good character, we're going to give you the lightest possible sentence of probation and a fine.'

I can't concentrate on anything else, because the word *guilty* just swims in my mind. It's the way he says it, like they're doing me a favour. I'm relieved I'm not being sent to prison, but am I supposed to feel lucky that my parents will have to pay out? That I'll have a criminal record and have to do probation? I don't even realize I'm crying but my cheeks are wet and I feel stupid for even having the tiniest bit of hope. It's all over so quickly and it's nothing like how you see it on TV. The magistrates leave the room and my mum and dad rush over to me and throw their arms around me, but it still doesn't make sense. How can you decide what's reasonable when you're scared? When it's all those people against you? When you're just trying to get away?

I feel empty and I don't notice that we've walked out of the gallery and we're heading into a meeting room.

My mum's crying and I see her rubbing my shoulder, but I feel numb.

'We have to fight this!' my mum says, and I can hear the pain in her voice. 'We have to appeal. I don't care how much it costs ... This is *ridiculous*! I mean, I know that miscarriages of justice happen all the time. But this is just— That conviction will be on Jackson's record for ever!'

For ever.

Sian looks sad. 'I'm so sorry,' she says, and I can see she genuinely means it. 'I really thought they'd see that Jackson hadn't done anything wrong.' She sucks in a breath. 'You can appeal,' she says. 'Of course you can. But, like you've seen, there's so much grey area in that aspect of the law and Jackson's been given the lightest possible sentence. If you do appeal and he's found guilty again, he could end up with a much worse conviction. It could be a prison sentence.'

I feel like I can hardly breathe. If I try to fight it, there's a chance that things could end up being worse? My head is spinning. Do I want to take that risk?

My dad shakes his head. 'That's insane!' he says. 'How can we possibly *win*?'

Sian gives him a small smile. 'If you decide to appeal, it will go to crown court and you'll have a jury, which means that there's a greater chance they will see Jackson was defending himself and that it was his only choice. But there's still a fifty-fifty chance. Whatever it is you decide,' she continues. 'Just take some time to think about it. You don't have to do anything right away.'

My mum and dad nod and they thank Sian. Even though I'm relieved that I'm not going to prison, what little hope I had in the justice system, at people believing *my* truth, is gone. I think that maybe this was what was going to happen all along. That as soon as I was arrested and the handcuffs were put on me, the outcome had already been decided.

When we get home I go straight up to my room and sit there for a while. I phone Chantelle and Marc and tell them what happened and they're as shocked and as angry as me. It still hasn't sunk in. I just feel so numb.

There's a knock at the door and my mum comes in carrying a tray of food.

'Thought you might be hungry,' she says, and she puts it on top of my desk.

'Thanks,' I say, and I realize I haven't eaten anything all day.

She comes and sits next to me and I can tell that she's been crying because her face is all puffy and her eyeliner is smudged. She doesn't say anything, she just pulls me into her.

'Mum,' I say, and the tears start to come again. 'What am I supposed to do? That's gonna be there for the rest of my life. No matter where I go or what I do, that box will be there. And people won't care about the reason, or the story, or what even happened. They'll just see that and think the same as the police and those magistrates and everyone else – *that I'm guilty.*'

My mum's crying too, I can hear her. Then she wipes away

some of my tears with her sleeve. 'Baby, I'm sorry,' she says. 'I honestly didn't believe it would come to this. It's so … unfair. I've been wanting to shout and scream and throw things since the moment we got back. We'll seek legal advice, and we'll figure out the best thing to do. If we should appeal it. Or … I don't want you carrying that around with you for the rest of your life.' My mum pauses. 'I know that this is awful, Jackson. But I want you to know that there are other ways to fight this. You can fight by going on and leading a good life. By making something of yourself, y'hear?'

She lifts my chin gently, and somehow through all the pain and sadness, I know she's right. For now, at least – the court, the charges – it's over, and for the first time since all this began, I can start feeling hopeful about the future

42

JACKSON

I've got my eyes closed and I feel like a bit of an idiot, standing here in the middle of some courtyard by these half-demolished flats with Marc and Chantelle. We decided to do our own celebration instead of going to prom, although this wasn't what I quite expected. I got the grades I needed to get in to Xaverian, and Chantelle and Marc are going there too.

I feel Chantelle fidgeting next to me. 'What's taking so long?' she asks. 'Can we open our eyes yet?'

'One sec,' Marc says, and then he goes. 'Right, now!'

I stare around at the concrete balconies and boarded-up windows covered in graffiti and I'm almost about to ask Marc what exactly were supposed to be looking at and why he made us close our eyes, when I see it, right there. A mural. I don't think anyone else would even know that it's us because they're only outlines, but it's proper amazing. There's all these different colours filing the shapes. It's the same style as the mural that was painted for Shaq and, come to think of it, some of the other ones around Manchester, too. Marc grins and then it clicks.

'Hang on a minute,' Chantelle says. 'That was you? You're the graffiti artist behind the mural? It's incredible!'

'Yeah!' he says. 'But don't you dare tell anyone. I'm trying to conceal my identity!'

Chantelle mimes locking her mouth. 'My lips are sealed,' she says. 'I can't believe you kept that hidden from us for so long.' She grabs my hand. 'Jax?' she says.

I wrap my fingers around Chantelle's but I can't take my eyes off the mural.

'D'you like it?' Marc says. 'I mean, we can *obviously* go and celebrate somewhere properly after this, but I wanted to do something for you both ...' He pauses. 'I've never had friends like you two before. I'm so glad that we were brought together, that day.'

I feel emotional and pretty speechless, because a few months ago Marc and Chantelle were total strangers and now they're the two most important people in my life.

'I *love* it!' I say and my eyes start to water a bit. 'Can't believe that's you, though! Why've you been hiding these special talents?'

Chantelle gives me a smile. 'Bring it in!' she says, and Marc runs over to us and wraps his arms around us both.

'You two are my favourite couple,' he says. 'But don't tell Kade!' I hear Chantelle laugh and I smile as I hold onto them both. I don't know what the future holds, but here, right now, with Chantelle and Marc by my side, things feel bright.

Acknowledgements

I'm so grateful to the entire publishing team at Simon & Schuster. I've been lucky enough to work with not one, but two wonderful editors on this book. Huge thank you to Jane Griffiths for seeing something (although I'll never know what) in that very first hot mess of a manuscript. Thank you for your encouraging words and initial edits. To Amina Youssef, thank you for your patience, incredible editorial eye and general brilliance! I feel so very honoured to have been able to work on this book with you.

To Chloe Seager, I really couldn't have survived 2020 and book two without you! Thank you for always being there, for having my back throughout everything and for believing that I would get here with this book (even when I didn't think so myself). You really are the agent of dreams!

Huge thank you to Raymond Sebastian for the most beautiful cover. Thank you to Jason Okundaye for reading an early draft of this book and for your insightful, helpful and perceptive feedback. Thank you to Aaron Cobham for not only being a wonderful friend, but for answering the endless questions I had while writing this book.

Thank you to Joyce Efia Harmer, Alexandra Sheppard, Lara Williams, Marie Basting, Steve Hollyman, Christina Hammonds Reed, Chloe Allen and Carly Baggaley. I feel so very lucky to have you all in my life. Massive thanks to Jahvel Hall for your invaluable input and encouragement.

To my dad, Stan Jawando, thank you for your love and support. Huge thanks to Julie Jawando for always being there, no matter what. Thank you for your advice and help with parts of this book. To Andy Forbes, thank you so much for your encouragement and support.

Last but not least, I'm always inspired by the many young people who I've been lucky enough to meet and work with over the years. Thank you all for just being you. Special thanks to the incredible group of young writers who I tutored on the Arvon course at Totleigh Barton back in 2019. Your resilience, bravery, determination and spirit is something that I will never forget.

Danielle Jawando is an author, screenwriter and Lecturer in Creative Writing at Manchester Metropolitan University. Her debut YA novel, *And the Stars Were Burning Brightly*, won best senior novel in the Great Reads Award and was shortlisted for the Waterstones Children's Book Prize, the YA Book Prize, the Jhalak Children's & YA Prize, the Branford Boase Award and was longlisted for the CILIP Carnegie Medal, the UKLA Book Awards and the Amazing Book Awards. Her previous publications include the non-fiction children's book *Maya Angelou (Little Guides to Great Lives)*, the short stories *Paradise 703* (long-listed for the Finishing Line Press Award) and *The Deerstalker* (selected as one of six finalists for the We Need Diverse Books short story competition), as well as several short plays performed in Manchester and London. Danielle has also worked on Coronation Street as a storyline writer.

DANIELLE JAWANDO

AND THE STARS WERE BURNING BRIGHTLY

'AN OUTSTANDING AND COMPASSIONATE DEBUT'
PATRICE LAWRENCE

TURN THE PAGE FOR A
SNEAK PEEK OF ANOTHER
OUTSTANDING BOOK FROM

DANIELLE JAWANDO

AL

prologue

When a star reaches the end of its lifetime, it explodes in this violent supernova. Sometimes the outer layer of the star blows off, leaving behind a small, dense core that continues to collapse. Gravity presses down on the core material so tightly that the protons and electrons combine to make neutrons, and they combine to make a neutron star. Something born from a death that ripples out from thirty-three light years away. The core of the star speeds up, and it spins faster and faster, up to 43,000 times per minute, so that eventually the universe just becomes this blur – a blur of time and space – where nothing can hurt you because you don't really exist. Not properly. You're just a floating cluster of subatomic particles, trapped in this perfect world.

Last summer, me and Nate went to the fair. We climbed on

to the Spin Master, one of those rides with the metal cages that catapult you forward, and Nate's face was all stretched out and weird. He kept shouting and yelling because he loved it so much. And, as the wind hit me in the face, I could feel the corners of my mouth lift and then I closed my eyes and thought, This is the closest I'll ever get to being a neutron star. *Me and Nate, together in this whirl of colour ... this rush of light and sound. Pulsating. Rotating. Orbiting. Lifting off the ground.*

I held on to the metal safety gate and thought of the patterns that were all around. I thought of the Fibonacci sequence and how everything in life is made up of numbers. I thought about how you can time travel in your mind with your memories. You do it, without even realizing. It's called chronesthesia. I thought about Van Gogh leaving out the bars on the windows of his room in his Starry Night *painting. I thought about how it can take ten million years for a star to form, but it can only happen once there's been the perfect gravitational collapse.*

And I thought of me and Nate on the boxing-gym roof. Me and my little bro up on that roof, and my chance to tell him everything, but not being able to find the right words.

Then I sat back and prayed that the ride wouldn't stop. Because I knew that when it did I wouldn't be a neutron star any more. I'd just be Al.

Al who was nothing.

Al who wanted to disappear.

Al who wanted to be up there instead ... where nothing can touch you and all you know is helium and nitrogen and dust.

NATHAN

chapter one

One day, little bro, you'll see. It will happen and you won't even realize it. You'll look up at the sky, stare at all those stars burning hundreds and thousands of miles away, and you'll think: I get it now. I get all that stuff that Al was banging on about – I really do.

'It is not in the stars to hold our destiny, but in ourselves.' That's what Al said.

It was the last thing he told me before he disappeared. He said it was from some play he'd been studying in English, and then he ripped it out his school book and tossed it to me. He'd scrawled all these drawings down the sides of the words, cramming his pictures into the margins. All these people with no faces. I hated reading more than I hated school, so I screwed it up and flushed it down the bog. Then I told Al exactly where he could shove his poetry. I didn't care that he thought it was a good one.

At least I didn't *then* anyway. Cause Al was always coming out with crap like that. Talking to me about some book, or a fact he'd remembered, or going into one of his weird moods when he couldn't get a drawing right. He'd get all stressed out and start running a hand through his thick Afro, pulling at the tufts of hair. Then he'd screw the whole drawing up and toss it in the bin. His room was full of half-finished faces and half-finished things, all split in two and scattered round the place. He had proper sketches, but he'd never let me see them. He kept them hidden, locked inside one of his desk drawers.

Al was full of secrets, but that didn't stop our mum from loving him the most. Al would be the one to get out of Wythenshawe. Al would be the one to do something with his life. To end up in one of those posh university halls and make her proud. Al, Al, fucking Al. Mum loves my little sister, Phoebe, probably cause she's the only girl. She loves Saul, probably cause he's the oldest. But, with me, it's like she didn't have enough love left to give. Maybe she doesn't love me so much cause I look most like our dad.

I turn over in the dark and I wait for it to stop hurting. Not the kinda hurt when someone gives you a dead arm in school and you laugh your head off, pretending it doesn't sting, even tho it kills. This is a different hurt. One that seems to come from inside and pull down on me. Like all these different parts of me are slipping away, and I can't do nothin to stop it. It's this hurt that takes over. That splits me right down the middle. That reminds me every minute that Al ain't here, and there's nothing I can do to change it.

I hear the muffled sound of the telly coming from downstairs, forcing its way through the cracks in the floorboards. Mum's probably fallen asleep in front of it again. Since it happened, she hardly ever goes upstairs. She doesn't even sleep in her room any more. She spends more time praying, tho, heading down to this crappy church round the corner from our house or bringing these old fogeys to ours. People who've never bothered with us before, who hold her hand, and bring her stuff, and tell her that *'Al is in heaven now'*. That *'at least he's with God'*. That *'he's in the best place'*.

Mum nods like heaven is better than our house, or Civic Town Centre, or the pop-up funfair. That Al's better off dead than necking as much alcohol as he can, or getting on the Spin Master or the Miami Wave. And all I want to do is tell her there's no point in praying to some idiot in the sky. That God is just a taker, like one of those idiots in your year, who nicks a new pair of trainers even before you've managed to break them in. God *took* Al. And, if anyone asks, that's all I'd say he is – a taker of brothers and trainers and really important shit. I never believed in God much anyway, but I believe in him even less now.

The floorboards outside my room creak. I watch as my bedroom door begins to open and the light from the landing floods in, making me cover my eyes. And, for a moment, he's there. Al. Standing in the doorway, his Afro blocking out most of the light, his body leaning to one side, his dark shadow stretched. He shakes his head slowly, like he can't believe wot a fool I've been, and I think I hear him say, '*Got you!*' Like this is all a joke. One of the stupid tricks that he'd play when he was messin around.

'Al?' I whisper, and my throat tightens. 'Al ... ?' But all I can see is a shadow.

'It's just me,' a small voice says. Phoebe.

The door opens wider and I suddenly feel stupid. Phoebe moves towards me, a bright yellow dressing gown wrapped round her, the end of her long plait slowly unravelling. She's clutching this old teddy. The thing looks like a rabid cat shoved into a small doll's dress. Al bought it for her one Christmas ages ago. I hadn't seen it for years, but the night it happened she came into my room with it. She didn't speak, she just lay there. Curled up on her side, with this teddy pressed to her chest.

'I can't sleep,' she says. 'I can hear Mum crying again.'

I move over and peel the covers back. I don't mind Phoebe coming into my room cause at least then I'm doing summat for her. At least then there's summat I can try to fix.

Phoebe climbs in next to me. 'It smells funny in here,' she says.

'Well, it was fine before you came in.'

'It's not my fault that you don't wash.'

'Nah,' I say. 'D'you want me to kick you out or wot?'

Phoebe goes quiet and, even tho she doesn't say anything, I can tell that she's thinking.

'Nate,' she says. 'Where do we go when we die?'

I shrug. 'Heaven,' I say.

'I know *that* . . . but how do you get there? Do you just wake up and you're there? Or does an angel come and take you away? Or do you just die and then . . .'

She pauses, and I think of Al for a minute. Drifting upwards, so awkward and lanky that, if you do float up to heaven, he'd probably get caught on summat on the way up. Tangled round an electricity wire like the old socks or school shoes that people throw up there. The thought makes me smile for a minute, numbing all those bits inside me, but it soon stops.

'Do you think it hurts?' Phoebe says. 'Dying . . . Do you think it hurt Al?' She pauses. 'Was he in pain?'

I look up at the plastic glow-in-the-dark stars on my ceiling. Al got them from one of those crappy pound shops the day Dad left. He'd stuck them down, taking ages to get them in the right places. He'd said that when he didn't understand life, or if things didn't make sense, he'd just look up and, somehow, everything would just feel different. It would feel okay.

Then he started telling me that there was no point in having stars on the ceiling if they didn't look like the real thing, and he kept going on about all these names. Saying how there was some star named after this guy called Ryan, and how everything was shaped like his belt.

And, when he'd finished, he just had this one thing left. A comet that he ended up sticking in the corner, at the far side of my room. He said that he didn't know what to do with it, but that he could tell that it didn't wanna be with the rest of the stars.

I think of how Al looked when I'd found him. The blueish tint to his face. The green-and-black school tie knotted round his neck. His silver prefect badge glinting in the light, and the stupid faded school motto on his blazer: *In Caritate Christi Fundati*. I could hear kids playing in the street outside: someone kicking a ball against a fence; the wheels of a bike skidding round a corner; the slapping of a skipping rope on the pavement; the *thud, thud, thud* of music from a car in the distance. The chanting of, '*Who are ya? Who are ya? Who are ya? Touch me again and you're dead.*'

I think of how me and Al had had a row that morning. How he'd called me after school and I'd cut him off. Ignored his call, then turned my phone to silent. All cause I wanted him to stop bothering me and piss off. All cause I was having too much fun, drinking and smoking in the park. All cause I wanted to stay with Kyle and these two fit girls we were with.

Al had always been there for me, but, when he needed me the most, I'd cut him off.

I feel Phoebe tug at the sleeve of my T-shirt and my eyes begin to sting.

'Nate, do you think it hurts?' she asks again.

I stare up at the comet, separate from all those other stars.

'Nah,' I lie. 'I don't think it hurts at all.'

WITHDRAWN

Hurstpierpoint College

1001412038